I0658433

STILETTO 911:

The Makeover Manifesto of a Career Woman

By Vivian Valtas Schmidt & Sue Publicover

This is a work of fiction. All the characters and events portrayed in this novel are products of the authors' imagination. In the event that you think differently, you are totally trippin'.

STILETTO 911

Published by Glamour Press House
PO Box 11743 • Chicago, IL 60611
www.glamourpresshouse.com

ISBN: 978-0-615-49478-4

Library of Congress Control Number: 2011914684

Book Design by Emily Johnson
Editing by Katie Gutierrez Painter

acknowledgements

This book would not have been possible without the insight, support and business savvy of our friends, mentors and family. A special thanks to Tarrie Adams, Zulma X. Barrios, Downtown Sheri Brown, Jan Cefalu, Katie Gutierrez Painter, IMERMAN ANGELS, Kim Jackson, Emily Johnson, Jennifer Kline, Andrea Klouman Coppola, Kathy Laramie, Stephanie Mollica, Lori Movsesian, Becky Neikamp, Rema Nelson, Patricia Schmidt, Christiana Schwab, Andra Simionescu, Cathy Solsaa, Anna Suarez, Evgenia Valtas, and Annette Wetherby. And to Ryan Publicover and Shirley Movsesian, thank you for keeping life in perspective when writer's block brought on the grumps. Lastly, a special shout out to Jeff and George Schmidt – my reason for each season!

To the powerful woman in you.

"Let's just think about this for a second, shall we?
I am out of your league. I'm so out of your league that,
if your league exploded, I wouldn't hear about it for three days.
So let us go on in a companionable silence, shall we?"

— NICOLE NOONE IN "THE LIBRARIAN"

introduction

The Purpose of a Makeover Manifesto and Why Stilettos are a Must...

There are no excuses in life—only choices. You can choose to lead or accept the role of follower. You can decide that "good enough" is a compromise you're not willing to make, or you can choose to be mediocre. Yes, we are each dealt our own unique set of circumstances, but I have seen too many people overcome adversity to believe that poverty, a bad family life, or even physical challenges are a foregone conclusion to failure. And by failure, I mean settling for anything less than achieving your true potential.

People talk about being dealt a bad hand. I'm not much of a poker player, but I understand enough about the game to know that if you are holding crummy cards, you either toss them back or cut your losses and fold. And then you start anew with a clean hand.

I can attest to this. I grew up with nothing but leftovers and hand-me-downs from strangers. I lived in a neighborhood where I couldn't ride a bike any farther than four cracks down the sidewalk because that's where the danger lived. I went to school every day, followed by my requisite attendance at Greek school—where all good little Greek-Americans go to learn about their culture—and then to work with my father. On some winter nights, I slept about four hours—after doing my homework—because I had to be up at three a.m. in order to help my dad with his snow-plowing business. I was shoveling sidewalks for strangers before the sun rose. At the age of twenty-one, I got married and discovered as early as the honeymoon that my supposed true love had an abusive streak.

But during all these times, I never looked to the heavens and moaned, "Why me?" Not even when I was lying in a dark basement after a beating from my husband, who thought I had the unmitigated gall to get pregnant (which turned out to be a false alarm) without his permission. Those were the times I looked inward and searched for a way to make my life better, to learn from mistakes, and to take action to achieve joy and success. The little voice in my head yelled, "Don't just sit there and take it. Get on with your life!"

And that's what I have done.

Step One: Divorced the abuser.

Step Two: Pursued the career that I desired.

Step Three: Refused to take "no" for an answer.

Step Four: Sought out mentors who could fill in the gaps of wisdom I would need to avoid more mistakes.

And I completed a homework assignment between each step: Learn from the experience.

What did poverty teach me? I knew I wanted more from my life than working every waking hour and scavenging for things that other people took for granted. It lit a fire in me.

What did I learn from working so hard at an early age? Money means independence, no matter what age you are. From the time I was seven years old, I was earning money and never, ever asked for a handout from my parents. I gained the power of being self-sufficient and enjoyed the pride that came with it.

What did I learn from choosing a bad mate? We all make bad choices at some point. That one was a doozy. But I discovered that you *can* right a wrong. Marriage should be a forever thing, but only with the right partner (luckily, I have discovered the true meaning of love and partnership). In any relationship, you have three choices: accept it at face value, work to improve it, or move on.

If you're ready to turn your life into something more joyous and fulfilling, park all those woes at the curbside with the rest of the junk.

For this book, I have brought along my friend, Sue Publicover, a woman who has almost two decades more life experience (we don't call it "age") than me. A woman with some "oh-woes" of her own, Sue knows what it means to be knocked down, only to get up, brush off, and charge forward with dirty knees and an unrelenting attitude. I've asked

Sue to join me on this journey to write a book that would inspire others to stop sitting still and start taking action. We both know what it means to overcome obstacles and surge ahead. And we both realize we didn't do it alone. We had mentors who provided wisdom and caveats, inspiration and warnings.

The purpose of *Stiletto 911* is to help other women develop life skills (goal setting, time management, business acumen, cultivating lasting relationships, and seeking and becoming a mentor). While the chapters tell the story, the "Footnotes" at the end of each one present exercises and some appetizing food for thought to fuel your own makeover. Chapter by chapter, you'll gain the insights to guide your journey to independence, self-awareness, finding your true passion, and developing business and social etiquette.

Stiletto 911 is both tale and truth. It tells the story of Morgan Demarest, a young woman who has never needed to make much effort to get what she wants. Suddenly, all her safety nets fall down, and she isn't equipped to make essential life decisions. Morgan Demarest embodies the characteristics of many women of her generation—the daughter of helicopter parents who hover too closely, an individual who relies on conveniences, and an adult who has not given much consideration to building her future. But the combination of a fiery ex-lover, a family member in distress, a new friend with a troubled past, and a suddenly-curtailed shopping habit cause Morgan to take another look at how she has been living her life and why she needs the emergency aid of *Stiletto 911*.

And what would a fable be without a fairy godmother? So, yeah, she's in there, too. But she's a twenty-first century spirit who has no patience for entitlement, attitude, or bad manners—though she can still appreciate the beauty of a fine pair of Italian leather stilettos and the value of properly accessorizing.

This is not a Cinderella story, however. If you want your happily-ever-after, you need to make it happen for yourself. Think of *Stiletto 911* as an introduction to your own fairy tale ending.

Here's your first choice for making your life better: Commit to reading this book in its entirety. Don't skim through it, or you might miss some "AHA!" moments tucked in paragraphs. We can't tell you where they are because these little nuggets will have different potency for you, depending on your perspective, experience, and desires. So we'll move forward together, telling you a story but also imparting some business smarts—like how to find and attain your dream job, get people to recognize and reward your talents, and build a network that keeps you as buoyant as a Victoria's Secret's bra.

One thing you won't find in these pages is the motherly hug of an Oprah-like sympathizer. Yes, we understand that change is hard, because we've been through it. We also know that coddling is enabling, not empowering. We offer empathy, not sympathy. It is our fervent desire to infuse you with energy, strength, and commitment to acquiring and living the best life you can. Think of us as your coaches, somewhere between a cheerleader and a drill sergeant.

So here goes:

Cheerleader: There's an exciting future waiting for you, and you deserve it! Come on; let's do it together!

Drill sergeant: Stop that whimpering, Trixie. Pull up those big girl panties and get going!

Why *Stiletto 911*? For one thing, Sue and I both love shoes. We know that no matter how bad you're feeling, you can perk up when you have something to strut about—and in. But, while shoes are fun, stilettos represent a challenge. You can't possibly slip on a pair of four-plus-inch stilettos and walk the walk without wobbling the first time around. That's what this book is about. Everyone starts in flats, because there's no challenge to walking around in them—nor do you enjoy the feel of red-hot femininity and admiring glances. You have to work your way up, and the same is true in business: Inch by inch, we get taller. Our confidence rises. We will undoubtedly stumble—that's called "experience"—but we will never give up.

prologue

On a typical Thursday morning, when most trade shows opened, a crowd of people milled outside the Edmonds Expo Center in Chicago. The first-comers to the show du jour (or du several jours) lined up to get first peek at the eye candy and free swag about to fill their almost-empty totes, computer bags, and oversized purses. While the savvier attendees knew that exhibitors, not wanting to re-ship the remaining products, were most generous on the last day of the show, they also knew that the best goodies were limited in quantity and it was worthwhile to do some serious schmoozing right from the start— something like marking their territory, minus the leg lifting.

Today was no exception. This group, readying for the annual DigiMart convention of business technology, reflected the usual mix of men in suits and women who sought to mimic them in trim, dark, unimaginative ensembles. The occasional khaki-wearers made a statement of relaxed notoriety, while still attempting to say "I'm a hip businessperson" by feverishly pecking at their smartphones and chatting on their Bluetooth headsets while also juggling their precious *venti* Starbucks—aiming for cool but achieving obvious.

The October morning sky was speckled with small clouds but was otherwise clear and sunny, a pleasant break from the normal autumn chill that slipped into Chicago in early fall. As pairs and groups of waiting conference attendees swapped handshakes and business cards, only a few people noticed the sleek car that pulled alongside the curb. But their sudden pause in conversation caused more heads to turn, and the silence spread through the crowd like an invisible trail of falling dominoes. Within moments, most of the attendees were looking at the sleek black Mercedes that had hummed to a stop before them. Indeed, it was not just any Mercedes but a true luxury car that was worth as much as some of their cozy condos.

Once the onlookers finished gaping at the exquisite automotive specter, their focus switched to the driver: Who in the world possessed such extravagance? A woman sat behind the wheel, with a pink scarf draped around her head—not quite covering her silky blonde hair—and cascading down her back in true Hepburn style. Her sunglasses covered most of her face. She reached across the front seat to gather up her oversized, equally pink Valentino bag and took a quick glance in her rearview mirror at her glossy pink lips.

Before she could touch her door handle, a man smoothly emerged from the crowd. The waves of his sandy hair were nicely tamed, with the exception of a stray lock that tickled the top of his wire-rimmed glasses. Dressed in a fitted white shirt that did little to mask his muscular torso—hallelujah—he smiled at the driver and opened the car door for her.

She swung her left leg slowly from the car. Her cream-colored leather shoe traced a graceful line on her foot, from the perfectly shaped peep-toe that gave only a tiny glimpse of her pedicured nails, to the top of the five-inch stiletto that bore the trademark red leather sole of Christian Louboutin's four-figure finery.

Bringing her other leg around, the mystery woman gracefully slid from the comfort of her Mercedes' black leather seat. The man extended a hand and helped her navigate to a stand. Her pale blue dress slipped into place with the ease of feathery silk, draping over the subtle curves of her slender figure. A small zipper in the shoulder displayed a hint of skin, more sensual than sinful. The dress ended inches above her knee, and the onlookers—particularly the men—couldn't help but follow the lengthy road from the hem of her dress down her calves to the tips of her stiletto heels.

She smiled back at her personal valet. The hint of intimacy that passed in her glance suggested that he was not affiliated with the conference center; their look said that he held her trust and she had his respect—and perhaps a bit more, but only they could know for sure.

The woman whispered something in his ear and slid her key into his hand with the seamless finesse of a relay runner. He reached behind her, lifted her bag from the seat, and handed it to her in a rhythmic motion that said they had danced this *pas de deux* many times before.

He lowered himself onto the driver's seat, watching as she walked around the front of the car to the sidewalk. He turned the key and revved the engine in what seemed to be a farewell salute to the woman, who smiled at the sound.

As he drove away, the woman started her walk through the parting crowd. Whispers rose around her:

"Who is she?"

"She must be married to one of the execs."

"Are you kidding? She probably *is* one of the execs."

"Check out those stilettos!"

"I saw those at Neiman's. They cost about a week's salary."

"Maybe *your* salary. Mine goes to pay the bills."

"Wouldn't it be nice to have that kind of money to throw around?"

"Yeah, but she was probably born into it."

Their object of envy took it all in, inhaling the commentary like oxygen. *If only they knew,* she thought. Her life was not the gift of a wealthy pedigree, or the luck of marrying well, or even the result of being in the right place at the right time. The wisdom of her mentor echoed in her head: Life is under no obligation to give us what we expect.

So true, she thought with a slight nod. *You make your own destiny. And if you don't like it, make a new one.* Which was exactly what she, Morgan Demarest, had done over the past year.

Morgan reflexively looked over her shoulder. She paused and surveyed the crowd, avoiding the glances of those who were casting judgments her way, but the familiar face that had been a key part of her journey was nowhere to be seen.

Morgan may not have seen me, but I had my eyes fixed squarely on her and this exquisite entrance. I chose to let this scene unfold without me. I wouldn't say I was gone for good. Just for the better.

CHAPTER *one*

Once upon a time in Chicago, there lived a young woman named Morgan Demarest. Like many of her peers, she enjoyed a life of fair luxury. However, Morgan was no princess—except, maybe, in her mind, as she had gotten so used to being doted on by her well-meaning parents. Can someone please ground those helicopter parents who hover over their kids and then swoop right in and handle every problem for them? It starts with cleaning up their diapers, and the messes just get bigger from there. Before these parents know it, they're telling Little League coaches what's fair—which only happens when their child's butt is collecting splinters on the bench—and accompanying their college graduate on job interviews. Not so long ago—before Baby Boomers became parents—kids were pushed out of the nest and forced to take off. Mama and Daddy weren't standing by with their checkbook and a lawyer on retainer to make sure their kids avoided life's pitfalls. And in those days, parents also knew that sometimes you lose. Get over it. Helicopter parents don't make my job any easier, I tell you.

Okay, I digress. But you can be sure we'll be talking about this later!

Anyway, Morgan Demarest was one of those copter kids. And she was a red-hot mess when we first met. She just didn't know it. Being airlifted all those years by her loving parents didn't help her one bit.

That girl had spent most of her twenty-three years following a path that was paved for her—and not too smoothly, I might add. She was popular in high school, a decent athlete but never a starter, just missed prom queen, and not quite in the top tier of her class but certainly nipping its heels. Like most of my clients, she partied her way through college but managed to earn a bachelor's degree in marketing, with a minor in communications. She did it because others had told her that this college and this degree would take her places.

The only problem was that Morgan had never taken the time to stop and think specifically about those "places" and what she would do when she got there. Quite simply, Morgan lacked goals. And without those goals, she had no focus or plans for her life. She lived day to day. And with her father's success as a real estate developer, she had the perfect fallback position in the event she needed a helping hand. Her parents had always had her back; at least, that was her opinion. In mine, however, they hovered so closely that Morgan never had to fear trouble, failure, or consequence. When she had a run-in with a teacher, Claire and/or Edward Demarest were in the principal's office making the problem go away. When Morgan was caught smoking pot in her sorority, her parents managed to smooth the ruffled feathers of the administration, which later benefited from some generous support to the renovation of their struggling theater arts building. And when Morgan maxed out a credit card, the balance was paid off within days of a call to her father.

What attracted me to Morgan Demarest was her lifelong status as an "Almost". Top honors had always evaded her by inches, and though the near-misses didn't seem to faze her, she hadn't set any lofty goals for herself, either. This told me she had accepted a less-than-stellar destiny that, in my humble opinion, sold her far too short. And my job—and my life's passion—is to never settle for less than what can be. So the night I met Morgan,   I knew I had my work cut out for me, but I also knew she would be worth the effort. Now, if only I could get her to share that vision.

If Pavlo Fyorchenko's heart and mind (and a few other things) had been as large as his ego, Morgan would not have found herself in this predicament. Cast out of their—well, his—loft on a rain-soaked street in Chicago's Gold Coast, she sat on the stoop among her precious little beauties, innocent victims of a heartless and selfish Ukrainian beast.

Morgan cradled a once-perfect pair of stilettos in her arms. How could Pavlo have treated her—and them—this way? After all she had done for this hot-tempered artist with only a modicum of true talent! Though . . . he did have the passion of an artist—no, he was never at a loss for passion. Or foot rubs. Or hot kisses.

She shook her head and reminded herself of the tirade that had led her to this desolate moment. She recalled the scene as if it weren't real and she had just confused her life with a Lifetime drama. Would Jennifer Love Hewitt play her? Well, maybe if Jennifer's colorist changed her brunette hair to Morgan's shade of blonde. Better yet, Reese Witherspoon! Or a younger version of Reese, someone who could pass for twenty-three years old. Morgan smiled at the thought of lunching with Reese's younger substitute, discussing her life and how the actress would portray her. She would be the center of Look-Alike-Reese's attention, and passersby, recognizing the actress, would wonder who Morgan was to be so interesting to an award-winning superstar.

A gust of wind shook Morgan out of her reverie and back to the horrific scene that had unfolded upstairs a short while ago.

Having just returned from a day of shopping, Morgan had been unpacking her purchases: a stunning Valentino bag in a subtle copper metallic, accented with perfectly placed floral adornments; the matching belt, of course, because that was a given—accessorize your accessories; a scarf that Morgan knew would bring out the blue in her eyes; and the moisturizing eye serum she could only acquire from Karina, her personal make-up consultant and an artist with concealer and a brush.

In the apartment, Morgan's mind had drifted to the necklace she had opted not to purchase at Neiman Marcus. The deep purple amethyst teardrop, framed in a graduating cascade of small diamonds, was stunning. Morgan knew that an amethyst this dark, this nearly black, could only have come from one place in the world: a South Korean mine. The rarity of the stone made the piece all the more desirable, but the salesman seemed distracted and did not give her the attention she expected—and deserved. Still, she baited him with the possibility, trying on the precious pendant, admiring its beauty and stroking her throat, a gesture that most men found quite sensual and inviting. Then, just as the salesman was whipped into a commission-induced frenzy, she abruptly put the necklace back on the counter, told him she'd think about it, and strutted away, feeling his perplexed gaze on her swaggering backside.

But now, sitting in the loft with her purchases, Morgan thought back to the one that had gotten away. Perhaps she should have thrown the guy a bone and returned to the counter to buy the necklace before heading home. Was the punishment she'd doled out worthy of the risk? What if the perfectly purple amethyst was gone by tomorrow morning when she planned to return? Wait a minute! Hadn't there been another woman standing at a nearby counter, eyeing the scene? At the time, Morgan had assumed that the somewhat simple-looking shopper was admiring her Karen Millen stilettos, but what if she had drawn too much attention to the necklace and lured this woman to sneak in and get it as soon as Morgan walked away? After all, that was probably what *she* would have done!

Morgan's hand went to her throat, stroking it in that thoughtful manner she employed when she pondered a decision. While her thoughts were solely focused on the scene playing out in her head, Pavlo came up behind her and began to softly kiss the back of her neck, moving slowly around to the line where the pendant should be lying right now. But his caress could not break her focus, and she ignored his touch. Pavlo took the indifference as resistance, a challenge that he welcomed. But when Morgan swatted away his advance and instead picked up her iPhone to direct dial the jewelry counter at Neiman's, the fiery Ukrainian's passion turned to rage. He grabbed the phone and hurled it across the room, and Morgan watched in horror as her phone connected with the brick façade, fell to the polished wood floor, and smashed into pieces. She scrambled over to gather what was left of her beloved device, particularly the SIM card that contained her lifeline of contacts, including Karina's personal number.

She didn't even hear the deafening roar of her crazed lover.

"Enough viz da phone! Enough viz da shopping!" shouted Pavlo, his arms waving wildly. "Iz MY time now!"

Pavlo stood with his hands on his hips and squaring his broad shoulders, his thick mane of brown hair adding to his stallion-like air. He glared at Morgan, who had knelt to gather the pieces of her shattered phone. She emitted only a tiny mewling sound. Having lived through a lifetime of her mother's "Pay attention to me!" thunderous rages against her workaholic father, Morgan was adept at tuning out voices she didn't want to hear, which only further ignited Pavlo's fury.

While he spat out a lengthy chain of Russian—which Morgan usually found very hot—she stood straight up. Using every inch of her five feet and nine inches (thanks to the five-inch heels she was still wearing), Morgan marched to Pavlo until she was so close she could feel his hot breath on her forehead. Even with the help of her stilettos, she was dwarfed by his height and broad frame. But fueled by her own fury, she faced off, pointed a perfectly manicured, pink nail in his face, and seethed, "You went too far this time, Pavlo!"

Stunned by her refusal to bow to his presence, Pavlo's dark brown eyes bulged so wide that she expected them to pop from their sockets and fall at her feet. *Ha*, she thought. *If only*. And then she would kick them across the room and watch them land right where he had hurled her phone.

"Too far? Too *far*?" he thundered. "I haf not gone far enough, you crazy leetle beetch."

Pavlo turned on his heels and stomped across the floor, his footsteps echoing through the loft as Morgan stood silent and motionless. He disappeared into the bedroom, and Morgan heard the sound of drawers and doors slamming. Fine, she thought. *He's packing. I could use the extra closet space.*

But when Pavlo emerged, he was not holding a suitcase. His arms were filled with clothes and shoes. *Her* clothes and shoes!

"What are you doing?" she demanded, her hands perched on her hips and her chin upturned in the defiant stance that usually led to her victory in a face-off.

"Vat I haf vanted to do for months!" Pavlo growled.

Pavlo walked to the window, and before Morgan's brain could alert her feet, she saw Pavlo yank open the window with one powerful flick of his hand and toss his armload out into the night air. Morgan stumbled to his side in time to see her favorite Prada wrap float down to the sidewalk, its perfect pale pink color disappearing into the darkness. Meanwhile, a Hermès scarf had caught on a windowsill on the floor below. She didn't know her downstairs neighbors but felt certain they would understand her plight and return it to her when she knocked on their door—unless the person living there appreciated the rare beauty of this vintage piece of wearable art and kept it for herself. Not that Morgan could blame her.

Morgan leaned out the window, oblivious to the light rain falling on her hair, and searched for her precious items below. She had spent more than two years hunting for the perfect shades, the perfect fit, the perfect accessories, so that she could achieve the look she so desired. She cherished her choices, kept them safe in her professionally organized closet to preserve their beauty. The way an art collector lovingly protects and displays his treasures, she had amassed and cared for her wardrobe, up until this moment when her crazed lover destroyed so much of what she held dear. Pavlo would never be able understand the severity of his action. He cared nothing for clothes. His grossly casual appearance, in spite of the shirts and slacks she brought him from Barney's, was a testament to that truth.

As she stared out the window, searching for her beautiful possessions, something powerful rose in Morgan; it swirled up from the tips of her painted toenails (in her favorite color, Good Morning Glorious), gaining momentum as it moved up her legs, past the heavy beating of her heart, and out to her hands, which had curled into white-knuckled fists. With fire in her eyes, Morgan turned and shot a lightning fast glance at Pavlo, who stood barely a foot behind her, arms crossed over his broad chest and a look of satisfaction on his perpetually unshaven face. She registered his victory face, raised her hands, and with the anger of a mother bear protecting her cubs, she lunged.

But not for Pavlo.

Instead, Morgan aimed her fury at the painting behind his back. On Pavlo's easel rested a disturbing self-portrait of the artist that showed far too many facial flaws for her taste. Inflamed by the image of her silk wrap now lying on the muddy ground, she hurled her fist through the nose on Pavlo's portrait, knocking it off the easel and onto the floor. Morgan lifted her foot and thrust her five-inch, dagger-like heel through the painting's frowning mouth. She pulled her shoe upward like a knife, tearing the canvas from the tip of Pavlo's chin to his unruly mop of brown hair. Then she kicked the canvas off her foot with the same distaste as if she had stepped in dog crap.

She had stepped in it, all right.

footnotes

So far, we've had a glimpse into two sides of Morgan Demarest: We've seen her strolling confidently through a crowd of admiring (and, yes, envious) glances, and we've seen a materialistic woman who values her possessions more than her relationship. As we venture into this tale, you'll learn more about Morgan, a woman who was raised to heal her wounds with shopping and to believe that there will always be a safety net to catch her when she falls. Morgan's life was stealthily piloted by helicopter parents who were intent on shielding their daughter from pitfalls and, therefore, never prepared her for real-world challenges. Although done out of love, their parenting still led to an adult who was clueless about how to navigate her life.

Morgan is a young woman who has yet to discover her life's goal. She has never ascended to first place in any endeavor and seems to have accepted that spot as her lot in life. Does it have to be? Only if you're willing to accept that "good enough" is as much as you can do.

CHAPTER *two*

Having destroyed Pavlo's painting, Morgan chose not to look back at what she expected would be a really, really pissed off Ukrainian. In all honesty, the brutal kick she'd just administered to his self-portrait had released a bit of her anger, but the relief was only momentary. Once she pictured her designer stilettos, clothes, and accessories lying in a mud-soaked pile on a pedestrian walkway, she felt the urge to levy a kick on the artist himself.

Instead, Morgan rose up to her full height, with heels. She pulled back her shoulders and tipped up her chin to the most defiant posture she could muscle. She grabbed her handbag off the sofa, along with the Neiman Marcus and Saks shopping bags from the day's excursion, and strode to the door without looking back at Pavlo. Her fired-up lover was strangely silent, but Morgan could hear his heavy breathing, like a bull's snort as it prepares to charge. She stomped out of the loft, making a concerted effort to slam the door. But the hydraulic hinges prevented the colossal bang she was aiming for to punctuate her dramatic exit.

Once outside the door, Morgan crossed the hall and hammered the elevator button with her fist, careful to avoid using fingertips that could conceivably break a nail. Why add more damage to this situation? Pressing the button repeatedly didn't make the elevator door open any faster but gave her something more to do than stare at the stupid arrow, waiting for the downward pointing one to light up. When the door finally opened, Morgan grabbed her bundles and shuffled in. On the short ride from the sixth floor to the first, her hands began to shake. Then her shoulders followed. She knew what she had just left but feared what lay ahead of her, outside the door.

Morgan stepped into the night air and paused on the cement step. The rain had turned to a light mist, but she didn't feel the moisture. She hesitated on the landing, preparing herself to view the fallen heroes on the battlefield, particularly her pink Prada wrap; those exquisite Christian Louboutin bejeweled sandals with a metallic gold platform and pink-and-gold straps and six-inch heels that fit her like Cinderella's glass slipper, but were crafted in much more durable Italian leather; and the Judith Leiber blue satin clutch.

Morgan walked down the stairs and shut her eyes when she reached the sidewalk. Her heart pounding and hand clutching the wrought iron railing, she opened her left eye, just a bit, and then wider, scanning the cement walkway and rain-soaked patch of grass beyond. Her vision hadn't yet adjusted to the darkness, and the streetlight behind her cast her own shadow on the scene, making it even harder to discern the damage. She opened her other eye and took a step closer. Then she gasped, holding her breath as her eyes sent the signal to her brain and it all registered.

Her once-shiny blue clutch had landed on the sidewalk and now rested at her feet. She slowly bent down and picked it up, moaning when she saw muddy spots scattered all over her designer precious-precious. She lovingly wiped the rain and dirt from the front, then reached into her shopping bag and removed a sheet of white tissue that had been protecting the handbag she had purchased just hours ago. *I'm sorry, Valentino, but Judith needs this more than you,* she thought. She wrapped the wounded clutch in the tissue and placed it in her bag, uttering a short prayer to the fashion goddesses.

A few more steps and Morgan found one of her Louboutins. One gold strap was gashed, and the sparkling jewels on the back of the heel were so covered with dirt that she could not gauge the true damage from the fall. No, not a fall, but a purposeful attack by a jealous artist—jealous of the true artistry of Christian Louboutin. Clutching the pink and gold masterpiece to her chest, Morgan scanned the area for its mate, hoping to find at least one survivor, but there was no sign of the once-perfect shoe.

She surveyed the area and saw that her clothes had scattered to the sidewalk and street. She started to pick them up and found slight solace in the fact that they were not among her most desired pieces. Ha. At least Pavlo didn't know the difference between new and so-last-season.

Laden with an armful of clothing, her worst fear was finally realized: The Prada had fluttered down the six-story descent and landed squarely in a puddle. Not just a small gathering of raindrops but an all-out vernal pool with God-knows-what living in it— probably some horrid amoebas that had already begun to feed on her precious pashmina. Morgan put her collected clothing into one of her bags. She then picked up the once-pink wrap with the tips of her nails, careful to avoid any of the mud and micro-critters in the puddle. She stood and held up the wrap, now a muddy mess, to examine the damage. Seeing the senseless destruction, Morgan wailed with the lung strength of ten mourners at the Wailing Wall. A few lights clicked on in the building above her, but she didn't care. She had suffered a tragic loss. *Call 9-1-1*, she thought. Maybe she'd have Pavlo hauled away for assault on an accessory.

"Why me?" she whimpered. "This is so unfair. And so mother-freakin' wrong!"

Morgan looked down at the puddle from which she had extracted the cashmere Prada wrap. And there lay the sad remains of the mate to her wounded Loub. While the left shoe had suffered scrapes, the right shoe was DOA. The once-sparkling six-inch heel was almost completely severed from the shoe, dangling by just a shred of Italian leather.

"Animal!" she screamed to the open window on the sixth floor where she knew Pavlo was pacing and grumbling in Russian. Morgan remembered the Russian word he spat when he was angry at someone who cut in front of him in line or performed some other gesture that insulted his very being. Morgan yelled, "Govnjúk!" She was fairly sure it meant "bastard", but at the very least, it was definitely not a compliment.

"Really, Morgan? Really? Is that the best you can do?"

Morgan whirled. "What?" she asked, looking at the windows in the building, expecting to see a neighbor looking down at her. The lights were on, but no one appeared to be home, which was how Morgan was beginning to feel about her own confused state.

"Seriously, girl! Look at you, crying over spilled Prada. Pull it together or I refuse to lift a finger to help you."

"Wh-who said that?" she demanded, looking unusually wobbly in her high heels.

I stepped out of the shadow of a tree by the sidewalk. Morgan looked at me, fearful at first. But I could tell she was surveying my appearance, like any self-respecting woman does in order to sculpt that first impression. Her eyes darted from my ebony hair, straightened and silky, down to the emerald dress that hugged my ample curves and exposed the décolletage that is only achieved with the help of a hard-working push-up bra and Mother Nature's generosity—sorry, Heidi Montag, but you can't fake girls like these. And let me just add here that my particular work does not allow me to drop designer names, but you can be sure this frock was not a blue-light, off-the-rack, special of the week. Morgan took it all in and stopped when she saw my stilettos. A pair of silver strappy sandals, fit for a princess . . . or maybe her fairy godmother.

I waited while Morgan tallied her mental measure. You get used to this response when you're bold, colorful, and, well, full-figured. And when the scrutiny ends with the hint of an appreciative nod that Morgan Demarest tossed my way, it's all good.

"I'm sorry, but do I know you?" Morgan asked, taking another envious glimpse at my stilettos.

I had been assigned to Morgan Demarest, and although I knew she was outgoing and quick to make friends, I didn't expect her to be Miss Congeniality, given the situation. But my research showed that she had far more potential than even she recognized, and could benefit from someone with more experience at tackling challenges. It's always hard starting with a new client. They don't believe in Fairy Godmothers (yet seem to believe in a Mr. Right). But you have to start somewhere, so I took a deep breath and extended my hand.

"My name is Divinity," I said.

Morgan was still unsure of me, but her good manners pushed her to accept my hand, albeit hesitantly. She shook it firmly.

"At least I know you've got a grip on something, girl," I added.

"Okay, Divinity, is it? Well, Divinity, I am in a bit of a predicament right now, as you can probably see, so I don't really have time to chat." Morgan abruptly pulled her hand from what she saw as an audacious woman in front of her.

"Of course, I see, Morgan Demarest! What do you think I'm doing here? Enjoying a walk in the rain? I don't think so. I just had my hair straightened, and any minute it's going to turn back into a black Brillo pad, so trust me when I tell you that I sure as heck wouldn't be taking a nighttime stroll in this weather! And let me just say that your hair is not looking too fine right now, either."

Morgan stared in wide-eyed disbelief. She couldn't take her eyes off me but reflexively reached up to feel her own hair and get a bead on the damage. Not fully wet, but definitely drooping, she surmised.

One shake of her head brought Morgan back into the moment, and she became a bit nervous. I was sure she figured me for some type of overdressed street person, because she abruptly turned away. It didn't even register that I had called her by name, but I figured she was still sorting out her thoughts, trying to make some sense of her situation.

Morgan picked up her shopping bags and started down the sidewalk in the opposite direction from where I was standing. But she halted when she found herself face to face with me again as I held my business card inches from her wide eyes.

Morgan blinked twice. She looked back over her shoulder, probably expecting to see my twin—who, to my knowledge, does not exist—and then back at me. She looked closer at the business card—mainly because I wasn't about to let her ignore it. She took a few steps back, but one heel became wedged in a crack in the sidewalk. Morgan lost her balance and started to fall backward. Her arms went up in the air, releasing her shopping bags, but just when she expected her size six posterior to come in hard contact with the sidewalk, Morgan landed in a soft, overstuffed chair that magically appeared beneath her. She moved her hands along the arms of the floral chintz and peered over the side to remind herself where she was. She looked up at the apartment building, over at the muddy patch where her Prada wrap had been lying just moments ago, and then shifted her gaze up to me. I pointed to a spot above her head, where her bags were suspended in mid-air. She leapt from the chair and grabbed the floating bags with the finesse of LeBron James making a slam-dunk.

"Well, Air Morgan, if you could have jumped like that in high school, you would have made starting varsity instead of sitting on a bench being a wannabe."

"How did you know about me playing basketball?" Morgan asked, dazed.

"Let me lay this one out for you. I am your guiding light, the little voice that people think is just their conscience—"

"Are you my guardian angel?"

"Do you see wings on my back, girl?" I snapped. "No, I am most certainly *not an angel*, guardian or otherwise. I should have known you'd have to stick a label on me, seeing as you are so driven by them."

"I'm not 'driven' by labels!" Morgan retorted. "I respect creativity and quality."

"Sweetheart, you can rationalize it any way you want, but those designer labels are your crack. And I didn't say there's anything wrong with that. I just said you're hooked on them. So here's one you can use, if you really have to call me something other than Divinity—Dee to my friends, and I'm not so sure you're gonna fall into *that category* any time soon if you keep this up." I tucked my card in her coat pocket. "I'm your Fairy Godmother."

Morgan pulled out the card, read it, tipped back her head, and burst into laughter. "*Stiletto 911*? Puhhlease! Now I *know* I'm dreaming. Maybe this whole thing is a dream, or a nightmare. Maybe I'm going to wake up and all my things will be exactly where they belong, in my closet and drawers. I knew Pavlo would never do something so heinous as throwing my clothes out the window. I mean, these stilettos cost more than his college education. And that kick! I would never put my foot through his painting. *Now* this makes sense. A dream!"

Morgan yelped in response to a sharp pain on her arm, coming from my pinch.

"Feel that? Still think you're dreaming? Don't make me pull out my wand! You don't want to know what I will do with *that*!"

Morgan, all damp and droopy like a poodle in the rain, was speechless at last. I rolled my eyes, having witnessed this spectacle more times than you can say "Cinderella's fantasy".

"Now let's save time, shall we?" I said. "We've got a lot of work to do, so you might as well just accept the fact that you have a Fairy Godmother, I am her, and you can either waste time making me prove myself, or we can put that energy into getting you past the wah-wah-woe-is-me bull."

"I'm not doing 'woe is me'!" Morgan objected.

"Seriously? I just told you that I'm your Fairy Godmother and all you heard was 'woe is me'? Lord, we've got more work than I thought!"

Morgan paced back and forth on the sidewalk, occasionally stealing a glance at me, as though hoping I would disappear. But I just glowered at Morgan as I grew increasingly impatient with her.

"Okay," I said, rolling my eyes. "I know this routine. I have to do something to prove that I am who I say I am—something other than materializing a chair under your falling butt or hanging your precious shopping bags in mid-air. So, what *else* do you want me to do? Wait. I have an idea."

I flicked my wrist as though delivering a casual backhanded slap to the air, and the mist stopped. "How's that?"

Morgan rolled her eyes right back at me. "The rain had almost stopped, so that's not convincing."

"Lord, help me! Even Diane Sawyer was easier to convince than this one." I waved my hand again and snapped my fingers. "Okay, Barbie, now take a look at your Louboutins."

Morgan looked into the shopping bag where she had placed the ruined stilettos.

She reached in and plucked them from the sea of tissue. The stilettos were once again perfect. No scrapes. No gashes. No mud. And both heels were firmly attached.

"OHMIGOD!" screeched Morgan. "Thank you, whoever you are! That's amazing!"

She did her happy dance, with one shoe in each hand, waving them over her head with unbridled glee. She stopped suddenly, hugging her stilettos to her chest. Morgan turned and peeked back into the bag, not touching it, and then looked over at me. "Did you . . .?"

"Yes, I fixed the wrap, and that very hot blue clutch. I could never let a Judith Leiber stay like that. That would just be damn cruel."

Morgan pulled the wrap and the blue satin clutch from the Saks bag. Both were as good as new, not a stain or tear or a missing crystal. "Ohmigod—*Stiletto 911*. I get it! You're the Shoe Fairy!" She squealed with joy and resumed her awkward dance.

I held up a palm like a traffic cop. "Enough! If you don't stop that twisting and shaking right now, I swear I'll throw those things back in the puddle and stomp on them myself. Child, has anyone ever told you that you have no rhythm? And I am *not* the Shoe Fairy! If I were, you'd be standing there in a pair of Birkenstocks right now."

Morgan gasped at the "B" word, and held the stilettos, clutch, and wrap even tighter. She stared at me, taking in the situation. After a lengthy pause, she smiled. "I can't thank you enough! I may be crazy, but I believe you are my Fairy Godmother. But I didn't make a wish or anything, so why are you here?"

"Girl, am I wearing a turban? Is there a lamp stuck to my buttocks?" I asked, twisting and pointing at my rear. "I'm not here to grant you wishes. I am your Fairy Godmother, not some fool game show host desperate to fill your crib with prizes. Honeychild, I've been around a lot more years than you can count and I can tell you one thing for sure: Every woman—myself included—can take away some type of learning from each situation. I'm sure when I am through with you, I will have picked up a few pointers myself—and I ain't talking about fashion, dear girl."

"So, what, you're just going to follow me around and tell me what I'm doing wrong? Isn't that what mothers are for?"

"Morgan Demarest, if I hadn't taken the Fairy Godmother Oath to be patient, you'd be feeling my sweet shoe connecting with your little butt. You are not my first client and you won't be my last—Lord give me strength. I seem to be constantly matched with the clueless young female."

Morgan frowned at my description, but I decided not to hold back. She needed a wake-up call from her wasteful ways—wasteful of time, money, and her life! Her mouth was open, but since no sound came out, I kept talking.

"I'm here to help you, like it or not. And if you had to pay for my wisdom, your deck of credit cards would crash and burn. Now step aside, you silly girl, open up your mind, and let me do what I'm supposed to be doing here!"

"And that is what, exactly?" she asked, pushing my buttons once more.

"My job is to help you become the person that, way deep down, you want to be."

Morgan gazed at me, clinging to her restored designer accessories like a drowning person with a lifesaver.

I shook my head. "Way, way, *way* deep down."

footnotes

What woman hasn't dreamed of having a Fairy Godmother? Wouldn't it be great to have someone step in and make everything right by just waving a wand, or, in the case of Divinity, a hand?

If you had a Fairy Godmother, what would you want her to help you with? What changes would you like to explore? These wishes can become goals, if they mean enough for you to pursue them. Changes don't happen magically. People have to consciously make the decision to affect the changes that will better their lives. For now, write down three wishes that you would request of a Fairy Godmother. Don't overthink this assignment! Just write them down. We'll come back to it a bit later.

CHAPTER *three*

While I watched with solid disapproval, Morgan wiped a tear from her eye, or maybe it was a raindrop. Her lip quivered slightly, a move, I knew, that turned most men into chivalrous masses of Galahad jelly. But having seen Leona Helmsley part with her thousands of shoes on her way to jail without shedding a tear, this little effort was wasted on me.

"Well, you can just suck it up and stop that whimpering," I said, "because I've seen women with far more to cry about pull up their big girl panties and move on. Did your golf star hubby cheat on you with more women than pledge into a college sorority? Did you lose your life savings to Bernie Flippin' Madoff? For crying out loud, even Martha Stewart sucked it up and knitted ponchos while she was in prison."

I paced back and forth in front of Morgan, mumbling to myself and waving my hands in frustration. "Dang divas . . . Barbie Dolls with credit cards . . . I'm gonna need a whole lotta chocolate for this one . . ."

Meanwhile, Morgan thought back to Pavlo and, more importantly, the warm, dry loft. That thought was like a loud voice yelling in my ear.

"You've got two choices, Morgan," I said, with less anger. "You can go back upstairs and make nice with your Russian Picasso or you can find some other place to stay. But we are *not* staying out here on the sidewalk all night."

Morgan looked up at the open sixth floor window and heard the sounds of Johnny Cash's "Ring of Fire", accompanied by Pavlo's off-key baritone.

"Love is a burning thing,

And it makes a fiery ring

Bound by wild desire

And I fell into a ring of fire."

Pavlo was probably on his third Stoli by now, channeling his cowboy-ex-con-singer-hero with the "I been wronged by a woman" pain that was just plain pathetic to Morgan. So going back upstairs was not an option, in spite of her desire to rescue more clothing before it joined her on the sidewalk. But, she reasoned, if he hadn't discarded any more items by now, Johnny Cash would keep him occupied until he passed out.

Morgan's best friend, Brianna Waters, lived a four-minute cab ride away—well, four minutes at this time of night. Morgan didn't know how many blocks because she measured everything in cab time; when you've committed your life to walking in heels, anything beyond two blocks justifies hailing a taxi.

Morgan and Bree had met nine years earlier at the Chicago Yacht Club, at a party after the annual Race to Mackinac, a time-honored tradition that both their fathers enjoyed. To the dads' mutual dismay, neither Morgan nor Bree had ever developed sea legs and only used the family sailboats to sun themselves. The teens instead spent their summers taking advantage of the many perks of the club, like wealthy young men, parties in the clubhouses, and the excuse to buy more clothes for those parties. After meeting at the Yacht Club, they discovered that they would be attending the same private school that fall; later, they became roommates in college. For years now they had been almost inseparable, except for the occasional family vacation or the first few weeks of a new romance, both of which were acceptable excuses for a true friend's absence. Even when Morgan had to be the one to tell her BFF that she'd seen her fiancé nuzzling another woman at a café, their friendship was not destroyed—which couldn't be said for the fiancé who had been eyeing Bree's family's wealth. Having been through so much together, Morgan knew that Bree would be there for her when she needed her most. Now, if only she could hail a cab.

Morgan looked at me and paused a moment. Once again, I read her mind.

"I don't change pumpkins into carriages or rats into white horses," I declared.

Morgan gathered her belongings and stepped to the edge of the curb, where she strained to catch a glimpse of an oncoming taxi. She never had to wait long, but tonight appeared to be an exception . . . Tonight was an exception to all the rules she had lived by for so long.

Two cabs passed, but both were occupied. A third slowed down as it approached her. It finally pulled to a stop half a block past Morgan, where it picked up a young couple dressed in evening wear—and carrying an umbrella to fend off the mist that was turning into a light shower. Okay, they looked like a better choice for the cabbie than the rain-drenched Morgan, but she needed a little break. In my own special way, via fairy influence, I summoned a cab, which pulled to the curb beside Morgan. She grabbed her bags, opened the door, and jumped in. Her manners at least extended as far as to wait for me to get in before slamming the door.

"1260 West Miller, please," Morgan said to the driver, who glanced quickly at his passenger before turning his attention to his ringing cell phone.

I looked at the driver's hackney license, posted on the back of the passenger seat, and nudged Morgan sharply in the ribs. "Are you sure that guy," I asked, jerking a thumb toward the driver, "is the same as the one on this picture? You can't be too careful, you know. You shouldn't just be jumping into cabs without paying some attention to who's driving."

Morgan shook her head and ignored me. In truth, she usually pretended to be on the phone when she got in a cab and gave the cab's number to her pretend caller, just to convince the cabbie she was alerting someone as to who was driving her. She'd picked up this tip from Brianna, who had had a bad experience with a crazy cabbie and had to use the guy's cab number to report him. But Morgan had no phone for her make-believe phone call. All she had was me, a Fairy Godmother who was tired and, frankly, getting rather irritable. I sniffed the stale air and shifted on the seat.

"Does this cab smell funny to you? I think it smells funny." I moved around to find the source of the smell and snagged the sleeve of my dress on a jagged shred of torn vinyl on the edge of the seat. I shrieked. "I'm stuck! And I'm stuck on cheap vinyl. Get me out of here."

Morgan reached over and freed my beautiful green sleeve from its trap.

"It wouldn't kill you to do a little walking, you know," I said, twisting the fabric around to check for damage. "Don't think I didn't notice you bought a size larger in those new pants."

"What?" screeched Morgan, in an octave that should have alerted the hounds. "Everyone knows that certain designers make their clothing on the small side."

"Uh huh," I replied, knowing full well the opposite was true. Let's face it: Designers need to make their wealthy clients happy. They don't do that by forcing them to purchase a very expensive outfit in a larger size than they care to accept.

"Just *shut up*, please!" Morgan erupted.

The cab driver shot her an angry glance in his rearview mirror. He mumbled something into his phone and quickly hung up.

"I'm sorry! I wasn't talking to you," she said. "I was talking to . . ."

Before she could finish her sentence, I hit her with an elbow to the ribs and said, "He can't see me. He can't hear me. Don't make a fool of yourself."

Ever the skeptic, Morgan ignored my advice. "Did you happen to see that woman I was with back where you picked me up?"

The driver looked at Morgan in the rearview mirror and then back at the road. "No, ma'am. I saw no one."

"And when I got in the cab, no one else got in with me," Morgan said.

"No, ma'am, no one." His eyes darted first with nervousness, then relief as he pulled to a quick stop at the curb in front of 1260 West Miller.

Morgan dug into her wallet for the four-eighty fare. She handed him six dollars, and we climbed out of the cab a split second before the driver screeched away.

"So, you're invisible, huh?" asked Morgan, watching the taxi disappear.

"Yup."

"You might have shared that with me before we got in the cab."

I smiled. "But that wouldn't have been nearly as much fun."

Morgan greeted the doorman by name, and he gave her a big smile in return, seemingly oblivious to her haggard appearance. Once inside the building, Morgan took the elevator to the twenty-fourth floor. When we arrived at apartment 2407, Morgan knocked on the door and waited for the sound of Bree's footsteps. She smiled in anticipation of sprawling on Bree's comfy couch and enjoying a bottle—or two—of shiraz while making jokes about Pavlo's big ego and short fuse. But the silence was longer than Morgan had expected and she began to fear that Bree wasn't home, which would leave her once again "on the street". She pounded more vehemently this time. Finally Bree came to the door, which she opened only enough for Morgan to see her wrapped in a raincoat. Her cropped auburn hair was disheveled, but Morgan paid no attention, immediately bursting into her tale of woe.

"Oh, Bree, I've had the worst night and thank God you're home because you will *not* believe what Pavlo did!"

If Brianna was listening to her friend, you couldn't tell by the distracted look on her face. After a few glances over her shoulder, Bree interrupted Morgan with a hushed voice. "Sorry, Morgey, but this really is not a good time for a visit, if you know what I mean." She grinned mischievously, jerking her head to her left.

Morgan stared at Bree. "I know I didn't call, Bree, but that crazy Ukrainian destroyed my phone and threw my things out the window. Out the window, Bree!"

"Honey, honey, honey. Whatever it is, just go back and bat your eyes at him and everything will be fine. We can talk tomorrow, but now is really, *really* not a good time."

"I *can't* go back!" Morgan exclaimed, causing Bree to give her the "hush" signal. Bree looked up and down the hall before stepping out the door and pulling it almost fully closed behind her.

"Listen," said Bree, her hands positioned on each of Morgan's shoulders. "I have a guy in my apartment, and he's a fireman. A fireman, Morgey. Do you know how hot those guys are? I mean, I have fantasized, but he is beyond my wildest dreams!"

"I'm happy for you, Bree, and under normal circumstances, I would never, ever impose, but *this* is an emergency!"

"No, this is an emergency." Bree laughed, again jerking her head toward the inside of her apartment. "Do you know how long it's been for me? And now I've got a fireman in my place. And if I let you in, looking like a drowned cat, he would get all knight-in-shining-armor and turn his attention to you, even though you look like hell—sorry, but you really do. Then you would dry off and start looking all gorgeous again, and my fireman would fall hook and ladder for you. And once again, good old Bree would be sleeping a in a queen-sized bed without a king."

"Oh, c'mon, Bree, I can't believe you would put some guy you barely know before your best friend!"

"Every woman for herself, Morgan. You taught me that," said Bree. "Seriously, you know in any other situation, anything, I would be there for you, but please don't ask me to do this. He is my *destiny*, Morgey!"

They stared wordlessly at each other, neither able to fathom the other's request. It was a stand-off with neither side ready to cave. Finally, Bree broke the silence.

"Listen," she said, as Morgan readied herself to accept her friend's apology and hospitality in one fell swoop. "Why don't you go to your dad's apartment? You know it's probably empty, and you can have some quiet time to figure out what to do next. If

I were you, I'd be thrilled to have a place all to myself right now. Well, not that I want *my* place all to myself right now." Bree giggled.

"If I were you," snapped Morgan, "I'd be more worried about that stray hair on your chin and whether or not your fireman has more whiskers than you."

Morgan snatched up her shopping bags, turned, and stomped down the hall to the elevator without one look back at her friend, who was standing agape and fingering her chin in horror.

footnotes

When life takes a bad turn, it appears that more troubles follow right behind. Morgan's world has done more than become misdirected by a failed relationship with Pavlo. Now it seems her best friend has also abandoned her. (And where was her Fairy Godmother? What kind of person do you have to be to get dissed by your Fairy Godmother?) Is it a string of bad luck or a reflection of the quality of Morgan's relationships? We can presume that, until this day, Pavlo and Brianna were two of the most important people in Morgan Demarest's world, but now both have disappointed her. If you look closer, the feeling is probably mutual.

The first step in determining who you want to be is to identify who you are, and your relationships are a key factor. Think carefully about the people who matter most to you and why that is. What do you get from these relationships? And what do you give? What brings you joy from these relationships? And what aspects would you like to improve? If you could wipe the slate clean with the key people in your life and start over, is there anything you would do differently? Take a few minutes to think about this as part of your personal inventory before we move on to the next chapter in Morgan's life.

CHAPTER *four*

Edward Demarest's city apartment was located on Dearborn Street in downtown Chicago, in the heart of the city's financial district. He'd bought the three-bedroom space fourteen years earlier so he could have a comfortable and convenient place to work, relax, and entertain clients and colleagues. Back then, Edward also owned a spacious home in suburban Hinsdale, but his wife, Claire, acquired that property—along with custody of their chocolate lab, Winston—in their divorce. The Chicago apartment had thus become Edward's primary residence. But not his home.

Morgan's younger sister, Emily, had moved to New Orleans, where she was teaching in a school for special needs children and volunteering for Habitat for Humanity to rebuild some of the homes destroyed by Hurricane Katrina. Two years younger than Morgan, Emily had finished college in three years and set off at the age of twenty to make a difference in the world. Morgan had never understood how two sisters who had been so close as children could grow to be so far apart as adults. Morgan appreciated Emily's ability to give up comforts, but she could never share that feeling. Morgan was more like their mother in this way. Shopping was an experience she shared regularly with her mother. For years, they'd gone on a weekly search for some treasure, like a new leather coat in a particular shade of brown or the perfect painting for a wall that had become a boring spot in their home.

But those shopping trips had become less frequent since Claire had discovered a passion for cooking. She had been spending more and more time in her newly renovated kitchen, testing new recipes and practicing her culinary skills. At forty-seven, Claire Demarest had been reborn. She had woken up from a sort of emotional coma and learned how to have fun—and to do it without shopping! Well, she still shopped, but her purchases were now investments in her desire to become a chef, or maybe a caterer. She shopped for cookware and cookbooks, not shoes. She hunted for hard-to-find ingredients, not the latest designer bags. Morgan still accompanied her mother on the occasional shopping trip but found it to be less satisfying without the stops at their favorite boutiques.

What Morgan didn't know was that those many shopping trips while Claire was still married to Edward were mostly Claire's effort to find joy in her life. Her husband worked six, sometimes seven, days a week. He had missed countless birthday parties, anniversary dinners, dance recitals, and other special occasions. And whenever Edward cancelled on Claire, she took her girls out to purchase solace in a store where the salespeople were sure to make Claire feel worthy of attention.

Claire eventually gave up waiting for Edward to come home after long days building his real estate empire. In the end, the things she bought couldn't fill the void of loneliness that she'd lived with for nineteen years, and she called it quits, if for no other reason than to put an end to her unfulfilled expectations and move on to a new phase in her life. Claire had always possessed culinary talent and decided, after the divorce, to pursue that interest. She studied at the renowned Northwest Institute for Culinary Arts and treated her friends to exquisite brunches, luncheons, and dinners in her home. And she was loving life with a *joie de vivre* that Morgan had never witnessed in her mother.

Meanwhile, Edward had remained engrossed in his real estate development business, the result of years of hard work stemming from his upbringing as a construction worker's son. Starting at the age of eight, Edward had done side jobs with his father to help support the family. In spite of his efforts, when the time came for Edward to go to college, the money wasn't there. He had the choice of getting student loans but didn't want that burden, so he worked for the same construction company as his father and eventually took college courses at night, until he earned his bachelor's degree in business management.

Edward had vowed to himself, even before he met and married Claire, that he would give his children a better life than he had experienced, and he worked tirelessly to make that promise a reality. He gave his wife and daughters every comfort he could acquire. With his income, his wife had the luxury of staying at home and raising Morgan and Emily, both of whom had far more "extras" than he had fathomed possible at their age. For Edward, success was a measure of what you could provide for your family. His own father, although a hard worker, had never realized that kids needed to be kids, to have time to play. Working long hours without reward had not made his dad a success; it had just made him tired and bitter.

Yet, Claire never seemed satisfied with all that he gave her. Not knowing how else to show his worth as a husband and provider, Edward worked even harder, developing larger and larger projects with greater profit potential. With his hefty income, he was able to afford the lavish lifestyle that Claire obviously relished. Their home was the showplace, masterfully decorated by an interior designer whose services were reserved for the top tier residences in the Chicago area. The Demarest gardens had been featured in a national horticulture magazine. But it was all a never-ending pursuit. His wife seemed happy when she was able to create something new and different, like the garden. But her joy was always short-lived, and she soon moved on to another distraction.

Emily, on the other hand, shared Edward's work ethic. She never shied away from a challenge; in fact, she seemed to delight in them. She didn't care about material possessions and rarely joined her sister and mother on their regular shopping jaunts. Emily, like her father, wanted to work toward a goal. When she became passionate about environmental concerns, he invested heavily in making his home the epitome of energy savings, without sacrificing one ounce of comfort and convenience. For that, Emily was proud of her father, a major coup for Edward, who had never found the formula for achieving that success with his youngest daughter. In truth, he didn't feel he had made any of the three women in his life truly happy. They seemed temporarily content, but his family lacked that tight bind that he had always envisioned. Did the perfect Rockwell family even exist? He comforted himself with the thought that such an idyllic home could only exist on a canvas. Reality ran far deeper than a few layers of paint.

When both Morgan and Emily were off to college, Claire chose to venture on her own as well. She asked Edward to move out, much to his surprise. With both girls and Edward gone, Claire feared she would be lonely in the big house. She made some changes in the décor but found that the kitchen gave her the most comfort. She began watching cooking shows on the television that Edward had installed inside the island when they'd renovated the room. With the push of a button, the flat screen rose from a hidden compartment, and Claire could spend hours cooking along with her favorite Food Network chefs. When she came up with a menu that worked, she invited her friends for lunch, brunch, dinner, or the devilishly delightful chocolate buffet.

With regular exercise and the blessing of a fast metabolism, Claire managed to stay trim in spite of her new passion for food. And the freedom that came when she stopped waiting around for her husband was truly exhilarating. She soon realized she was happier on her own than being his wife.

In spite of his tireless efforts as a provider, Edward had been left without a family, and he discovered that his work lacked some of the joy he'd felt when he had purpose. As much as he tried to reignite his excitement for developing new real estate projects, he couldn't spark the flame that had long been fanned by his desire to succeed for "his girls". And then the recession hit, and real estate development skidded to a halt. It was hard enough to rekindle his passion for his work without the doom and gloom of a soggy market adding to his woes.

Emily was living, working, and volunteering in New Orleans—with the same energy for her work that Edward had once had—which left little time for her to stay connected with her father. Edward had remained close with Morgan; that was, until she met Pavlo and became immersed in his art, his life, and his—well, as a father, he chose not to think about what else Morgan was immersed in with the burly Ukrainian painter. Still, Edward had to admit that he genuinely liked Pavlo. In spite of Pavlo's loud, brash ways, he was bright, charming, and loved life. The two men in Morgan's life had occasionally spent time in the loft, drinking beer while Edward explained American football to Pavlo, who enjoyed the heavy contact of the sport. Pavlo had also sailed with Edward a few times. The artist in him reveled at the sight of the sun setting over the horizon of Lake Michigan, and he vowed to paint the vision.

As a successful artist, Pavlo was enjoying some of the riches that Morgan had become accustomed to, so Edward couldn't deny that the man could be a provider. And Edward could tell that Pavlo had a warm heart and genuinely cared for Morgan. He saw the way Pavlo stole appreciative glances at his daughter when she wasn't looking, and it reminded him of the early days with Claire, when life was simpler, before the need for "things" got in the way.

I had studied the Demarest family closely as I prepared to step into Morgan's life, and couldn't help but wonder if Edward needed me more than Morgan. Both had seen people exit from their lives, and neither knew how to reconnect. But I decided that if I could help Morgan, then perhaps I was also granting a silent wish for her father. And maybe someday he'd either be paired with one of my colleagues or figure out life's challenges on his own.

footnotes

Most people have wishes. They wish for better things for themselves, hoping for a more satisfying life. Those desires come in the form of wanting a good job, making more money, looking better, or being healthy. Having a wish and turning it into reality, however, are two distinctly different activities—unless you're Cinderella, but even she had to scrub a lot of floors and put up with some nasty she-devils to pay her dues. (You may have noticed that the Evil Stepmother and Ugly Stepsisters didn't earn their own Fairy Godmothers.)

Think back to the vision of yourself that you began to create after Chapter One. Now stir in the wishes you listed after Chapter Two. Blend them together—stirred, not shaken—and write down three goals that can guide you toward achieving your vision. Did you wish for a job that could get you excited about going to work? Did you want to be healthier, in better shape? Think about turning those wishes into goals. What would it take to make them reality? Put your thoughts on paper. What changes must you make today? A week from now? Next month? "Plans" are useless until you put your pen to paper, setting clear goals and rolling up your sleeves to put your thoughts into action. Just wishing is not enough.

CHAPTER *five*

The next cab ride, from Bree's apartment to Edward's, was less stressful, for me anyway. The cab was almost new. It didn't have the new cab smell but, thankfully, it didn't have the old one, either—that unseemly blend of stale coffee, tobacco, and the many perfumes and colognes that combine to create a low-lying stench of "public place".

We arrived at 442 Dearborn Street at about 9:30 that night. From the nasty sounds coming from Morgan's stomach, she clearly hadn't eaten dinner. And, spiritual entity or not, I am never one to skip a meal. I suggested we take a short walk to grab a bite, but Morgan pushed on.

When we entered the lobby, surrounded by marble and polished brass, Morgan made a beeline for the elevator, passing by the doorman who was in a heated conversation with a maintenance man. (Something about a resident with a plugged-up toilet who had been waiting far too long for relief—nothing a plunger and some fiber wouldn't cure, but that was none of my business.) Morgan smiled and waved at the familiar little man who was trying to explain the importance of customer service to a man with a soiled uniform and an untucked shirt that, judging by the droop of his pants, was certainly masking the inevitable repairman butt crack. I didn't hang around to find out if my theory was correct but hustled behind Morgan as she got into the elevator and pressed 14.

"Would it have really hurt you to stop for a bagel or something?" I asked.

Morgan stared at the panel overhead, watching the progress of numbers. Fascinating viewing, but my hunger was making me cranky.

"Five minutes. There was a coffee shop less than a block away. And don't tell me you're not hungry, because that God-awful sound coming from your belly is telling me otherwise."

"Okay. This is a little weird! So, you're telling me you *are* my Fairy Godmother and you can't magically conjure up a meal?"

"My magic is for emergency purposes only," I said. "If it weren't, you would expect me to make all your problems go away with a flick of my wrist. Honey, that's *not* how life works. So let's just reserve my skills for 9-1-1, and food ain't no 9-1-1. But we have to hurry. My stomach is about to eat its own lining!"

"Just chill. I'm sure you can find something to eat in my dad's apartment. He always has a stash of frozen dinners," she said, still focused on the numbers. 40. 41. 42 . . .

"Wonderful. I don't even want to *think* what's in the fridge of a single man who hardly ever eats there. Do you know what freezer burn does to food, girl? Even ice cream gets nasty when left alone too long."

44. 45. 46. Ding!

"Well, hallelujah, and don't block the door to the kitchen!" I exclaimed.

The apartment was located just a few steps from the elevator. Morgan knocked on the door and waited for an answer. All we heard was the *a capella* sound of two hungry bellies in an unharmonious duet. She knocked again, and still there was no answer. Morgan fumbled inside her handbag and retrieved a key. She inserted it into the lock and turned the knob. Or, I should say, she *tried* to turn the knob. It didn't budge.

"What the?" Morgan removed the key, took a closer look, and put it back in the lock. Still no movement.

"Are you sure that's the right key? Maybe you're so used to going into Pavlo's place that you grabbed that key instead," I offered, trying to hide my hunger-driven impatience.

Morgan took another look. "This is the key. I think I know which key unlocks my father's door. I've been here a gazillion times, Divinity."

It was the first time Morgan had called me by name, which startled me. It sounded so strange to hear it come from her mouth; my babygirl was one step closer to acknowledging that she actually had a Fairy Godmother. With this itty-bitty baby step, I felt a warm surge, like a miniature hot flash. Not that I am old enough to know what that's like. In people years, I'm in my prime.

Morgan jiggled the knob, then knelt in front of the door and peeked into the keyhole to look for something broken. I squatted behind her and looked over her shoulder. Neither of us heard the "ding" of the elevator or the footsteps behind us.

"That's a switch. I usually have women trying to get *out* of my apartment, not break in."

Morgan responded faster than I did to this comment. She jumped up so fast that I didn't have a chance to get out of her way. I bounced backwards and landed on my backside against the opposite wall. Thankfully, I did so with grace and kept my dignity intact, if only for the benefit of Morgan, the only person who could see me at the moment.

I focused my attention on the source of the voice. He was about seven feet tall, or so it seemed from my low vantage point on the hall carpet, something like a dog's eye view. He was more likely a foot shorter than that, but, height aside, this was one fine tall glass of water on a hot day. His short, thick, wavy hair was a blend of about twenty-seven shades of blonde, and judging by the sun-kissed tan on his face, those highlights came from nature and not a stylist. Behind a pair of wire-framed glasses, his eyes were more green than hazel, and he had a strong jawline that sported nothing more than a hint of five o'clock shadow. Maybe more like seven o'clock. He was dressed in a pale blue oxford shirt, with the sleeves rolled up to his elbows, exposing well-toned forearms that were as tanned as his face.

Morgan was giving him the same once-over as me, while she regained her composure. I expect she was startled as much by the sudden interruption as by the appearance of its source. He was good-looking in an aw-shucks sort of way. Not knock-me-to-the-floor hot stuff, but there was something warm and welcoming about his gentle face—in spite of the concerned look that furrowed his brow and squinted his eyes.

"Ohmigod, you scared me!" Morgan blurted, leaning against the apartment door.

"And imagine *my* surprise to come home and find a strange woman trying to break into my apartment," he replied, his arms folded across his chest and his green eyes looking far less amused than his tone would appear.

"What do you mean, 'your' apartment? This is my father's place. Edward Demarest." Morgan's eyes darted to the number on the door, quickly making sure that she wasn't, in fact, at the wrong apartment. 4608. Nope. No mistake.

"Well, you're partially right. This *was* Edward's place, but I bought it two months ago," the man replied, relaxing his posture as he realized he was not confronting an attractive, if scruffy, burglar.

"No, that's not possible." Morgan shook her head. "Dad would never have sold this place and not told me."

"Well, I assure you, he did. Why don't you call him? Obviously, the two of you haven't spoken in, well, at least two months." He stepped to the door, gently nudging Morgan away from the knob.

"Are you inferring that I am not a good daughter just because it appears that my father made some ridiculous move and didn't feel the need to share it with me?" Morgan was using that same defiant, chin-in-the-air posture that she had pushed on Pavlo two hours earlier. Two hours? It felt like two days, or maybe even two weeks.

"I'm not 'inferring' that. If anything, I simply *implied* that you lacked that father-daughter bond since you had no idea your dad moved out of here two months ago," he countered, clearly enjoying the opportunity to jab at the frazzled young woman on his doorstep. He opened the door and pushed it slightly ajar, as Morgan still blocked the entrance. He placed a hand on Morgan's shoulder and guided her two steps to the left, making a path to squeeze past her and into his home. "Now, if you'll excuse me, it's been a long day, and I'd like to go inside *my* apartment. And do give your father my regards."

The door closed softly as Morgan stared at it, her nose practically touching the peephole.

"This is not possible. It's not possible," Morgan muttered to herself. Again, she looked at the key in her hand and then the number on the door.

"I can't help you here, honey," I said. "I can fix some things, but I can't evict that man from his home."

"But that's what this guy did to *me*! Aren't you supposed to be *my* Fairy Godmother? When are you going to start making *my* wishes come true?" she demanded, and with much more whine than I cared to hear at the moment. I half-expected Morgan to throw herself on the carpet in the hallway and sink into spoiled brat tantrum mode, which, in my famished state, would only make me want to conjure up a wand with which to smack her upside the head.

"Oh, please! First of all, I told you I am here to help you become the person you can be, and that does *not* include breaking and entering or putting some guy on the street because poor little Morgan has been so wrapped up in her own life that she didn't bother to call her daddy for the past few months. Get over yourself and let's figure out a solution to this highly undesirable predicament."

"I need to get in touch with Dad," she said. "I'm sure there is a perfectly good explanation for all this. I'm sure it was a big mistake. I must have just missed the email when he moved. I probably deleted it by accident and he thought I was mad at him so he left me alone. That's what this is, you know—a ridiculous misunderstanding. Now, if you can just do that thing with your hand and get me a new cell phone, I can call Dad and get everything straightened out."

I looked at this poor, delusional woman-girl as she reshaped her woes into something all nice and neat and tied up in a little pink bow. Knowing she had always relied on others to make her life easier, I was reluctant to give her this wish. I would only be enabling the spoiled behavior that I was trying to help her erase. Morgan had yet to appreciate the many comforts that were so frequently bestowed upon her.

"Morgan, this is the root of your problem. You ask and you receive. And you just expect everything to work that way. Well, I'm here to tell you that it doesn't. The reason you are in this particular predicament is that you have never learned how to fend for yourself, to be independent," I said, more heatedly than I'd intended. I think my hunger was getting me more worked up than usual.

"Excuse me?" Morgan's voice was raised in indignation, some sort of prelude to a tantrum. "Is there some place I can go to file a Fairy Godmother complaint? You clearly are not what I need right now. In fact, you're just pissing me off. So if you can't conjure up a flipping magic wand and make this living hell disappear, then you might as well leave me alone. I'm sure there is some lunatic woman somewhere who would appreciate your type of help, but it's not doing it for me."

She was right there, in my face, coming at me with the fury of a PMS-driven woman who has been denied her chocolate.

I looked at her and mentally counted to ten. Then twenty. I had learned to park my temper after an unfortunate incident with a woman at the DMV who'd closed her window just when it had finally become my client's turn. Let me just say that thanks to modern medicine and a good proctologist, that woman had the stick extracted and is now sitting comfortably.

"And it's this spoiled brat attitude of yours that has put you in this situation," I continued. "No boyfriend, because he's fed up with your selfish spending. No BFF to tell you that you're right and everyone else is wrong. And no daddy to make it all go away. Well, *boo hoo*, Morgan. And now you're shoving aside the one person who *can* help you. Well, that's fine. I've got better things to do with my time than stand here and get old while you whine."

I stepped back and made a waving motion with my arms. I'd seen this done on "Bewitched" many years ago and it looked so dramatic. When I wanted to make a memorable exit, I channeled my inner witch—spelled with a "w". I was also buying a little time in case Morgan changed her mind. And she did.

"Wait!" Morgan held up her hands, motioning me to stop. Thank goodness, because I knew that my boss would send me back here anyway. I had been personally charged with guiding Morgan Demarest to reshape her life. Someone back at the office had honed in on Morgan and decided she was worthy of some extra help to pull her life together before she ended up so deeply in debt that she exhausted her father's last resource, drove her friends away, and ended up as a miserable, bitter, unfulfilled woman instead of the influential young woman she had the potential to be. It was an extremely rare occasion when a Fairy Godmother was allowed to bail on a client, so I didn't expect to challenge the Powers That Be. But it would be easier for Morgan to ask me to stay than to convince her she needed me.

"I'm sorry. Don't go yet!" She paused, gathering her thoughts into some order that she could make sense of. Clearly tired and confused, she sagged to the floor in a rumpled clump of hurt and frustration. Morgan pulled her knees up to a seated fetal position and tucked her face into her lap. "You're right. Pavlo. Bree. Dad. Strike three!" I saw her shoulders shake as she started to sob

footnotes

Luck, good fortune, or whatever you want to call it can only take you so far. Without a clearly defined set of goals and a plan to achieve them, your life can easily spiral out of control. And when that happens, you're not in the level-headed mindset to make the right choices to get your life back on a positive route. Take a look at your current position. If you lost your job, could you survive until you found something else? If you had to move suddenly, could you maneuver that? Think about your own 911 strategy. A life plan with goals is like a blueprint for happiness and fulfillment.

When you are clear about who you are and what you want, it's a whole lot easier to make smart choices. For example, when things come crumbling down, how will you react? If you have never taken the time to get to know your strengths and areas of opportunity (what some might call "weaknesses")—it is time to start! Go to and take the personality profile quiz. It is a fun exercise and will teach you so much about yourself.

CHAPTER SiX

I actually felt sorry for Morgan at that moment. It wasn't entirely her fault that she had grown up to be a helpless young woman who depended on others to take care of her and grant her every wish. Her parents had worked hard to make her life as enchanted as possible. But what they'd succeeded in doing was to prevent their little girl from growing up to be independent. Morgan really didn't know how to function without someone hovering overhead and pulling the strings of her life.

And here she was, a puppet with her strings cut, heaped in a sobbing pile on the floor in front of a strange man's apartment, with no place to go. I knew that my Fairy Godmother Oath would direct me to save her from this homeless predicament, but I also felt that my real job required me to do more than be one more "fixer" in her life. Yes, this girl was certainly a fixer-upper, but she was going to have to learn how to use some power tools and become a do-it-yourselfer!

I sat down beside Morgan and stroked her tangled, damp mess of hair, trying to offer comfort while I mentally sorted out a solution. I could feel her body shaking as she wept quietly into her hands. The trembling subsided after a few minutes, and her sobs turned into small whimpers. Finally, she picked up her head and looked at me. Amazing, I thought. She had been through rain and tears, but her mascara was still intact. I had to find out what brand she used!

"Everything has turned to shit!" she spat out. "Stinking, steaming shit!"

Her eyes narrowed, and she looked at me as if I was the pile she had just stepped in.

"Why is this happening? What did I do wrong? Am I such a rotten person?" she asked in a manner that seemed to be daring me to blame her. But I couldn't. Her situation was the perfect storm of all the choices she had made, which were based on the only reality she had ever known: Someone will pick me up when I fall. With this type of safety net, she'd never had to worry about taking risks. Without the fear of consequence, there *was* no risk. Compared to "real world" problems, her predicament was laughable, but knowing my boss, she had a plan for Morgan. She must believe that this girl, or someone whose path she would cross, would make a difference in the lives of millions. Morgan just needed some confidence in herself, and as much as I felt like preaching, now was not the time. It was hard to see her at such a low, and at a place where she didn't have the help of her parents. The safety net was gone, and Morgan had hit the floor hard, without the ability to bounce back.

"Is this all just some nightmare?" Morgan asked. "Will I wake up soon, back in my bed? Are you, like, one of three spirits who are going to visit me and show me the error of my ways?"

Good old Charlie Dickens. He had gotten a lot of mileage out of the night I'd gone to set him straight when he'd been about to give up on his writing. Course, in his twisted tribute to my work, he turned me into three spirits. Typical: One is never enough!

"Honey, you are *not* dreaming. If you were, I would probably look more like Brad Pitt. But the younger, finer Brad Pitt, not that scraggly one who looks like he's been living on a deserted island," I said. "Or maybe George Clooney. Time has no problem with *that* man!"

Morgan squinted at me and then broke into a small smile. "I'd take either one right now," she said softly.

"I'm just curious, Morgan—why haven't you mentioned your mother?"

"First of all, she's in Italy, at a cooking school in Tuscany. And she would just tell me to 'Find your passion! Find your passion!' That's her big thing now, ever since she 'found herself' with cooking," Morgan said, applying the air quotes with a side order of sarcasm. "What does that *mean*, anyway? I *am* a passionate person. I love life. I have fun." She looked around her before adding, "Well, until now."

"I think your mother wants you to find something that brings you the kind of joy she is experiencing, and like your sister is experiencing in New Orleans."

"How do you know about Emily?"

"Puhhlease!" I glared at her, waving my finger in her face. "I do have *some* job privileges.

And did you think I didn't do any homework before I accepted this assignment? Girl, I got more info on you than your own parents, 'cause I *know* where you went when you told them you were going to your friend's house for the weekend, and I know what happened on spring break in Cancun!"

Morgan's mouth opened, but nothing came out but a tiny squeak.

"As I was saying," I continued, "Emily is following her passion for helping others. Your momma is following her passion for cooking, and, might I add, it's about time she did something that didn't involve a credit card, 'cause that just wasn't working for her."

"Retail therapy," Morgan said. "And it did work for her, and for me. We both found that joy in shopping."

"But what meaning did it bring to your life?"

"See? Now you sound like my mother. Why does everything have to have meaning? Why can't 'fun' just be fun?"

Morgan was still seated with her back against the apartment door. She leaned her head back and bounced it gently off the door to punctuate each mention of the word "fun". She then rested her head on the door and stared at the ceiling, as if the answer could be found somewhere among the acoustic tiles overhead. Whatever she was pondering was interrupted when the door jerked open. She fell back and landed flat in the carpeted doorway, looking up into the face of the tall stranger who had taken over her father's home. He stood over her, with a look of concern on his face and a chilled can of Diet Coke in his left hand. He squatted beside her.

"I figured that after all this conversation out here with yourself, you might be thirsty," he said, handing her the soda. "I took you for a Diet Coke kind of girl, so I hope that's okay."

Morgan sat up, shook off her embarrassment, and coldly replied, "Actually, I'm a Pepsi kind of girl, but thank you, anyway."

"I would have offered you a glass of wine, but since I haven't yet decided if you're delusional, drunk, or just distraught, I thought it would be better not to feed any of those conditions," he said, lifting one eyebrow as if still trying to make the evaluation. He glanced up and down the empty hallway, then at his watch. "So, here's the thing. I can't have you sitting out here in front of my door talking to yourself. Someone is going to complain. I'm going out on a limb here, but judging from what I can tell—and the fact that you're still sitting here—you don't have anywhere to go. And you haven't been able to call your dad yet, I take it?"

Morgan shook her head.

"Okay, well, if you want to come in and take a little break from your misery, you can use my phone to call him," he said. "My name is Sam, by the way. Sam Baxter."

He extended his hand to Morgan, who was still sitting on the rug, halfway in and halfway out of Sam's apartment.

"Well if you don't take him up on that very lovely offer, I will!" I said to Morgan, who was uncharacteristically silent.

Finally, Morgan took his hand and shook it. Sam held on and pulled her to her feet. They stood for a moment, measuring each other up. Morgan broke the silence.

"I don't even know you. For all I know, you're a serial killer or a rapist," she said.

"And for all I know, Edward Demarest's daughter is an escapee from the psych ward. At least I know you're not a burglar, unless you're a really lousy one."

"If I wanted to get in there, I could have," Morgan countered, raising her chin so high she had to tilt back her head. She lost her balance and Sam reached out a hand to steady her. But I shoved her forward, practically into his arms—not for a romantic moment but to get her the heck out of the hall and into a place with a kitchen and a fridge.

Morgan shot a nasty look back at me and then told Sam, "Must be the shoes. I'm still breaking them in."

Sam looked down at the five-inch heels, which were now looking pretty scraped up and mud-splattered, thanks to the evening's cross-town trekking. If he noticed their condition, he was at least gentleman enough not to comment. A point in his favor.

He stood back, holding up the hand with the Diet Coke and extending his other arm to invite Morgan inside. She took the can as she walked in slowly, surveying the place that had once been so familiar. The furniture had changed, looking more casual than her father's style, which was intended not for comfort but to impress visitors. The hardwood floors looked newly refinished. But the walls remained the same soft mocha color; the kitchen counters were still the rich, dark granite she remembered; and the cabinets were the same curly maple and cherry that her father had custom built.

"Does it look very different?" Sam asked, noticing her surveying the area.

"The furniture mostly," Morgan said softly, a thousand memories flooding her mind. She remembered sliding down the hall in her stocking feet with Emily, pretending they were figure skaters. Sitting on the kitchen counter, melting Belgian chocolate into their hot cocoa to warm up after the Christmas tree lighting ceremony on Daley Plaza. Spending a girls' weekend here with their mother, shopping in the city for the annual back-to-school wardrobe update.

"Your father kept this place in great shape, so I didn't see any reason to change it," Sam answered.

"Well, I, for one, am going to check out the kitchen!" I declared. "I'm starved!!"

Sam picked up the portable telephone handset and handed it to Morgan. "Here you go."

"Thank you," she replied, staring at it.

Sam watched her. "Um, unless you have special powers, you have to press the buttons to make a call."

"I know!" she snapped back at him, adding a nasty glare. She bit her lip, trying to remember her father's number.

"You don't even know his number, do you?" Sam shook his head in a show of mild disgust. "You don't know your father's phone number? Wow! I bet Father's Day was quite the party in your house, huh? Listen, can you show me some identification so I know that Edward really is your father?"

Still clutching the phone in one hand, Morgan dropped her bags on the sofa and rummaged through her handbag, which was like a magician's hat. She pulled everything from there but a rabbit. At last, she found her license, which she held inches from Sam's nose.

"I am exactly who I say I am," she said. "For your information, I've got my dad on speed dial so that I don't have to remember phone numbers."

"Yeah, and how's that working for you?" Sam asked.

Morgan didn't respond. She just stared at Sam, her bottom lip quivering as she held back tears. I wasn't sure if she was using the damsel in distress ruse or genuinely wanted to cry. Whatever the reason, it worked. What American male with half a heart could resist the waiflike sadness of an attractive young woman in need?

"All right, don't cry." He walked over to his desk and rummaged around the top drawer. He pulled out a fistful of business card, flipped through them, and took one. He handed it to Morgan. "Here's your dad's business card. His cell number is right there. Try that."

Morgan took the card and read the number out loud as she dialed, turning her back to Sam for a modicum of privacy. There was a pause as she waited for the connection, and she looked over her shoulder at Sam. She smirked only slightly, having enjoyed his moment of weakness when she'd turned on the tears. Ha! It *had* been manipulation. My ESP—Estrogen Sensory Perception—was like radar, detecting when a woman was using feminine wiles to get her way.

But Morgan's smile faded with each ring as she waited for her father to pick up on the other end. When she finally began to speak into the phone, her face reflected full-out disappointment. "Hi, Dad, it's me. Morgan," she said. "I'm at your apartment on Dearborn. At least, I thought it was your apartment. There's some guy here who says you sold it to him. I'm really confused, and, oh yeah, I moved out of Pavlo's place, so call me. Wait. Oh, no. Um. My phone is broken, and I have to replace it. I'll call you back."

She clicked off the handset. Looking crestfallen, she handed the phone back to Sam. "He wasn't there."

"Sorry," said Sam.

"Yeah, well, whatever. That seems to be about the luck I'm having tonight." Morgan's stomach interrupted with a growl. She put her hand on her stomach, horrified. "Oh, jeez, excuse me!"

"Well, isn't *that* the hallelujah chorus?" I bellowed. "That sound tells me dinner is served."

I walked past Sam and gave him an appreciative once-over. He was built like a runner, long and lean. His shoulders were broad enough to be masculine but not so much to take on the body-builder look that I'd always thought was narcissistic. He was in good shape but clearly didn't obsess over it. I was hoping his kitchen stash would prove me right, although, at this point, even a handful of granola would taste like a fistful of buttered popcorn. Well, okay, I'd have to use my imagination for that one—or maybe a little magic.

footnotes

Who can't use a little "retail therapy"? When you're feeling down, there's nothing like a new pair of shoes, a bag, or some other reward to perk up your spirits. Never underestimate the instant healing power of a shopping trip! But how long does the joy last? In most cases, the purchasing euphoria is short-lived and merely a Band-Aid on the real cause of the problem. Think about your own joys. Make a mental list of the ways you like to have fun. Then dig a little deeper and see if you can understand the passions that fuel your spirit. Emily Demarest's passion lies in helping others. Claire Demarest has discovered that cooking makes her feel alive and fulfilled. Passion can ignite your ability to overcome challenges. It can guide you through times when you question yourself. Passion is crucial to lifelong joy. And I guarantee you that it cannot be purchased in a store. Start a journal and write down the things in life that make you happy. Is it singing? Perhaps you enjoy building or fixing things. Once you've written down all the things that make you happy, peel back the onion, one layer at a time, and ask yourself, "Why?" Write down your response. Then peel back another layer of that onion and ask "Why?" again.

CHAPTER *seven*

Having been charged with Morgan, I decided to do a little 411 on this Sam character. As quickly as the thought crossed my mind, I knew my boss would have the information in my file, so as the two of them were sparring, I conjured up the file and took a quick peek at his profile. Being a Fairy Godmother has its perks: I've got access to the Wikipedia version of any person's life, plus all the dirt. Pretty sweet gig.

With three older sisters, Sam had been raised to respect women. But, while he probably understood the female species more than his friends did, he knew there was only one basic truth: No man could ever fully understand a woman. You could try to guess what they were thinking—which was what they expected a man to do—but you would probably be wrong. You could ask them about their feelings, but the answer would be sprinkled with hidden cues that no man could completely read. The key was remembering one tried and true rule: Women were consistently inconsistent.

And, he learned—more from watching his sisters than listening to their complaints—women seemed to prefer bad boys. Nice Guys were the doormats on the threshold to fun—always one step away from what the coarser, thoughtless, self-centered guys enjoyed and took for granted. Because of his upbringing, Sam had become the Nice Guy. His outspoken Italian mother, Loretta, had taught him that, in spite of women's liberation, chivalry was not dead; at least, not in *her* household. Stand up when a lady enters the room, she'd told him. When he'd asked, quite innocently, "Even you?" she'd swatted him upside the head.

Sam's father, Scott, was a man of few words, perhaps because in a household dominated by four women, he'd realized he could rarely sneak in his opinion. And

Sam's sisters—Leah, Maggie, and Tessa—were like add-on mothers, so he'd had more lessons in how to treat a woman than he'd wanted. One by one, the girls had come home from dates and told their younger brother what not to do if he wanted to do well with women. Most of the things *to* do on their list had included the Nice Guy traits, like call when you say you will, send cards, remember special dates, and basically treat a woman like a goddess. He'd taken it all in but put his own twist on it. After all, his buddies had told him that girls only pretended to want all that stuff so they could suck you in and stomp all over you.

Sam knew he was a good guy but didn't want to spend his life stuck in the Nice Guy group. He'd already been bitten squarely on the backside as a result and had no desire to fall into the trap of wearing his heart on his sleeve, where it could be snacked on by women who said they were looking for a Nice Guy but kept returning to the bastards. As he had always known, the only sure thing to understand about women was that you could never understand them. So, don't try, he'd realized. Just be yourself.

I liked this man already and could see that he might be helpful for my task of rehabilitating my girl—that was, if he could get past her attitude. I slipped into his thoughts to see what was on his mind at this moment and found that he was torn:

Here was this sad, hungry woman with nowhere to go and no one to help her. His instinct told him to cut her a break, maybe give her a little something to eat. But his experience told him to steer clear of a woman with baggage. Been there, done that. Divorce papers showed how successful it had been. Still, Sam was feeling a tinge of interest in this woman who talked to herself. Morgan was certainly unusual, he thought. He knew he should just show her the door and let her be Edward's concern. But what if she couldn't reach him? What if she had no place to stay and returned to her boyfriend, who was possibly abusive?

While his brain played the "What If" game, I saw Sam's gaze follow Morgan as she glanced around the living room and kitchen, clearly absorbed in her memories. His look was a combination of curiosity about the stranger and enjoyment of the moment. He had a kind face, and my instincts told me he was a person to be trusted.

Morgan ran her hand along the kitchen island. When she looked up, her eyes met Sam's and she was jerked back to reality. Her meditative trance broken, she resumed her defensive posture. Sam caught the transformation but continued to stand back with an appreciative smile.

"You must have a lot of memories here, huh?" he asked.

"Some," Morgan replied, a bit too curtly for my refined sense of etiquette.

"You know, I could continue to call you 'Edward Demarest's daughter' or you could tell me your name."

After a hesitation, she said, "It's Morgan." She didn't see me move behind her. I pushed her right elbow forward, forcing her to extend her hand to Sam, who took it. "Morgan Demarest."

"Well, Morgan Demarest, have a seat, if you'd like." He pointed to a dark green and burgundy paisley printed sofa that looked quite inviting to my tired body. But not as inviting as the Chinese food containers in his fridge.

Morgan, however, accepted the invitation and carefully set her bottom on the couch. I could tell she was restraining her desire to stretch out and get comfortable. She was doing her best to keep up her defenses in front of Sam, unwilling to let him see how emotionally and physically drained she was—which did not slip past the watchful Sam.

"So, Morgan, I guess you've had a really bad day, or at least a really bad night," he said, sitting opposite Morgan on the matching loveseat. He leaned forward and picked up his own drink, as well as a handful of popcorn from a large bowl on the coffee table. He saw her eyeing the popcorn and nudged the bowl closer to her. "Help yourself. I was just going to watch the game."

"I didn't think the Cubs were playing tonight," she replied, pecking at a few kernels of popcorn with her fingertips.

"So you assumed I'm a Cubs fan," he said with a smile that carried on up to his eyes. "What about the White Sox?"

"In all honesty, I would have taken you for a Yankees fan," she said. "You have an accent that gives you away."

"That's painful! I'm a New Englander, so don't confuse me with the Evil Empire. That accent—which I've tried to hide, obviously without success—is Bostonian, which makes me a diehard Sox fan. Red, not White," he added, exaggerating the Bostonian accent so that "diehard" came out as "die-hahd". He paused. "Do you follow baseball?"

"I'm not a 'die-hahd', but my dad and my sister are big Cubs fans," Morgan said. "I used to tag along once in a while."

"Then you can appreciate what it feels like to have your heart broken every fall."

Morgan finally allowed a hint of a smile to grace her tired face. "At least the Red Sox gave you two World Series championships recently."

"Aha! So you *do* follow baseball!"

"Muscular guys in tight pants. What's not to like?" Morgan took a sip from her soda and raised one eyebrow as she peered at Sam over the top of the can. There was a hint of that fire I knew was still smoldering in my girl!

Sam chuckled. And I did a quick inventory of Sam and his pants. Not exactly baseball spandex, but he was sporting a pair of jeans that had been worn often enough to become just so familiar with his long legs and fine posterior. Put that man in a baseball uniform and I would be swinging for a homerun, too.

"So, I've learned your name, determined that you're a quasi-baseball fan, prefer Pepsi over Diet Coke, haven't spoken with your father in a while, and appear to be lacking a residence." Sam ticked off each point on his fingers and then reached for another handful of popcorn.

"I am *not* homeless," Morgan protested.

"Did I say 'homeless'? I did not say homeless. I just meant that you seem to be in some kind of . . . life transition." Sam sat back on the loveseat. "Everybody goes through it. You hit a bump in the road and it throws you for a tumble. Believe me, been there, done that."

"Exactly! It's just a small bump. I'll get everything figured out and this night will just be a bad memory."

"And thank you very little," Sam mumbled, shaken back into the reality that his Nice Guy goodness made him forgettable to the women he was attracted to. Morgan had fired the warning shot and he assumed the guarded position. Defenses up! Now there was a chill in the room, unnoticed by Morgan, who was still so wrapped up in her own woes that she was oblivious to those of others.

I had been watching this rally from the kitchen. Well, I half watched and half ate, having found some leftover pork lo mein and an eggroll in the fridge. Normally, I knew better than to rummage around in the refrigerator of a single man because you never knew what lurked in that cold void. I hoped the food hadn't been there too long, but I figured I'd find out soon enough. Hunger topped common sense in my current state. And, since no one was watching, I added a few fried dumplings to my meal, and a little chicken teriyaki, two more eggrolls, and crab rangoons. A girl had to eat, and I needed fuel to keep me going with *this* situation.

When I saw the hurt look in Sam's eyes after Morgan's blatant failure to appreciate his kindness, I yelled across the room to her. "Hey, girl, you just told this very nice man who welcomed a soggy stranger into his apartment that he is going to be part of a bad memory. Did your mother teach you no manners whatsoever?"

My mouth was filled with noodles, so my words were a bit garbled, but Morgan sat up and looked in my direction, leading me to believe my message had been received loud and clear. She shook off her "woe is me" attitude as if suddenly remembering that both he and I were in the room.

"Of course I didn't mean *you*, Sam. It was very nice of you to let me come in and see what you've done with my dad's apartment."

"My apartment," he corrected, still a bit annoyed with Morgan's stubbornness and refusing to release his chokehold on the Nice Guy who was struggling to get free.

"Whatever," she sniffed, rolling her eyes until she caught my stare of whole-fired disapproval. I was shooting her the full tilt, hands on hips, don't-make-me-come-over-there-or-you'll-be-sorry posture that intimidated clients far tougher than Little Miss Prada.

Morgan stiffened when she caught my visual chastising. I followed up with one sharp point of my index finger, ready to pull the trigger on what could be an etiquette lesson this girl would not forget.

"Listen. I'm sorry. I really have had a crappy night. I'm tired, hungry, frustrated, and, as much as I hate to admit it, confused about what to do next."

"Fuggedaboutit," he said in an accent that could be New York or maybe Boston. What the heck, for all I knew, it was the south side of Outer Mongolia. Regardless of locale, I could tell by the way Sam pulled up short after that statement that he had a tale to tell but, like Morgan, wasn't ready to put everything out there to a stranger.

As if reading my mind, he continued. "Listen, we don't know each other. You seem to be in a jam. Do you have some other friends you can call? Somewhere to go?"

"Well," Morgan started, remembering Bree's betrayal of her, "I thought I did, but she's busy entertaining a fireman right now."

Sam's eyebrows shot up at this last tidbit. His mouth opened, but before he let a word out, he snapped it shut and regrouped. "Okay. Well, there's nobody else? C'mon, you must have tons of friends."

"Of course I do! But they all have, well, uh . . . situations."

"Situations? What does that mean?" he asked, wondering if he'd been mistaken in letting this strange woman make herself at home in his apartment.

"You know, situations. Like, they're married and don't remember what it's like to be single and I just can't deal with getting advice from a blissfully married person, or they live out of town, or don't have room, or whatever. Why do I have to explain this to you?"

"You don't have to explain anything to me," Sam said, holding his hands up in surrender. "I'm just trying to help. Maybe you call your friends as often as you do your father and that's why you're stuck right now."

Zing! I watched this volley land squarely on Morgan, whose face immediately contorted. "My friends are *none* of your business!" Morgan stood up, grabbed her bags, and headed to the door. But her heel caught in the rug and she stumbled, landing face first on the carpet. Sam jumped up from his seat on the couch and hurried over to help her up.

"Are you okay?" he asked gently.

"I'm fine. It's the damn rug. That always happens in here, you know. This carpeting is *not* stiletto-friendly." She tried to regain her composure and shake off the embarrassment of her stumble.

"Listen, we got off on the wrong foot. Literally. Why don't you try calling your father again? Let him know he can try to reach you at this number. You can sit here for an hour or so and see if you can get in touch with him."

Damn. The Nice Guy had sneaked out when Sam's guard was down. Just when he was almost free of this woman who was definitely . . . interesting.

"I can at least help out with a little food." Sam headed toward the kitchen, where I had just chucked two empty Chinese food containers in the trash. Tasty. A bit too salty, but not bad. "I've got some Chinese food that can be reheated, if you like. I've got lo mein, kung pao chicken, fried rice, and I think an egg roll."

Sam wandered into the kitchen just as I took the last bite of the egg roll. He opened the refrigerator door and rummaged around. The refrigerator wasn't very full, so it was fairly easy to see that the Chinese food supply had been somewhat depleted.

I stood behind Sam as he bent over, hunting around in the fridge. I stretched up on my tiptoes to peek over his shoulder.

"I don't remember any kung pao, but the lo mein and egg roll are history," I whispered in his ear.

He grabbed two containers and opened them on the counter. "Well, it appears the lo mein and egg roll are history, but I've still got a little kung pao and some fried rice. Would you like some if I heat it up?"

Morgan chucked her stubborn pride aside and answered, "Sure. Thanks."

While Sam emptied the containers onto plates and stuck them in the microwave, Morgan dialed her father's number. Once again, she got his voicemail. She left a short message and Sam's number, which he had written down for her. She wandered around the room again, browsing the books on the shelves and framed prints on the walls. Sam had a collection of novels by popular mystery and suspense writers, like James Patterson, Ken Follett, and Harlan Coben, along with an ample array of business and motivational books. She noticed a grouping of titles on mentoring and pulled one off the shelf: *The Mentor In Me*.

Sam had arranged the food on two plates and was carrying them to the living room when he noticed Morgan thumbing through the pages of the book.

"Do you like to read?" he asked, placing the plates on the coffee table and reclaiming his spot on the loveseat. He was a book fanatic and loved spending a Sunday afternoon poking through a bookstore.

"I used to, but I don't read much anymore," Morgan said, resting the book on the couch as she sat down.

Sam glanced at the title and smiled. "That's a great book," he said, as he shoveled a forkful of chicken into his mouth. "It was written by one of my mentors."

"Mentors? Plural? How many do you have?" she asked with surprise. Morgan picked up her fork and stabbed at the chicken with cannibal-like zeal.

"I don't know; five, six, maybe seven. I never stopped to count."

"Really? So what do they do? Give you advice? Introduce you to people?" asked Morgan, whose hunger had overtaken her manners: Her cheeks were puffed out like a chipmunk's, but she continued to load up on the bounty like a starved homeless person—which, in truth, she was. But a better dressed one than most, I must say.

"Different mentors do different things. My finance mentor helps me evaluate opportunities, and we talk about how to avoid certain mistakes. Then there's Carl, a semi-retired corporate executive. He's been helping me improve my management skills."

"Like what?" Morgan put down her fork and picked up the book, beginning to scan the table of contents.

"He helped me learn how to deal with conflicts. He's a great manager. And he taught me to take time to pay attention to other people's positions and perspectives so I can understand what motivates them to act and respond the way they do."

Morgan was listening intently. I could hear the creaky wheels starting to crank in her head. Books. Learning. Awesome!

"What is it you do, Sam—I mean, when you're not taking in strange women?"

Sam chose to ignore the last part of Morgan's question. "I'm a marketing consultant for Smithson/Bell. And I manage a group of account executives and train them to basically take my job some day."

"Why would you do *that*?"

"Because I'm training to take my boss's job." He smiled and took another forkful of food while Morgan processed his response, trying to gauge its level of sarcasm. Sam pointed his now-empty fork at the book in Morgan's hand. "Andy, the guy who wrote that book, helped me figure out what I wanted out of life and how to find the things that really matter." Sam's voice softened, and he looked with fondness at the book in Morgan's hands. "I'm not sure what my life would be like if I hadn't met Andy. I know, at least, that I would never have met Anthony, and that would have been a big loss for me."

"Who's Anthony?" Morgan asked.

"My little brother."

footnotes

Finding perspective can be a real challenge, particularly when your life seems to be a tangled jumble of craziness. When you're too close to a situation, you can't objectively evaluate it. A good friend or family member might be able to help, but let's face it, her first concern is probably to make you feel better, which means telling you what you want to hear: "No, those pants don't make you look fat!" "Oh, that guy didn't deserve you." "French fries are a vegetable."

Seeking out and building relationships with mentors enables you to connect with people who can understand your situation and offer their own experience and expertise to help you make the right choices. Whether for career or personal purposes—or both—a mentor's knowledge, experience, and wisdom can be a valuable resource to help you avoid certain mistakes.

Where are the gaps in your own life that a mentor could fill? What knowledge, experience, and connections would be helpful to you in pursuit of your goals? What types of people possess those attributes? And how could you use your experience to mentor others? Make a list of those categories and list the types of people who might make good mentors. There is no limit to the quantity; it's *quality* mentors you need to find.

CHAPTER *eight*

"Your little brother? You mean you had never met your own brother before?" asked a startled Morgan, reminding herself to call Emily soon.

Sam smiled as he looked into Morgan's wide eyes. He walked over to the credenza, picking up a framed photo, then handed it to Morgan. She put down her fork and looked into the face of a sweet-faced young boy who, with dark hair and eyes, appeared to be about eleven years old.

"Anthony is my little brother, as in the Big Brothers/Big Sisters program. He's a great kid who's had some tough times. His dad died when he was three, and his mom works two jobs, so she doesn't have much time to do fun things with Anthony." There was such warmth on Sam's face when he spoke about Anthony that I just wanted to go over there and hug him, but I opted for a mental one instead. I beamed a little warmth his way. He stood up straight, still smiling, and I knew my gift had been received.

"Is it warm in here?" he asked Morgan.

"Feels fine to me," she answered.

Sam shrugged and sat back on the loveseat.

"How did you get involved with Big Brothers?" Morgan asked.

"I knew about the program and felt like I wanted to do something more when I got to Chicago than just work and hang around. One day, I was walking down my block and saw some kids hanging out on a street, looking really bored, and it made me think about Big Brothers. So I made a call, went down for an interview, and was introduced to Anthony about ten days later. That was a little over a year ago. We get together at least twice a month."

"And what kinds of things do you do with him?"

"Sometimes we go places, like the movies or a ball game. I'm trying to turn him into a Red Sox fan." Sam smiled. "Other times, I help him with homework or projects, or we play video games and just talk."

"I'm sure it means a lot to Anthony," said Morgan softly, looking at Anthony's photo again and then back at Sam.

"It means even more to *me*, I think," Sam replied. "Anthony is such a smart, fun kid. He makes me laugh and gets me out doing things I might not otherwise do. And I think it's good to remember what it's like to be a kid. I'm trying to help Anthony enjoy his childhood, but he is making it a whole lot more fun for me to be an adult."

Morgan was clearly taking this all in. She had *The Mentor In Me* on her lap and placed Anthony's photo on the coffee table in front of her. I could sense that something was cooking inside her brain but wasn't sure what would come out of her mouth.

"This man has some serious niceness, Morgan," I cautioned. "Maybe you can show him a little in return."

Morgan turned around and glared at me. "I *am* nice!" she shot back. The instant the comment was out there, Morgan realized she was talking to somebody Sam couldn't see. She turned back to Sam with the "uh, oh" look on her face.

"Excuse me?" Sam asked.

"I'm sorry," she said, thinking quickly. "I was wondering if I could have some *ice?*"

"Oh, of course," said Sam, apologetically. "I should have thought to give you a glass."

Sam came into the kitchen, and I watched him grab a glass from the cabinet near the sink. Out of Morgan's sight—but not mine—he gave it a quick inspection to make sure it was clean. Either he decided it was okay or hoped Morgan wouldn't notice if it wasn't, because he filled it with ice and brought it to her. She thanked him and poured the small amount of soda remaining in her can to the glass.

"So tell me more about this mentoring thing," Morgan said. "It sounds like you have mentors, and you're one for Anthony, so it must be a big part of your life."

"I believe that no one thrives in isolation. You have to reach out to others, to learn from them, and to teach them," Sam explained, becoming more impassioned as he continued. "Mentoring allows people to connect and share the benefits of their experience and knowledge. Imagine helping someone avoid the kinds of mistakes you've made or discovering something really valuable from someone else that could help you in your career or your life."

Sam was gesturing with his hands, like a preacher at the pulpit. He seemed to recognize his zeal because he put down his hands and looked a bit embarrassed.

"I guess you can see I get excited about this subject," he said with a puppy dog look.

Morgan smiled, leaning forward with her elbow on her knee and her chin on her palm. She was measuring up this man and processing everything he had just said. Sam Baxter had a kind face. There was a natural warmth about him, and a calmness that I found comforting. His green eyes sparkled, and he had small laugh lines beginning to grow at the corners. But I knew that he had achieved this peaceful manner after overcoming some struggles along the way. He possessed wisdom that you don't come by without enduring powerful life lessons. I had looked into Sam's life and seen him overcome challenges but thought it better not to divulge them to Morgan. She needed to learn to ask questions, show interest in others, and listen. So far, she was showing great promise in this regard.

There was a mildly awkward silence as Morgan and Sam looked at each other, neither sure how to proceed with the conversation.

"Oh, for God's sake, just grunt or something, will you?" I shouted, unable to endure this pause that was so pregnant it was in labor!

"I wish I could find that kind of energy," Morgan finally put forth. At first, I thought she was referring to me but then realized she was complimenting Sam. And that was okay, too. "I think I've just been following my life and not leading it, and here you are, all in control, and I have to admit: I'm kinda jealous."

Now where was all this candor coming from? It appeared that Sweet Sam had hit the Talk button and my girl was ready to open up. Well, hallelujah and pass me a margarita.

"Jealous? Well, if you only knew how hard it was to get here, and how much farther I have to go, I don't think you'd be envying me, Morgan," Sam said with a chuckle. "The hardest part is taking a good, honest look at yourself, from the inside out, and seeing who and where you are in your life. Once you can do that, you can start to map out your path. It's not easy, but it's really worth it."

"I can see that." Morgan swirled the remaining ice cubes in her glass, watching the little whirlpool she was creating. Sam watched her, sensing that she was pondering her next statement. He picked up their empty plates and carried them to the kitchen sink, giving her a moment to consider. Then he took two more sodas from the fridge and walked back into the living room, handing one to Morgan. She thanked him and poured half over her remaining ice, still pensive.

"If you don't mind my asking, what is it you do for work?" asked Sam with some apprehension.

"Right now, I work part-time at an art gallery," Morgan answered, with little enthusiasm. "It's okay, but certainly not my dream job."

"And what is your dream job?" Sam asked with obvious interest.

Morgan dropped back, sinking into the cushy sofa. She looked up at the ceiling long enough that Sam turned his gaze there as well. At the same time, they turned their eyes back to each other, and she sighed before responding. "I wish I knew."

"Like I said, it's not always easy to figure these things out. I had a *lot* of help." He paused and smiled. "A lot of help."

"You make it sound like you were a miserable wreck." Morgan said. She looked down at her once-beautiful stilettos and ran a hand quickly through her tangled hair, realizing just what kind of wreck she must appear to be at the moment.

"I learned not to dwell on where I was." Sam's smile instantly disappeared, and Morgan was startled by the somber introspection that had replaced the happy, handsome, inviting face. "I couldn't move forward if I carried too much baggage, so I learned some lessons and have moved on."

She waited for him to offer more, but he shut down. Silence returned, far more uncomfortable than any previous moments. I finally left my observation post in the kitchen and took a seat next to Sam. I wanted to look Morgan in the eye and, at the same time, give Sam a little good karma to bring him back to his happy place. I put my arm around his shoulder and he shrugged slightly, sensing my presence but unable to see me.

I whispered in his ear, so softly that even Morgan couldn't hear, "You're a good man, Sam Baxter. Your past doesn't define you. It's only a starting point."

Sam took a long gulp of his soda, looked squarely at Morgan, and stood up.

"I don't know about you, but I could use something more substantial than a Coke and that measly amount of Chinese food. I'm going to order a pizza and grab a beer. Care to join me?" His question was a combination of invitation and challenge.

Knowing Morgan, I thought she'd be up for both. I was right.

"As long as it's Giordano's deep dish and anything except light beer, I'm in!"

"Is there any other kind?" Sam responded, all smiles once again.

footnotes

Holding onto the past can be a heavy weight. When you spend too much time and energy on regret, you might be missing opportunities that present themselves to you. We all make bad choices—that's part of being human. The important thing is to learn from those experiences. Write down some of the regrets you've been carrying around with you. Maybe you wish you hadn't treated someone a certain way or that you hadn't accepted a job or a task (like being a bridesmaid again). Put those regrets on paper. Then cross them off, one by one. Make them go away in front of your eyes, and promise yourself to leave them in the past.

CHAPTER *nine*

Morgan awoke to morning sun streaming through the window and smacking her dead in the face. She grabbed the first thing she could reach, which happened to be an empty pizza box, to cover her eyes. She whacked her forehead with the box, compounding her existing headache.

With the pizza box over her throbbing eyes, Morgan groped blindly to find something softer. She felt a pillow on the floor. She brought it to her face and tossed aside the cardboard box that reeked of sausage and onions, two ingredients that had sounded wonderful last night but gave off a pungent odor the morning after.

The morning after? What had happened? With one hand clinging to the pillow, the other hand reached down to see what she was wearing. With a sigh of relief, she realized she was still fully clothed—except for the shoes, but let's not worry about accessorizing right now.

I heard the loud groan and waited for Morgan to emerge from beneath the pillow. It took a bit longer than I anticipated, but after more groans and some unintelligible mumbling, she tossed the pillow back on the couch and slowly sat up.

"Where am I?" Morgan squinted and took a slow, panoramic scan of the room. Then her eyes landed on me, sitting comfortably on a stool at the kitchen counter, where I was sipping coffee with a triple shot of espresso—anticipating a long, trying day—and wearing my favorite fluffy white bathrobe that I'd acquired from a short yet eventful stay at the Ritz. Morgan eyed me up and down and then scanned the room again. A mixture of recognition and disappointment took over. "So this wasn't all a weird dream. Shit."

"And good morning to you, sunshine," I said, with enough perkiness to emphasize her painful state. "Are we feeling a little morning-after ugliness?"

"Puhhlease, leave me alone!" She flopped back down on the couch and covered her face again with a pillow.

"Babygirl, I told you not to try going toe-to-toe drinking against a Scotsman. It's in their genes, you know. And he wasn't even drinking much. You're just a lightweight. Probably more used to a little appletini than Guinness Stout," I chided.

She yelled something into the pillow, which I choose not to share with you lest you think my girl had that kind of potty mouth. At least, I resolved, she wouldn't have one when we were through with our journey. Expletives wouldn't get her where she wanted and needed to go.

She took the pillow from her face and shot me an evil glare. "What kind of fairy godmother *are* you? Aren't you supposed to protect me?"

"What? From your own fool self? You're a big girl, Morgan Demarest, and I am *not* your babysitter. My job is to guide you down a path to create your own future. Now, if you stepped in front of a bus, I would grab you back—unless, of course, you're still giving me this attitude, in which case I might even give you a little shove."

"Okay, okay. I get it." She buried her face in the pillow. "This is all new to me, Divinity. I'm so confused!"

I looked up and saw Sam standing in the hall, just beyond the living room. He was dressed in Red Sox pajama pants and a grey t-shirt, looking a bit scruffy with his unshaved face and tousled hair. But still mighty fine. He was barely awake, scratching his chest and trying to make sense of Morgan's diatribe. He shook his head and wordlessly shuffled to the kitchen. He put a K cup in his Keurig coffee maker, grabbed a mug from the cabinet above, and leaned on the counter, staring at the machine as though willing it to work faster. The hazelnut blend smelled heavenly when the machine started to dispense the dark nectar into his cup.

Sam took his coffee and sat beside me on the other stool, his gaze fixed on the groaning woman hiding under a pillow on his sofa. After a few minutes, the brew started to take effect on him. He sat up a little straighter and appeared more composed when he finally broke the silence.

"So, how long have you had this problem?" he asked, loudly enough for Morgan to hear him through the pillow.

Morgan threw back the pillow and sat up. Instinctively, she shook out her hair and ran her hands through the tangled mop to make some sense of it. She looked at him and zoomed in on the coffee cup. "What problem? And is there any more coffee?"

"Talking to yourself. And yes," Sam responded. He slid off his stool and returned to the coffee maker. "You have your choice of hazelnut, dark roast, and donut shop. We don't serve latte, cappuccino, or caramel macchiato here." He paused, and I saw a slight grin creep on his face as he called back to Morgan, "Or I could pour you another stout."

"Don't even *say* that word!" she said. "I think there was something wrong with that beer. Maybe it was stale or something. I never get this reaction from good beer."

"*Good* beer? *Good beer?*" Sam repeated. "Guinness Stout is *the* beer. You've probably only been drinking those trendy beers with fruit in them. They only pretend to be beer. It's like those powdered drinks that taste like a watered-down version of what they're supposed to be. You've been drinking powdered beer, Morgan."

I enjoyed this energy between Morgan and Sam. They were like sparring partners, both looking for that open spot to hit with a jab. And I thought Morgan over-estimated the power of the punch she packed.

"Whatever," was her ripping comeback, confirming my belief. "Can I just have some coffee, please?"

A few minutes later, Sam returned to the living room and handed her a steaming cup that wafted the delicious aroma of hazelnut in my direction. He sat down on the loveseat and watched Morgan take a gulp. She closed her eyes as the hot liquid worked its way down her throat. Her expression went from a lioness about to pounce to a purring kitten.

She opened her eyes and looked at Sam. "Thank you for the coffee, Sam. I should become human again shortly."

"I'll just sit here and wait for the transformation," he replied with a smile.

Morgan took a few more sips before responding. "Listen, I know you gave me some really great advice last night, Sam, and I appreciate you letting me stay here on your couch, by the way, but I can't remember where we left off."

"Well, you were cursing someone named Pavlo and said you could do better artwork with finger paints and a blindfold," teased Sam. "And I think you said something about a fairy godmother who doesn't know her wand from her, um, I believe you said that stick up her butt."

Well, this was the first I'd heard about *that!* I must have been dozing when the Diva of Darkness had gone on her rant.

I sneaked around behind her. "*Stick* up my *butt?*" I screamed into her ear.

She jolted upright, turned around, and glared at me with her hands over her ears.

"You think I've got a stick up my butt? That's some real sass talk from a girl who looks like she's been living on a street. And, if you don't watch yourself, that's where you will be!"

"I'm sorry," whimpered Morgan. "I was drunk. I didn't mean it. Please! I'm really, really sorry!"

"You don't have to apologize," said Sam, who had just turned his back to walk away. He disappeared down the hall momentarily.

"You'd better apologize," I said to her, wagging a finger in her face. I made a mental note to include some basic etiquette lessons in her upcoming Fairy Godmother education.

Sam returned to the living room and stopped short when he saw Morgan: Her hair was puffed up like Snookie on steroid mousse. I had hit her with a coiffure that only a Jersey girl could love, striking right at the heart of my hungover fashionista.

"Whoa! What happened to your hair?" Sam stood a few feet away, just in case she was standing on a live wire that he didn't want to touch.

She reached up and felt the pouffed-out do that I had given her. Her mouth formed a perfect "O" but nothing came out. She pulled, tugged, and smoothed her helium hair until it was back to normal. "Must be the static electricity in here," she said, shooting me a venomous glare when Sam wasn't looking. He handed Morgan two pills and a glass of water. "Here, take these. It's just Tylenol but should help that hangover— I mean, headache."

She took the pills without even looking at Sam. "Thanks."

"So, listen," Sam said, sitting down once again and putting his feet up on the coffee table. "Your dad called back while you were, uh, sleeping. He's going to pick you up here in a little while."

"Dad? Here? What did you tell him?" she asked, her mind swirling with excuses for her situation.

"The bare minimum. I told him you showed up here looking for him, that we talked for a bit, and you fell asleep on the couch. He wasn't in the city, so I told him you'd be fine until the morning," Sam said, casually sipping his coffee.

"That's it? He didn't grill you about, um, you and me?"

"There is no 'you and me,' so there was nothing to tell. I know Edward, and I think he knows me well enough to know I wasn't about to ravage his drunken daughter," Sam said, annoyed that Morgan was taking the offense when he was clearly trying to help. *And this is why I shouldn't stick my big nose in and help people,* I heard him think.

"I wasn't drunk." The raised volume of her own voice rattled her head. She put her palms on her forehead to push back the pain.

"No, of course not. But I don't think a sober person would do the things you did," he said slyly.

Ooooh, I liked this man. He could play dirty.

"What? What did I do?" she asked, horrified.

"You don't remember? How could you not remember? It was one of the most memorable nights of my life and you don't even remember. See, you *were* drunk," he said, pointing an accusatory finger in her direction.

"Well, maybe a little. But I was really just very, very tired. It was a long, exhausting evening."

"So you remember that much."

"Yes, but I don't remember anything . . . else." Her eyes were pleading with Sam to end her misery and unlock the secrets of her late-night drunken revelry.

He smiled. "Because there wasn't anything else. Like I said, I don't ravage drunk women. You basically ranted about your stupid Ukrainian boyfriend, someone named Bree who put her sex life before her friends, and something about calling the fire department to put the hose on some hot stuff. I think that's about it."

Morgan plopped back down on the couch and covered her face with the pillow once again. And she noticed for the first time that it smelled of Sam. His cologne was light and clean. He had obviously lain on this pillow many times. She inhaled the scent and started to imagine what *could* have happened the night before.

Sam walked back down the hall to the bathroom, leaving Morgan in her hungover state.

"Well. Aren't you a mess, young lady?" I said with a sneer. "And, by the way, I am still waiting for an apology. Or do I have to play hair stylist again? I'm thinking this time, maybe a Mohawk."

"I already apologized! I'm sorry! Don't touch my hair. It's connected to my head, which is throbbing so badly right now that I can barely hear you talking at me. Gawd, make that pounding go away!"

I stopped and listened. I heard the pounding, too. But it wasn't inside her head. Someone was at the front door.

And then we both heard it: "Morgan! Morgan! I know you are there. Open za door!"

It was Pavlo. He was pummeling the apartment door.

"Shit." That was all she could muster. Morgan dropped the pillow and hurried to the door, barefoot and scruffy in her slept-in clothes. She whipped open the door to Pavlo's raised, meaty fist, ready to pound again.

"Pavlo!" she said in a sort of hushed yell. "What are you doing here?"

"I go to Bree's apartment because I am thinking you be there. She tell me you come to stay viz your father." Pavlo's eyes were bloodshot, a combination of too much Stoli and not enough sleep. He looked at her with anger and relief. He was not accustomed to being walked out on but was glad she was okay.

"Well, you found me. Now you can leave." Morgan put her hand on the man's broad chest and tried to push him backward toward the elevator.

"Nyet!" he pronounced. "You come viz me now. Come home and I vill forgive. Come back where you belong."

The thing with Pavlo was that he really was a Russian (okay, Ukrainian) bear: a hulk of a man who looked like a professional wrestler, but with the loving heart of an artist. However, the link between the two sides got all jumbled up when he spoke. Morgan knew he wasn't the Neanderthal that many of her friends took him to be. But at the moment, all she saw was a bully who had no regard for her or her cherished possessions.

"*You* forgive *me?*" She was still pushing him but not moving the man an inch. "You threw my things out the window. You pretty much kicked me out on a rainy night. And now you're standing here looking for an apology? Get out, Pavlo. Just get out."

"You destroyed my artwork. You can buy new shoes and scarves. My painting cannot be replaced," he said, his dark eyes bearing down on her. "But I am here to say that I luff you so I vill forgive you, dis time."

"Dis time?" she said, mocking his accent. "And what happens the next time you get mad at me for something—and I don't even know what I did to tick you off last night—and you explode? What next, Pavlo? Do you throw *me* out the window?"

"You are being shtoo-pitt," he said, spitting out the syllables like watermelon seeds. "I neffer hurt you. Is me who is hurt."

"Just go now, Pavlo. I can't talk to you right now." Morgan shoved him harder, and he took a step backward. She looked over her shoulder to see if Sam had emerged from wherever he'd gone. She wasn't sure, but she thought she heard the shower running. "Go now. I need time to think."

"If I go now, and I go alone, it vill stay dat vay, I promise you, Morgan," Pavlo said, steadying himself in the doorway. He reached up with his muscular arms and held onto the top of the doorway, filling it with his presence. "I am varning you."

"You are warning who?" came a voice from behind Morgan. She turned to see Sam standing there, with just a bath towel wrapped around his waist. His hair was wet and tousled, his chest gleaming with water droplets. But his face was rock solid in anger. "Who are you, and what are you doing in my apartment?"

"*Your* apartment? Dis iz Edvard's apartment." Pavlo glared at the nearly naked man.

I stood at the ready to jump between these two unlikely centurions. Pavlo was all heaving manhood and Sam was a shining, nearly-naked knight. My money was on the towel.

"This is *my* apartment, and you will leave or I will call the police," Sam said, taking three steps toward Pavlo, his hands balled tightly into fists.

"So, I spend da night vorrying and you are shacking up viz another man. Forget every-sing I haff said. I am *not* sorry. I do *not* vant you to come back. You vill get all your leetle things and get out of my life!" Pavlo waved an angry fist in the air to emphasize this last statement.

Instantly, Sam stepped in and grabbed Pavlo's wrist, presumably to prevent it from striking Morgan. Through gritted teeth, he seethed, "Get. Out. Now!" He released his grip and pushed Pavlo out of the apartment, slamming the door in his face. Then he whirled around to look at Morgan. "Are you okay? Did he hurt you in any way?" Sam's voice was charged with adrenaline. His anger still sputtered, but he was clearly concerned for Morgan.

"I'm fine. It's just. Well. I'm sorry he barged in like that. He gets crazy and . . ." Morgan, still shaken up from the confrontation, tried to find the words to both apologize to and thank the innocent man who'd ended up fending off her pissed off boyfriend.

"I'm glad you're okay. Now, I think it's time you left as well. I really don't want any more drama in my life."

Morgan was stunned by the sudden change in Sam's demeanor. He had shifted from sweet, likable guy to a bitter man without empathy.

"But . . ." she said, her voice quivering.

"No. Just go. Your father can meet you in the lobby." Sam tightened the towel around his waist and walked back toward his bedroom, slamming the door.

I walked over and put my arm around Morgan, who was standing there, her head down, fighting back tears.

"C'mon, sweetie. It'll be okay. Let's get your bags and go. Everyone is upset right now. You all need time to cool off and clear your heads. Let's just go downstairs and wait for your daddy."

Morgan nodded. She moved like a robot over to the couch where she had left her handbag and shopping bags. She took one more look at the photo of Anthony on the coffee table and the mentoring book that lay beside it.

"I'm a mess, Divinity. A total flipping mess."

And that was why I was there, I thought, as she heaved a huge sigh and walked toward the door.

footnotes

The first step in making a change is acknowledging that a change is necessary. You can go about making excuses and blaming others for your problems, but the truth is that you are the mistress of your destiny. Don't waste energy placing blame or making excuses. Channel that energy into making **change**. Fuel your future with positivity, not negativity. Negative thinking is a toxin that you need to push out of your life. If you haven't done so already, start making a list of things you'd like to achieve, including those changes you want to make in your life. It doesn't matter who did what in the past; it's what you do from here on in that counts!

CHAPTER *ten*

The lobby was very familiar to Morgan, though she was always just passing through on her way to or from her father's place. The marble floor was accented with a Persian rug with an intricate pattern in shades of deep blue, gold, and dark crimson. The walls had been faux-finished in soft shades of cream and gold. As she waited for her dad to arrive, Morgan sat in a burgundy velvet chair and glanced at the outdated magazines on the glass-topped coffee table in front of her. The summer issue of *Chicago Magazine* featured a cover for a festival that had already passed. She had wanted to go to that event but had been busy. Doing what? she asked herself. What had she been doing? Shopping? Sipping martinis with Bree at their favorite bar? Watching Pavlo paint?

One thing was for sure: She hadn't been busy spending time with her family. Or she might have known about the apartment being sold.

She wondered how long it would be before her father showed up. Had Sam mentioned that? He'd been so quick to push her out the door that she hadn't thought to ask. Or had been afraid to.

What a mess. What a horrible mess. Damn Pavlo. Damn Bree. Damn Guinness.

Morgan stared at the marble floor, tracing with her eyes the white veins in the deep green stone, following them to the door where Jeffrey, the doorman, stood with his back to her. He wasn't much taller than she was in heels, and he had hints of gray peppered through his short, dark hair. She tried to remember when she had first met him. Had he been there when her family had first started coming here? Why had she never given him more than a passing glance and quick greeting? Now she noticed that Jeffrey had wonderful posture and wondered if that was a requisite for the job.

Did one have to know how to stand at attention? And could she possibly do that? Nope.

But Jeffrey seemed content. He always smiled. He was in a low-stress job that probably met his needs. But did it feed his passion?

Oh no, she thought. There's that word. Passion. Why had it crept into her vocabulary like a pesky mosquito? She'd lived this long without worrying about finding her passion. Why should she start fussing about it now?

"Maybe because you know you need to make changes," I said, interrupting the little conversation she was having with herself in her head.

"How did you . . .?" she asked.

"Honey, your thoughts might be inside your brain, but they are screaming out loud at me! If I had to rely on just the things you decided to share with me, it would take me a lifetime to get the job done," I said. "So I listen both to what you say and what you don't say."

"Isn't that eavesdropping? Don't I get any privacy?"

"Sure. When you need it. And trust me, I'll know when you need it. We're trained to help, not be busybodies."

Morgan just stared at me.

All of my clients had trouble learning and understanding their Fairy Godmother's modus operandi at first. They all wanted me to grant their wishes. Everyone wants her own Cinderella story. And when I had to give them a dose of reality—explaining that Cinderella hadn't been all she was cracked up to be—they were disappointed, but backed off. You see, Cinderella had been a bit of a doormat. She'd let her stepmother and stepsisters push her around. The true story is that I'd tried to get her to grow a spine and stand up for herself. She hadn't needed a Prince Charming to take her away from her woes. She'd needed to learn to do it for herself. And she had. Which was a good thing, because her Prince had been far from perfect. He'd loved her, definitely, but that "happily ever after" stuff had been way overblown. They were in marriage counseling less than a year after the wedding. Additionally, she had trouble adapting to life as a princess after spending most of her life scrubbing floors and hanging around with singing mice. And as much as she liked having servants, she never forgot her roots and tried to do as much as possible by herself.

I knew that Morgan wanted me to wave my magic wand and make all this trouble go away. But I hadn't done it for Cinderella—in spite of what you've heard—and I wasn't about to be just another quick fix for Morgan. It was time for her to wake up and face the responsibility of being a grown woman.

"So," I said. "We might as well get started. You don't have a place to live, you need a better job, and, forgive me, but your life skills could use some polishing."

"My life skills are just fine," she shot back.

"Morgan, your primary activity is spending money. And right now you don't have the money to spend, and you can't keep running to your daddy. So, yes, you need to rethink how you live. Now, we can sit here and argue, or you can suck it up and let me help."

I paused, waiting for the return volley, but Morgan said nothing. She was tired. The fire in her eyes was gone. Her expression shifted from one of defiance to acceptance.

"I'll take your silence as choosing the latter," I said. With a quick flick of my wrist, I conjured up a pad of paper and pen and handed them to her. "Don't worry. This won't hurt you a bit, but you might feel some slight bruising to your ego."

She remained silent, which I counted as a blessing.

"Let's start by taking a personal inventory of your life," I said. "First, you need to count your blessings."

"I can't imagine right now what those would be," she grumbled.

"Let me help you. Are you healthy? Do you have family and friends? Do you have to worry about where your next meal is coming from? Have you been ravaged by a flood, hurricane, or earthquake that has destroyed everything you own?"

"Well, I have no place to live, my bank account is low, my boyfriend—excuse me, ex-boyfriend—is playing ring toss with my belongings, my father apparently has forgotten I exist, my mother is off in Tuscany learning how to cook pasta al dente, my sister is in New Orleans saving the world one person at a time, and my best friend is getting her fires lit by a fireman instead of helping me. And I don't, in fact, know where my next meal is coming from." Morgan ticked off each item on her fingers. When she got to the end of her list, she shook her hands like she was flicking away flies. "How's that for my 'personal inventory'?"

I grabbed the pad from her. "I'm sorry, but I'm not hosting a pity party here, Morgan. I didn't ask you to share your 'oh-woe-is-me' list. I asked about your blessings. You actually *have* a family, even if you aren't the center of their universes right now.

Be thankful for them, because many people are truly alone. You are healthy. Be thankful for that. You have, I think, intelligence. You have a job, even if it's not perfect. And your current situation is only temporary."

I scribbled quickly on the pad and tossed it back to her. Morgan fumbled to catch it. The pages fluttered as she grabbed them.

"I'm not going to play secretary here. This is your work, so you write these things down," I instructed.

She straightened out the sheets and looked down at what I had written:

Life is under no obligation to give us what we expect.

Her brow furrowed as she stared at the words.

"Someone told me that a long time ago," I said. "It's a valuable reminder whenever you're feeling sorry for yourself—like now!" I held out the pen for Morgan to take. She kept staring at the notepad. Her eyes were becoming moist with tears. I wasn't sure if she was feeling that downtrodden or if my words had touched some emotion that she had been keeping buried. She wiped her eyes, picked up the pen, and started writing:

Parents

Emily

Health

Education

Bree (when she's not shtupping the fire department)

A job

Happy memories

My wardrobe

She paused and studied the list before adding:

Sam opened the door

Divinity

She clutched the pad to her chest, apparently not ready for me to see what she had written—as if I didn't already know.

"Okay," I told her. "Now, next to each item on your list, write down what that particular thing you're thankful for means for you."

"What do you mean?"

"For example, having a family that loves you means you have support for times when you need it," I explained. "You have people who will always love you, no matter what. Isn't that worth a lot?"

Morgan looked at her list but didn't write anything. She scratched her head with the tip of the pen (the non-writing end; I checked). Then she started adding to her notes:

Parents—a lifetime of love and support

Emily—the voice of wisdom; she loves me no matter what

Health—no medical bills; I'm healthy enough to take care of myself

Education—a college degree should help me get a better job; I've got skills I'm not using (not sure what they are, though)

Bree (when she's not shtupping the fire department)—a good friend who deserved to have last night; someone who understands me and (usually) is there to listen

Happy memories—childhood, vacations, family stuff, traveling, good times with Pavlo

My wardrobe—makes me feel good

Sam opened the door—a stranger gave me a break when I needed it

Divinity—ditto (I hope)

She stopped writing and looked at her list, then up at me. I was thumbing through an issue of *Cosmopolitan* from last spring and rethinking my hair color and style. If Beyoncé could have long blond hair, why couldn't I?

"Okay, I'm done. Now what?" Morgan asked.

"Now I want you to start thinking about goals for yourself. Make four columns. At the top of the first one, write 'Today'; on the second one, write 'This Week'; the third one, 'This Month'; and the last one, 'This Year.'" I watched and waited while Morgan did as I instructed. "Now, I want you to write three things under each column: Write down goals that you want to have accomplished by the end of today, this week, this month, and at the end of a year." I paused a moment before cautioning her. "And if I see the words 'shop' or 'manicure' anywhere on that list, I will turn your precious Prada wrap back into a rag. This is your chance to grab some meaningful think time. Don't waste it."

Morgan rolled her eyes and then glanced toward the doorway. Jeffrey turned and smiled at her. She gave him a little wave and watched the door for a moment, expecting her father to come walking in.

"He's stuck in traffic," I said. "Get back to work."

Another eye roll.

Morgan found that the first part of her list—the things to do today and this week—were the easiest items to come up with. The longer-term goals, however, were proving to be a challenge. I looked at her progress.

Today	*This Week*
Get a new cell phone	*Get my stuff*
Find a place to stay	*Call Bree*
Talk to Dad	*See what I've got in my bank account*

Morgan's stomach was awake now and announced that it was time for breakfast. She thought about last night, eating Chinese food and pizza with Sam. It had been comfortable. Maybe part of that feeling had come from being in the apartment where she had spent so many good times. The furnishings had changed, but the memories still lingered through the apartment. She thought back to the Sunday breakfasts she had enjoyed at the kitchen counter. Her dad had been in charge of making breakfast on Sundays, and it had always been a treat. Cinnamon-raisin French toast. Belgian waffles with strawberries and whipped cream. His famous "Name Your Poison" omelet station. But her favorite as a child had been watching her father create letters and shapes with pancake batter. He had become masterful with a spatula, artfully making their initials, a heart, Mickey Mouse, and a snowman—and a question mark when he had a surprise planned that day. Pancake Sundays had been the very best.

Her reverie was broken as Edward Demarest dashed through the door and hurried toward her. The sight of his normally perfectly groomed daughter sitting in a wrinkled mess and—horrors—without makeup, surrounded by equally wrinkled shopping bags made his fatherly heart skip a beat. Suddenly, Morgan was a little girl again, and Daddy was coming to the rescue.

footnotes

When you start any new project, it makes sense to organize your tools so you know what you have to work with. Men, who never have enough tools, will make lengthy trips to Home Depot, where they ogle things that most humans don't even know exist. (But that's another story.) When you are doing a life makeover, you need to start with the same approach. Take a look—an objective look—at what you have to work with. List your strengths, whatever they are. Are you dogged when pursuing a task? Great! You're not a quitter. Are you able to see different sides of a situation? That could make you a good negotiator. Take the time to look at yourself through the eyes of someone who is just getting to know you. What would they notice about you? And remember that even a rusty tool can be polished up, so think about the skills you haven't used in a while or those abilities that simply need a recharge. Make your inventory as complete as possible.

The exercise of getting to know yourself can be very uplifting. Most people don't give themselves enough credit for being remarkable. They take things for granted. Now is the time to celebrate who you are and what you have to offer.

Once you have worked through your personal inventory, use that knowledge to shape your goals. The short-term ones that can be quickly accomplished provide instant gratification—the ability to check a few things off your list and get that sense of accomplishment. As you start looking farther off into your horizon, identify goals that can pose a bigger challenge. When you put them together, you're on the right path.

CHAPTER *eleven*

"Morgan, are you all right?" Edward grabbed his daughter and pulled her from the chair. He wasn't a tall man—a bit under six feet—but he was strong. He was handsome, with hazel eyes and dark brown hair that was peppered with gray. His broad-shouldered, stocky frame had thickened a bit with age, but he was definitely not fat. I knew him to be in his late forties. Dressed in a pastel blue golf shirt and navy slacks, Edward appeared to be a man who could fit in with the elites at a golf club or tossing back beers with the guys at a local pub. Although a successful businessman, he had the hands of a worker, someone who didn't hesitate to get dirty.

Edward wrapped his arms around Morgan and gave her a bear hug. "I was so worried. I'm sorry I couldn't get to you last night. I was in Bloomington with a client, and when I got your message and called, Sam said you were sleeping. Are you okay, Pony Girl?"

Edward released his grip but kept his hands on Morgan's shoulders as he inspected her. Morgan's hair was a mess, but he saw no bruises; nothing to indicate that she had been physically hurt. That was a relief. He smoothed her tousled hair and smiled.

Morgan gave him a tired smile at the mention of her pet name. Her father called her "Pony Girl" because Morgan was the name of a strong breed of horse, known for its proud carriage, intelligence, and spirit. He used to tell her that she possessed that same strength and character. That was his encouraging way of saying, "You can do it!"

"I'm fine, Dad. It's just been a long night. I am so glad to see you!"

"C'mon. Let's go get something to eat and you can fill me in on everything." Edward took her bags in one hand, draping his other arm around her shoulders.

Morgan snuggled into her father's hold, feeling like a little girl again. Daddy always made everything feel better. Whether it was scraped-up knees when she'd fallen off her bike or when Dylan Brewster had decided to go to the prom with another girl, Morgan had always known that she could count on her father to make the pain go away.

Edward gestured to Jeffrey, who effortlessly hailed a cab. That was the magic power of being a doorman at a posh building in Chicago: Taxis just appeared, even without a magic wand to summon them.

I squeezed in next to Morgan, who was huddled close to her father. En route to the café Edward chose for breakfast, she told him the whole story—well, almost everything. She left out the part about the amethyst necklace she had wanted to buy at Neiman's and downplayed the part where she'd shoved her heel through Pavlo's painting. And she certainly put a lot of description into Pavlo's hurling of her clothing and cell phone. Morgan spewed a litany of colorful details, readying for the "poor girl" sympathy she felt she had earned.

But Edward smiled, which took her aback. "I'm sure there's more to it than that, honey. Pavlo doesn't seem like someone who loses his temper that easily. He's always saying he's an artist, not a fighter."

"So now you're defending him?"

"I just think I need more information before I go charging in to confront a two hundred and twenty pound Russian to preserve my daughter's honor. That's all," Edward said.

"Pavlo is Ukrainian, Dad. Not Russian. He hates it when people call him Russian," Morgan said. "And I don't need you to defend me. I just thought you might be a bit more concerned that your daughter's boyfriend threw her out on the street."

Edward sighed. His face shifted from jovial to serious. "Believe me, Morgan, I am concerned. I want my girl to be safe and happy. I'm sorry if I reacted wrong. I figured it was just a lover's quarrel and you both needed to blow off steam. God knows I know what *that's* like!"

"I know, I know. Mom had a temper. But maybe she had a reason for being that way. And maybe *I* have a reason for feeling the way I do," snapped Morgan, making no attempt to veil her accusation.

"I don't want to get into a sparring match with you, young lady, nor do I need to defend myself," Edward volleyed back in the "I'm the father, that's why" tone that was all too familiar to Morgan. Edward was a gentle man, a proud man, but he had limits to his calmness. He'd always had a long fuse, but when it was finally touched off, the women in the Demarest household knew enough to back down to quell the fury they'd ignited. Then Edward's anger would subside as quickly as it had erupted.

"Okay, I'm sorry," Morgan said.

Eight minutes of silence later, the cab came to a stop in front of Tavern on the Rush, a lovely little café where Morgan often met up with friends for an after-hours drink or Sunday brunch. It was almost noon, and Tavern on the Rush was busy as usual, with a steady stream of diners enjoying sandwiches, mimosas, gourmet coffees, and luscious desserts al fresco.

We were greeted by a pleasant-enough hostess, although she looked a bit bored. She wove her way through the maze of tables as gracefully as a model on a catwalk. She presented the table and told Morgan and Edward that Janine would be their server.

A perky waitress came to the table, introduced herself as Janine, and took their drink orders: iced tea for Morgan and a Sam Adams draft for Edward. I was dying for a Bloody Mary and conjured it up myself, with extra Worcestershire.

"Listen, Dad, I don't really want to talk about Pavlo right now. I want to know what's going on with you."

Edward squirmed in his seat. He fidgeted with the saltshaker. The pause only made Morgan more anxious.

"Dad, please, what is it?" she asked.

"My business is failing and I might have to declare bankruptcy," he said, finally making eye contact. Edward held Morgan's gaze, hoping to find some comfort in his daughter's eyes. He had always been a proud man, and I knew this confession pained him deeply.

"Dad . . . how . . . what happened?" Morgan reached out and took his hand with both of hers. Her mind grappled with the news. The sound of a massive bubble the size of Jupiter burst in her brain as she sorted through how this life-quake was going to impact her.

Janine returned at that moment, breaking the connection between them. She served their drinks and quickly took their orders—Tavern "stacked" burger for Edward, grilled chicken pesto wrap for Morgan. She smiled at them both and bounced away to the next table. Edward's tone, which had been pleasant for Janine's benefit, switched to serious.

"The market tanked, honey. No one is investing in real estate, so it's hard to develop new projects. Most of my properties have high vacancy rates, so I'm working to plug that hole. There are a few retail projects keeping me afloat right now, but that's only because I've had to lay off almost half my staff." Edward rubbed his face with his palms as he struggled with the pain of his situation. "I'm pretty much broke."

Morgan sat there in total disbelief, trying to make sense of his words. *It's not possible*, she thought. *Maybe this really is a terrible nightmare. Please, please wake me up now*, she screamed in her mind.

"I sold the apartment in hopes of riding out the recession without drowning," he admitted.

"Why didn't you call me, Dad? I'm your daughter. And where are you living? You need to share these things with me." Morgan's voice cracked as tears began to well in her eyes.

Much better, I thought. I had been worried that Morgan was overloaded with spoiled brat DNA and couldn't focus on the crushing blow that this situation had dealt to her proud, honest father. I knew there was a good reason I had been summoned to bring my *Stiletto 911* skills to this young woman!

"I had hoped to protect you from all this. I didn't think, at first, that it was as bad as it has turned out to be. I figured I could get it all sorted out and not have to tell you, but this mess just keeps getting uglier," Edward said, shaking his head.

Perky Janine returned with their sandwiches and inquired if they needed anything else. Edward smiled and said, "A million bucks would be nice."

"He's joking," Morgan said.

The waitress shrugged and went on her way.

"Does Mom know what's going on?" asked Morgan.

"Yes, I told her. She's been very understanding and supportive, which kind of surprised me. I thought she'd be shrieking at the thought of not having the Bank of Edward to rely on."

"Dad, that's not how she sees you. I think that's how *you* see you." Morgan looked her father in the eye as she wondered if he felt the same pressure from her own spending. He often slipped her extra money, with or without her asking, though with Pavlo's generosity and the income from her own job, she hadn't asked her father for anything in months. Did she only call him when she needed money? If she had called him just to say hello, would she have learned this news earlier? "What can I do to help, Dad? Is there anything, anything at all?"

That's my girl, I thought.

"That's my Pony Girl," Edward said, reaching across the table to take her hands. "This will all get straightened out. It has to. The economy will bounce back and people will start regaining confidence in real estate. And I'll be building big developments and the world will be rosy once again. Now eat your lunch before it gets cold."

"It's a chicken wrap, Dad. It's supposed to be cold."

"Then let me shut up and eat my own lunch, okay?" He winked.

Morgan shook her head and picked up her wrap. As she took a bite, she looked over her father's shoulder. A man at the next table was reading a newspaper, and an advertisement on the back gave her a sudden, unexpected idea. She knew just where her next step would take her.

footnotes

There is always more than one way to respond to a difficult situation. Finding the path to a reasonable solution, however, is usually the best route to take. Look back at a big challenge you've had to face. Maybe you struggled to pay your bills, had trouble at work, or a run-in with someone close to you. How did you handle it? Looking back, is there anything you wish you had done differently? Is there a way you could have prevented the problem to begin with? Although you shouldn't dwell on the past, be sure you learn from it. Pull out your personal journal and write about a difficult situation that you overcame, and how you did it. What did you learn? What can others from learn from your mistakes?

CHAPTER twelve

Elizabeth Tanner-Freitag was usually the picture of organization, but today was an exception. Before she'd even left for work, her day had begun to spiral out of control. It started when her eight year-old son, Erich, told her at breakfast that it was his turn to bring in cupcakes for the class party that afternoon. Then four-year-old Lara picked this morning to become a fashion diva, insisting that she wanted to wear her ballet costume with her favorite purple sneakers and denim jacket. Elizabeth's husband, Tom, had been delayed on a business trip to San Francisco, which meant she was on her own to do battle with the kids, the dog, the leaky faucets, the clothes dryer that didn't dry, and the plumber he had hired to replace the outdated pipes in their townhouse.

While she trusted Tom's choice of repairman, she found Vince creepy from the moment he stopped by to do an estimate. He had a nervous eye twitch, smelled like cheap cigars and day-old coffee, and kept looking around as if someone were following him. A friend of Tom's, though, had highly recommended Vince, saying he had been a real lifesaver when his house's pipes had burst last winter.

Vince had called this morning to say he had to increase his estimate because his regular supplier couldn't get what he wanted so he was using "another guy who's got good stuff but it's gonna cost more but he's got me by the balls, you know?"

Elizabeth didn't know. And she couldn't reach Tom to get his take on Vince's change in plans. As it was, Vince had already delayed the project a week because another project had turned into "a freakin' nightmare." When Elizabeth had expressed reservations, Tom said she was being too sensitive and encouraged her to give Vince the benefit of the doubt. *Easy for him to say,* she thought. He didn't have to deal with the guy.

And on top of these challenges, Oscar, the dog Elizabeth and Tom had rescued from the animal shelter three weeks earlier, had dined on one of her Manolo Blahnik pumps. The soft gray suede stilettos with the three and a half inch heel were the perfect pairing with her new suit, which she had planned to wear to her presentation to a new client the next day. When she stumbled upon Oscar this morning after finishing her frays with the kids, the dog had already opened the shoebox on the floor of her closet. He'd gnawed the leather-covered heel and was at work on the floral appliqué on the toe when Elizabeth found him. She let loose a screech that could probably be heard all the way to the street corner. She grabbed the chewed-up, slobber-covered shoe from under Oscar's paws and engaged in a tug-of-war to release the once-perfect floral appliqué from his vice-like jaw.

"Bad dog! Bad, bad dog!" She waved the flower in front of his muzzle, which Oscar took as a game. He grabbed the flower from her hand, and Elizabeth smacked him on the nose before taking it away once again.

Elizabeth stepped back and sat down hard on the bed, with the remnants of her shoe in one hand and the tattered appliqué in the other. She glared at the little black and white dog that was now cowering in a corner of her closet.

"Don't give me those big sad eyes. I'm the one who deserves to have the sad eyes. These stilettos cost ten times as much as your bail! How'd you like to go back to puppy prison? Huh? How about a little 'dead dog walking', huh?"

"Mommy, *no!*" wailed Lara, who was standing in the doorway, decked out in her pink sequined tutu, green ankle socks, and purple sneakers. "You can't give Oscar back! He didn't mean it."

Lara ran over to Oscar and knelt next to the dog, wrapping her arms around his neck in a protective embrace.

Elizabeth watched the scene and softened. "Honey, I'm not sending Oscar back, but he did a very, very bad thing. He needs to learn what he can't do."

"Are you going to put him in a time-out?" Lara asked in a tiny voice, her cheek pressed up against the puppy's remorse-filled face.

"I think that's a good idea. Let's put him in his crate and let him think about what he did wrong," Elizabeth said. Then she muttered, "While I think about getting his little teeth yanked."

She looked once more at the bitten Blahnik and sighed. "Is this my punishment for buying something special for myself?"

Elizabeth arrived at her desk feeling exhausted. But she had to prepare for her presentation tomorrow, which reminded her once again of the demise of her Manolos, collateral damage in her battle to have it all—the loving husband, great kids, nice home, good job, and, after much debate, the consummate family pet.

She spent the remainder of her morning retooling her PowerPoint presentation and checking the progress of her latest project. Elizabeth had founded IdeaWerx Software, a company that specialized in software development for small businesses. Her assignments ranged from small applications for ecommerce sites to moderate enterprise projects, but she had recently taken on some projects for the latest computer tablet innovation. Clients came to her with challenges, and she pulled together a team of software engineers that never failed to soar over the bar with stellar results.

Immersing herself in her work allowed Elizabeth a temporary escape from the household disasters that had turned her otherwise organized self into a frazzled female. Here, at her office, she was able to regain her balance and resume her leadership role.

A little after one p.m., a young woman slipped into Elizabeth's office as she was staring out the window at the Chicago skyline, pondering her American dream. Rosaria Vega stood a bit on the short side at five-foot-four-inches tall, and had broad shoulders, a hefty chest that she attempted to mask beneath an oversized blouse, and small hips. Her flawless skin was the color of mocha latte, and her thick dark hair was pulled back into a no-nonsense bun. "No-nonsense" summarized Rosaria. She wore no make-up, dressed plainly in a loose white blouse, simple navy skirt, and what most women would call "sensible shoes"—code word for boring. She didn't smile easily, a fact that was reinforced by the frown line between her brows. Overall, she gave the appearance of a woman much older than her twenty-three years.

"Excuse me, Elizabeth. I'm sorry to interrupt you, but there's a woman out front who says she urgently needs to speak with you. She didn't make an appointment but says you know her. I suggested she make an appointment and that you are in a meeting right now. She's very pushy," added Rosaria, with obvious distaste.

Rosaria was tightly wound and always the guardian of her boss's time. Elizabeth sat back and listened to her gatekeeper launch into a monologue about respecting the value of someone's time and the importance of keeping to a schedule if you expect to meet your goals. Elizabeth smiled, because these words echoed the numerous lessons she had imparted to Rosaria since hiring her three years ago. Rosaria had learned these lessons all too well, Elizabeth thought. Now if only she could learn the ones about joy and passion, she might discover there was more to life than a rigid schedule.

"I think you're too busy to talk to people who don't respect your time enough to make an appointment," Rosaria continued to grumble.

Elizabeth took a quick inventory of her morning:

She'd been late getting to the office because she had to stop at the market and buy cupcakes for Erich's class, knowing full well that other mothers presented home-baked treats decorated with all sorts of fun candies and colorful frosting. *Well,* she thought, *I'm not an "other mother" and never will be.* And the kids would be just as happy with store-bought cupcakes.

Next, she'd given in to Lara's style choice because she'd decided her young daughter needed to feel in control of something in her life more than she needed a lesson in fashion sense.

She'd left a message on Vince's voicemail that she would get back to him about the revised costs to determine whether they were going to proceed with the project, hoping he would get the underlying message that she knew he wasn't the only plumber in town. In spite of what Tom had said, Elizabeth knew she was not going to be yanked around by the likes of Vince.

Elizabeth had then contacted the appliance repair service and made arrangements for a service technician to arrive on Friday morning to fix the clothes dryer. With enough advance planning, she could work from home while the dryer was being fixed. And she'd ensured that the window of arrival for the technician was not open-ended, securing a guarantee of "on time or free".

And Oscar, well, that problem wasn't so easily handled. They were both going to need a period of adjustment. In the meantime, she needed to dog-proof her possessions. She planned to charge the kids with wearing him out with more activity, and keep a closer eye on his whereabouts—and ensure that her closet door was securely closed.

Elizabeth's conclusion? She was, indeed, busy. Still, she interrupted Rosaria. "What's her name?" Elizabeth asked.

"What? Oh, uh, it's Morgan Demarest. She says you told her she could stop by if she was ever ready to stop settling for less. Did you actually *say* that?"

Elizabeth remembered this conversation. It had been after her presentation to an organization for women in business. This particular attendee had seemed out of place, not driven by the same passion as the others in the group, who were like caged animals ready to unleash their potential on an unknowing world. The young woman hadn't spoken up during the presentation but afterwards had approached Elizabeth with definite interest in topics like goal setting. Elizabeth had known there was something brewing inside this person—the spark of a quiet ember—but she'd also sensed that Morgan wasn't yet ready to take the steps necessary to make a significant difference in her life. Perhaps her "someday" had sneaked up on her.

Having pondered the successes she had already achieved this morning, Elizabeth was feeling better about her day. Yes, she had been slammed with challenges, but she'd met each one head on and was satisfied with each outcome. Now she was feeling as though Rosaria needed a lesson on flexibility.

"Well, now, Rosaria, I appreciate your care and concern for my time and schedule. Your focus is invaluable to me, but you know what? After the morning I've had, I think I could use a little distraction; why don't we see what this woman needs so urgently?"

footnotes

How many times have you been hit with a string of challenges and asked, "Why me?" Everyone has bad days, but the people who can turn those lemons into lemonade are more likely to succeed. When you see a problem as an opportunity, you give yourself the chance to learn and grow. Not every test is a punishment. Quite often, there's a valuable lesson buried underneath the mess you're staring at. Once you take time to work on a solution rather than bemoan the situation, you've made progress. When's the last time you lost your cool? What was the cause? What do you do when you're having a really bad day? Do you assume the world is against you, or do you try to fend off each challenge as it comes? Right now, be your own coach and come up with a motivational phrase to repeat to yourself when life gets tough. And be sure to include a reminder of how you've survived and thrived in the past.

CHAPTER *thirteen*

A few moments later, Rosaria reappeared in Elizabeth's doorway. She blocked the entrance a moment before allowing Morgan to step past her and into the room.

Morgan looked considerably better than she had the night before. Thanks to a short stop at Brianna's apartment—thanks to the spare key that Bree had bestowed on her for the "just in case" moments—she'd been able to shower, do her hair and makeup, and borrow an outfit from her best friend, who appeared to have left for work in quite a hurry. Morgan had spied telltale signs that last night's date had included more fire than just the candles left around the bedroom. Exhibit one: empty wine glasses on both nightstands. Exhibit two: a pile of wet towels on the bathroom floor. Bree wasn't the neatest person on the planet but never left towels on the floor. She'd left them there as a "marker"; Morgan was quite certain. Although still irked that her friend had not provided refuge when Morgan had needed it most, she couldn't help but smile at the romp with the fireman Brianna had clearly had experienced.

Brianna did not have the shapely curves that Morgan was endowed with, so finding something to wear had been a chore. Outfits that looked great on Bree were too tight where it mattered on Morgan. Finally, she'd chosen a cream-colored jacket with wide notched lapels and a single button at the waist, over a pink camisole with loose-fitting black slacks. And, of course, stilettos. She'd found a pair of black patent leather Miu Mius with a beautiful off-white ribbon that ran from the back of the heel to the toe, where it create a two-toned bow. Fun, yet professional. And she knew Bree had worn the shoes on several occasions. By unwritten law, you never borrow a pair of shoes that have not yet been worn at least once by the owner. And how great to have a friend who not only had great taste in shoes but wore the same size as Morgan. Serendipity at work!

So, Morgan arrived in Elizabeth's office looking polished, professional, and together. But her exterior only masked the nervousness that Elizabeth sensed in the young woman. She extended her hand to welcome Morgan.

"Nice to see you again," she offered in a polite, reserved voice.

"Thank you so much for taking the time to see me." Morgan glanced over her shoulder at Rosaria, who was shooting daggers with her eyes. Morgan quickly turned back to Elizabeth. "I know I should have made an appointment, but this was a very, uh, spontaneous decision. I actually saw your photo on the front of the *Times'* business section, and it reminded me of that presentation you made to the Chicago Businesswomen's Cooperative."

Elizabeth motioned for Morgan to take a seat on the tapestry chair across the room. Morgan kept chattering as she walked over and sat down. I had already reclined on the comfy sofa where I could watch the two of them. I figured I'd keep out of this conversation so as not to distract Morgan. She had taken a big—and positive—step by coming to see Elizabeth Tanner-Freitag, and I wanted to let her make the most of it...but still under my watchful eye, just in case.

"You were really inspirational at the talk," Morgan said. "I think I was a bit overwhelmed by the women there, so I didn't get involved much after that, but I always remembered your story—how you built your business, and everything you overcame to get what you wanted."

"It's always good to know when you have an impact on another person." Elizabeth was still sizing up Morgan, trying to compare her with the vague image of the young woman she had met last year. Morgan had a sense of urgency that hadn't been there before; it could be passion or panic—or a little of both. But Elizabeth was intrigued.

Rosaria was still standing in the doorway, surveying the situation and clearly displeased that Morgan had shoved her way onto her turf. Elizabeth shot her a look that told her to pull back her claws. Wordlessly, Rosaria turned and left the office.

"So," continued Elizabeth, "are you here about the article?"

"Article? Oh. No. I'm sorry. Actually, I didn't read it. Someone else was holding up the paper, and I saw your photo," Morgan said awkwardly.

"Don't apologize," Elizabeth said. "I just thought perhaps you were here about the fundraiser. I'm raising money to build a new shelter here in Chicago for victims of domestic abuse, and the paper was kind enough to give me some space to get up on my soapbox and plead my case."

"That's wonderful, uh, Ms. Freitag," said Morgan.

"You can call me Elizabeth."

"Thanks. Elizabeth. I know that this cause is very personal for you." Morgan stopped, unsure if she should continue. Elizabeth had been quite public about the beatings by her father and, later, at the hands of her first husband. She'd used her past to inspire other women to escape such abuse, to find the courage and confidence to reshape their lives, but Morgan felt that now was not the time to delve into such sensitive issues, particularly when she herself had never experienced similar violence.

"I think that you are an amazing woman, Elizabeth, and I'm in a situation where I feel I need to find inspiration or direction or something to start making sense of my life," Morgan admitted. As she spoke the words, I sensed that Morgan was sorting through a web of thoughts—about her father, Pavlo, and her life. While some people internalized, Morgan was a "heart-on-my-sleeve" woman. Which made my job easier, because I didn't have to waste a lot of time reading her thoughts, something I had encountered with many other clients who were either pouty or aloof. Morgan, although confused and misguided, was at least genuine.

"Thank you, Morgan. I appreciate the kind words, but I'm wondering the reason for your visit. You said it was urgent," Elizabeth said.

"Okay. So here's the thing. I haven't done a great job so far with my life. I've been just kind of going with the flow. But in the past twenty-four hours, I had a break-up with my boyfriend, who tossed my stuff into the street, and found out my dad is in serious financial trouble. I don't have a place to live, my bank account is pretty sad, and I just don't know what to do," Morgan said.

"I don't understand. What is it you want me to do? Are you looking for a job?" Elizabeth paused before adding, "Did your boyfriend beat you?"

"What? Oh, *no!* Nothing like that. It's just—I met someone last night who told me about mentors and mentoring. He has several mentors, and it seems to be really valuable for him. So I thought, maybe, well, maybe you might consider being my mentor," said Morgan, half-stating and half-asking. "I could really use someone who has it all together to help me sort out this mess of a life I have."

"Hmmm...well, I hope you know that working with a mentor and being a mentor both require real commitments. You would need to take a good look at your life and be prepared to make changes—and that's not always easy or fun. I'm speaking from experience. Change can be scary," Elizabeth said.

"And sometimes *not* making a change is even scarier," replied Morgan in earnest.

"That's very, very true. So, you've clearly made the decision to do something more with your life. Have you given any thought to what you want?"

"A little," said Morgan. "I think the past twenty-four hours have done more to show me what I *don't* want. I've spent my life a bit frivolously. I'm not going to lie: I love to shop. And I don't want to give that up. But right now, shopping is the only thing that seems to make me happy, and I know in my heart there should be more."

"There *is* more, but you have to know what those things are. You need to figure out what it is that you're chasing or you'll just continue to waste time. Then, before you know it, you're thirty years old and all those childhood dreams have become distant memories."

Elizabeth was speaking about her own past. As a child, she had hidden from her emotional and physical pain by dreaming about the happy home she would someday have. She'd pictured kids running around the yard, playing with the dog, and the front porch where she and her loving husband would sit and watch this perfect picture. She'd been so anxious to make her dream a reality that she'd married her high school sweetheart right after graduation. He'd gone on to study to become an electrician while she'd worked as a receptionist at a local manufacturing company. She'd wanted to go to college at night, but Brad had said they couldn't afford it. In truth, he'd feared she would outgrow him, so he kept tight reins on her. Elizabeth had been used to obeying. It had been the only way she could escape some of the beatings at the hands of her father, by getting his beers for him—in hopes he would pass out before becoming mean. Sadly, her mother had taken the brunt of his anger.

After the first two years of their marriage, Brad, too, had started to drink. Elizabeth was anchored in a déjà vu world: At first, it was a backhanded slap, and he was deeply apologetic afterwards. Before long, however, the slaps turned into punches and the apologies became accusations. He blamed her for being a drain on his life, even though he himself had pushed her into the submissive role.

When Elizabeth started calling in sick at her job, her co-workers suspected something was wrong. Several had noticed the bruises on her arms, and they believed that her sudden penchant for wearing scarves was less of a fashion decision and more of a cover-up.

But no one spoke of it.

At least not until Elizabeth ended up in the Emergency Room after Brad threw her down the stairs of their apartment building and left her bleeding and unconscious at the bottom. A neighbor who had heard the fight called 9-1-1, and Brad was arrested for assault. While he was in jail, Elizabeth was visited in the hospital by a victim's advocate who outlined the ways in which she could escape her husband and start over, without fear.

That felt like a lifetime ago. Now, at forty-two, Elizabeth looked back at her life as though it had all happened to someone else. The little girl with the dreams. The young woman who lived in fear. Those were both very different people than who she was right now.

After her divorce, Elizabeth had managed to go to college at night, attain a degree in computer technology, and find a job with an up-and-coming software firm that recognized her potential. The company funded her MBA education, and she met Tom when he was guest lecturer in one of her business classes. Tom was a successful executive on his way to becoming CEO of a well-established company. Once her heart had healed, she married him, and Erich was born just over a year later. Tom encouraged her to stay home with their infant son, which she gladly did. During that time, she freelanced for her former employer, working on developing and testing software applications while also playing peek-a-boo and changing diapers.

When Erich was three, Tom supported Elizabeth in venturing out and launching IdeaWerx. The company was barely underway when she learned that she was pregnant with Lara. Her plans slowed down, but they didn't stop. She built her business plan, connected with prospective clients, talked to other developers, and conducted lots of market research. While she was redoing the nursery, Tom was building an office for Elizabeth over their two-car garage.

That had been five years ago, and more than sixteen years after the awful night in the emergency room. Now here she was, with a woman who was at a turning point much like Elizabeth had faced many years ago, when she'd had to decide which way to guide her life. It took only a moment for Elizabeth to give Morgan an answer:

"I'd be happy to be your mentor, Morgan. And we can start right now."

footnotes

Every day, we have choices. We decide what to wear, eat, and do. Sometimes, those choices are more complex and the outcome is more meaningful. But no matter what the decision, you have to weigh the consequence. Think back to seemingly simple choices in your life that actually led you to a major change. Perhaps it was accepting one job over another. Maybe you went to a place you'd never been and ended up meeting someone who struck a major impact on your life.

Have you procrastinated about something in your life? What is on your backburner right now? Tackle something today that can give you a sense of accomplishment.

There might be fate, destiny, or serendipity—or even a Fairy Godmother looking after you. But you are still the one who is in control of your own life. You must take charge of it, value it, and live each day with purpose.

CHAPTER fourteen

Morgan sat up straight like an eager student on the first day of school. And, like the new teacher, Elizabeth asked Morgan to share a little about herself. Morgan launched into the same story of yesterday's journey into her personal hell. Elizabeth listened and then asked her to go back a little further in her life.

"What have you been doing since you graduated from college?" Elizabeth asked.

Morgan looked past Elizabeth, reflexively chewing on her lip and thinking about how she had been living the past two years. She struggled to find significant details that would impress her newfound mentor.

Elizabeth waited patiently but stepped in when she sensed the discomfort that Morgan was experiencing. "This isn't a test, Morgan," she said. "I just want to get to know you."

Morgan exhaled and told Elizabeth how she had traveled for a while, so she could see "what's out there before settling down." She'd then taken a job at an art gallery, where she greeted visitors, assisted with displays, wrote the descriptions and promotional materials, and organized receptions. That was where she'd met Pavlo.

"Which brings me to now," Morgan added, fidgeting and looking down at the borrowed Miu Mius.

Elizabeth commented, "Nice shoes, by the way."

Morgan gave the shoes an admiring look and smiled. "Thanks. Yours, too. Versace?"

"Yes. And, thankfully, my dog has yet to discover them, unlike the Blahniks that turned into his breakfast this morning."

"No!" Morgan and I gasped simultaneously.

"Yup. I'm in mourning."

"And is the dog still alive?" Morgan asked.

Elizabeth laughed. "He's on probation."

"If those were my shoes, he'd be on life support," Morgan quipped.

Elizabeth walked over to her desk and picked up her laptop. She paused and then reached into a desk drawer. She extracted a worn-looking journal with a red leather cover, and brought both the journal and the laptop back to her seat across from a curious Morgan.

"So, is that the all-knowing 'Guide to a Happy Life'?" joked Morgan. Standing behind her, I couldn't help but smile but also gave her a quick thwack on the head to tell her to take this help seriously.

"Pay attention, girl!" I said.

Elizabeth didn't see Morgan's head jerk slightly at the tap but heard her quick, "Hey!" in response.

Morgan reached up to smooth her hair and covered quickly with, "Sorry. There was a fly buzzing around."

"In answer to your question, this is not the all-knowing 'Guide to a Happy Life.'" Elizabeth gently stroked the cover of the book in her lap. "It's '*My* Guide to a Happy Life.'"

Morgan looked at her curiously.

With a knowing smile, Elizabeth said, "It's my journal—well, my current journal. I write down thoughts, ideas, questions, goals, and other notes that help me sort through where I am and where I want to go with my life."

Elizabeth paused. I could tell she was revisiting her past. Judging by the slight smile on her face, she was recalling good times. Morgan and I both gave her time to enjoy her reverie.

"You've got to get yourself one of those books, Morgan," I whispered.

She nodded, still respecting the thoughtful silence in the room.

After a few moments, Elizabeth looked up again and resumed seamlessly. "I started journaling when I was a teenager. Back then, it was an escape. I think maybe more of a *hope* for an escape. Anyway, I found that putting my thoughts into words on a page where I could see them helped me to focus, to pull things together and make sense of what I was dealing with. This is my first piece of advice for you. Get a journal. Use it. Write in it. You don't have to be eloquent, and not every entry will be an epiphany. But I guarantee that if you keep it up, you will benefit greatly from the effort and the experience."

"What kinds of things do you journal about?" Morgan asked. I knew she was dying to grab that book and thumb through it. I have to admit, I was just as curious, but also knew that journals were meant to be private places, where the writer could share his or her most intimate thoughts and feelings.

"Some days, I write about my experiences. I had a difficult time with a project not too long ago and worked through it here in my journal. I wrote down all the things that were making me crazy, and when I saw it on paper, the solution started to appear."

"Like magic, huh?"

Elizabeth chuckled slightly. "Yes, like magic. Sometimes, I ask myself questions, like, 'What do I want to gain from this experience?' or 'How could I have reacted better?' It's an ongoing conversation. My journal is the place I go when I need to either figure out a problem or celebrate something good in my life. I took it with me to the hospital when both my kids were born and recorded my feelings during early labor and then after each was born. Someday, I will share those pages with the kids."

"Do you take it with you, or do you keep it here in your office?" Morgan asked.

"Actually, I have a couple of journals. This one stays here in my desk, and I use it for my work things. I have another journal at home for more personal thoughts. And I use my cell phone to record notes for my journal when I'm on the road."

"How often do you go back and reread what you've written?"

"Depends. On days when I'm struggling with a particular issue, I might flip back to earlier entries and read my thoughts at that time, to see if it helps to get a reminder. Once, when I did that, I thought, 'What was I thinking?' Other times, I just like to go back and see how much I've progressed—or even if I have progressed at all. You know, some issues seem like such a big deal at the time and I do a lot of journaling about it, but then they fizzle or work themselves out, or I just find a new perspective and whatever was bothering me back then doesn't matter anymore."

Elizabeth opened her journal and began skimming an early entry in the book. She furrowed her brow, and I couldn't resist the urge to wander over there and peek over her shoulder.

> *Rosaria needs to find a different focus in her life. She is an amazing person, with so much potential, but she is holding herself back. What can I do to nudge her along without pushing her away?*

Morgan watched as I spied on Elizabeth's private moment, and I wasn't sure if she was mentally spanking me for peeking or hoping I would share some insight with her. Either way, when I noticed her watching me, I suddenly felt ashamed and moved away.

"Okay, so I promise I will get a journal and start writing down my thoughts, starting today," Morgan interjected eagerly. "What's the best way to start getting results?"

Elizabeth laughed. "This is not a quick fix, Morgan. How old are you?"

"Twenty-three," Morgan said, although it sounded like more of a question.

"Okay, well, you're not going to detangle twenty-three years of experience and confusion in a day. As I said, you have to make a commitment to change, and there are no shortcuts, like it or not."

Morgan was crestfallen. She'd come here hoping to find answers to relieve the pain and anxiety she was experiencing, and I knew she had expected more than Elizabeth could realistically give.

"I know that's not the answer you want, Morgan, but I assure you that the investment of your time will pay off for you. I know you're going through a rough patch right now, and I wish I had some magic wand to wave and make it better, but I don't. And frankly, you wouldn't learn a thing if that were the case."

Morgan's jaw dropped, and she looked from Elizabeth to me and back again, as though there were some conspiracy happening here.

I looked at her and shrugged. "Don't look at me. I didn't do anything. She's just telling you what I've been trying to get through to you: You don't need magic, girlfriend; you need guidance."

Morgan sighed. "I'm sorry. I don't mean to be impatient, Elizabeth, but this is all new to me. I don't know where to turn or what to do, and I can't stand feeling so confused and disconnected."

Elizabeth leaned forward and took Morgan's hand. Her warm eyes held Morgan's as she spoke. "I know. Believe me, I know. Your life feels out of your control and you just want to rein it all in, in one fell swoop."

Morgan nodded.

"But that's not going to happen."

I could see tears welling up in Morgan's eyes. I knew she had been spoiled her entire life, that things had come easily for her, and that it was a good reason for people to resent this young woman. But I also knew that it wasn't entirely her fault. Claire and Edward had carefully shielded her from life's woes, and she'd accepted their protection. They were loving parents who thought they were doing their best for their daughter. But now, here she was, vulnerable and unprepared for the challenges that were hitting her square in the face. Like her parents had done on so many occasions, I wanted to give her a hug and tell her everything would be okay, but I also knew that my job was to give her strength and guidance. I settled for gently patting her shoulder, letting her know I was close by but not interfering with the lesson that Morgan's new mentor was imparting.

"Morgan, I was in your position once, a long time ago. And I wanted a quick fix, just like you. I was impatient, just like you. But I discovered that that impatience just got in the way of making clear decisions. So, right now, I'm just going to ask you to take a deep breath, shake off the tears, and make me a promise."

Morgan held Elizabeth's gaze, wiping away her tears with the back of one hand. She forced a small smile and nodded.

"Promise me that you will make every effort to turn your life into something wonderful, and not settle for anything less than utter joy."

Both women had moist eyes, and I have to admit that I was a bit choked up myself.

footnotes

If you've ever lain in bed at night and tried to sort through a tangle of thoughts, to-do lists, and emotions, you know the frustration and confusion that swirls around in an overloaded mind. Journaling presents the perfect opportunity to sort out your thoughts, work through solutions, and celebrate even the smallest triumphs in your life. When you realize that no one understands you better than yourself, you can appreciate that having these "conversations" can be a far sight better than talking to someone who brings his or her own issues to the discussion. Start now by creating a journal that will provide a lasting record of your challenges and successes, keep you focused on your goals, and give you a little lift from time to time.

CHAPTER *fifteen*

Morgan walked out of Elizabeth's office feeling both exuberant and drained. Her hopes had risen and fallen—and risen again—and the roller coaster ride had exhausted her. She walked down the hall toward the lobby, where Elizabeth's assistant was seated. Rosaria saw Morgan approaching out of the corner of her eye but kept her focus on her computer. Her body language clearly said, "Leave me alone!"

Morgan, however, chose to ignore the sign. "Thank you, Rosaria. I hope I didn't create too much of an interruption, but I have to say that I am so glad I came here. Elizabeth is amazing and inspiring and so helpful! You're lucky to work with her every day."

Rosaria raised her eyes but not her head. "Yes, she is a wonderful, patient, and *very* busy woman." Her gaze shifted back to her computer screen, shooting off more venomous body language like a pygmy with a blowgun.

"I appreciate that." The chill in the room had turned sub-zero. Morgan struggled to deal with the uncomfortable silence. "Well, have a nice day."

Rosaria did not wish her well in return. I turned back and saw her glare at Morgan as she walked away. I was surprised that her evil eye didn't burn a hole into Morgan's backside, but my girl just ignored Rosaria's rudeness and went back to her thoughts about Elizabeth's advice.

But I couldn't let it slide so easily. I had insight into Rosaria's life, which was one of the reasons I'd planted the idea in Morgan's head to seek out Elizabeth after all that time. (Who do you think arranged for that interview with the *Sun-Times* that Morgan saw? I may not always wave a wand, but I do have my wily ways.)

Hooking Morgan up with Elizabeth wasn't just for Morgan's benefit. Rosaria was a young woman I had noticed in my research, and I thought she would be a good match for Morgan—and vice versa.

"She's an interesting woman," I said to Morgan as we stepped into the elevator.

"Amazing. I am so excited about connecting with Elizabeth!"

"Of course," I said, "but I was talking about Rosaria."

Morgan grunted. "Please. Underneath that unibrow and sensible shoes is a bitter woman who will spend her whole life being miserable."

"Is that what you see?"

"Absolutely! She looked at me as if I'm some kind of empty-headed Barbie doll who was put on this earth just to irritate her. Who is *she* to judge me and act all Miss Important?"

"So she shouldn't judge *you* by the way you look, but it's okay for you to do the same to her?"

"Well," Morgan stumbled, realizing the irony.

"Let me tell you a little bit about Rosaria Vega before you dismiss her as a fashion failure and therefore unworthy of your consideration."

We stepped out of the elevator, and I launched into a long-winded tale that I felt Morgan needed to know, beginning with one blunt fact: Morgan represented everything that Rosaria was not: fun-loving, frivolous, beautiful, stylish, and seemingly spoiled, a woman who appeared to have gotten by on her looks, not her smarts. To Rosaria, Morgan's sense of entitlement was vulgar, and her stunning self-esteem was unearned over-confidence. But underneath Rosaria's crusty exterior lay a truth that she kept hidden from those in her office—everyone except Elizabeth, who respected Rosaria's privacy.

As a young girl growing up in a predominantly Latino neighborhood in Chicago, Rosaria had been a light-hearted, spirited, and very creative child. The daughter of Felipe and Selena Vega, owners of a small bodega in their neighborhood, Rosaria had spent most of her time after school helping in the store. Her favorite job had been creating interesting displays with the inventory, and her parents had encouraged her inventiveness. When flowers bloomed in the spring and summer, she often picked bouquets to give to customers who seemed to need a pick-me-up. Rosaria brought joy into the lives of her parents, her older brother Luis, and everyone who knew the little Latina with the bright eyes and big smile.

But everything changed for Rosaria in one brief moment, when she was eleven years old. She was in the bodega on a Friday afternoon in early June, rummaging in the storage room for some cigar boxes to use for her Father's Day display, a little surprise for her dad. While Rosaria was conducting her search and her mother was away on an errand, a young man walked in the front door of the bodega and nervously looked around. From a few feet away, Felipe Vega asked if he needed help. Then the man pulled a gun and ordered Felipe to open the cash register.

"I will do what you ask. You do not need that gun." Felipe's glance darted to the storage room door. The thief, his hand trembling, kept the gun pointed at Felipe, who was slowly reaching for the cash register's drawer. But Felipe's biggest fear was realized when the storage room door opened and Rosaria walked into the store, her arms so loaded with cigar boxes that she could not see what was happening.

The thief whirled, turning his eyes and gun toward Rosaria. Felipe dove across the counter and tackled the robber, and the gun went off in the struggle. The sound startled Rosaria, who dropped the boxes to see her father lying on top of a strange man.

"Papa?" she called.

She heard a moan, not sure which man was making the noise, and saw her father slowly move off the stranger. She ran toward him to help before she realized that he was only moving because the thief had rolled him aside. There was blood on both men, and Rosaria was paralyzed with fear as she stood over them—her father lying still and the thief looking wildly from Felipe to Rosaria. He pointed the gun at Rosaria, his hand shaking. Rosaria stared down the barrel of the pistol, hypnotized by the dark metal cylinder. Then she heard an explosive pop and was certain she was dead but felt nothing. She wondered, *Is this what death feels like?*

But it was her father who had taken the bullet. As Rosaria had held the thief's gaze, neither had seen Felipe's hand reach up to yank the intruder's gun hand down, away from Rosaria. The intruder's finger already on the trigger, he lost his balance and put one more bullet into the chest of Felipe Vega.

When the thief realized what he had done, he stumbled to his feet. He rushed to the open cash register, grabbed the thirty-seven dollars in the drawers, and ran out the door.

Rosaria fell to her knees beside her father and screamed, "Papa! Papa! Wake up!" She ran to the door and yelled for someone to help, her face and hands covered with her father's blood. The shopkeeper next door had heard the shots and already called the police, but they were never very fast to respond to calls in this neighborhood.

Rosaria ran back to her father, trying to remember what she had learned in school about CPR. She tried frantically to breathe life into Felipe, whose dark eyes stared unblinkingly at the ceiling. Intent on her efforts, Rosaria didn't hear the gasp of her mother entering the scene, returning from making the bank deposit.

With the detailed description from both Rosaria and the shopkeeper next door, the police eventually tracked down the killer, a drug addict who was sentenced to life in prison. But the penalty did nothing to restore peace to the Vega family. Luis, just fifteen, dropped out of high school in spite of his mother's protests and took over his father's responsibilities at the store. Committed to being a provider, Luis worked hard but couldn't turn the same profit that his father had done so adeptly. His frustration led him to deal drugs to earn more money to support his family. When Rosaria discovered this truth, she confronted her brother and reminded him that it was one of those drug addicts who had killed their father. Luis had become part of the problem!

But her brother didn't listen. The bodega became known as a place where drug deals took place, so honest people stopped shopping there. As much as they wanted to support Felipe Vega's family, they feared the danger: Drive-by shootings were too common, and it wasn't worth the risk in a place already known for gang activity.

Three years later, Luis was killed in one of those drive-bys.

The community, triggered by the latest tragedy, jumped in with a collaborative neighborhood watch effort and together drove the drug dealers from the small area—including the bodega. Selena Vega took over running the store, but her joy was gone. She had aged terribly with the losses she had experienced in the past few years. Selena refused to let Rosaria drop out of school, like her brother, but welcomed her to work in the store after school and on weekends. Rosaria gave up her plans to attend college and study interior design. She couldn't justify spending money on her own dreams when her mother needed her.

So Rosaria graduated high school, with honors. A year later, her mother sold the bodega to a developer who saw the potential for the neighborhood to become the next-best-thing in Chicago. She offered to use some of the money from the sale to pay for her daughter's college education, but Rosaria refused. She found a job with an emerging company, IdeaWerx, and decided not to go to college—at least, that's what she told her mother, wanting her to keep that money for a secure retirement. Selena Vega, however, had spent her whole life living sparingly and was not about to sit back and do nothing now. She took a job as a housekeeper for a family in the wealthy section of Chicago. They were generous and appreciative, so Rosaria felt that her mother was now in a better, safer place, and was able to focus more on her work—but not on rebuilding the joy in her life. She had forgotten what that even meant.

"Rosaria believes that hard work is the only way to live," I said, finishing the tale. Morgan had been listening intently, her eyes wide at discovering that the stern Rosaria had lived through such tragedy.

"I feel so bad." Morgan shook her head, imagining the pain that Rosaria had endured. "I had no idea."

"So much for the book and its cover, huh?" I said as we continued walking down the street.

footnotes

Appearances are frequently deceiving. How many times have you misjudged someone? And think about the last time that someone didn't give you the benefit of the doubt. How did that feel? Before you jump to conclusions or judgments about a person or situation, take the time to consider a different perspective. Ask yourself: What are the other possibilities here? Is there something I might be missing?

If you met someone right now, for the first time, what impression do you think you would give? How do you look at this moment? Would a person who doesn't know you appreciate your sense of humor? Would you be judged by your accent or your clothes? Maybe it was a colleague you misjudged or were misjudged by. How can you change a bad perception? What's preventing you from doing so? Take a moment to do some deep reflecting and write in your journal.

When you open up your mind to other views, you might discover new, unexpected opportunities.

CHAPTER sixteen

We walked to the end of the block and into a sprawling two-story bookstore, where we followed signs to the journal section. Morgan was amazed at the wide variety of blank books, from floral printed fabric covers to leather-bound volumes. Morgan picked them up one at a time, examining covers and flipping through pages.

"I can guarantee you that they will all have blank pages, Morgan. What are you looking for?" I asked several minutes later, a bit impatient with her prolonged browsing.

"It's got to be perfect. It has to be *me*," she said, still examining one book after another.

"What makes it *you* are the words you put inside, not the outside. Didn't we just have a discussion about not judging a book by its cover? Why don't you pick out something that *isn't* you so it stands out?" I suggested, more to challenge Morgan than to inspire her. It never hurts to get someone to think in a different way.

"Hmm . . . interesting," she replied. "Then I am going to pick this sort of ancient-looking one, because maybe it will remind me that I can learn from older people." She had picked up a brown journal that resembled a rare volume, with gilded pages and antiqued gold embossing on the leather cover.

"And by 'older people', I assume you mean anyone over thirty?" I sniped.

Morgan gave me one of her "whatever" glances. She had the journal in her hand and was walking toward the front register. Then she stopped short. As I wasn't watching her but looking at the magazine display—hoping for a newer issue of *Cosmo* than I had seen in the lobby of Sam's building—I rammed into her. She lurched forward and hit a table that held a nicely arranged pyramid of books with a sign that said, "Top Picks".

The books toppled around Morgan, who tried unsuccessfully to catch them. After scowling at me, she bent down to pick up the scattered volumes. A middle-aged man with a nametag that said "William" hurried over to help, and while a few other shoppers looked on in amusement, William and Morgan replaced the books on the table.

"Don't worry," William said in a hushed tone. "I knew that pile would fall sooner or later. And I think people were afraid to pick up a book here because they didn't want to be the one to trigger the domino effect."

"Thank you, but I am so sorry for the mess," Morgan replied, offering him her sweetest smile.

When all the books had been returned to the table, Morgan started to walk away but remembered what had made her stop in the first place. She turned back to William and, with the same face that had already made him weak in the knees, said, "I'm looking for a book a friend had. What was it?" she wondered aloud. "*The Mentor In Me*! Could you help me find it?"

William smiled and said, "Of course!" After returning to the counter and typing the title into the computer, he announced, "It's in the Self-Help section. I can show you."

"Self-Help, huh? I think that means you're supposed to do this on your own," I quipped.

Morgan rolled her eyes and followed William. He found the book and handed it to her. She snapped it up excitedly, as though she had in her grasp the last pair of red Louboutin stilettos in her size.

I spied a display of greeting cards and suggested that Morgan might send a thank-you card to Elizabeth for her help.

"I was just going to text her," Morgan responded.

Now it was my turn to roll my eyes. "Texting is fine for your friends, but it doesn't belong in this type of business situation. An email, maybe, but a good, old-fashioned handwritten note is a breath of fresh air, girl! I'm assuming you know how to write 'manually,'" I replied with a snippy little sneer that matched hers.

Morgan shrugged, tucked the book under her arm, and picked through the cards on the rack. Luckily, it didn't take her as long to find the card as it had to choose the journal. She paid for her purchases and we left. When we hit the sidewalk, Morgan reached inside her handbag to grab her cell phone, only to remember the demise of the device. She groaned.

"I have to get a new phone, thanks to Pavlo," she said, looking around to see if there was a store within view. She spotted one a few doors down and across the street and headed in that direction.

We were barely inside the store when we were approached by a salesman with an over-worked smile and black hair that had been spiked a bit too much. "Welcome to Cell City!" he said with perkiness that was as annoying as it was artificial. "How can I help you today?"

"How about backing off and giving us a little room, grabbing a breath mint, and picking the leftover lunch off your teeth," I shot back. "Is that spinach or pesto?"

Morgan tried to mask her amusement. For once, I didn't get an eye roll—probably because she was thinking the same thing. But Mr. Happy took her smile to mean she was pleased and pushed on. "We are having a killer special, today only, on the latest smartphone when you sign up for a two-year contract."

He leaned in as though he was telling her a secret. "And you can pick a case from a choice of spectacular colors!"

Mr. Happy took a quick glance down and perked up even more. He leaned in once again, putting his hand to his narrow chest. "Oh, my goodness. Great shoes!"

As a reflex, we both looked down at our feet. Mine were decked out in orange platform sandals, courtesy of Alexandre Birman, with a crisscross strap that was drop-dead gorgeous. Morgan eyed her borrowed Miu Mius, doing the little toe point to show them off a bit more. We responded in unison, "Thank you!"

"I can see that you know quality, so forget that special and let's look at what's really hot right now," he said, gesturing for Morgan to follow him to the display counter. He reached in and pulled out a sleek silver phone with a touch-screen. He poked it once and showed her a scheduling app, which caught her attention. He tapped it again and held it in front of her so she could see how the phone could locate the closest Starbucks. Nice. Then he pressed a button and slid his finger over the glass screen and, with a broad smirk, held the phone right in front of her face.

"Shopper Search," he said proudly. "Find the best sales in Chicago on whatever you're in the mood for. It's a brand new app just for this phone. It's a must-have."

Morgan's jaw dropped. She took the phone from him and tapped a link. The screen switched to a display of closeout shoes, with prices and locations. She pressed another link and found a similar list of handbags. Mr. Happy watched his mesmerized customer slip into a moment of shopping ecstasy.

After she tapped and browsed for a minute, he chimed in. "So, should I sign you up?"

Morgan didn't say a word. She nodded, still enjoying this shopping fantasy. From beneath the counter, the salesman pulled a box containing an untouched phone. He opened it up, found the serial number, and started typing into the computer on the counter. She gave him her current cell number and automatically offered Pavlo's address.

"Is that really the address you want to use?" I asked her.

"Oh, you know what?" Morgan said to the man. "I'm in the process of moving. That's my old address. Is that okay?"

"Of course. Trust me, honey, the phone company will catch up with you, wherever you go," he said, and kept tapping away at the keyboard. When he finished, he asked for her credit card. Morgan reached inside her wallet and instinctively grabbed a card. Mr. Happy swiped it through the card reader and paused. He furrowed his brow, swiped again, and frowned when he read the computer screen.

"I'm sorry." He held the card out. "There's a problem with this card. The system is rejecting it. Do you have another one we can use?"

Morgan took the credit card and examined it. She had just used it yesterday when she'd bought that gorgeous Valentino bag. She didn't think it was over the limit. She reached into her wallet and handed another card to Mr. Happy. He repeated the process and held it back out to her, this time with less patience.

"This one isn't working either," he said. "I don't suppose you have another one, do you?"

"What is going on?" Morgan sputtered. "I just used these cards yesterday!"

"I don't suppose those are Pavlo's cards, are they?" I asked.

"Oh, no! That's not possible. He wouldn't!"

"Let's remember that you destroyed his painting last night and he found you with a half-naked man this morning," I reminded her. "I'm guessing that not only *would* he cancel the cards, but it appears that he *did!*"

Morgan's face turned beet red. She looked out the store window, as if the answer could be found on the street. Was she expecting to see Pavlo standing outside, laughing? Or perhaps hoping her father would be there, waving a credit card?

"My *ex*-boyfriend," she whispered across the counter to the salesman. "I can't believe he cancelled my cards so fast. I mean, it all just happened, like, this morning!"

Mr. Happy's look of disapproval took a u-turn to empathy. "Oh, honey, I feel your pain. Been there! But I still need a credit card in order to process this for you."

Morgan dug around in her handbag. She found a fistful of rewards cards, a Neiman Marcus credit card, and a Zappos gift card. She held up the Zappos card and squealed, "I wonder if there's anything left on this?"

"Sweetie," Mr. Happy said, "We don't accept Zappos here."

"No, but there's a pair of really cute boots I've been thinking about," Morgan replied.

I elbowed her to shake her out of this momentary shopping distraction. "Don't you have your *own* credit card?" I asked. "It's not like you're eighteen years old!"

"I *do* have a card in here somewhere. I haven't used it in, like, well, when did Pavlo give me those cards?" She dug around, unzipped two pockets, and pulled out an array of lipsticks, keys, pens, a tiny flashlight, a nail file, and some loose change. "Aha! Here it is!" She proudly handed a credit card to the salesman.

He swiped it through the reader, waited again, and gave her a pouty look. "Sorry. This one is over the limit."

"Ugh! But that can't be. I haven't used it since last year and would have received notices or something."

"Let's see if we can put a smaller amount on it." Mr. Happy typed and waited. He shook his head and entered another number. Morgan leaned over the counter to catch a peek at the screen. Finally, after a few attempts, he said, "Phew. Okay, we can put seventy dollars on the card. That leaves a balance of eighty-eight dollars and fifty-seven cents."

Morgan dug around in her almost empty handbag and handed him an American Express gift card. "My mother gave me this for my last birthday and I was saving the balance for something special. I hate to use it on a phone, but I guess I have no choice."

"You *do* have a choice," I said. "Buy a cheaper phone!"

Morgan pulled back before Mr. Happy could take the card from her hand. "Wait a minute. Is there a phone that is less expensive?"

Mr. Happy was no longer happy. "Well, I could sell you one of those other models, of course," he said gesturing with distaste to a display in the bottom of the kiosk, where one had to bend way down just to see the phones. "I mean, if you're not going to use your phone for anything but making calls, I guess it doesn't matter."

Morgan bit her lip: It was either the very hip phone with the luscious shopping app or the bare-bones cell that wouldn't max out her limited resources.

"Well, I can upgrade later, can't I?" she said in a tiny voice.

"You can *always* upgrade, honey!" I exclaimed. "They tell you that you can't just so they can suck you into a contract. If he wants to sell you a phone, he can do whatever you need."

"Sure," he said flatly. Mr. Not-So-Happy retrieved a simple black phone from the bowels of the display case and laid it on the glass counter like it was two-day-old muffin: stale and undesirable. "Forty-nine ninety-five and no contract."

Morgan picked it up and pressed a few buttons. "Can I text?"

"If you've got two thumbs, you can," he sniffed, his attention span clearly shot. He looked around the store like he was hoping someone would save him from a first date gone horribly awry.

"Okay, I'll take this one," Morgan said. "But I'll be back when this whole mess is straightened out."

"Of course you will," he said, trying to appear sympathetic but coming across as a shrew. He wordlessly completed the transaction, put the lesser phone into a small bag, and handed it to Morgan with a tiny smile. "Have a nice day."

She took the bag. I could tell she was embarrassed, and this sales guy's behavior wasn't helping the situation. As her Fairy Godmother, I felt it was my duty to protect Morgan from such callous disregard for her feelings. At the same time, she didn't need to know how I used my magic. As we headed out of the store, I looked back and swatted my hand in the wrongdoer's direction. When he stepped from behind the counter, he felt a chill from behind. His co-workers and several customers found the source before he came to the realization that the seat of his slacks was ripped wide open, exposing a red sequined thong and tattoo of SpongeBob SquarePants on his left butt cheek.

If one is going to act cheeky, I thought, why not go all the way?

footnotes

Making positive financial decisions isn't always easy. There will be compromises and even sacrifices, but when things get tough, just remember your goal. Picture how you'll feel when you achieve that goal, and then weigh the consequence of the moment. If you put aside the money that you might have spent on something that probably won't matter to you in six months, you're investing in your future, rather than spending money with no return. There will always be obstacles along the way—whether those are shiny objects you dearly want to possess or distractions that detour you from your plan. Learn to identify those hurdles so you can soar over them.

If you need help and some direction, go to and search for "financial calculators". The site has calculators for retirement, savings, paying off debt, and lots more. Remember to take the time to put together an action plan for you, 'cause if you don't, no one will do it for you!

CHAPTER *seventeen*

After Morgan had left her office, Elizabeth thought about the conversation they'd just had. Morgan had been filled with energy and excitement, but Elizabeth wondered if she had a clue about the challenges that lay ahead. The workplace could be tough, particularly for a woman. And, despite positive changes, women like Morgan were often judged by their good looks more than their smarts. Elizabeth could tell that Morgan had plenty of brains but hadn't relied on them to get ahead. She had simply been gliding through life with the help of others.

Elizabeth's road had been bumpier. She'd grown up as the middle of five children, and their idea of "frills" had been a new pair of shoes at the beginning of the school year. It was partly due to the stress of supporting five kids that her father had occasionally lost his temper and taken out his frustrations by slapping around his wife or one of his kids who'd seemed to misbehave—which could mean forgetting to restock his favorite snacks or not mowing the lawn to his liking.

Anxious to get out of that environment, she'd married Brad soon after graduating from high school. Elizabeth—who'd gone by the name "Lizzie" back then—had worked full-time as a receptionist during the day and waited tables a few nights a week for extra cash. She'd then gone home to a husband who accused her of flirting with her customers. Like her father, Brad had a temper. And like her father, he'd beaten her when she got "out of line".

No one at work suspected the domestic violence because Lizzie hid the bruises very well, but the emotional scars ran much deeper. Still, while she had to hand over her paycheck to Brad, she gave him only a portion of her tips. He complained about the "cheap bastards" at that restaurant while she squirreled away dollars in her secret getaway fund.

At the office, Lizzie was the coffee-fetcher and office "mommy". When any of the men needed help, they relied on Lizzie to solve the problem. Many of them had ideas but no ability to execute, and only a handful made an effort to try. For a long time, Lizzie didn't mind, but when she saw them get raises and promotions on the merits of the work she had done for them, she became resentful—just not enough to stand up for herself. At the hands of her father and her husband, she'd learned what happened when she tried to voice an objection. Although she didn't expect to be physically beaten in the workplace, Lizzie knew that emotional blows could be just as damaging.

So Lizzie was everybody's savior. She wasn't able to work late because of her waitressing job, nor could she take work home because it angered Brad, but she *was* able to work feverishly throughout the day, skipping lunch when necessary and producing far more in eight or nine hours than her colleagues did in a week!

Management recognized Lizzie's talents but didn't adequately reward them. And they didn't need to, because she never complained. Instead, management invested in the employees who voiced their needs.

When Lizzie finally escaped Brad and hid in a safe house provided by the local women's shelter, she called in sick for a few days while the restraining order and other matters were in the works. When she felt it was safe, she returned to work. She advised human resources of her new address and gave them a copy of the restraining order, as instructed by the attorney at Legal Aid, but she offered nothing more. She didn't want sympathy, nor did she want her colleagues to have yet another reminder of the fact that she was a woman—and a battered one at that.

She took back her maiden name, Tanner, and started using "Elizabeth" to remind herself that she was a different person than the victim she had been. She changed the nameplate on her desk and corrected her co-workers when they referred to her as Lizzie.

Elizabeth also decided to pursue her bachelor's degree and then her MBA at night, and she requested tuition reimbursement, which she knew was available from her employer. She had long wished to continue her education, but her circumstances prevented it. Free of Brad, she was ready to move forward. Her boss approved the request and she enrolled at Northwestern. Once she didn't have to fork over every penny of her income to Brad, she discovered that she didn't have to work two jobs, so her evenings were free to study. She did take a work-study position with one of her business professors, Margaret Braxton, but mainly because the woman intrigued her.

Professor Margaret Braxton was an imposing figure who commanded respect in the classroom. The attractive African-American woman dressed in vibrant colors and gestured madly when she was passionate about an issue. She nurtured curiosity, slapped down arrogance, and cultured an environment of collaboration.

Margaret became a mentor to Elizabeth, encouraging her to speak up and take charge of her life. And she played matchmaker when she saw the spark that shot up when Elizabeth and Tom Freitag came in contact with each other.

When Elizabeth was once again passed over for a promotion in favor of a less deserving colleague, Elizabeth sought the advice of her mentor.

"Liz, my girl," said Margaret, peering over the lime green reading glasses that matched her shoes, "it is time for you to pull up those big girl panties that I know you have and just move on."

Elizabeth discussed the situation with Tom—now her husband—as well. Like Margaret, he agreed that Elizabeth was talented, knowledgeable, and connected enough to start up her own software development company. Tom and Margaret told her to follow her passion for problem solving and find a niche that wasn't yet served well enough.

Four months later, after spending night after night building her business plan and executing the steps necessary to launch her business, Elizabeth brought IdeaWerx to life. She catered to smaller enterprises that needed software but couldn't pay the same price as the big companies. She used her network to connect with people she knew in the industry, and then to connect with *their* connections. Word spread, and her client list grew. Within two years, she had added three developers to her staff, as well as Rosaria, a young woman who needed the same encouragement and support as Elizabeth had received. But Rosaria was a challenge. She was tightly wrapped in her own cocoon, believing that hard work was the measure of her worth in the world. While Elizabeth respected Rosaria's unyielding work ethic, she had also discovered in her own life that it wasn't the number of hours you put into your job, but the results you got from that investment of your heart and soul.

Morgan was truly a contrast to Rosaria: two women of the same age but very different backgrounds. Rosaria seemed much older than her twenty-three years. She was far more serious than Morgan, but Morgan had a positive energy that would truly benefit Rosaria. With both of them, Elizabeth had the chance to pay it forward. She could use the lessons she had learned to help Morgan and Rosaria discover their potential.

The trick was to put these opposing forces together and see if they could ignite great results—or would they just erupt in an explosion?

footnotes

You've probably heard the phrase, "No man is an island." Well, no woman is, either! We have a natural pack mentality and thrive in groups. Success is a collaborative effort. We learn from one another, support our gal pals, laugh, cry, and cheer together. This incredible network is not just a personal one. Reach out and use those connections as part of your toolkit for success—along with your talent, knowledge, experience, and skills. Wield these special tools with confidence and use them to guide others along a positive path. And remember that if you want to make a significant change in your life, you can't do it from the safety of your comfort zone. You need to take a risk. What risks have you taken to advance in your life and/or your career? What were the results? And how can you pay that forward to someone else? If you haven't yet taken a risk, think of a reason to step out of your comfort zone. Write it down and turn it into a goal with a set of actions and a deadline. Then push yourself to grow by taking this risk, and journal the experience and results.

CHAPTER *eighteen*

Morgan reached in her handbag and pulled out a business card. I glanced over her shoulder and read the name on it: Sam Baxter, Vice President, Smithson/Bell Marketing.

"Why, you little devil!" I said with a smile. "Nice grab."

"I just saw it in his book and thought, well, just in case. But then Pavlo showed up, and you know the rest. Maybe I should throw it away. It's not like he'll ever want to talk to me or see me again." She held up the card as if willing it to answer her question: Do I call or do I not call? She sighed and replaced the card in her handbag.

"I need some caffeinated courage," she said as she spied a Starbucks across the street.

"For what?" I asked, although I suspected her answer.

"I've got to go back to the loft and get my things. Or I could just stand outside and catch them."

"Well, it has to happen sooner or later. I guess you chose sooner," I responded, feeling proud that she was tackling the challenge with such initiative.

"Well, I can't live in Bree's wardrobe. I love the girl, but she's smaller where it matters." Then she declared, "And I miss my accessories."

"It's been twenty-four hours and you're missing your accessories already?"

"Yeah. I'm just not comfortable when things don't come together right. It's like I'm not in my own skin." She was whining a bit, but I understood. Clothing and appearance were important for Morgan, and she was feeling as if she were wearing a costume rather than the items of her choosing.

"What about Pavlo? Have you thought about what you're going to say to him?"

"I've thought about it but haven't come up with the right words," she admitted.

A young couple walked by and looked at Morgan, who appeared to be talking to herself. She saw the odd look, pulled her cell phone from her handbag with one hand and cupped the other around her ear, pretending she was talking into a Bluetooth—even though she wasn't wearing one. "And I'm afraid."

She looked at me with eyes that were brimming with tears. I had never stopped to think that this strutting woman had to worry about abuse from her scorned lover, and I felt a bit ashamed.

"Oh, Morgan," I said, taking her hand in mine and patting it gently. "Nothing will happen. I promise. I know I haven't used my powers to do much more than fix your shoes and wrap, but I would never, ever let Pavlo or anyone else lay a hand on you."

"It's not that," Morgan said, with a bit of shame on her own part. "Pavlo is big and loud and strong, but he's not physical in that way. He's a teddy bear, really. A big, sexy, *proud* teddy bear, and I know I've hurt him—if nothing else than by ripping the shit out of that painting."

We both recalled the moment and couldn't restrain smiling before regaining our serious composure. We walked into the coffee shop and waited while the barista prepared Morgan's caramel macchiato. When it was ready, she picked up her coffee and walked toward a table by the window.

She continued, "Don't get me wrong. He deserved what he got for throwing my things out the window. That was inexcusable! But he is a good man, usually, and I do care about him."

"But you don't love him, do you?" I asked softly.

"You know, I don't think I ever stopped to think about our relationship like that. I love his passion, I love his excitement for life, I love his accent and the way he says my name like it's exotic," she said, slipping back into the lustful reverie she'd enjoyed a few moments ago when Sam had been on her mind. "I love so much about him."

"But you haven't said you loved *him*, Morgan. And as for stopping to think about how you feel, well, if you were in love with the man, there would be no need to think about it. You'd just *know*. That's how it works. Love is an emotion, not a practical thought. If it were practical, more men would change diapers and do housework," I said.

Morgan sipped her coffee. The caffeine must have started to connect with her brain, because she sat up straighter, with more confidence. "You're probably right. But it makes me sad that this man can't make me happy when he has all those things going for him. Maybe it's me. Am I the problem? Do I want too much? Is there anyone who could possibly make me feel the way I want?"

"So many questions, girl. There's nothing wrong with you—okay, maybe a little attitude adjustment, but that's a whole other discussion. Pavlo is a good man, but he's like wearing a gorgeous black dress with perfectly wonderful turquoise Sergio Rossi pumps and also carrying a to-die-for red bag—all at once."

Morgan winced as she visualized the color combinations.

"They're all great items on their own," I continued, "but just don't work together. That's you and Pavlo. You don't accessorize each other."

Morgan reached over and hugged me. The couple that had been eyeing her caught this moment when the strange woman grabbed onto the air across her table. They nudged one another and shook their heads. Morgan didn't notice the exchange, and I certainly wasn't one to turn away a well-deserved hug.

"While we're having this nice-nice moment, may I make one little observation?" I asked—quite sweetly, I might add.

Morgan was back on her guard. Okay, I admit, I spoiled the moment, but I was afraid that if I didn't speak what was on my mind, it would slip away into a senior moment of oblivion.

"First of all, I think there is someone out there who will accessorize you perfectly and vice versa." Morgan relaxed when I opened with an ace. "But right now, you are focusing on pulling your life together and discovering the woman that you want to be. Until you figure that out, this might not be the best time to jump into a relationship or spend more time with one that isn't going to make your dreams come true." I paused before adding, "As tempting as that might be right now."

"You're probably right."

I arched my brow. "Your real opportunity for happily every after is to find out what will make you happy and keep you happy. That doesn't come from anyone in your life— not a man, not a friend, not your father, and not a Fairy Godmother, Lord help me for saying. You have to find that joy inside yourself, Morgan. That's where it lives. The outside stuff is just icing. Yeah, it's sweet, but your cake would still be wonderful without it."

footnotes

Happiness doesn't come with the wave of a magic wand, nor from the people in our lives. Happiness, like passion, comes from inside. Once you discover who you are, you can explore the right ways to accessorize your life. That means evaluating the relationships that fit you right, the career that brings out the best in you, and the life that makes you beautiful, inside and out. Make a list of the people in your life who wonderfully accessorize you—family members, friends, co-workers. What are the qualities that make each of these people special to you? Now, consider what these qualities say about what you need from your relationships. Do this exercise to continue learning about yourself!

CHAPTER *nineteen*

After leaving Starbucks—and the curious gazes of the coffee elite who'd seen Morgan's odd behavior—we hailed a cab. When we got in, I expected Morgan to give the cabbie Pavlo's address, but instead she said, "Celestial Sky Gallery, West Lake and LaSalle." I looked at her curiously, but she didn't make eye contact.

"I thought we were going to see Pavlo." I folded my arms across my wonderfully ample chest, bumping Morgan in the act. She opened her mouth to respond and remembered her newfound trick: She pulled out her cell phone and pretended to dial, so the cabbie would not think he had a crazy lady in his back seat. I wondered how he would feel to know he had a Fairy Godmother breathing down his neck.

"I have to stop by the gallery and take care of a few details first," she said.

The cabbie looked in his rearview mirror and seemed satisfied that this attractive, well-dressed woman was talking on the phone. He returned his attention to the road in front of him.

"Are you sure you're not avoiding Pavlo?" I asked.

"No, I have an artist's reception coming up in a few weeks and need to check on the invitations, call the caterer, and make sure Celeste isn't pissing off someone she shouldn't."

Celeste Bourque owned The Celestial Sky Gallery. She tended to shift from moderately mellow into panic mode in four seconds flat. She was rather scattered, with the attention span of a toddler, and she often blamed her inability to get things done on the perceived incompetence of her staff and vendors like the florist, caterer, parking valet, electrician, carpenter, cleaning crew, printer, window washer, and pretty much anyone else who attempted to do work for her. Celeste's tantrums meant that Morgan was steadily apologizing to vendors and schmoozing new providers who had already been clued into Celeste's reputation by their colleagues. Yes, Celeste was difficult, but thankfully, she trusted Morgan and willingly turned over those tasks she considered bothersome to this young woman who innately knew what her boss wanted and when she wanted it—the answer to the latter always being *immediately!* Celeste never told Morgan how much she valued her talent and relied on her. The shrewd business-woman feared that disclosure would make her vulnerable to higher salary demands—which she would gladly pay—or, worse yet, the painful acknowledgement that she actually needed to rely on someone else.

Morgan, for her part, was able to keep Celeste separated from the most necessary people she might otherwise alienate with her caustic remarks, ridiculous demands, and backhanded compliments. (She once told a caterer that the goat cheese tartlets weren't nearly as bad as the ones she'd had at the dinner party of a well-known artist, an event that this same caterer had managed. She had also asked an electrician if she could deduct ten percent off his bill for every inch of butt crack he exposed to her clientele.) So, most of Morgan's part-time job at Celestial Sky was to keep Celeste and her comments away from everyone except the clients and artists who seemed to love her. Her customers loved Celeste's ability to grasp their taste and find those works of art that truly "spoke" to them. To the artists, she was a divine patron who recognized how difficult their lives could be, putting their hearts and souls into creating fine art that might be exposed to the culturally bereft if it weren't for her own keen ability to skim la crème of collectors from the less serious clientele.

Morgan also knew another side of Celeste—formerly known as Celia Durbin. She was a fifty-ish woman who had grown up in a small town in Ohio, gone to art school, and taken a job in a museum after realizing that her own artistic talents were too limited to make a living from. She'd married Stefan Bourque, a much older, celebrated artist, who had brought her into the inner circles of the art world. After he'd died from a massive stroke nine years earlier, Celia-Celeste had opened a gallery to exhibit some of his lesser known works and pay homage to his life by cultivating new talents.

When Morgan and I entered the gallery, we heard Celeste's throaty voice bellowing from the loft office that overlooked the gallery floor. "Oh, puhhlease, Charles, I could print better business cards with a box of Crayolas. How could you deliver these to me? I simply can't use them!" she said.

Luckily, no customers were there, but Morgan dashed up the spiral stairs in full sprint. She tapped Celeste on the shoulder and gestured for the phone, with a "May I?" look. Celeste sighed dramatically and handed the cordless receiver to Morgan as if it were an overripe banana that she had no use for. Morgan took the phone and smiled as Celeste strode away in a graceful huff.

"Hello, hello? Charles? No, it's Morgan. I know, I know," Morgan said, turning away from the exiting Celeste and lowering her voice to just above a whisper. "I asked for these cards to be delivered tomorrow for a reason. Today was supposed to be my day off. I don't know. Hold on." She reached over to the box of business cards and pulled one out. She examined it closely and compared it to a business card pinned to the memo board above her desk.

"It's not terrible, Charles, but it's not an absolutely perfect match to the sample I sent you. It's the logo, and you can't mess with the blue. Take a look and compare them, and I think you'll notice the difference." She paused and listened for a moment. "Thank you! And just so you know, the die-cutting is perfect, which is why I always rely on you!"

Morgan clicked off the phone and put it back on her desk. "What next?" she said aloud.

Meanwhile, Celeste had returned to the main floor of the gallery and was chatting with a well-dressed businessman who had walked in while Morgan was on the phone with the printer. Realizing she had a break from discussing the business card fiasco (in Celeste's eyes), Morgan went through some notes on her desk, crossed off "call Charles re: biz cards" from her To Do list, and scrolled through her cell phone in search of a number. I noticed how orderly her workspace was, a definite contrast to the disheveled kitchen and living room in Pavlo's loft. Morgan's living space reflected a "drop it and go" lifestyle, but her desk had color-coded files neatly stacked, directories in perfect order on the shelf above, and not even an extraneous paperclip in view.

"Pardon me," I said, "but how come this space looks like it belongs to Miss Neatnik and your apartment looked like the aftermath of Hurricane Morgan?"

She answered in a hushed tone. "Celeste insists on order. Believe me, it takes a *lot* of effort to keep it this way, but it's worth it not to hear her whine."

"Maybe. But it shows you *can* be organized. You just choose not to in some places."

"Okay, enough lectures for the moment. I've got some calls to make."

While Morgan smooth-talked the caterer and florist to get what she wanted for the upcoming reception, I walked downstairs and browsed the artwork. Celeste did have an eye for talent. The pieces on her walls were powerful in those works where the artist was communicating a strong message. Others were wonderfully calming, with delicate strokes and harmonious color. And I liked that Celeste opted for quality over quantity, not feeling the need to stuff the walls in order to make more sales.

While Celeste spoke with her customer, I came upon a wooden sculpture of two long arms reaching upward. Nestled in the cupped palms was a tiny bird at rest. The rich, dark mahogany of the arms contrasted with the lightness of the curly maple carving of the bird. This piece was begging to be touched. I ran my palm along the backs of the arms, feeling the smoothness of fine wood. I wrapped my fingers between the open hands of the sculpture and then reached down and, with one finger, grazed the head of the sleeping bird. When I did, a sense of calm and quiet joy seeped inside me. This was the feeling that art should bring.

"Home," Morgan said, startling me back to the present. "That's the name of the sculpture."

"It's wonderful," I breathed.

Morgan pointed to the card at the base of the podium. I looked closely, blinked, and read the artist's name again: *Pavlo Fyorchenko.*

"But I thought he was a painter," I said, quite surprised that this gentle artistry had come from the hands of the burly Ukrainian.

"He paints when he's passionate, but he carves when he's calm," Morgan explained. "He did this shortly after we started dating. We were snuggled together one morning and he told me that even though he enjoyed what he had here in America, he sometimes missed his life in the Ukraine. I said something about a bird in the hand and he asked me what that meant. I explained that you're better off enjoying what you have than missing what you don't. It's something my sister always told me when I talked about the things I wanted to have someday," she said. "And maybe I just wanted him to appreciate having me around."

I looked at Morgan and then we both looked back at the sculpture.

"I'm ready to go now," Morgan whispered. "I've got to talk to Pavlo." She stroked the wooden arm once more before walking away.

footnotes

Life is what you make it. Yes, it's a cliché, but for good reason. You choose to live a certain way. You choose the relationships you keep—including some that are not pleasing but do serve a purpose—and those you eschew. Your life is not about what is given to you but what you make of it. Face up to the challenges. Recognize that you have the power to make changes in your life. And know that it's all about choice.

Make a list of three difficult people in your life—currently or in the past. Write a list of adjectives that describe the characteristics in each person that frustrate or irritate you the most, such as: perpetually late, dishonest, short-tempered, opinionated, argumentative, or stubborn. Are there common traits among them? If so, consider how you can deal with this type of person in the future—and also ask yourself what your distaste for these traits says about you.

CHAPTER twenty

After Morgan had left his apartment, Sam paced around the living room, scratching his head and fuming about what had just occurred. He chided himself over and over again, "I just *had* to let her in, didn't I? I couldn't just let her sit out there and figure things out for herself. What a freaking idiot I am!"

Yes, Sam Baxter was a chronically Nice Guy. Not a pushover but not a jerk, either. While sticking to his own personal commitment to "no games" and remembering the advice of his sisters, he'd collected a stash of ex-girlfriends who had opted for the guys who were more challenging. The Bad Boys.

Like Stacey. When he'd met her at his running club in Boston, Stacey was involved with a Bad Boy. She was beautiful, spirited, and smart, but she put up with being neglected by a guy who was clearly not worthy of her. Week after week, while she and Sam jogged along the Charles River, she complained about the latest gaffe, slight, or insult from Rotten Rick, as she had dubbed him. And when she learned that Rotten Rick was also seeing other women, she cried on Sam's shoulder. His empathy sparked a night of passion between the two. And he officially became Rebound Guy.

They dated for six months, a blissfully sweet courtship. Stacey was thrilled to have a break from the heartache that came from being with one Bad Boy after another. She loved his honesty and the way he listened to her opinions and made her feel important and special. And Sam felt he had found a soulmate with whom he could just be himself.

When Sam announced their engagement to his family, his sisters all pasted on the artificial smiles, but not one of them was sold on Sam's choice. Leah felt that Stacey wasn't worthy of her brother. Maggie thought her future sister-in-law was still hooked on her ex-boyfriend. And Tessa, the sibling Sam was closest to, believed that Sam was in love with the idea of being in love and couldn't see that Stacey, at only twenty-two, was too immature to be more than a girlfriend—certainly *not* a wife.

As it turned out, all three were right. When Sam came to his parents' house alone for Thanksgiving dinner, just two and a half years into their marriage, he announced that he and Stacey were getting a divorce.

"What happened?" exclaimed his mother, grabbing her son in a bear hug. His response was garbled by the fact she was clutching his head to her shoulder.

"Ma, let him go. He's suffocating," said Tessa.

Loretta Baxter released Sam, who towered over her but still bowed to the wishes of his cherished mother. She held his face in her hands, smooshing and smoothing his cheeks.

"Mom, it's okay. Seriously. We just had, um, a problem with our beliefs," he started to explain. Sam had been prepared for the scene, or so he thought.

"What do you mean, a problem with beliefs? You're both Catholics," Loretta said. "What? Did she decide to become a Buddhist or something?"

"Loretta, let the boy talk," Sam's dad interjected. And, as was always the case, when Scott Baxter spoke, everyone listened. Just like E.F. Hutton.

"See, I thought that after we got married, we'd stop dating other people. Apparently, Stacey didn't have the same belief."

Every jaw in the room—except Sam's—dropped in a wordless chorus. A few gasps. Leah's husband sprayed a mouthful of beer on Loretta's apple pie, which had been cooling on the counter. Sam's dad looked down and shook his head. And one by one, each sister took their brother into a warm, loving hug that brought him to the threshold of tears.

That Thanksgiving Day was one that Sam would never forget, as much as he tried. His sisters' comforting words had the hint of I-told-you-so's that each tried to refrain from blurting at their poor, guileless baby brother. His mother spent the afternoon shaking her head and hugging her son. Scott patted his son on the back and told him, "You'll get over it. You'll be happier." And that was the end of his attempt at comfort.

After his bad luck with Stacey, Sam was very careful about relationships. He dated, but decided not to think about pursuing anything long-term. And when he got that old, gnawing knot in his stomach that signaled all was not right with a relationship, he ended it. Sam had honed his radar to know when he was just a stopover on some woman's journey to the next Bad Boy.

In his heart, he knew better than to assume that every woman was the same. Just like there were Nice Guys and Bad Boys, he knew the same was true for the female counterparts. The trick was sifting through and getting past facades to find out which was which—and he frankly didn't have the energy or desire to do that right now.

Since his divorce from Stacey three years earlier, friends had forced him into fix-ups, which only served to make him wonder what kind of image he projected to those friends. The women they told him were just perfect for him were either too focused on climbing the ladder to success as quickly as possible, too anxious to dive into a deep relationship, or just plain flaky. Somewhere in the middle of those types was the magic blend, but he wasn't sure he'd recognize it if he saw it. Morgan Demarest had looked pretty good—until this morning. Seeing Pavlo arguing with Morgan in his living room, after he had listened to her vent about his crazy behavior the night before, was a flashback to the many cry-on-my-shoulder nights that he would rather forget.

"Shake it off, Sam," he said out loud after Morgan had left. He had to get packed. He was flying to Tampa that afternoon to meet with a client who was launching a new line of nutrition bars. *As if the world needs more tasteless junk*, he thought. But as a marketing pro, he had the sense and savvy to keep his personal feelings out of the process of building a brand. (Although allergic to shellfish, he had managed a shrimp company's marketing account for five years.) He was good at convincing people, the mark of a true salesman. His success was the result of being a good listener and paying attention to the customer's needs. He often considered himself a chameleon, with the ability to put himself in someone else's position and figure out what made that person tick—or buy. He'd taken the job at Smithson/Bell after deciding that Boston held too many memories. Too many old connections he'd just as soon leave behind. So he'd started over, with a new job in a new home.

Since coming to Chicago last year, Sam had also tackled his goal of securing speaking engagements. His passion for creating a sustainable business with a multiple bottom line—fiscal profitability, good employee relations, eco-friendly practices—made him a popular presenter at business gatherings, which helped grow his network and further fuel his confidence. While many of the speakers on this circuit were pumped up with their own imagined superiority, Sam's "Nice Guy-ness" proved to be a real plus when it came to business networking.

Sam had met Edward Demarest at one of these meetings, and their paths crossed again a few weeks later at a gallery opening for an up-and-coming Russian painter. Sam had stopped in briefly because the gallery owner was a client, but he didn't linger; the vivid artwork of Pavlo Fyorchenko was not to his liking, and he had an early meeting the following morning. He and Edward chatted briefly and exchanged business cards. Ten minutes after Sam left the gallery, unbeknownst to him, Morgan had hurried in, late as usual, and spent the evening playing first lady of the artist.

Shortly afterward, Sam had made a call to Edward with the intention of pitching his marketing firm to Edward's development company. They met for lunch a few days later. During the conversation, Edward mentioned he was selling his downtown apartment and made subtle suggestions that business was not very good, but he was too proud to go into any detail. Seeing that the possibility of securing Demarest Development as a profitable client was not going to happen, Sam expressed interest in the apartment. Edward's description was enticing, and he invited Sam to look at the place later that day. The apartment was ideal for Sam, and the two closed the transaction without the need for a realtor.

And then Morgan Demarest had shown up on his doorstep, literally. She was funny, smart, and definitely attractive, but also combative—although he had to admit that he had enjoyed the verbal sparring. Still, he reminded himself that he had to stay committed to his goals. He had a full life with his work and relationship with his "little brother", Anthony, who helped Sam escape from life's stresses. And clearly Morgan had unresolved issues with her artist boyfriend. He knew that being the Rebound Guy would undoubtedly lead to more pain. *Nope, no way*, he thought. Morgan Demarest was one risk he was not willing to take.

But...

footnotes

Everyone has baggage. You can't go through life without gathering some tough experiences and nagging memories along the way, but until you can put them in the proper perspective, you'll just be needlessly weighted down. How has your past colored your present? Do you have fears that you'd like to conquer? What's standing in your way? Is it a legitimate obstacle or one that you have placed there to protect yourself from hurt? Stop right now. Look at the baggage you're carrying—the hurt, the fear, the prejudice. Write it in your journal, and set a goal to work on lightening that load.

One of the reasons that young children can do a Rubik's Cube or learn a new language so easily is that they don't over-think the challenge; they just do it! While it's important to weigh the consequences of an action, you also need to know that just about anything can be repaired—including a broken heart.

CHAPTER twenty-one

After Morgan had stomped out of the loft last night, Pavlo had flip-flopped between anger and worry. But following this morning's scene with that other guy, the worry had faded and he was just plain pissed. *Foolish, impetuous girl*, he brooded. How dare she think that tossing a pair of shoes out the window was reason for destroying a work of art? Shoes could be replaced. The painting was gone forever.

Ah, who am I kidding, he thought. That one was crap. He had left it on the easel hoping to see some way to turn it into something that could sell, because it was nothing he would want to keep. But Morgan would never know.

Morgan. She was spoiled and self-centered. What had he seen in that scrawny American? What? The answer was a light heart filled with joy at the simplest things— like shoes. She overflowed with excitement when she brought home a new pair. He had never known a woman so in love with her shoes.

And that was the problem. She was in love with her shoes, with her clothes, with her *stuff*, but he could never tell if he was included among her beloved belongings. Well, he was no longer going to play second fiddle to anyone named Christian Louboutin or Sergio Rossi, men that Morgan had never met but adored just the same.

Now he stood in their bedroom, staring at her closet. The rest of the room was in total disarray, but the closet was orderly. Shoeboxes were neatly—lovingly—stacked. A few blouses and a pair of jeans had been tossed on the floor, but the others were hung on padded hangers that Morgan had color-coded: mauve for blouses, mocha for jackets, dusty blue for dresses, ivory for skirts, and sage green for pants.

Pavlo smiled at this attention to detail and recalled her excitement when she'd explained her new system. Silly girl. Silly, crazy, wonderful girl.

Pavlo reached in the closet and pulled out a shoebox that contained a pair of her favorite stilettos. He remembered the time a man had stopped her outside a café and just said, "Nice shoes!" She'd beamed. Pavlo had wanted to tackle the man but then assumed he was probably gay and thus posed no threat to his manhood.

He opened the shoebox and sifted through layers of pink tissue until he unearthed the shoe, a cream-colored peep-toe with an ankle strap. The shoe's sole was made of crimson red leather, the signature of a "Loub", as Morgan called it, like some hip insider. He rubbed his calloused hand along the strap, which was incredibly soft leather, and then felt the smooth sole. He had to admit that it was a nice-looking shoe—even nicer on Morgan, who wore them with such pride.

Again, that annoying thing with Morgan and her wardrobe. He was jarred back to reality. He put the shoe back, with none of the care that Morgan would use, and tossed the box back into the closet, where it landed with a soft thud.

Although it was not yet noon, he made a beeline for the liquor cabinet. He had finished the Stoli last night but found another bottle of vodka. He poured a glass and gulped it, then spat it right out. He looked at the label. Blueberry.

"Who the hell puts fruit in vodka?" he roared. This must be some of that booze Morgan used for her girly drinks. He rummaged around the cabinet and found a bottle of Jack Daniels. It would have to do.

While he tossed back three shots in a row, Pavlo thought, *Now what?* He knew he had thrust a dagger in Morgan's heart when he'd thrown those things out the window. It had felt so good at the time, but when he'd seen the look of horror on Morgan's face, he'd immediately regretted his action. Still, stubborn and proud, he'd stood firm. No apology.

And then the way she'd brutalized his self-portrait. He had never seen her so enraged, which aroused him. If she had stayed a few minutes longer, he would have dragged her off to the bedroom for some steamy make-up sex.

But she'd left. She'd chosen her designer things over him. At least, that's how he saw it. Or maybe that was just an excuse so she could run off to her new lover. The sting in his chest wasn't from the Jack Daniels he was drinking. Morgan's betrayal had ripped open his heart, leaving him feeling mortally wounded. He knew he loved her, which made the pain of losing her almost unbearable.

Pavlo wanted to lash out. The painting that she had torn with her fist and her foot was still lying on the floor. He picked it up and heaved it at the wall, the same wall that had taken the hit from Morgan's cell phone last night. The corner of the canvas hit the wall, and the wooden stretcher holding the shreds of material together broke apart. He picked it up off the floor and shredded the remainder with his hands.

When he was done taking out his anger on objects, Pavlo flopped onto an overstuffed chair and buried his face in his hands. He wanted to make Morgan hurt so she could feel the way he did. But she wasn't in pain. She was tucked away in her father's apartment with some other guy, probably laughing at him.

Laughing. He couldn't bear the thought of being the butt of her jokes. He had to do something.

And then it hit him. Pavlo saw a pile of mail on the coffee table. Right on top was a credit card bill, addressed to him. He opened it and perused a long list of purchases: Gucci; Victoria's Secret; Saks; and, of course, Neiman Marcus. Not one of them was anything he had bought. They were all Morgan's.

"Vell, ve vill put an end to dis right now," he announced out loud. He took out his wallet and grabbed his credit cards. One by one, he called the toll-free numbers to cancel every credit card that Morgan had, courtesy of his generosity.

When he was satisfied that he had cut her off completely, he returned to his studio in the far corner of the loft and thrust his angry energy onto a canvas, which he struck with powerful strokes of harsh colors, piling one over another like a boxer pummeling his opponent. By the time the late afternoon sun was sending amber rays through the windows, he was drained of energy, void of anger, and pretty well anesthetized with whiskey. He put down his brushes and looked out at the glistening towers of the Chicago skyline and the pedestrians hurrying along Lakeshore Drive. Was Morgan among them? Hand in hand with her new lover?

His heart was so heavy it felt like a cement block in his chest. Although hurt and furious with Morgan, he already missed her smile, her laugh, and the sweet smell of her hair. His throat felt tight, and there was a dampness around his eyes that blurred his view. Pavlo inhaled long and slowly. He held his breath a moment and blew it out, as if he were extinguishing an unseen candle. Perhaps, he thought, he should fight to keep her. Maybe he could win her back.

But did he want to? He didn't know the answer to that question, and his mind was getting as fuzzy as the skyline, so he decided to table his mental debate. For now, he just needed rest. He lay down on the sofa in his studio and drifted off to sleep.

Pavlo was already snoozing when Morgan slipped her key in the lock. Her hand was trembling, and I whispered to her, "I've got your back, girl. You can do this!"

She was holding her breath as she slowly pushed open the heavy metal door to the apartment she had been sharing with Pavlo for the past ten months. She had come through this door on so many occasions without even a thought as to what she'd be walking into. Most of the time, Pavlo greeted her with a big smile and warm kiss. She knew for certain that would not be the case today.

When we entered, the space was quiet. We both stopped and surveyed the area. The painting Morgan had kicked was lying in shreds by the wall. There was an empty bottle of Stoli on the floor by the sofa, and some magazines thrown on the floor. It was otherwise just as she had left it.

I paused and listened. "Do you hear that?"

"What?" Morgan scanned the room.

"Sounds like a truck," I said.

"Divinity, we're in downtown Chicago. Of course, there are trucks," she said. Again with the eye roll.

"Do they all drive through the apartment?" I shook a warning finger at her to knock off the sass.

""What are you talking about?" She paused to listen, and a knowing look came over her face. "That's not a truck. Pavlo is snoring."

So he *was* here. This was one more wish of hers that hadn't been granted. (Like I said, I'm not a genie. I've got much more important things to do than to continue helping clients avoid difficult situations.)

She stood frozen in place, her gaze fixed on his studio, where the sound of his snoring was coming from. I knew she was wondering what to do next. Should she wake him up to talk about their fight? Did she need to reassure him that nothing had happened between her and Sam? And what about their relationship? Did they still have one?

If she was going to embark on a new future, with fresh goals and smarter choices—with the help of her very own mentor—Morgan had to release herself from a relationship that didn't fulfill her. And Pavlo's last outburst this morning at Sam's apartment made her next step even easier. If he truly meant what he said about her being silly and selfish, Pavlo didn't respect her, nor did he understand her. In his eyes, she was a toy, a doll—not a woman to be taken seriously.

After a few moments, Morgan went to the bedroom and pulled out two large red suitcases. She took every item hung in her closet, hangers and all, and plunked them into the bags, which quickly became unfeasibly stuffed. She sighed, trying to decide what to leave behind. I could tell the dilemma was killing her and decided she could use a little help: I waved my hand and everything magically fit. Hey, it worked for Mary Poppins.

Like someone who was told she didn't have to pay for checking extra baggage, Morgan gleefully gathered up her colorful stash of scarves and handbags and tossed them into the suitcases. Then she opened the dresser and emptied the contents of her underwear drawer into one bag and put her entire jewelry box into the other.

And then she looked at her shoe collection and back at the suitcases that were once again filled to the top. "Well?" Morgan asked. "Can't you make more room for my shoes?"

Not liking the entitlement in her voice, I answered, "Honey, that's as far as I can stretch it. Time to improvise, girlfriend!"

"Hmph," she grunted, and looked back at the towering stacks of shoeboxes. It would be easier to take the shoes out of their boxes and pack them loosely, but she couldn't part with their homes, their safe havens. She sneaked to the kitchen, careful to avoid waking Pavlo, and grabbed a box of trash bags. Back in the bedroom, she packed one box after another into the plastic bags.

"I'm sorry to do this to you, girls, but it's the only way I can get you out of here safely!" she whispered inside the bag.

When she was done, Morgan wheeled her luggage out the door and into the hallway while I followed behind with one of the trash bags. She then returned for more of the treasure-filled bags. Like a high-heeled Santa Claus, she dragged them behind her, one in each hand, and I walked out with the last one.

Once her worldly belongings had been moved from the loft into the hallway, she stepped back inside and felt the energy of Pavlo's stare. He was awake and sitting up on the sofa in his studio, watching her. Their eyes met and held with a grip that neither person seemed able to break. His face was drawn, but his eyes were filled with pain. It was hard to tell if he was too tired to be angry or had found it in his heart to let his feelings for Morgan take over.

Neither Pavlo nor Morgan moved from their positions. Morgan stood near the doorway, her oversized handbag hanging from her shoulder and the keys to the loft in her hand. Pavlo returned her stare, not budging from the couch. It was a stand-off.

"Say something," I whispered to her out of the corner of my mouth, even though I knew Pavlo wouldn't be able to hear me even if I screamed it.

She looked at me and then at Pavlo.

"I'm sorry," she said in a choked voice. "It's not what you thought. I never cheated on you. But I'm sorry you think I did."

She laid the keys on the table near the door and walked out.

footnotes

When you make a plan, be clear about your objectives. Then, when opportunities arise that challenge that plan, stop and consider them. Is the "opportunity" actually a distraction that is taking your focus away from your goal? Is it perhaps a means to refine your goal and make it better? Take the time to write down your goals, rather than just keep them in your mind. Use your journal! And post them on notes in places where you can see them. Do the same thing with these speed bumps along the way. Determine their value—or lack thereof—and put them in perspective. Weigh them against your goals and determine how they align with your plans. Anything that does not contribute to you reaching the vision you've created is an obstacle. Clear those obstacles away so you can keep moving forward—whether that is with a task or a relationship!

CHAPTER twenty-two

Morgan and I hauled her two suitcases and four trash bags into the elevator. Once in awhile, I don't mind a little manual labor, as long as it doesn't interfere with my manicure. Of course, I have to be careful that passersby don't see things like bags moving themselves because it draws unwanted attention to my client.

When we got to the lobby, I gave everything a hefty nudge when the doorman wasn't looking so that neither of us had to drag every bag out again. I sat down on the suitcases while Morgan called her father. He had insisted on picking her up after she got her things together. He'd offered to come to the loft but Morgan decided it was best for everyone if she went alone—well, almost alone.

"Hi, Dad. I've got everything and I'm in the lobby . . . No, it's fine . . . Yes, Dad, I'll wait inside until you get here . . . I love you, too." She clicked off the phone and looked at me. "He'll be here in a few minutes. I'm guessing he's been circling the block so he would be close by in case I needed him."

"That's so sweet," I replied. "And then what?"

"Then we'll head to Hinsdale. I'm going to stay there, with Dad, for a while, until I can get things figured out. We'll commute together to the city for now. I just need to get a good night's sleep so I can think straight. Although you have to admit, I've made a lot of progress for one day!"

I stared at Morgan, saying nothing. I figured I'd let her have the discussion with herself. Personally, I had no issue with her going home to Dad in this case, but it wouldn't be nearly as fun to tell her that. And since we had ten minutes to kill, I'd let her work through her issues.

"I am not running home to Daddy, if that's what you're thinking. He could use some support right now, and so could I, right? So we're just going to hang together for a while. This is not a long-term thing, okay? I know you think I am hiding from my problems, but that's not true." She paused. We did a mutual, wordless glare. I could hold on as long as Miss Stubborn, which wasn't much of a challenge because she broke the silence in little more than ten seconds. "You know, you are *so* judgmental!"

"Who are you talking to?"

Morgan swirled around and was face-to-face with her father, who was curiously eyeing his daughter.

"Who is so judgmental, Morgan?" Edward asked again.

"Um, me. I am, Dad. I was just thinking out loud," she stammered.

"Now, why would you say that, Morgan? You're certainly a woman with an opinion, but that doesn't make you judgmental." He looked past Morgan and the suitcases and saw the four trash bags. He put his hands on his hips, assuming his fatherly "and what do we have here?" posture. "Are you taking out the trash?" he asked.

I was still sitting on the luggage, taking in the situation.

Morgan looked at the green bags. "Those are my shoes, Dad."

"You're throwing out your *shoes*? Wow! What *happened* up there? What did Pavlo say to you, sweetheart?" He put his hands on her shoulders and looked her in the eye, which was easy since her five-inch heels closed their difference in height.

Morgan looked at him quizzically. "What? No, Dad. I am *not* throwing out my shoes! I just didn't have anything else to pack them in."

"Oh," said Edward. "So, this is your luggage." He reached down and picked up three of the trash bags. "At least you have a matching set. But where is the rest of your stuff? You couldn't possibly fit everything you own into two suitcases and a few trash bags, C'mon, Pony Girl, I know you have lots more in your closet than this. Or should I look out on the sidewalk to see if it's raining Prada again?"

"This is everything, Dad. Everything I need." She smiled sweetly.

He took the bags out the door to the car as we watched.

"I like your father, Morgan."

She smiled. "Yeah, me, too."

Once Morgan's belongings were packed into the car, we all hit the road. Although Edward Demarest was facing some definite cutbacks in his life, he had yet to give up his Infiniti, and the back seat was quite comfortable. I stretched out my legs as if I were in a limo and he was my driver. Meanwhile, Edward and Morgan exchanged pleasantries for a few minutes. They talked about the sudden chill in the air, the amount of traffic heading out of the city at this hour, and the possibility of grabbing Chinese takeout from their favorite place on the way home. And then they drove in silence. But it wasn't uncomfortable. There was a common bond that connected father and daughter without the need for small talk. It was okay for them to just hold back the words for a bit, feeling safe and happy in each other's company while immersing themselves in their individual thoughts.

For his part, Edward drifted back into his world of worries. He saw his business as a tangled mess he didn't know how to fix. He had always been able to solve his challenges by working harder, like burrowing a tunnel. But this problem was a crumbling wall he couldn't push through; he would have to fully reconstruct it. He felt as if he were going back to the beginning, twenty years ago, and didn't want to start over. He had come too far, worked too hard, made a name for himself. He couldn't go back. Maybe he should just get out. Retire.

But that would be giving up, and that wasn't in his DNA. So Edward was back to the tangled mess. He had already laid off two project managers, both of whom had been with him for years, as well as three administrative people. He had let them down. Sure, he could blame the economy, but Edward believed he should have seen the recession coming. In fact, he had, but he'd somehow felt impermeable. Edward had assumed that he would do what he always did: doggedly bulldoze through and come out strong on the other side. He thought back to some of his decisions. Had he taken his eye off the ball? Should he have been more aggressive about cultivating new business? Had he done enough to take care of the clients he had? A few had gone on to other developers, companies that were less expensive, but only because they couldn't match his quality, experience, and depth of services. Still, he should have tried harder to hold onto them. If he had found ways to increase his value to those clients, he would have had the cash flow to keep his staff intact.

Edward shook his head, disgusted with his inability to manage the situation. He just kept coming back to the same question: What do I do? The answer still eluded him.

Next to him, Morgan reran the episode with Pavlo. She thought about what she could have said, should have said. She imagined different outcomes. What if they could work it out and go back to those fun days in the beginning? Was that possible? Did she want that? Nah, she answered back. She was moving forward, and Pavlo was slipping into her past—regretfully, painfully, but almost certainly. After all, he'd made it clear he thought she was nothing but a paper doll. *I'll show him*, she thought. There was a new Morgan Demarest emerging, which was both exciting and scary. She wondered what parts of herself would be left behind in this post-Pavlo world. Certainly not her stilettos; that was for sure!

Morgan thought about what lay ahead. Elizabeth must have seen something of value in her to be willing to invest time in her as a mentor. Elizabeth—or maybe just having a mentor who could give Morgan hope that her life would get better—felt like a medication, and it was taking effect. Morgan already felt more confident.

She thought about her journal and rummaged around in her handbag until she found it. What would she write in this book? Her first entry should have significance. This was one of those "Ta-da, look out, world!" kind of moments, and she wanted to start out strong. She held the journal on her lap, rubbing the leather cover with her thumb while she pondered.

Edward glanced over and noticed the book. "What's that, honey?"

"I met with this amazing woman today—Elizabeth Tanner-Freitag—and she agreed to be my mentor. She suggested I start a journal, so I bought this one today," Morgan explained.

"How did you meet this woman?" Edward asked, trying to mask his concern that his daughter might be getting sucked into a scam.

"She spoke at a seminar I went to a while back, and she told me to come and see her when I was ready to make some changes in my life."

"What kind of changes?"

"Getting my act together. Planning my future. Elizabeth is a successful entrepreneur. She runs a software development company here in Chicago. IdeaWorx. Have you heard of it? Well," Morgan continued without waiting for a response, "I checked it out, and she has definitely made a success of her life, and after having been abused by her husband and going to college at night. Anyway, I'm just thrilled she agreed to work with me. Now I'm just wondering how to start the journal and what to write."

Edward was pleased with Morgan's enthusiasm and felt confident that Elizabeth—and mentoring—was a good step for his daughter. "There are some classic openings," he said. "How about, 'Call me Ishmael'? Or, 'It was the best of times, it was the worst of times.'"

Morgan smiled, knowing he was joking with her.

"Or how about, 'It was a dark and stormy night, and there was Prada in the air—literally,'" Edward continued, enjoying the exercise.

"Ooh, I like that, Morgan! What do you think?" I chimed in.

She glanced over her shoulder and, for once, gave me a smile and nodded in agreement.

"Actually, Dad, that's not such a bad idea." She opened the book and wrote that down on the second page, leaving the first one blank, just in case she came up with something else.

When she was done, Morgan watched her father for a few moments. He looked older than she recalled, more tired, but he was still the strong force she had always relied on to keep her safe from harm. And she hoped that she could find it in herself to stop taking and start giving back to this man who had always been there for her.

She reached over and gently placed her hand on her father's arm. "Thanks," she said softly.

"My pleasure, honey. Go ahead; give me another challenge. I'm on a roll!" His spirits picked up as he enjoyed the one moment today where he felt he was able to solve a problem, albeit a little one.

"I mean thanks for everything, Dad. You're always there for me, and I want you to know that I appreciate what you do. And who you are. You're a good guy and a great dad. I hope you know that."

He smiled broadly and put his left hand over hers, giving it a squeeze. "We're a team, Pony Girl. We just have to figure out our game plan."

footnotes

Change can be great, but it is also scary, and taking the first step is a tough one. Use your journal to work through a change that you'd like to make in your life. Write about why you want the change and what it will mean in your life. Journal about the challenges you'll need to overcome to get there and remind yourself that the work is worth the journey!

CHAPTER twenty-three

When Morgan walked in the door of her childhood home, the house felt wonderfully familiar and yet unexpectedly strange. Her parents had divorced when Morgan was away at college, so she'd spent little time there without her father. Yet, in the few years preceding the divorce, Morgan had already begun to notice steady changes when she'd come to visit—usually when retreating from a problem and seeking solace from her mom, who had always been good for retail therapy when life sucked.

When the four Demarests had lived under one roof, the living room had held a burgundy leather sofa with the dark wood accents that Edward preferred. The den had been Edward's office, where he displayed his awards, a few golf trophies from local tournaments, and photos of himself with family and friends.

Within two months after Claire asked Edward to leave, she had redone the master bedroom, replacing the Polo bedding with blue toile and Battenburg lace shams. She had made the room "girly girl", as Morgan called it.

Soon after, the beige walls of the living room became pale yellow, and the leather sofa was replaced by one in red jacquard, covered with toss pillows in shades of red, sage green, and ivory. The heavy drapes that had adorned the windows were retired in favor of gently flowing sheer jabots in varying hues of the same sage green as the toss pillows.

Claire then converted Edward's den into a creative space. She removed every stick of furniture, which she offered to Edward. He declined everything except the personal items, and donated the furniture to a local charity auction. Like Claire, he didn't want to carry over memories that would pain him. And the loss of his family—as it felt at the time—cut so deeply that he couldn't bear more reminders of the life he had been forced to leave to behind; forced more by his own myopic vision and workaholism than his wife's divorce decree.

So Edward's former den morphed from man-cave to feminine retreat. Claire had a window seat installed under the bay window where Edward's desk had been. The cushions were a floral print reminiscent of a Monet watercolor. Those shades of lavender, periwinkle, mauve, and emerald set the tone for the room. Claire had a sofa and chair covered in the same fabric. Once Edward's books were removed from the built-in shelves, she replaced them with colorful pottery, small sculptures, and her own reading material, including travel guides, cookbooks, chick lit, and interior decorating how-to guides. And every week, she placed a fresh bouquet of flowers on the coffee table in the room. The space that had once smelled of Edward's cologne now held no hint of the previous occupant.

But the most noticeable difference in the post-divorce home was the absence of the family portrait that used to hang above the fireplace in the living room. In its place was a painting of a vineyard at sunset, a piece of art Claire had purchased on a trip to California's Napa Valley during her "healing" phase after the split. Morgan had often thought about asking for the family portrait but knew she had no place to hang it since she had yet to truly find "home".

Edward had been staying in "the Hinsdale house", as he preferred to call the former family home, for about six weeks. After selling his apartment to Sam Baxter, he'd stayed at the apartment of a friend who was traveling in Asia. When the friend returned, Edward decided not to potentially over-stay his welcome in the event he needed to return later. Meanwhile, Claire was preparing to leave for Tuscany and knew that Edward was contemplating his next move, so she graciously offered to let him stay at the Hinsdale house during her absence. Knowing it was hard for Edward to accept anything he felt was pity or charity, Claire called him and couched her invitation in a manner that made it easier to swallow: "You know, Edward, I had been thinking about getting a house-sitter to stay here while I'm gone. I'd rather have someone here who can also take care of Winston so I don't have to board him. And enough people know that I will be away, and I don't really trust that security system," she began.

"It's a very good system, Claire. You shouldn't worry," Edward replied, sensing where she was going but not willing to devour the humble pie too zestfully.

"Be that as it may," she continued, "you would be doing me a favor by staying here while I'm in Tuscany. I know it's not the most convenient place for you, but please consider it. I thought of asking Morgan, but she would never want to stay out here without Pavlo and immediate access to her social circle. The suburbs are no fun for a single woman." Claire paused, realizing that she herself was now single. "A *young* single woman, that is."

Edward recognized Claire's attempt to preserve his pride. In spite of all the pain that had passed between them, they had managed to retain respect and kindness. *Hmm,* he thought, *maybe that marriage counselor wasn't a total waste of money.*

Although he knew it would be painful to return, Edward also relished the idea of getting away from the city, of sitting on the porch where he used to contemplate life, and eating in the same old kitchen, the one thing that Claire hadn't changed after he left, mainly because she had spent several years investing in its renovation to make it exactly as she wanted it. And so he had accepted Claire's invitation and moved back in just hours after Claire left for the airport.

Tonight, after towing in the suitcases and trash bags, Edward and Morgan stopped in the foyer and looked around. Morgan expected to feel something different. Instead, a rush of memories returned, erasing the new furnishings that couldn't mask the feeling of being home again. Dad was here, and that just felt right to her. Edward, too, felt the comfort that Morgan's presence brought to this empty house.

An overjoyed brown dog hurried into the foyer, skidding to a stop on the wood floor at Morgan's feet. She rubbed his ears and nuzzled his soft face. "Hello, Winston. I'm so glad to see you, too!"

While Winston greeted his family, I wandered around. The house was a lovely colonial, with beautifully maintained hardwood floors in the foyer. Antique accents complemented the new furniture, blending seamlessly. Claire loved color, and that was evident in her choice of paints, furniture, and decorative accents. I could feel the positive energy that came from a woman's renewed passion for life. I'd seen it often enough, when clients made a life change like Claire's. It was hard for them to work through the hurt of a failed relationship and see that there could be a brighter future ahead. Yes, although I had come to specialize in young women like Morgan, I did my training helping women who felt paralyzed by the end of a relationship, those women who gave so much of themselves in an effort to please someone else that they ended up empty and fragile shells when left on their own.

For all of these women, the power surge came shortly after they stopped asking permission to do something that might be perceived as selfish—like take an hour-long soak in the tub, away from the kids, or going out for an occasional evening with friends, or just deciding *not* to cook dinner. Perhaps one of my colleagues had helped Claire Demarest rediscover herself, but there was no way to know for certain. The Fairy Godmother Code is similar to the oath that doctors, lawyers, and therapists take: Client confidentiality is essential. Still, I suspected Claire had had a little voice somewhere telling her to seek out her passion for life. And she'd found it right there in her kitchen.

And here I was with her daughter, in the same kitchen—helping myself to a little snack of chocolate-dipped pistachio biscotti (well, three, actually)—trying to figure out how to help Morgan experience a similar epiphany.

While I was looking around the kitchen, admiring the colorful cookware and pottery, Morgan and Edward wandered in. He took a bottle of shiraz from the cabinet, poured two glasses, and pulled up a stool at the kitchen's custom marinace countertop. Meanwhile, Morgan rummaged around the fridge and pulled out a block of cheese. She next grabbed a box of crackers and a plate and sat down next to her dad.

"So," Edward began, "tell me more about the meeting with Elizabeth."

"Like I said, I met her at a conference where she talked to a group of businesswomen, and she talked about how anyone can achieve a dream if they're prepared to do the work. At the time, I wasn't really thinking about change. I went with Bree because she was looking for a new job and thought it would be a good place to network with successful women," Morgan said.

"And how'd that work out for her?"

"She made some connections. I know she was Facebooking with one or two of them. And she got help on her resume from someone she met there." Morgan swooshed the wine around in her glass and watched the small whirlpool rise up and settle.

"And Elizabeth was the guest speaker?"

"Yup. She was really inspiring, too. She came from nothing and basically built her life by working hard and never letting anyone push her down. She's amazing, Dad. So smart and successful. I felt smarter just being there with her."

"Hmm, maybe I should stand in her presence then," said Edward, thinking once again about his business dilemma.

"Dad, please. I'm serious," Morgan said, thinking he was mocking her.

"And so am I, sweetheart. I'm sorry, tell me more. What do you hope to gain by having Elizabeth as your mentor?"

"I want to find my passion, set goals for myself, and get my life together. I'm twenty-three, and I've never put much thought into what I wanted for my life. I see Emily all excited about her work in New Orleans. And now Mom is off in Tuscany taking cooking classes and acting about as happy as I've ever seen her."

The last comment stung Edward. Claire was happier without him than with him.

Morgan realized the effect of her words and reached over to put her hand on her father's. "Dad, it's a different kind of happiness. I think Mom spent years not knowing what she wanted, so she couldn't tell you what it was that she needed. I know you think you failed, but that's just not true."

I chimed right in. "It's like I said, when you don't accessorize each other, nothing is going to make a plaid and a stripe work together. And horizontal stripes will never ever be flattering, so why do they even use them in clothing? And spandex—well, don't get me going on spandex."

Morgan pretended to be yawning as she stretched out her arms behind her, but whacked the side of my head in so doing.

"What? Is it not true? Spandex might feel like it's holding you in, but the truth is that your goodies are hanging out way more than they should," I said.

Maybe I was having a sugar rush from the biscotti. But it felt pretty good, so I just helped myself to another one.

Morgan turned her attention back to her father. "As I was saying, Dad, I know the divorce hurt you. It hurt all of us. But maybe not as much as seeing you both unhappy," she said softly.

"I didn't know we were unhappy," he replied. "Why didn't I know we were unhappy?"

"Well, you were working all the time and Mom was shopping all the time, so neither of you stopped to realize why you did what you did." Morgan sliced off a piece of cheese and nibbled at it. "I guess I'm guilty of the same thing. I've been doing everything I can to ignore my future. I've been living day to day. And now I find myself without all the safety nets I've always had, and I can't ignore it anymore."

"Ahem, with a little help from yours truly," I interrupted.

"Whatever," Morgan mumbled. "Anyway, I want to find that passion that makes people love their jobs and their lives. I want to do more than *pretend* to be an independent woman."

"I'm proud of you, Morgan," Edward said with a smile. "It takes a lot to make a change. And I don't know whether to help you or stay out of your way. I have a feeling I've been one of those safety nets, and that isn't exactly a good thing." He took a bite out of a cracker. "But I'm your father, and I only want to be there for you, to help you when I can."

"Dad, I love you, and I know you'll always be there for me, but a little voice keeps telling me I have to do this on my own"—Morgan glanced in my direction and I nodded to her—"so maybe you can be there to tell me what I'm doing wrong and then keep an eye on me when I try to fix it. If I screw up, tell me."

"Like a mentor," Edward responded.

"Yeah, I guess. Like a mentor."

"Okay. Speaking as a fatherly mentor, have you given any thought as to what you might want to do?"

"I've given it a lot of thought but found no answers."

"You know, you've always been creative, like your mother."

"But I don't see myself as a chef, Dad."

"I'm not saying that," he protested mildly. "I'm just saying that you're the type of person who needs to have some creative thinking in her job and her life. I don't see you as someone sitting behind a desk or doing the same task one day after another."

"Ugh, no!"

"So, think about ways you can use that talent in a career. Maybe interior decorating, running a boutique, or even teaching," he offered.

"Hmm, not sure. I never thought about teaching. A boutique would be fun, but I'm afraid I would spend my entire paycheck there. Interior decorating is possible. I'll think about it," she said.

"You know, even dog walking can be a creative job if you make it that way," I suggested, hoping she wouldn't limit her options too much.

"I am not going to be a dog walker!" Morgan pronounced.

Startled, Edward replied, "Well, I hadn't suggested that, but at least you can cross it off your list since you've obviously made up your mind."

Morgan scrambled. "Sorry, Dad, I don't know why I thought about that. Weird." She gave me another "butt out" look.

"Don't give me that look, girl, unless you want another session with my hair styling," I warned her, wagging my index finger in front of her nose.

Morgan sat up straight and returned her attention to her father. "Dad, I'm just afraid that I won't find this passion that everyone is obsessing about. What if I just don't have it?"

"Honey, it's not an obsession. Passion is part of everyone, including you. It's in there, sweetheart, because you are a passionate person. Maybe you need to do like your mother did. Stop shopping and start listening to your heart," Edward said, with a tinge of remorse.

"Except for the 'stop shopping' part, you sounded just like Mom," Morgan responded with surprise.

"You don't stay married for all those years without learning one or two things." He smiled, taking a sip of wine.

"Well, seeing as I need to save some money to pay for an apartment, I have no choice but to"—Morgan slowly took in a deep breath and exhaled before finishing—"not shop for a while."

"Now, that didn't hurt so much, did it, Pony Girl?" Edward smiled at her again.

"Saying it? No. Doing it? You have *no* idea."

footnotes

The first step in sculpting your life is to uncover your passion, which is not always an easy task. Some people just know what it is, while others have to search more diligently. The only way to uncover what drives your excitement is to stop, clear your head, and think. Peel away the layers and get to the core of your energy. When you take the time to explore your own interests, skills, talents, and passion, crafting your goals becomes much easier.

Think about the things in your life that bring you joy. Make a list of ten surefire things that get you so jazzed that you can't wait to get started. Your list might include gardening, hiking, and sailing, which means you need a job that keeps you outdoors. Or you might find joy when you make things yourself, which tells you that you would do well in a job that presents a creative, hands-on challenge. Once you have your list, look for the common threads and see if you can determine passions that you have overlooked in the past. Once you know what that powerful driver is, shape your goals around it. Then determine what steps you need to take reach your happily-ever-after.

CHAPTER twenty-four

Later that night, Morgan returned to her childhood bedroom. Unlike the rooms that had undergone the post-divorce makeover, Claire had left her daughters' rooms untouched. Morgan's canopy was still draped with pale pink and white sheer valances. The silver stars she had pinned to them were there as well. She recalled many nights when she'd played on the bed, imagining that she was a fairy princess in a castle or that the mattress was a magic carpet where she was flying with Aladdin. One spring, after a visit to Disney World, this bed had been transformed into Cinderella's attic, where Morgan/Cinderella waited for Prince Charming to arrive with the glass slipper. And another time, Morgan had used her imagination to pretend she was in a tent on an African safari. This bed had been many things to Morgan, and she was flooded with happy memories as she lay there, surrounded by a mound of plump pillows—square, round, and oblong—in a range of pinks, some with giant poppies, others with stripes, and a few solids.

The queen-sized bed was looking might comfy, so I lay down beside Morgan and propped myself up on a few of those pillows. I gave her a little hip nudge and, to my surprise, she moved without complaint.

"Nice room, Morgan," I said. "But what's with Pillow Land here?"

"I like pillows," she said. "And when I was younger, it made me feel safe to snuggle in with all of them around me."

She grabbed a round pillow and hugged it to her chest, then lay there on her back staring at the canopy above.

"This reminds me of when Emily used to come in here and snuggle into bed with me," Morgan said. "We'd lie here and fantasize about our lives. She wanted to be a veterinarian and was going to get an RV and travel the country helping strays."

"That's sweet," I said.

"Yeah. Even then she had real goals." Morgan paused, still staring upwards. "I thought she was crazy. I couldn't understand why she would want to live like that, without all the things we had—you know, a full bath, a closet, and a for-real bed. I always loved my sister, but I didn't get her."

"Are you saying that now you do?" I shifted the pillows a bit so I could look at her.

"Maybe. I can see that she had a real vision for her future, because she had this desire to help people. She was a kid, but she had passion. And here I am, an adult, and I still can't figure it out."

I could hear the sadness in Morgan's voice. She was feeling as if she was lacking something, but I knew she had more in her heart and her mind than she gave herself credit for.

"Okay," I said, sitting bolt upright and getting in her face. "It's time to stop the moaning and start putting your brain to work. Time to get over this mental block that has you believing you don't have passion. Think. What gets you excited?"

She smirked. "Besides shopping?"

"One more mention of shopping, shoes, or clothes, and I'll turn them all into little mice and watch them scurry away."

"Okay, okay. Geez, Dee, you do get testy sometimes."

"Testy? Girl, you haven't *seen* testy, but you're creeping up on it." I got off the bed and paced back and forth in front of the footboard. "Now, think about the things in your life that have made you go, 'Hey, this makes me feel really good about myself.' I guarantee that shopping does not make you feel good about *yourself*. That stuff makes you feel good, but admit it: It's a momentary feeling."

Morgan contemplated what I had said—or was she just trying to come up with a snappy response? I walked over to her handbag, reached in, and pulled out the journal and a pen. I tossed them both on the bed.

"Maybe this will jump-start your brain. Start writing," I commanded in my bossiest, no-excuses tone.

Morgan picked up the journal and pen. She stared at the book's cover, not opening it.

"Morgan, the journal isn't a mind-reader. It's not going to absorb your thoughts. Open it and start writing, will you?"

She opened the book, flipped a couple of pages, and started to write—slowly at first, stopping frequently to find the words. After a few minutes, however, she was writing away, her face switching from smile to frown and back again.

I made myself comfortable in a wooden rocker across the room and watched Morgan write with the unbridled excitement of a maestro conducting a symphony orchestra. I picked up a fashion magazine on the shelf below the nightstand. Just like it would be in a waiting room, the issue was outdated by two years. The happy celebrity couple featured on the cover had already divorced, and the hairstyles and clothing were so two-years-ago. I flipped to the Do's and Don'ts to check out the fashion faux pas. Then I read a story about Martha Stewart and how she had gone from Connecticut housewife to lifestyle maven to millionaire businesswoman to convict and then back to being synonymous with style and class. That journey hadn't been easy, I knew. Its success had taken hard work, commitment, passion, a great publicist, and a relentless Fairy Godmother who now knew ten ways to prepare an artichoke.

I must have dozed off because I was startled awake when Morgan pronounced, "Done!" and snapped the journal shut.

She hopped off the bed and rummaged around in her bag, pulling out the note card she had purchased earlier. She went back to the bed and penned the first note:

> *Dear Elizabeth,*
>
> *Thank you so much for taking the time to talk to me today. I know you are a busy person, and I can't tell you how much it meant to me that you would consider helping me. I just finished my first journal entry. It's more like a chapter, I think. And I can see why this has been so useful to you. I look forward to talking with you again soon.*
>
> > *All the best,*
> >
> > *Morgan Demarest*

She slipped the card into the envelope and sealed it. She found Elizabeth's business card, addressed the envelope, and set it on the bed beside her.

footnotes

Communication has turned from talking to texting. But just because something is quick and easy doesn't make it the best solution. When it comes to saying thank you, there's nothing like a handwritten note. Once in a while, try reconnecting with a pen and send someone a note, postcard, or card. The message can be simple: hey, thanks, or wish you were here. Admit it: You like getting that kind of snail-mail! Why wouldn't someone you care about feel the same way? Take the time to think of a few special people and send them a note—a *manual, handwritten* note, not a text or a Facebook message. The small gestures you make in your life have a way of becoming meaningful moments in the lives of others. Do something today for someone other than you.

CHAPTER twenty-five

For the first time since moving back to Hinsdale—albeit temporarily—Edward was able to drive to work without the rising feel of dread as he neared his office.

Every morning of late, he'd spent his commute worrying about how he would salvage his business, which clients were going to put their building plans on hold, and how he was going to make payroll. It was dizzying. All he could see was one big mess, one massive dark cloud that had been raining down on him for the better part of a year, ever since a big retail development project had tanked. One of the anchor stores had filed for bankruptcy, and another had been bought out by a conglomerate that was currently investing in overseas expansion, where people were actually buying. Without the anchors, other retailers weren't willing to risk going into a center that might not draw the shoppers they needed. So the investors pulled out. Edward had spent two years working on this project. He should have pulled the plug earlier, he chided himself, before he'd sunk so much time and money into a losing proposition.

But on this morning, with Morgan seated next to him, Edward's usual woe-filled drive became lighter. His daughter was energized by the belief that she could make her life what she wanted. He was not going to let his downtrodden attitude squelch her excitement.

"What are you going to do today, honey?" he asked, forcing himself to erase the worries that plagued him every day—at least for the duration of this drive to Chicago.

"I've got a reception coming up and need to take care of some details. This artist is really exciting. She's a fiber artist named Siobhan Findlay, and she does these amazing works with fabrics, threads, paper, and all sorts of media. They're like these mosaics of different materials, but with so much texture you just want to get right up close and touch them and then stand back and see the big picture," Morgan said with such animation that Edward couldn't help but smile.

"And the invitations are so cool!" she continued. "I needed something that would really reflect Siobhan's artistry, so I had our graphic designer come up with a layered design, with handmade paper as the base and then this sheer vellum with the invitation printed on that. Then the paper and vellum are tied together with some cool ribbon-y yarn I found, with little beads and flecks of color. And *then* I had envelopes made out of fabric. The invitations go inside the fabric envelope, and then the whole thing goes into a vellum envelope so you can see through to the fabric."

As she described the invitation, Morgan gestured like a person playing charades to show how each piece would go together, and Edward tried to keep up with the image his daughter was painting. "Wow, that's pretty intricate," he said.

"I know, but that was the point. I wanted something really different that would get people's attention but also keep with the theme of the exhibit," she explained.

I had been sitting quietly—so far—listening to the conversation and giving Edward a chance to keep connecting with his daughter. But, hearing Morgan's description gain even more enthusiasm with the description of the different colored yarn and how pretty and unique it was, I leaned forward and planted a thought in Edward's ear: "Don't look now, but I think Morgan is discovering her passion," I whispered.

Edward smiled. He didn't take his eyes off the road but reached over and patted his daughter's knee. "Don't look now, Morgan, but I think you're showing that passion you've been trying to find."

Morgan stopped, looked at her dad, and tilted her head. I could see that she wasn't quite sure what he meant, so I hurled myself forward and put a hand on each of her shoulders to grab her attention.

"Morgan, you just got yourself worked up into a passionate tizzy just now—and all because you were describing this invitation that is so far away from average and boring. Honey, you *are* creative, and you definitely love coming up with ideas like that thing with the yarn and the paper and fabric envelope and whatever. That's a big, fat start on your search for passion, girl!" I said with as much energy as I could muster without having had a decent breakfast.

"Do you mean I should be an invitation designer?" she asked to either or both of us.

Edward and I responded in unison. "Maybe."

I let him continue. I'd have time to speak my piece later.

"But maybe you could use your talent to help people who aren't creative put on really great events, like you do for Celeste at the gallery," he offered.

"Bingo!" I exclaimed.

"You mean like a party planner?" Morgan said, her mind starting to imagine the possibilities.

"Or an event planner or a conference planner," Edward added. "I've worked with several of them over the years when my clients have receptions or grand openings. They leave all the details to their planners. I think you'd be great at it!"

By the time Edward double-parked in front of the gallery, Morgan's head was swimming with ideas. She gave her dad a quick kiss on the cheek and confirmed she would meet him later for the ride back to Hinsdale.

She hurried into the gallery and up the spiral stairs to her office cubby. She hadn't even sat in her chair when she pulled out her journal and started writing.

> *So maybe I should be an event planner?!?! What fun! I could spend my days coming up with ideas for events that people would be dying to attend. And I'd get to do it all with someone else's money AND get paid to shop for all the stuff. Can't wait to talk to Elizabeth and get her thoughts.*

Elizabeth. *Hmm*, Morgan thought, *should I call her?* Would she be excited to learn about this great discovery?

"Before you dive for your cell, Morgan, let's just remember that Elizabeth is a busy businesswoman. You can't be dialing her or texting her every time a thought pops into your head," I warned her.

"Ever the buzzkill, Dee," she said. "I just thought that she might want to know about this breakthrough. After all, she *is* my mentor."

"Exactly!" I put my hands on my hips and assumed my power stance. "She's your mentor, not your BFF. Respect her time. Make notes about the things you want to discuss with her. If you pick up the phone and call her every time you experience an epiphany, she is going to send you packing."

Morgan's shoulders slumped. She picked up her journal again and wrote "Things to Tell Elizabeth" on one page and underlined it three times. Then she added:

Event planner??

Buzzkills suck.

"I saw that!" I said, pointing a finger in her face. "And for the gazillionth time, I am not a buzzkill. I am your voice of reason, something you most definitely need! Sometimes you remind me of one of those great big hot air balloons. You get this head of steam for an idea and float up and away. Well, I tell you, girl, if you don't learn how to harness and focus that energy, you'll end up so far out there that you can never get back."

"Whatever." Morgan turned back to her desk and looked at her To Do list. "Now I've got things to do, so can you please go find someone else to bug?"

"Like I want to stand around and watch you work? I think not!" Just as Celeste appeared behind Morgan, I disappeared with a "plink" and went off in search of a chocolate croissant.

"I'm sorry? What did you say, Morgan?" asked a clearly affronted Celeste.

"Oh, Celeste, I wasn't talking to you. No, I, um, I had this stupid song stuck in my head. You know how you hear a song and then it sticks in your brain all day? It was the last one before I got out of the car, and I can't stop hearing it."

Celeste eyed Morgan suspiciously but chose to accept the odd excuse. Besides, she had much more on her mind this morning.

"Morgan, I went to a dinner party last night, and the food was phenomenal. Now, I knew that Deirdre's regular chef was off for some family event, so I slipped into the kitchen to see who was doing the cooking. Well, she had this caterer who looked like he was barely past puberty and I thought, 'Ohmigod, Deirdre, did you get a kid from the vocational center?' Well, anyway, it turns out he's twenty-four and has been working for Deirdre's regular caterer for just a month. I tell you, he's an artist—an absolute *artist!* He made a flambéed vanilla-poached pear with a raspberry sauce that was like heaven. Heaven!"

"Sounds wonderful," Morgan managed to squeeze in.

"Yes, well, I want you to get in touch with him. I want him—Perry or Terry, I can't remember, whatever. He *must* be the one to cook at Siobhan's reception."

"But, Celeste, I've already booked Molly!"

"I don't care. I want *this* one. He is going to be up-and-coming, I tell you, and I want to be on his A-list when that happens." Celeste put the caterer's business card on Morgan's desk, leaving her palm on top of it as if guarding a secret. "Just make it happen, Morgan. I want him here on the twenty-sixth, and make sure his boss understands that no substitute for Jerry-Perry-Terry is acceptable. Just remind him that I am a very good customer."

"But, Celeste, we've never used this caterer before!"

"Tell him we *will* be a *very* good customer. Do your magic."

Magic. Now where was Morgan's Fairy Godmother when she needed her?

footnotes

When faced with a problem—whether it's trying to hire the right caterer or salvaging a failing business—the best way to find a solution is to look at your challenge and dissect it. Start by identifying the problem and writing down the outcome you want to achieve. Now take baby steps. You can eat an elephant one bite at a time—hypothetically. So, before over-thinking a task and deciding it's too daunting, grab a fork and dig in! Maybe you are stuck in a dead end job. How can you change that situation? Instead of moping, start sending out resumes daily. Ask your mentor to take a look at your resume for suggestions. Research interviewing strategies before going in unprepared. Take a moment and write down a major stressor in your life. Then stare it down. Put it in perspective with the rest of your life. Are you going to let it dominate you? No! Now put on your big girl panties and write out all the possible solutions you can think of. Consider each one. Then start executing those solutions, one by one.

CHAPTER twenty-six

Elizabeth's presentation to her company's prospective client went very well. She felt she'd succeeded in convincing them that IdeaWerx had the expertise to not only handle the immediate project but the increasing volume of development jobs that were looming on their horizon; this one client could add thirty percent more revenue to her company's bottom line, Elizabeth estimated. She would have to expand her staff, but a few of her team had mentioned that they knew programmers who would gladly jump ship on their current companies to join IdeaWerx. Elizabeth had established a reputation for being a visionary who welcomed new ideas and treated her employees fairly.

If the contract came through, Elizabeth would promote Rosaria and find someone to take over her current job. If only she could find another up-and-coming Rosaria—a smart self-starter who didn't need much supervision, someone with a powerful work ethic, a dedicated professional who could be as reliable as Rosaria. Elizabeth smiled, wondering if she could be so lucky to find someone with even half of Rosaria's smarts and commitment.

Elizabeth recalled the day Rosaria had come in and applied for the job of administrative assistant. She'd been dressed in a navy blue suit and white blouse, looking more like a somber novitiate at a convent than a twenty-year-old woman. Elizabeth described the job to Rosaria, just as she had to the other eleven applicants who had earned an interview. Most of the others seemed to view the job as a steppingstone to greater things—either at IdeaWerx or another company—asking about the possibility, frequency, and timing of promotions. Elizabeth explained that her company, although still small, was growing and that opportunities would be available for people who could prove themselves. Elizabeth sensed that none of them would be willing to stick it out for more than a year or so; they were young, fired up, and impatient, just as she had been at their age. But as an employer, she was looking for someone who would be willing to do more than use IdeaWerx as a bridge to some greater goal. She couldn't build her company by hiring, training, and cultivating short-timers.

Rosaria Vega was different. She didn't seem to have long-range goals to rise to the top of the corporate ladder. She wanted to earn her pay, prove her worth, and have the stability of a steady job. Elizabeth sensed a deep desire to please, which was appealing. Who didn't want an employee who would bust a hump to impress the boss? Not a brown-noser but an honest-to-goodness hard worker!

Rosaria didn't have the college degree that the other candidates had, but she possessed enthusiasm, the desire to learn, and the ability to listen and take direction. Elizabeth thought back to her earlier days when she'd gone to college at night because of her detour from the conventional route after high school. She felt in Rosaria the same hunger to survive and thrive that she had experienced. So she hired the young woman—and had never once regretted that decision.

Now, Elizabeth called Rosaria to her office and asked her to sit down. Rosaria looked a bit nervous and hesitated before taking a seat in the chair opposite her boss.

"Rosaria, the presentation to Palladex went really well," Elizabeth said. "I think we have a very good chance of landing this contract, and I want to thank you for all of your help."

Rosaria, as usual, tried to hold back her smile, but Elizabeth saw the corners of her mouth turn up slightly. Even more telling was the sudden spark in her eyes. *For once,* thought Elizabeth, *I wish this girl would let loose and laugh—just a giggle would be nice!*

"You did all the work, Elizabeth. I didn't do much at all," Rosaria said with the sincere humility that Elizabeth had come to expect.

"You kept everything else going around here so I didn't have to worry about anything except the presentation. Without your hard work in managing so many other things, it would have been much, much harder to concentrate on this proposal," Elizabeth said.

Rosaria sat with her hands folded in her lap, ever the picture of the serious employee. She took direction like no one Elizabeth had ever known and seemed able to read Elizabeth's mind, always keeping up with—or staying one step ahead of—Elizabeth's thoughts and needs. Elizabeth remembered the reruns of "MASH" and how one of the characters, Radar O'Reilly, could finish his superior officer's sentences and complete tasks before even being commanded to do them. That was Rosaria—almost.

Elizabeth had been able to piece together a snapshot of Rosaria's past, and she understood that the younger woman's spirit had been stolen along with her father's life. But that had been twelve years ago, and Elizabeth hoped that Rosaria could somehow rediscover joy in her life. And she wanted to help. She reached into the top drawer of her desk and pulled out a lavender envelope. Then she stood up and walked around the desk, leaning on the edge and facing Rosaria.

"To thank you for your help, I would like you to take this gift certificate to my favorite spa and treat yourself to any of the services you want. Get a massage, a manicure or maybe get—" Elizabeth stopped just short of suggesting Rosaria have her unibrow waxed. That might make the young woman even more self-conscious and uncomfortable. "—a facial. It's so relaxing! Honestly, I treat myself once a month and feel like a new person afterwards."

"Oh, no, I can't." Rosaria pushed back the envelope that Elizabeth was trying to hand to her. "You don't need to give me anything. I'm just doing my job. Use that for yourself. Honestly, I don't need to go to a spa."

"I insist, Rosaria. This is my gift to you, and I want you to use it. There is a list of spa services on the brochure, and the phone number is there. Make an appointment and just enjoy it. Okay?"

Rosaria looked at the envelope in Elizabeth's hand. She seemed to think some awful surprise was going to jump out. Elizabeth took Rosaria's hand, pulled it forward and turned the palm up. Then she slapped the envelope on it and curled Rosaria's fingers around it.

"Rosaria, you can take all the fun out of giving a gift. You give new meaning to 'Tis better to give than to receive,'" said an exasperated Elizabeth.

"I'm sorry," Rosaria said in a sad tone.

Elizabeth shook her head and put an arm around her employee. She ordinarily avoided any physical conduct that might sniff of too personal a connection with her staff, but Rosaria was different.

"Don't be sorry," Elizabeth said. "Be happy. If for no other reason than I am asking you to." She went back around the desk and reclaimed her seat. "I also wanted to talk to you about the future of the company—and you." She smiled at Rosaria, knowing her first reaction might be a nervous one. "If we get this account, I'm going to need to make some changes with your job."

Elizabeth held up her hands like a traffic cop directing Rosaria to stop. "Before you get worried, this is a good thing. You are amazing at your job, but I think you should be moving forward with more responsibility. I would need you to be the Office Manager. No, that sounds too mundane. Maybe Director of Operations. How does that sound?"

Rosaria didn't know how to respond. All this new information was coming at her like a meteor shower, and she felt like she should be dodging each piece.

"But . . . who will do my job?" Rosaria asked in a small voice.

"Rosaria, we will hire someone else to do that. You can train your replacement and then be in charge of that person. This is your chance to take charge and be a manager. You could have more decision-making powers. Maybe even manage some of the programming projects, or the staff—or both. I haven't quite figured it out."

Elizabeth was usually very organized and calculating. But she felt intoxicated with the idea that she could help shape Rosaria's life, possibly fill it with more opportunity for growth and success. She was giving Rosaria chances that she herself had never been handed—but that Rosaria had certainly earned. When Elizabeth stopped thinking out loud, she realized that she was the only person in the room who was overflowing with excitement. Rosaria sat in the chair, hands once again folded, looking confused and even a bit hurt.

"Rosaria, have I said something to upset you? Are you concerned about taking on new responsibilities?"

"I don't know. I like my job, and I'm not sure what this new one would require. But if you think it is a good idea, then I will do it," said Rosaria, trying her best to muster up enthusiasm. She even managed a small smile.

Elizabeth softened her enthusiasm, feeling as though she was pushing Rosaria too hard. "I'm not forcing you into anything, Rosaria. Why don't you think about it? I still have to wait for Palladex to make their decision. We can talk more then, okay?"

Rosaria nodded, still trying to force a smile. "Thank you, Elizabeth."

A few minutes later, back at her desk, Rosaria looked at the lavender envelope that held the spa gift certificate. She didn't have time for something so frivolous, and Elizabeth should know that. Why did her boss suddenly feel the need to give her something extra? And if she wanted to do that, why give her something she had no intention of using? A facial? Rosaria's face would still look the same way. A manicure? ¡Qué loca! A hard-working woman did not get manicures. That was reserved for the pampered people who had nothing else to do with their money.

Speaking of pampered, Rosaria thought of Morgan Demarest. Had Elizabeth offered that new job so she could make room for Morgan to waltz in and take over? Oh, great. Just what Rosaria needed. A useless, empty-headed bimbo who wanted to play at being a professional. Rosaria felt sure she would spend her days cleaning up after Morgan, who would be too busy filing her nails and texting her BFFs to get any real work done.

Maybe Rosaria wouldn't take the new job. Then there would be no place *para la princesa*. But if she *didn't* take the job, would Elizabeth give it to Morgan? *¡Dios mio!* Rosaria thought. *Would she do that to me?* No. Never. But maybe.

Rosaria knew she could either cave in and accept the unwelcome newcomer or pull herself up and fend off the enemy. The answer was easy to decide but would be more difficult to live with.

footnotes

How many times have you bitten your tongue because you did not want to stir the pot? Or, conversely, have you ever spoken up for yourself, only to be viewed as a "troublemaker" for using your voice? *Effective* communication is key to thriving in the workplace—or anywhere, for that matter. Be open in your communication. When you need clarity, ask questions. This simple step will help you better understand the direction your team is headed. One caveat: Before you open your mouth and insert your foot, think about the best approach to take in order to NOT burn the bridge. Take a minute and write down some of the blunders you have made with your communication style. Maybe you inadvertently criticized your boss when you asked a question. What are some strategies you can implement to keep the lines of communication open?

For more help with improving your communication style, go to *Stiletto911.com*.

CHAPTER twenty-seven

Morgan was hurriedly writing thoughts in her journal, probably over-preparing for her noon lunch date with Elizabeth. We were at the gallery, and I told her that all her efforts would be erased if she walked in late.

"This is not the time to make an entrance," I said while she was writing.

Morgan swatted at me in that familiar way that told me I was intruding on her personal space.

"You shushing me? Don't you dare shush me, girl!"

Morgan ignored me. I gave her one of my own backhanded waves in return. Morgan's hand kept moving across the pages of the journal, but she was writing faster and faster. And the words on the page were not the thoughts in her head.

"Hey!" she exclaimed. "What's going on?"

I just smiled and watched her fill pages with the same two lines:

R-E-S-P-E-C-T.

That's what I owe Divinity.

"Divinity, *stop!* My hand is getting tired!"

"I'm sorry? Are you talking to me? Because when I was trying to talk to *you*, you swatted me away like a pesky mosquito. And I think you need a little reminder that I deserve better than that," I said with my hands-on-hips, don't-mess-with-me posture.

Morgan was looking at me, but her hand was working as if controlled by a remote. "Please, Divinity. I'm sorry if I was rude, but I was trying to finish a thought." "Then perhaps that's what you should have said. And for your information, if you're not early, you're late." I flicked one finger, and her hand stopped in mid-sentence. "That doesn't make sense." Morgan shook out her hand, flexed her fingers, and packed her journal in her bag.

"I mean that arriving at the time a meeting or appointment is supposed to start makes you late. Be in your seat, on location, or where you're supposed to be five minutes ahead of time," I advised. "So, as I tried to tell you a few minutes ago, we *need* to get going so you can get to the restaurant before Elizabeth and show that you respect her very valuable time. Are we clear on this one?"

Morgan's face went from what-the-heck-are-you-doing to rather contrite. A little tough love once in a while doesn't hurt—well, not too much.

We grabbed a cab from the gallery and somehow managed to arrive at the restaurant about one minute before Elizabeth walked in the door. She was dressed beautifully, in a tailored red suit, black camisole, thin black belt, and a pair of stunning black Blahniks that had apparently escaped the notice—and jaws—of her shoe-eating dog. On the outside, she looked perfectly put-together, but her body language was screaming, "Stressed!"

Morgan and Elizabeth were seated immediately. "I'm Jared, and I will be taking care of you today," a waiter said. "Can we start with something to drink?"

If he were really "taking care" of these guests, I thought, he'd offer to do a little housework, fend off demanding customers and vendors, handle family matters, and generally simplify the two working women's crazed day-to-day lives.

Morgan was wise enough to wait for Elizabeth to order before deciding whether or not to choose alcohol. Elizabeth ordered a glass of sauvignon blanc and Morgan did the same.

"So, Morgan," Elizabeth started, with her take-charge voice. "What have you accomplished since we last spoke?"

"Well, I've been writing in my journal several times a day," Morgan started.

"Mmm hmm," Elizabeth acknowledged, while her eyes darted to the cell phone she had placed on the table to her right. I hoped Morgan hadn't caught the hint of Elizabeth's disinterest; I wanted her energy level to stay positive.

"And it has been so helpful! I've worked through some questions I had about my future," Morgan continued, clearly oblivious to Elizabeth's distraction.

"Okay, and have you thought about setting your goals?" Elizabeth interrupted.

Morgan was taken aback. Elizabeth had been so calm and attentive during their first meeting. Today, she was coming on like a drill sergeant. Morgan was flustered but tried to regroup her thoughts and maintain an air of composure.

"I'm thinking that becoming an event planner would be a great use of my skills and interests. I've discovered that I have a passion for creating different types of events and organizing all the details," Morgan said, her enthusiasm beaming through the momentary disruption. "I plan events, like artists' receptions, at the gallery, and it's the best part of my job."

"That's good, Morgan. I can see by the look on your face that you've found your passion." Phew. Elizabeth was bringing Morgan back into focus. "Now, the next step is to build your goals. Think about what you need to do in order to become an event planner."

Jared arrived with their wine and asked if they were ready to order their lunches. Elizabeth chimed in, holding fast to her alpha-female demeanor. "I'll have the pear and gorgonzola salad, with the dressing on the side, and peanuts instead of pecans, please."

Jared smiled, not writing down a word but nodding to acknowledge that he had processed the request in his memory. Morgan added Thai pasta to the order. He picked up the menus and sauntered away.

Elizabeth dove right back into the discussion without skipping a beat. "Once you determine your goal, you have to set about creating a series of smaller goals that will lead you to your ultimate destination, which, in your case, is becoming a successful event planner," Elizabeth said. She was more focused now and had stopped stealing glances at her phone.

"I'm not sure how to get from where I am to where I want to be," Morgan confessed. Clearly, she wanted Elizabeth to draw out a roadmap but was afraid to ask.

"Let's start by defining your goal more clearly. What types of events do you want to plan?"

"Anything, I guess," Morgan stumbled.

"Anything?" Elizabeth's brows shot upwards. "So, you would do a Bat Mitzvah, for example?"

"I don't know what that is." Morgan looked crestfallen that her mentor seemed to be taking pot shots at her.

At that moment, Elizabeth's cell phone buzzed. She grabbed the phone, looked at the caller ID, and clicked the Talk button.

"Yes? No. I told you, Tom. I need you to pick up Erich and take him to his scout meeting this afternoon. No, I can't. No, Tom, he can't just skip it. Oh, please, you can switch that appointment. I'm just asking you for once to pitch in here and help out. Fine. No. Yes, I will be home in time for dinner and I promised to help Lara fix her dance costume for the recital. Yes, the recital. It's next Tuesday and you *have* to be there. Can we please talk about that later? Okay. Goodbye."

She punched the button on her phone to end the call, with force that was obviously intended more for her husband than her mobile device.

"I'm sorry, Morgan. I'm just having one of those days. I have never ever been one to believe the myth that you can't have it all, but some days it's harder than others to keep all those balls in the air." Elizabeth sighed, looking tired and much less the highly composed entrepreneur that Morgan had expected. I wasn't sure if Elizabeth's words were meant as a confession or an apology—maybe a little of both.

"I think you have a lot of responsibility and you're doing an amazing job keeping everything together," Morgan said gently, treading carefully on the boundaries of the mentor-mentee relationship.

"Thanks, Morgan. It's been a hard week with a lot of things going crazy. One thing I would advise is to always have a contingency plan to allow for changes. And if you are going to be an event planner, that contingency plan will play a huge part in your success."

Elizabeth paused, briefly closing her eyes in an attempt to refocus on her mentor role. "Now," she continued, in her Elizabethan way, "tell me why I should hire you to plan my daughter's Bat Mitzvah, which, incidentally, is a rite of passage for a Jewish girl at the age of twelve, when she is considered an adult."

"I thought your daughter is in preschool," Morgan said.

"This is hypothetical, Morgan. Assume I am the mother of a twelve-year-old Jewish girl. I want to put on a memorable event for my daughter. Why should I hire you over other event planners?"

"I'm creative, enthusiastic, and detail-oriented," Morgan said, listing qualities as though she were reciting the days of the week.

Elizabeth pounced. "That's a given, Morgan. Those are traits I would *expect* of an event planner. Tell me what makes you distinctive. What other Bat Mitzvahs have you planned? How were they different? Can I call the other mothers for referrals? And how do you charge your clients? Is it a flat fee, hourly, cost-plus?"

Morgan was dizzied by the barrage of questions, none of which she was prepared to answer.

"I-I-I don't know," she replied, turning into lifeless lunchmeat for the lioness her mentor had morphed into.

Elizabeth realized she had pushed too hard. She eased up, her eyes softening. "Morgan, I'm sorry. I didn't mean to push, but the answers are not always going to come off the top of your head. You will have to be prepared. You have to understand your prospective clients. What do they want, expect, and need from you as the professional event planner? Before you can begin to take the journey to your ultimate goal, there are many, many smaller goals to achieve. For one, you should better understand the job of an event planner. Do some research. Look at websites of other planners. Talk to people who might hire an event planner to find out what they like and don't like."

"I see," said Morgan, who was perking up now that she had some tangible assignments. "So I should start by doing some homework."

"Exactly! No matter what you do, you need to be prepared. Anticipate the needs of your clients. Have the answers ready before the question is asked. Remember what I said about contingency planning? Always, always, *always* have a Plan B."

Jared returned with their lunch plates. He set them gently on the table. "And here you go, ladies. Can I get you anything else?"

Elizabeth stared at her salad while Jared waited for an answer. She looked at him, frowning. "Well, you can start by bringing me an EpiPen. Do you happen to keep those in your kitchen?"

Elizabeth waited while the smiling Jared became less composed and more confused.

"I'm sorry?" he said.

"You should be sorry. Because I'm allergic to tree nuts, which is why I asked for peanuts instead. Had I taken a forkful of this salad you just gave me, I would need a shot from an epinephrine pen to avoiding dying right here in your restaurant." Elizabeth's controlled voice masked her anger, but the stabbing glare she gave Jared communicated it quite clearly. "Fortunately, I happen to carry an EpiPen in my bag for contingencies like this. But please take this salad back to your kitchen and remind them that I asked for a salad without pecans. Thank you!"

She dismissed Jared, who hurried off with her plate in his hand. When her eyes met Morgan's, she was clearly less infuriated. Morgan, however, was unsettled by the exchange, which Elizabeth noted.

"Okay, I'll clue you in on something here that will help you in your new venture," Elizabeth said. "You can judge the big picture by looking at the small details. I did not tell Jared why I didn't want pecans. He should listen to my requests and follow them, because that's his job. I shouldn't have to offer my medical history, because that's personal."

Morgan was listening intently and nodding.

"There was some rock star—I forget who—and he always asked for there to be a bowl of M&M's in his dressing room, with the brown ones removed," Elizabeth continued. "Well, everyone thought he was being a pretentious jerk, but his reasoning was that if the crew could follow a simple instruction like pulling the brown M&Ms from a bowl, then they could be trusted with more serious things, like the staging that could collapse if there was a minor flaw. He measured the quality of the crew by using the brown M&M barometer."

"Oh! I get it!!" exclaimed Morgan.

"And I have this friend who is a real estate agent. She has a client who buys investment properties. She says he does a quick walk-through and makes a purchase decision in about ten minutes. He doesn't go into extensive inspection. He told her that he can weigh the value of a property by some very simple details. He said that if the things he can see are in perfect order, then those that aren't visible will likely follow suit."

"That's fantastic! So you just have to know what to look for . . ."

"Pay attention to the small details, because every single one matters," Elizabeth finished.

Jared returned with the revised salad. Elizabeth looked at the plate, noting the peanuts as well as the dressing on the side, just as she had ordered. She smiled and thanked Jared, who was still nervous.

"I'm very, very sorry. And we are not charging you for your lunch," he groveled.

"I'm happy to pay for my lunch. I just want you to do two things for me in the future,"

Elizabeth said. Jared nodded like a bobblehead doll. "One, make sure your kitchen has a supply of EpiPens. Two, write down the orders. It really doesn't impress people when you attempt to memorize them."

"Of course. Thank you," Jared responded, and sped away.

Elizabeth stabbed at the salad with her fork while Morgan watched.

"That must be tough, having a food allergy," Morgan said.

"I don't have a food allergy. My son does. So I got in the habit of not eating tree nuts."

"But how come you—or your son—can eat peanuts?"

"A peanut doesn't grow on trees. And it's technically a legume, which is a bean," Elizabeth explained, holding out a fork with peanuts.

The women finished their lunches. And I went off in search of a big bag of Peanut M&M's.

footnotes

Creating a "big picture" goal is a major step toward achieving what you want from your life, but there are a lot of baby steps you need to take in order to get there. Once you find that vision for your life, scale it down and build a series of smaller goals to lead you to that ultimate destination. Make lists of key details and steps. Set daily, weekly, monthly, and annual goals. As you plan, measure each smaller goal against the outcome you desire. Revisit your goal plan periodically to check in on your progress and make changes as needed. Remember that you can never achieve goals if you don't clearly set them right in front of you.

CHAPTER twenty-eight

Morgan finished the painstaking task of hand-addressing the last of the invitations to Siobhan's reception at Celestial Sky. She used her most artful penmanship—gentle strokes, but no swirls—for the job. She'd learned from Pavlo that there is artistry even in handwriting. She used to love reading his notes, not so much for the words but because he didn't just write; he *lettered*.

Pavlo. She thought again about her now-ex-boyfriend. She remembered their first meeting, downstairs at this very place. She looked over the railing at the spot where he had walked up to her, complimented her shoes, and engulfed her entire being with his eyes. She'd sunk into a trance right from that moment, although she'd tried very hard to hold back. He was a force of nature, so strong and driven. He put every ounce of his heart and soul into everything—whether it was when he was creating new artwork, cooking up something in the kitchen, or just loving Morgan. There was never a gray area with Pavlo, no wishy-washy indecision and no second chances. When he was served a bad dish at one of his favorite restaurants, he never returned. When a friend he had known for years suddenly cancelled a lunch date, he never invited that friend to lunch again. That was Pavlo.

And yet he'd tried to offer Morgan a second chance. He'd asked her to come back with him the morning after their fight. But she knew that when Pavlo had seen her and Sam there, in a compromising yet innocent position, the door had been shut forever. She was sad that their relationship had ended that way, but knowing the powerful, passionate way he lived his life, there would never have been a gracious parting of ways, a day when they amicably agreed that the connection was broken. Morgan cared deeply about Pavlo, but she wasn't in love. It was a wonderful situation to be loved by a passionate man who would give anything to make her happy. But as she was turning the corner to a new life, would Pavlo support her goals? Would he understand her need to be something more than the object of his desire?

Morgan shook her head, knowing that she had made the right decision but feeling true sadness at the loss. She wiped a tear from her eye.

"You know," I said, putting a hand on her shoulder, "it's okay to mourn. You spent almost a year with this man. You do care about him. Whether or not you loved him, caring counts for something. Don't hide from your feelings, honey."

Morgan grabbed a fistful of tissues from the box on her desk and buried her face in them. I rubbed her back as she cried, while keeping an eye out for Celeste; I didn't want the woman's lousy timing to interrupt my girl's moment of grief.

Eventually, Morgan's sobs turned to short whimpers. She took a few more tissues, blew her nose, and dabbed at her eyes. She took a deep breath, looked up at me, and said in a tiny voice, "Thanks."

"It will all be okay, Morgan." I put one arm around her shoulder and pulled her closer to me, kissing the top of her head in a motherly gesture. "You have a good heart, and someday you will give it to the right person. The same will be true for Pavlo. Just remember: plaids and stripes, girlfriend, plaids and stripes."

Morgan smiled, nodded, and returned to the task of preparing the invitations. She inserted the personal notes that Celeste had written for each of her VIP guests into envelopes and placed them in the box for the mailman, who would be arriving shortly.

Celeste had been a bit skeptical about the idea of adding the colorful ribbon yarns to each invitation. Now, coming upstairs, she eyed the final product carefully, stroking the burgundy and gold ribbon on the sample that Morgan presented.

"This isn't acrylic or polyester in any way, is it?" she asked, making that sour face that always accompanied even the tiniest thought of something distasteful. And polyester was high on that list.

"It's pure silk, Celeste. The fabric envelopes are made from organic, hand-dyed cotton, and the vellum inserts and outside envelopes are made from recycled materials," Morgan said.

Celeste's puckered lips eased into a small smile.

"Are you gonna mail those invitations or eat them, for crying out loud?" I chimed in. "I wonder if she is as *particular* about the dye she puts in her hair."

Morgan tried to hold back a smile, but I saw the corners of her mouth twitch.

"I can always count on you to read my mind, Morgan. If only more people understood the value of details. Is it really so much to ask to *not* be ordinary?" Then Celeste's cell phone rang, giving Morgan an easy out of the conversation.

Celeste continually managed to forget her simple roots. She had somehow erased her years as a failed art student named Celia, who was the daughter of an auto mechanic and grocery store cashier. Celia's exit from the ordinary had come by meeting and marrying her husband. She had transitioned into the role of the elite easily and never spoke of her life prior to becoming Mrs. Stefan Bourque.

Morgan thought it sad to be so unhappy with your past that you could no longer accept or acknowledge it. She had been blessed with a wonderful family that loved her and that she loved in return. She thought about the list of blessings I had asked her to compile. She needed to tell her parents and Emily more often that they meant the world to her.

When Morgan had completed all the invitations and placed them in the appropriate boxes to take to the post office, five invitations remained on her desk, separate from the ones to be mailed. She put one in her drawer, to keep as a sample. The other four would be hand-delivered. She tidied up her desk, grabbed her handbag, and slid the four envelopes inside.

"Are we taking the afternoon off?" I asked. "Because I wouldn't mind a little window-shopping on North Michigan. And maybe grabbing a hot pretzel along the way."

"We're not taking the afternoon off, Divinity, although now I'm feeling tempted." Morgan smiled. I knew there were visions of stilettos dancing around in her head. "I'm taking my lunch break to deliver an invitation to Elizabeth."

"Just remember that you can't barge in on her when you feel like it. She's a busy woman." I didn't want Morgan to get in the habit of showing up when the spirit moved her.

"I *know* that, Dee. I am just dropping this off. That's all. I can leave it with Rosaria, although I don't know if I trust her to give it to Elizabeth. Rosaria just doesn't like me." Morgan frowned, staring me smack in the face. "You're a nag, you know? Do you think I'm a total idiot, or can you give me just a teeny bit of credit for not being a dumb blonde?"

She hailed a cab and got in without looking at me.

"I didn't mean to hurt your feelings, Morgan," I said, resting my hand on her arm, which was folded across her chest. "I don't think you're a dumb blonde. You're a smart woman who has so much going for her. I'm just here to guide you, and if my comment upset you, I am very sorry."

Morgan was looking out the cab window. She didn't face me as she spoke. "My whole life, people have never given me the benefit of the doubt. I've never been taken seriously. Emily was the smart one. I was just silly Morgan who loved to play dress-up. Was it such a crime to enjoy nice things? Does that make me useless to the world?" Her voice cracked. She was on the verge of tears but fighting hard to hold back the flood.

The cab driver peered in his rearview mirror, trying to determine if his fare was talking to him. She had forgotten her usual ruse of pretending she was talking on the phone, but he seemed satisfied that she was speaking with someone else—or at least he chose to ignore a woman in crisis.

"Morgan, Morgan, Morgan," I said, patting her arm and reaching for her hand. "This is a new day. You don't have to apologize for who you are, and you never should. But if people underestimated you, it's probably because you did the same thing yourself."

"What do you mean?" Her head whipped around until she was looking me straight in the eye.

"It's not a crime to take care of your appearance, but when you don't make an effort to show the world the woman inside, you don't give them the chance to see past the wrappings," I explained. "You're starting to take charge of your life. I think that in the past, it was much easier for you to just let things happen. But doesn't it feel good to be in control now?"

Morgan nodded, her eyes brimming with tears.

"I'm proud of you, Morgan. And you should be proud of yourself, too."

Morgan reached over and hugged me. The driver looked in his mirror, clearly confused. I flicked my wrist and altered his perspective a tad: Rather than seeing Morgan in an embrace with an invisible being, he saw an oversized female wrestler who darted forward and growled at him to "Keep your damn eyes on the road!"

When we arrived at Elizabeth's office building, Morgan handed the driver the fare, along with a reasonable tip. After we got out of the cab, he turned around and looked in the back seat to see where the burly beast of a woman had gone.

Ah, yes, appearances can be deceiving.

footnotes

Eleanor Roosevelt said, "No one can make you feel inferior without your consent." You are in control of the image you convey to the world. If people are not giving you credit for excelling, maybe it's because you don't give yourself the credit you deserve. When you believe in yourself, you exude confidence, and the world believes in you. Show doubt, and the world doubts you as well.

One of the toughest tasks a person can tackle is to write about herself. Whether it's a resume, college essay, or social network profile, it's often difficult to say good things about yourself. Start right now by making a list of ten things you do well. Are you a good listener? Can you multi-task with the best of them? Is there a particular dish you cook that your friends love? Write it down. And then celebrate each one with a mental pat on the back, or drink a toast to yourself.

As you build your goals, be confident that you can achieve them. Put your full force behind reaching out and grabbing everything you desire.

CHAPTER *twenty-nine*

When Morgan and I entered the reception area of IdeaWerx, Rosaria was focused on her computer screen—or was just trying really hard to ignore Morgan; I wasn't sure which.

Although Rosaria was not a receptionist, she had taken on that role since the intern who would normally handle those tasks had returned to college and Rosaria had not yet selected a replacement. Her office was adjacent to the lobby and had a large window that overlooked that space. I was certain that no one entered the inner sanctum of IdeaWerx without first being scrutinized by Rosaria Vega, with or without a receptionist seated in the lobby.

Morgan stood in the reception area, waiting for Rosaria to come out and welcome her. Morgan glanced in her direction several times, hoping to trigger eye contact, which Rosaria avoided. She was probably hoping Morgan would go away, and when she didn't, Rosaria finally emerged from her watchtower.

"I didn't realize you had an appointment with Elizabeth," Rosaria said curtly. "Unfortunately, she is heading out to a meeting in a few minutes, so she really can't take the time right now."

If I had been Rosaria's Fairy Godmother, that girl would be getting a lesson in manners right then.

"I just came to drop off this invitation to a reception we're having for a wonderful artist at Celestial Sky Gallery, where I work," Morgan said, stumbling a bit. She was intimidated by Rosaria. Heck, I was intimidated by Rosaria. That woman could suck the life out of a room with one unibrowed glare. "I didn't intend to just barge in," Morgan added, shooting an accusatory glance my way. I rolled my eyes in a "get over yourself" response.

"If you want to leave the invitation with me, I will see that Elizabeth gets it." Rosaria stuck out her hand to take the envelope from Morgan, with the same distaste as a teacher holding out her hand for a student to spit out his gum.

"Actually," said Morgan sweetly, "*this* one is for you. I thought you might like to come, too. The artist, Siobhan Findlay, does these brilliant works with mixed media, like fabrics, fiber, handmade papers, and watercolors. The art is really inspiring. I just thought you might enjoy seeing it, and these opening receptions are a lot of fun." Morgan sounded as perky as she could under the circumstances. She extended the invitation to Rosaria, who was speechless.

"Um, well, thank you." Rosaria took the envelope. She flipped it over and examined the vellum, with the colorful fabric envelope peeking through the opaque paper. She also studied the handwriting on the envelope, looking at her name written in an artful script.

"I can't tell if she's admiring it or trying to give herself a paper cut just to blame it on you," I said, irritated with Rosaria's odd response to a very courteous invitation from my girl.

"I really hope you can come," Morgan added, ignoring me. "And here is an invitation for Elizabeth, if you wouldn't mind giving it to her. I just wanted to personally deliver both, and not rely on the mail."

Rosaria took the second envelope and seemed to be regaining her normal rigid composure. "I will give it to Elizabeth, but we both have very hectic schedules."

"What are you going to give to me?" came a voice behind Rosaria. Elizabeth had come down the hall and obviously caught the tail end of the exchange. She was dressed in tailored black slacks and an ivory silk blouse, perfectly accessorized with tasteful gold jewelry. She set her red leather computer bag—a stunning Valentino, I might add—on the carpet and looked from Rosaria to Morgan. "Hello, Morgan. Nice to see you. And Rosaria, what am I too busy to do?"

"Morgan has brought us invitations to a reception at the gallery where she works," said Rosaria, handing one to Elizabeth.

Elizabeth took the invitation and flipped it over, just like Rosaria had done. Unlike her office guardian, however, Elizabeth removed the inner envelope, rubbed her hand across the fabric, and then took out the invitation. "This is lovely, Morgan! So imaginative!"

"Thank you. I wanted to do something out of the ordinary, and this artist really inspired me." Morgan seemed to be holding back any gush of pride in Rosaria's presence.

"*You* designed this?" Elizabeth's eyes widened.

"Well, it was my idea, but I had a graphic designer actually do the design," Morgan said humbly. She almost seemed embarrassed to admit that she hadn't actually crafted the invitation herself.

"It's a beautiful invitation, Morgan. Very inventive," Elizabeth said, stroking the ribbon on the card.

"I really hope you both can make it. I think it will be an interesting evening, and I'd love for you to meet Siobhan and see her work."

"Thursday, the twenty-sixth? I think I'm free," Elizabeth said. "Actually, Tom will be out of town that night, so, Rosaria, why don't we go together?"

"I don't know my schedule. I have several commitments that week, so I can't say for sure." She was scrambling. It was easy enough for her to refuse Morgan, but Rosaria was less inclined to say no to her boss. And she certainly didn't want Morgan and Elizabeth to spend an evening socializing when she wasn't there to keep watch over her perceived adversary. She finally said, making eye contact only with Elizabeth, "I will check and let you know for sure."

"Wonderful!" Elizabeth picked up her red bag and took a few steps toward the door. She paused and then turned back to the two women who were standing awkwardly in each other's presence. "I just had a thought. Morgan. If you have a second, can you come to my office?"

"Sure!" Morgan perked up like a dog about to go for a ride with the windows wide open.

She followed closely behind Elizabeth as they headed to her office. Rosaria was still standing in the reception area, watching the two walk away. When Elizabeth reached the threshold of her office, she turned and called, "Rosaria, can you please join us?"

Rosaria was briefly taken aback, but she hurried down the hall and into Elizabeth's office, where Morgan had already taken a seat opposite Elizabeth's desk. Rosaria stood until Elizabeth motioned for her to take the seat next to Morgan.

"I've been thinking," Elizabeth started, smiling broadly. "And this invitation made me decide. I want to throw a party when we finish the development on the software program for Family First Software. Morgan, this is a program where parents can manage their children's growth and development and compare it with accepted standards. You can measure your child's growth with the norm for their age and see what skills your child should be gaining. There are also games and activities that promote learning and teach children computer skills. Anyway, it's a big project and we're in the beta stage right now—that means it's being field-tested," she explained.

Morgan was nodding. I knew what she was thinking: *You had me at "party".*

"This project has really shown that IdeaWerx is a player in the software development field. Building a consumer-based program, as opposed to enterprise software designed for the corporate world, gives us the opportunity to stretch out and go after a lot more clients," Elizabeth continued. She'd lost me right after "beta", but at least Morgan was paying attention. In fact, she seemed to be hanging on every word, and I could tell her gears were already cranking ideas.

Rosaria watched with both interest and confusion. This announcement was obviously news to her, and I doubted she liked the fact that she hadn't been privy to such information prior to Elizabeth sharing it with Morgan.

"So, Morgan, we've talked about your aspirations for being an event planner, and I'm giving you a chance to tackle a corporate party. What do you think?"

"Oh, Elizabeth." Morgan clasped her hands together and beamed. "Thank you! I would *love* to plan this party for you. Let's see, well, first, when do you want this to happen? And how many people? Do you want something fun and casual, since it's a family type of product? Are you going to have the party here, or should I look into some other place?"

Elizabeth was pleased with Morgan's enthusiasm, but she held up her hand and turned to Rosaria. "What do you think, Rosaria? I didn't mention this to you before because I wasn't sure yet that I wanted to host an event, but with the possibility of adding Palladex to our client roster, I think it's time that we make ourselves more visible."

Rosaria was processing everything and framing a response. Elizabeth held her gaze, waiting for a reply. Morgan, too, was looking at Rosaria, who appeared more and more uncomfortable. I knew Rosaria was emotionally constipated but wondered if the grimace on her face resulted from a digestive issue or her obvious distaste for Morgan.

"I think that's a great idea, Elizabeth, but I can handle the details. Morgan is obviously very busy at her gallery, so why don't you just let me take care of this?" Rosaria forced as pleasant a smile as she could. Even an over-Botoxed face couldn't be more frozen.

"Actually, I would like the two of you to work together," Elizabeth said.

The faces of both women fell. The idea of collaborating had not been on either of their minds.

Uh oh, I thought. Elizabeth was pitting two hissing felines against each other, and Rosaria's claws were sharp and already extended. I could feel the negative energy in the air like a lightning storm about to strike on a hot summer night. Both women were agape, trying to find a way to mark their respective territories.

"I figured that you, Rosaria, know the business and our clients, so you can guide Morgan on our corporate persona and take care of the guest list. Morgan, I love your creativity and would like to see what you can come up with to make this event really memorable. So you both have important skills, and I think that if you team up, the party will be something that gets everyone talking—in a good way, of course!" She smiled at the two women, making it clear that there was no compromise to her equest. This was an all or nothing proposition; she would not allow either one to take on the project and fly solo.

"I'd be happy to team up with Rosaria," Morgan finally said, shooting a strained smile at her new frenemy.

"Of course," said Rosaria, struggling to shape a smile. She still looked more constipated than happy.

"Wonderful!" Elizabeth stood up, adjourning the meeting. "I've got to get going; I've got an appointment across town. Rosaria, why don't you and Morgan look at your schedules and see when you can get together to start discussing ideas? I'll put together my own thoughts as far as dates, number of guests, and anything else I can think of, but I really want this to be something the two of you create. I've got plenty of other things to do, so I will rely on both of you to handle the details and just keep me posted, okay?"

"Of course," Rosaria replied.

"Great! And thank you!" Morgan extended her hand in gratitude, and Elizabeth smiled and accepted the gesture.

"I'd like to see an overview of your thoughts by next Tuesday. That gives you a week to brainstorm, okay?"

Both women nodded and said "Sure" in unison—the first thing they'd been able to do together so far. I just hoped it wouldn't be the last.

footnotes

As they say, there is no "I" in T-E-A-M. The best outcomes result from true teamwork. And it's not always easy, particularly when the participants bring their own personal agendas into play. But a successful team is one that can leverage the strength of the individuals to the advantage of the group. Consider how you've worked in teams in the past and ask yourself how you might have performed better. Think about this the next time you're invited to join a group activity. Remember that teamwork is about knowing yourself and those around you. Log on to Stiletto911.com and complete the personality profile to get a picture of who you are and what drives you to do what you do. This snapshot of your personality will also show you how to effectively work with other individuals.

CHAPTER *thirty*

The afternoon of the twenty-sixth, Morgan was triple-checking every detail for Siobhan's reception. The artist herself had spent the last five days arranging, rearranging, and re-rearranging her works. Celeste had been offering her input as well, which only seemed to confuse the young woman. This was Siobhan's first major exhibit, and she was hyper-charged. Morgan made a mental note to switch her to decaf for the rest of the day.

In preparation for the event, Morgan confirmed the arrival time and menu with the caterer. She also made sure that Jerry-Perry-Terry—who actually turned out to be Gary—was going to be the chef. So far, so good. Meanwhile, the bartending service would be arriving one hour before the opening. The vendor had had some difficulty with Celeste's wine list but told Morgan that they had located most of the wines.

"Most?" Morgan asked, when she called him to confirm that the delivery would arrive as scheduled. "What do you mean by most?"

"Well, we have everything except for the Shaw & Smith sauv blanc, but we're substituting another one that we highly recommend," said Colin, a newcomer who was filling in for Morgan's regular rep, Tess, who was on maternity leave.

"I'm sorry, but we *have* to have that wine. The artist is from Australia, as is the wine, and it is her favorite. Celeste always insists on serving an artist's choice. She will not be happy about this," Morgan said, her mind shifting into "uh oh" emergency mode.

"Our distributor simply wasn't able to get it in time. I'm sure your guests will be happy with the other wine. Our clients have been very complimentary of it." Colin spoke to her in the I-know-better-than-you tone, which automatically sparked Morgan's ire. She was smart enough to know when someone was Barbie-ing her, although she didn't always rise to her own defense. But today, I saw a different young woman.

"You might be right, Colin, but that is not the wine I requested when I hired your company over a month ago. So you can either hustle around and find this particular wine, or I will have to take the time today to chase it down myself, which will be reflected in the fee that we pay to your service, and, of course, our future relationship." Morgan's voice was sweet, but her message was crystal clear.

"You go, girl!" I cheered her on.

"I'll see what I can do and call you back," Colin replied flatly.

"Thank you," Morgan said and disconnected.

She looked at me with deep frustration. "You know, I'm guessing he didn't try all that hard and is pushing something on me that he's getting better pricing for or just has overstock. And it might be a better wine, but it's not what I wanted, and besides, I'm the customer, and he shouldn't be telling me what I want! I suppose I could call Siobhan and ask if she has another preference, but then I'd have to explain the change to Celeste, because she notices these things, and she'd be really ticked off, so I'm going to stand firm and make this guy do what he's getting paid to do." She finally stopped for a breath, chewing on her lower lip. "But I could make a few calls to wine stores in the meantime and see what they have, just in case this guy doesn't come through."

"Do you have time to do that?" I asked, already knowing the answer based on the pile of notes Morgan had on her desk, which had become more cluttered as the date of the event approached.

"Not really," she sighed. "I've got a bunch of calls to make and need to oversee the set-up downstairs when the caterer, florist, bartender, and musicians arrive. I've also got to fill and arrange the baskets with the exhibit programs, which finally arrived, and set up the PowerPoint presentation about Siobhan."

"So then it sounds like you should just let Colin do his thing, huh?"

"But what if he can't?" Her voice rose as her nerves started to show.

"Okay, stop for a second here. No one handles Celeste like you do. Just think. What could you do to steer her away from a meltdown over a bottle of wine?" I asked, trying to spark her to work this one through on her own. Morgan chewed her lip a bit longer, and just as I thought she was going to hurt herself, she stopped.

"Worse comes to worst, I could ask Siobhan for another suggestion and grab a few bottles of that; tell Celeste that I found something even better that Siobhan loves."

"Perfect! That uppity she-devil would be happy as long as she can stick her nose higher in the air."

"You're right. Maybe I'll save time right now and ask Siobhan. She's downstairs. But I have to get her when Celeste isn't able to listen in."

"Which means outside a three-mile radius," I sniped. "That woman has the hearing of a hound dog."

Morgan peered over the railing in the loft and motioned to Siobhan, who was looking frantic. Celeste was waving her arms in grand gestures, probably offering yet another suggestion that was about to send the poor artist over the edge. Siobhan looked up and saw Morgan waving her over, then putting a finger to her lips and nodding her head in Celeste's direction. Siobhan clearly got the message. She excused herself and pointed toward the bathroom—one sure way to get out of a conversation, because no one questions it, although since women are pack animals, they often follow. Luckily, Celeste was a lone wolf, at least when it came to bathroom breaks.

Siobhan scurried up the stairs, looking relieved to be away from Celeste but still very stressed. "I truly appreciate everything Celeste is doing," she said with her lilting Aussie accent, "but she's making me bloody nuts. She probably thinks I've got something wrong with me because I keep telling her I have to run to the dunny, but it's just to catch a break and avoid screaming like a banshee right in her face. I think me brain's gonna explode, and knowing Celeste, she'll wipe it up with a canvas and hang it on the wall."

Morgan and I listened to Siobhan's rant. Her accent, combined with the Australian slang, made it hard to tell exactly what she was saying, but we got the gist of it.

"I think she's saying that Celeste is a pain in her butt," I said to Morgan.

"Yup," Morgan agreed.

"Sorry to pop off on ya. I'm just nervous," Siobhan said, finally taking a breath. She was a redheaded ball of energy packed into a five-foot-three-inch frame. Her thick, curly hair tumbled past her broad shoulders. She had tied it back today with a braided string of multi-colored fabric strips. She was wearing a gray Chicago Cubs t-shirt and well-worn jeans that were baggy enough to hide the extra fifteen pounds that she carried mostly in her hips and thighs. I took an instant liking to Siobhan, maybe because she'd clearly taken a dislike to Celeste. Or maybe just because she was a spitfire. Well, both, actually.

"Siobhan," Morgan jumped in, "I might have a problem getting that wine you requested. I'm not sure yet, but just in case, is there another Australian wine that we could substitute?"

"If it were up to me, I'd be slugging down longnecks," she grunted. "It was Celeste's idea to serve an Aussie wine. I just picked the one my sister always drinks. If you'd like, I can run down to the bottle shop and grab something."

"Oh, no, Siobhan, thanks, but that's not necessary. If it doesn't matter to you, then I'll just get whatever I can that is a quality wine. I just need to be sure that, if Celeste says anything, you tell her you prefer whatever it is we end up with. Is that okay with you?"

"No worries, Morgan. As I said, toss me a brew and I'm happy. I couldn't tell the difference between plink and that fancy stuff."

"Thanks so much." Morgan smiled at Siobhan. "Is there anything I can do to make this evening easier for you?"

"Got any Xannies?"

"If I did, I'm not sure I'd share," Morgan said with a smile and a sparkle in her eye. I didn't think she was kidding.

Celeste caught sight of Siobhan chatting with Morgan and called up to her. "Siobhan, we need to finish here so you have time to get your hair done!" Her shrill squeal echoed off the high ceilings and seemed to smack Siobhan in the face.

"Getting my hair done usually means a shampoo and a brush, but I'm guessing that's not what Celeste is thinking, eh?" asked Siobhan with a wink. "Damn, I wish I hadn't shaved my legs 'cause I'd sure like to give her a start."

Siobhan turned and hurried down the stairs to a waiting Celeste. A few minutes later, Colin called and told Morgan he had located one case of the Shaw & Smith. He made a point to mention that he would have to pay extra because it wasn't coming from his usual distributor.

"Well, since you quoted me a price for that wine, I assumed you already had a source for it," Morgan said sweetly. "Maybe you should tell them that they cost you money by not making it available when you needed it."

Colin grunted in agreement, although it was clearly not the response he'd wanted from Morgan.

A bit later in the afternoon, the florist arrived, right on schedule. Morgan loved that she never had to do more than give Renee a rough idea of what she wanted for her to come through every time with exceptional results. Today, among the vibrant arrangements that complemented the brilliant colors in Siobhan's work, there was a vase of bright pink peonies. The big magenta blooms were encased in a blue and white pitcher that Morgan had found in the window of consignment shop we'd passed on the way to lunch two weeks ago. Morgan had never been in the store, but the pitcher caught her attention. And she was surprised at how inexpensive it was for a piece of pottery in excellent condition. She'd expected the piece to cost about eighty dollars but paid only twenty-seven. When I explained to her that there was a whole world of secondhand stores out there, clothing stores included, her eyes grew wide.

"Seriously?" she asked. "I just assumed they were like thrift stores with old stuff."

"It's where some great designer things go when women have over-shopped or gained a little too much weight and don't want to be reminded by all the size fours in their closets," I explained. "And some of the clothes have never even been worn."

Morgan was getting all tingly with this shopping foreplay. I reminded her we'd have to take this treasure hunt another day, when there was more time—though, like her, I was almost drooling with anticipation! The whole trip back to the gallery, Morgan kept looking at the pitcher to find flaws that would justify the crazy low price.

When she met with Renee to discuss the flowers for Siobhan's reception, she handed her the pitcher and made a special request for it. So today, when Renee arrived at Celestial Sky loaded down with stunning floral arrangements, Morgan hurried downstairs. She gently picked the peony arrangement from the large box that Renee had set on the table by the door. She sniffed the flowers and intercepted Siobhan, who was coming back from yet another "dunny break".

"I heard you mention that you love pink peonies," Morgan said. "I figured that by now you'd be getting pretty worked up, so I thought I'd give you a reason to stop and smell the flowers." Morgan held the pitcher by the bottom and handed it to a surprised Siobhan.

"Goodness! Thank you, Morgan. They're bloody beautiful!" Siobhan wrapped one arm around the pitcher and the other around Morgan. "I'm going to put these in a place where I can see them when I need a mood lifter. Could I tie them to Celeste's arse?"

"Have I mentioned that I like this woman?" I said to Morgan. She nodded. I didn't know if she was responding to me or to Siobhan. And it didn't matter, because both answers were right.

footnotes

Women have a natural ability to multi-task. Brain mapping studies have proven this trait to be stronger in women than men, so it's not just your imagination that men think in a straight line and you're always juggling like a carnival performer. How do you use your genetic advantage to keep all those balls in the air every moment of every day? It's not easy, and sometimes a few come crashing down. You can save yourself some angst by planning ahead, building in contingencies in the event of an emergency. If you wait for that ball to fall, you rely on your ability to react. But if you are proactive, you can better manage problems and avoid shifting into panic mode.

Try this. Starting first thing tomorrow morning, make a log of how you spend your day. Briefly account for every activity and result in fifteen-minute increments. You may be surprised at how much of your day is spent productively versus unproductively. And go to Stiletto911.com for Time Management Spreadsheets to help you account for your day.

CHAPTER *thirty-one*

Morgan managed to slip away to Bree's apartment two hours before needing to report back to Celestial Sky and welcome the guests. Every aspect of the reception had been checked and re-checked. Morgan may not have been thorough about covering all bases in her life, but she was masterful at managing minute details of events such as this.

Since Morgan wouldn't have time to drive out to Hinsdale and back, she'd left the outfit she planned to wear to the reception at Bree's apartment. Her best friend was working late this evening but would meet up with her at the gallery. Morgan had the apartment to herself, giving her a quiet respite before the bustling that was sure to come that evening.

Morgan took her dress from Bree's closet, where she had left it after their shopping trip two weeks ago. Having been introduced to the joys of upscale consignment shopping—courtesy of yours truly—Morgan had shared the discovery with Bree, taking her for a trek among the many boutiques she had located with one Google search. The two fashionistas on a budget were amazed at what they could get for a fraction of the original price. And most of the dresses had barely been worn. Bree even discovered a Karen Millen jacket with the tags still attached, but paid only about one-third of that price. For her part, Morgan found a sapphire cotton dress with a square neckline, wide straps, and a matching blue sequined inset on the bodice. The princess seams flattered her fuller figure beautifully. The dress was in like-new condition, and Morgan delighted in getting such a great deal on such a great dress; after all, with neither her father nor Pavlo providing a revenue source for her credit cards, she had to cinch up her expenses considerably but didn't want to compromise her standards for style and quality.

Morgan completed her look with four-inch silver strappy stilettos—a necessary staple in any wardrobe, she believed. She loved the shimmer of silver shoes and owned a variety of them—silvery white, silvery gray, strappy, peeps, and sandals, so she could go from jeans to slacks to nighttime chic and still enjoy shiny stilettos.

Finally, she decided to wear the dangling diamond earrings that Pavlo had given her for her birthday. She knew that Pavlo might show up at the opening, but the earrings looked stunning with her outfit and hair—an elegant updo with curled tendrils framing her face. The look outweighed the risk of having Pavlo take her choice as some sign of her pining for him.

While she worked on her makeup, Morgan's mind shifted to Sam. It had been weeks since the argument with Pavlo at Sam's apartment, and she desperately wanted a chance to both apologize to Sam and possibly re-connect. After stopping in to give the invitations to Elizabeth and Rosaria, she had gone to his apartment to deliver one to him—as both a peace offering and an excuse to see him again—but he wasn't at home. She'd slipped it under his door, and there had been no word from him since. She had never admitted it out loud, but I knew she was interested in Sam—and not just for business advice. Neither of us expected him to show up after such a long silence, but if he didn't, I would encourage her to keep trying.

It would be a shame for him not to see Morgan tonight. She was stunning. Although nervous, she beamed with confidence, the epitome of the gracious hostess—even though she knew that was Celeste's job. But Morgan would play hostess to her father, Elizabeth, and even Rosaria—and possibly Sam—and wanted to make a striking impression.

At Celestial Sky, Morgan was standing near the entrance, ready to greet people and offer each one an exhibit program. Siobhan was nibbling on appetizers and flirting with Jerry-Perry-Terry-Gary—that was, until Celeste snatched her away and reminded her caterer that his time would be better spent preparing the overpriced food she was paying for.

While Morgan watched this exchange, she felt a hand on her shoulder. Startled, she turned to see Elizabeth in a black pantsuit with a brightly colored scarf and cascading crystal earrings in a spectrum of colors. Rosaria looked as though she had come directly from work, wearing a gray dress that Morgan recognized from a previous visit to IdeaWerx. She had on her ever-present sensible shoes with the one-inch heel and a black messenger bag strung across her chest. Poor Rosaria, thought Morgan. She just couldn't allow herself to pay any attention to her appearance.

"Honey, that woman is wrapped tighter than my control top pantyhose," I whispered in Morgan's ear. "Someone should parole her from that prison matron's wardrobe."

"I wish!" Morgan said.

"You wish what?" asked Elizabeth.

"I wish you would try the food. This caterer is amazing! I'm thinking of hiring him for your launch party."

I had to give the girl credit—she recovered quickly.

Morgan waved at one of the servers, a young woman in a tuxedo. The server hurried over with a tray of goat cheese tarts. Elizabeth picked one, tasted it, and closed her eyes with that euphoria that usually only comes with exquisite chocolate.

"This is incredible! Try one, Rosaria," said Elizabeth.

Rosaria plucked a tart with extreme hesitation, probably trying to guess which one Morgan had poisoned. She took a tiny bite and did her best to mask her pleasure, something I was sure she had done most of her life. Poor thing.

"Mmm hmm," she mumbled. But Morgan and Elizabeth could tell she was enjoying the appetizer.

"This new chef is fantastic," Morgan bubbled. "He's young and inventive and loves to try new things. Maybe you can talk to him at some point this evening and see what you think."

Behind Rosaria, Sam walked in the door. He was dressed in a tailored blue and white striped shirt and navy slacks. His sleeves were rolled up to the elbow, but he didn't look sloppy. He was just perennially casual and pulled it off nicely.

A tingle danced down Morgan's back, and her palms felt damp. She kept her gaze fixed on Sam, who was thumbing through a program and glancing around the gallery. Morgan wondered if he was looking for her. She stammered as she excused herself from Elizabeth and Rosaria, directing them to the exhibit and the bar. Then she slipped up behind Sam and tapped him on the shoulder.

He turned. It took him a moment to process Morgan. The last—actually the only—time he had seen her, she'd had the appearance of a scruffy waif. She had literally come in from the rain and, although he'd found her attractive, he certainly hadn't expected to see a polished sophisticate emerge from the caterpillar. But here she was, glowing and gorgeous. Sam finally reconnected his mouth to his brain.

"Oh, hey, wow! You look, uh, great!" he said.

"Thanks. I am *so* glad you came tonight." Morgan did the flirtatious hair toss, flicking one tendril off her forehead, only to have it land over her eye and stick to her eyelash. She swatted at it unsuccessfully and then picked it off with her nails and brushed it behind one ear. "I've been hoping we'd have a chance to talk again."

"Well, yes, I guess we didn't leave it on a high note, but that's one reason I wanted to come tonight," he said, a bit nervously. "I shouldn't have been so quick to shove you out the door that day."

"No, really, I understand. I can imagine what it all looked like, and it wasn't fair for you to have to put up with that scene—not after you were nice enough to let me in and help me out after such a bad night." Morgan gently laid a hand on his forearm. "I'm sorry, Sam."

Their eyes held. Watching them was like seeing hot water poured over an ice sculpture: The chill melted so fast that it was hard to remember it had ever existed.

"Can we maybe start over?" Morgan asked him, her eyes pleading.

Without allowing his eyes to shift from hers, he reached out his hand. "Nice to meet you. Sam Baxter."

Morgan looked down at his hand and took it gently, holding on as she replied, "Morgan Demarest."

"And I now pronounce you hot single guy and hot single girl," I announced. "You may now hit on each other."

"So, Sam Baxter, what brings you to the gallery tonight?" Morgan asked coyly, still holding his hand.

"I found this very unusual invitation under my front door and had to come see the person who was creative enough to make it and nice enough to personally deliver it." Sam smiled in return. "So, what else have you been up to, besides putting together this party?"

So relieved at this second chance with Sam, Morgan excitedly shared her new goal to become an event planner and talked about Elizabeth's launch party. She told him that she and Edward had been staying at the Hinsdale house and spending some quality father-daughter time. "And how are things with you?" she finished.

Sam responded with a quick summary of his work, brushing quickly past a recent "non-memorable" speaking opportunity. He had more energy for his latest get-togethers with Anthony, like their taste-test of Chicago pizzerias to find their favorite. "We've narrowed it down to three places. I think Anthony is just milking it to keep eating pizza with purpose," he said, chuckling. "You know, you might consider becoming a Big Sister at some point. I bet there's a young girl who could learn a lot from you."

"I'm afraid what that girl would learn from me," Morgan said with a smile.

Sam grabbed two glasses of champagne from a passing server's tray, handed one to Morgan, and sipped from the other. "Oh, I think you could teach someone some very interesting lessons," he said with a grin.

I was getting restless watching this way-too-subtle flirtation. Someone needed to jump in there and push this whole thing into high gear.

"Will you stop tippy-toeing around, girl, and just invite the man to lunch or something? If you two moved any slower, they'd be putting toe tags on the both of you!" I shouted. Morgan was caught off-guard by my outburst and jerked her arm in response, spilling champagne on Sam's shirt.

"Oh, Sam, I am so sorry!" she exclaimed, reaching out to wipe it off. "I must have been bumped or something. Can I help? God, I'm such a klutz!"

Sam found a couple of napkins on a nearby table and dabbed at his shirt. "Don't worry, Morgan. It's not a big deal. It's fine. Really."

"Let me make this up to you. Can I buy you a drink sometime, or lunch, or something? Maybe a new shirt?" Morgan was stammering. I knew it was hard for her to take this step, but she was doing just fine.

"You don't have to make it up to me. And I'm not sure if I trust you to buy me a drink," Sam said, smiling. "I don't know if I have enough shirts. But lunch sounds good. You know, I'm just going to go get a cloth or something and see if I can do a better job drying this off. I'll be right back." With that, Sam wove through the crowd toward the restroom.

Morgan watched him go, a look of embarrassment on her face, although she still managed to give him an appreciative evaluation as he walked away.

"Don't worry, Morgan. I think he likes the clumsy side of you," I whispered.

"I am just such a screwball," she replied.

"But such a lovely screwball," crooned a deep voice behind her. Morgan turned to see Pavlo standing within kissing distance behind her. "You look amazink, Morgan."

"Uh, hi, uh, hello, Pavlo. This is a surprise." Her eyes darted around the room to see where Sam had gone, but he was nowhere in sight.

"Shouldn't be. I come to all of these parties. Celeste is a vunderful patron for me. She luffs my work and vill usually find vun or two pipple here to introduce me to." He was still uncomfortably close to Morgan's face, his brown eyes taking in her every feature.

"Yes, I remember. Well, so, anyway, what's new? How's your work going?" Morgan was trying to pull back from his tractor-beam hold on her. She had been taking small steps backward but had edged herself up against a wall, with nowhere to go.

"Not as good as ven I had my muse. I miss you, Morgan," he said breathily, his mouth moving closer to her ear. "Haf you been missing me?"

"I've been really, really busy getting this reception organized," she stammered. She couldn't deny the heat that was rising from her toes from this closeness with Pavlo.

"Vat? You make calls. Vy haf you not called me? Did you sink I'd not forgiven you? Belief me, I haf. Vy don't you come back viz me and be my muse again? You can shop. I vill paint. All vill be vell."

Pavlo's raw sexuality was tempting. She considered her past life with him. It had been fun. But it felt like so long ago, although just a few weeks had passed. She loved the loft and always enjoyed watching Pavlo at work. His creative energy was intoxicating.

"Snap out of it!" I shouted. "This man is devouring you with his eyes and you're letting him. Do you want to go back and be his sweet thing or do you want to be taken seriously? C'mon, Morgan, you've come too far to stop now. You deserve more than some hot Russian who wants a love slave. Although I think I might be available, if he's man enough," I added slyly.

Morgan shook off Pavlo's spell. She put one palm on his chest, and he leaned in even closer. She gave him one strong push and he bumped into Siobhan, who was passing by behind him. His massive size almost toppled the little artist. He managed to grab hold of her before she rammed into a pedestal with a vase of flowers.

"Oh, Siobhan, I'm so sorry!" Morgan hurried to Siobhan's aid, but Pavlo was already steadying her.

"No worries," said a flustered Siobhan. "But are you going to introduce me to this freight train?"

Morgan made a hasty introduction and then turned to go in search of Sam, who should have returned by now. A hand reached out and grabbed hold of her arm. It was her father.

"Honey, where are you going in such a hurry? Is everything okay?" he asked.

"Oh, I was looking for Sam Baxter. He was just here, and, well, then Pavlo, you know. Anyway, have you seen him? Sam, I mean?" she asked, straining to look over the crowd to find him.

"Actually, I did. I spoke to him when I was coming in the door and he was heading out," Edward said.

"Heading *out*? Sam was leaving?"

"Yeah, he said he had to go."

"When was this? How long ago?"

"About two minutes. Why?"

"Uh, oh." I said. "I bet he saw you snuggling with Pavlo and beat his feet for the door. Damn!"

Morgan groaned. "Great. Just great. I could just smack him."

"Sam?" Edward asked. "Why do you want to hit Sam?"

"No. Pavlo. He has the most rotten, lousy timing in the whole world," she grumbled.

Celeste picked that moment to sidle up next to Morgan.

"And who have we here, Morgan?" she asked in a voice so sickly sweet that Morgan had to do a double-take to make sure it was coming from her boss.

"Celeste, this is my father, Edward Demarest. Dad, this is Celeste Bourque. She owns the gallery." Morgan's voice was matter-of-fact. She was trying to find a way to extract herself and see if she could catch up with Sam.

"This can't be your father, Morgan. He's far too young," Celeste cooed.

"This woman is putting the moves on your dad, Morgan! You've gotta save him!"

Celeste beamed her most flirtatious smile at Edward. He looked startled—not from the fake grin, but the lipstick that had somehow become smudged all over her teeth. Celeste slipped her arm through Edward's and said, "Come with me, dear Edward. Let me show you the wonderful works of Siobhan Findlay. I'll give you my personal tour and introduce you to the artist herself."

"Does she not think his own daughter could do the same?" I snipped.

Morgan was still too distracted, so I had to step in.

As Celeste and Edward turned to head off in the other direction, we heard a few snickers from the crowd. Celeste was in full strut, unaware that her skirt had become tucked into her underwear, providing quite the show for her guests.

"Ohmigod!" said Morgan, elbowing my side. "Did you do that?"

"What?" I asked innocently. "That woman always likes to be the center of attention. I'm just giving her what she wants. I *am* a Fairy Godmother, after all!"

footnotes

There will always be distractions in your life. Take a look at the spreadsheet you built in the last chapter. Highlight the distractions that caused you to lose grip on your time. As Benjamin Franklin said, "Lost time is never found again." If you could manage your distractions, what more could you accomplish with that "found" time? Investing some time to analyze your day/week/month will help you identify areas of potential growth. You may be surprised at what you learn about yourself.

CHAPTER thirty-two

While most eyes were trained on Celeste's exposed rear end, Morgan wove through the maze of people and hurried to the gallery's entrance. She whipped open the door and flung herself into the brisk October night air.

And smack into Sam.

He instinctively reached out to catch her as she fell backwards.

"What? Oh! Sam! I thought you . . . I thought you left. And I was, well, I was . . ." Morgan's voice trailed off as she looked into his eyes. "I thought you left."

"I did," he said flatly. He let go of her and took a step back, then looked up and down the street before turning back to Morgan. "I did leave, because I saw you with your boyfriend, and he wasn't looking all that 'ex' to me."

"No . . ." Morgan started to protest, but Sam held up a hand to stop her.

"I've been running away from possibilities for a long time, but suddenly, tonight, when I went out that door, I felt like such a wimp, like a coward or something. I saw you and that guy, and I just thought, here we go again."

"What do you . . . " Again, he stopped her from continuing, which was an impressive feat, I have to admit.

"I've been a doormat when it comes to women," Sam said. "I'm the one they come to when their boyfriends piss them off or hurt their feelings or break their hearts. And I tell them what idiots those guys are, how they deserve better, and then after I've been that white knight for a few minutes, hours, or days, they run on back to the jerk. So I get a little twitchy when I think it's going to happen again. And that's what it felt like a few minutes ago."

"But that's not what it was," Morgan said in a tiny voice.

"And that's why I didn't actually leave. Because I think I decided not to be a pussy—sorry, a wimp. I like you, Morgan, and I think you deserve better than some guy who wants to own you. You need to be yourself, and whether that's being with me, someone else, or no one at all, I just had to tell you that."

Sam stopped, but his breath was visible in the cold night air. Morgan studied his face and saw pain. But she also saw determination, honesty, and genuine feeling. And if it weren't for the fact that she was way too young, I might have thought she was experiencing a hot flash as a red blush ran up her neck to her face.

She reached down and took both of his hands in hers, pulling him closer. When she was so near that his breath warmed her face, she whispered, "Thank you."

He met her gaze and replied just as softly, "For what?"

"For what you said, for who you are, and mostly for not leaving."

And she kissed him, softly at first. Then he pulled her closer, wrapping her like a blanket with his coat, arms, and passion. Not necessarily in that order.

When she came back inside, arm in arm with Sam, Morgan made me fix the little fashion mishap with Celeste's exposed backside, so the haughty woman never realized what had happened—although plenty of guests had gotten an eyeful of her black thong panties and butterfly tattoo on her thigh—a remnant of her college years, when she was still Celia from Ohio.

The morning after Siobhan's reception, Morgan sat at her desk, contemplating the events of the evening. Celeste was ecstatic after having sold three pieces, with prospects for two more. And, unaware of the depths of her exposure at the reception, Celeste was so happy with the event that she suggested Morgan plan her daughter's sixteenth birthday party. Rather than offer to hire her, however, Celeste simply said that Morgan could find time during her workday to make the necessary calls. But, Morgan thought, if she did a good job, she might connect with some for-real clients from Celeste's vast network; for all her demands and snide comments, Celeste was very skilled at spreading the word about young talent.

Meanwhile, Siobhan was bubbling over with excitement after selling her works and receiving high praise from one art critic who loved the rawness of her mixed media.

She had also managed to charm Pavlo—and vice versa. To her surprise, Morgan felt very little jealousy—she was basking in the afterglow of her new connection with Sam. Yes, it was strange to see Pavlo giving Siobhan the same look that had, not so long ago, been hers, and it wasn't exactly painless, but another part of her was a bit relieved, which told her that the past had passed.

Her mind returned to Sam. For the rest of the evening, she'd wanted so much to be with him but felt obligated to mingle with the guests, which he encouraged her to do. Sam did some mingling of his own, talking with Edward and even striking up a conversation with Elizabeth when they were admiring the same work.

Just as Morgan was enjoying a rerun of that first kiss, her cell phone buzzed with a new text message: *Nice job last night. Party was great 2. Wanna do lunch 2moro?*

She smiled and thumb-typed her reply: *Thx. Maybe we should go buy new shirt 4 u. Lets get 2, just in case.*

They agreed on a café a block from the gallery, far enough out of Celeste's line of sight to prevent snooping. Sam told Morgan he'd call her in the morning to confirm, and as she tucked away the phone, her smile couldn't have stretched any wider across her face.

"Feels good to go after something and get it, huh?" I asked smugly.

"We're just having lunch," she said.

"But you took a risk last night and went after what you wanted. That's important, Morgan. There was no game-playing, You didn't have to waste the day trading texts with your BFF or passing notes in school. You're an adult now. Decide what you want and go for it."

"Thanks, Dee," she said softly. "You're right."

"Well, stop the presses, I think I'm gonna faint. Morgan Demarest actually said I was right about something!" I wobbled a bit and pretended I was about to drop.

Morgan rolled her eyes. "Well, enjoy this moment, because I don't know when it will happen again."

My girl was making bigger-than-baby steps in her stilettos. So I took the opportunity to nudge her a bit farther. "Okay, big shot, so why not tackle the next big obstacle and call your little friend, Rosaria?"

Morgan sighed and tipped back her head, looking at the ceiling.

I bent over her and got right in her face. "You're on a roll. You're feeling powerful. Go ahead and rope in that mustang." I swung my arm like I was twirling a lasso.

Morgan looked over her shoulder at me. "You really know how to kill a great moment, you know."

But she grudgingly found the number for IdeaWerx in her directory, picked up the phone, and hit Call. As Morgan suspected, Rosaria answered.

"Hi, Rosaria, it's me. Morgan," she said, hopeful that the brief social interaction last night might have melted some of the chill between them.

"Yes."

Okay, the temperature was still below freezing.

"I just wanted to touch base with you about the details for Elizabeth's party. What did you think of the caterer last night?"

"Elizabeth said she was happy, so I guess we'll be going with him, but I'll need to see a menu and budget."

"Okay, I'll talk to Gary. Now what about the themes we discussed? Did Elizabeth give you any feedback on the list we presented?" Morgan had actually created the list. Rosaria hadn't seen the need to build in a theme for a party: You have food and drinks, and that's it. Morgan had to wonder what help, if any, Rosaria would be in the planning process. So far, she had only been a hindrance.

"She said she liked your idea about having stages of a child's life and creating stations around that idea," Rosaria answered, with zero enthusiasm.

Morgan continued to probe for feedback, but Rosaria made it impossible. This woman simply didn't understand the fine art of conversation. Finally, in exasperation, Morgan got to the point. "Listen, Rosaria, Elizabeth has asked us both to work on this. I need your help here, and I think you need mine."

"I am perfectly capable of hiring a caterer and doing decorations," Rosaria said. "A party is a party. I don't see the need to go overboard."

"Of course you don't, but you should! This is important to Elizabeth and to the company. I would think that you'd understand that."

"You don't need to lecture me on what's good for this company. I have been here practically since the doors opened—while you were off shopping or getting a manicure or something. This is my job. It is not some silly experiment or game to play."

This was the most Morgan had ever heard Rosaria say at one time. It confirmed everything that Morgan believed about Rosaria. The cards were on the table.

"This is not a game for me either, Rosaria. This is my life, not a shopping spree or whatever it is you think I do," Morgan said. I was impressed that she had yanked out that doormat and was standing tall, even though she was sitting down. "I am not your enemy, Rosaria, You need to know that."

"And I am *not* your friend!"

"And why is that, exactly? What did I do to you that made you dislike me so much?"

"We have different values," Rosaria said.

"You *assume* we have different values. How do you know? You have never taken the time to get to know me. You look at me and assume that I don't work as hard as you, or I'm not as serious as you, or that I'm just a silly shopaholic. Well, let me tell you something. You don't know me. I am a good person with real values, so don't go thinking you're better than me just because we don't look alike."

Rosaria was quiet. I was sure she hadn't expected this response from the shallow woman she'd taken Morgan to be. Finally, Rosaria broke the silence:

"I have to go. I have work to do."

She disconnected. And I ran through my mental address book to see if I could find Rosaria a Fairy Godmother, because she was right: She *did* have work to do!

footnotes

When you set goals, there will be challenges en route to achieving them. You will likely have to step out of your comfort zone from time to time. Taking a risk is going to be crucial to creating change for your life. If you continue with the same behaviors, repeating the same actions, you will never see different results. The next time you are faced with taking a risk, don't skirt around it. Stop and consider the potential consequences. What do you stand to gain? What might you lose? Weigh the two possible outcomes against each other. Remember that faltering here and there still provides a valuable lesson. Learn from those missteps and they will not be wasted effort.

CHAPTER thirty-three

Elizabeth was struggling with a four year-old complaining of a tummy ache. She ran through the litany of Mommy responses, starting by first feeling her daughter's forehead, which was no warmer than usual, but she stuck in the ear thermometer anyway. As Elizabeth suspected, 98.6°. No fever.

"Do you have to make a poopy?" Elizabeth asked, in her loving Mommy voice.

Lara shook her head.

"Did you already make a poopy?" she asked, wondering if Lara was plugged up. She used to give her daughter apple juice on those occasions, something she came to refer to as "Baby Drano".

Lara shook her head once again.

"Does it hurt anywhere other than your tummy?"

Lara paused and thought a moment. She pointed to her head and then opened her mouth and pointed toward her throat.

"Hmm, so your head and throat hurt, too? I wonder if you're coming down with the flu. God, I hope not, because that means your brother will get it, too."

Then Lara bent over and pointed to her knees. "Mommy, it hurts here, too."

"Well, I guess you'd better not go to school today," Elizabeth said. She was already envisioning her calendar and mentally re-juggling her schedule to stay with her ailing daughter. "Let's get you back to bed."

"I don't want to go to bed. I want to watch TV, Mommy. Will you watch Dora the Explorer with me?" Lara asked.

"No television right now, honey. You need to rest," Elizabeth told her, while also calculating the tasks she had to complete today, which would now have to happen from home. She had the option of managing her work remotely, largely because Rosaria was so competent at keeping everything moving smoothly in Elizabeth's absence. But she also resented that *her* schedule—not Tom's—was the one that was usually compromised when it came to handling family matters. Whenever one of the kids was sick or needed help with schoolwork—or cupcakes at the last minute—it was assumed that Elizabeth would handle the parenting. What was the point of being married, she thought, when she always had to deal with these emergencies on her own? Tom was a good father, but he was gone so much that Elizabeth often felt like a single parent. She loved being a mother, but it trying to "have it all" was a real challenge.

Lara's cherubic face twisted into a pout, and she folded her arms across her chest. "I want to watch TV, Mommy. Why can't I watch TV?" she insisted. " I want to stay home with you and watch TV."

"When you're sick, you have to rest, Lara, and that's that!"

"Then I don't want to be sick," Lara said.

If only it were that simple, Elizabeth thought. If only wishes could come true just by willing them to happen.

It suddenly dawned on Elizabeth that perhaps her daughter wasn't sick. Maybe she only wanted Elizabeth's attention, some motherly love. Elizabeth received the message that Lara was sending, but she also realized that she couldn't cave in to her daughter's demand or she'd be feeding what could become a manipulative little monster—like the ones she had seen have temper tantrums in stores, only to have the parent give in and reward the bad behavior just to silence the wailing child. Elizabeth sat down on Lara's bed and wrapped her arms around her daughter.

"Sweetheart, I would love to stay home with you today and have our special time. I think, though, that we need to plan a day when you and I can have fun when you're not feeling so, so sick. Why don't you stay in bed today and get all better? And then we can have Lara's Special Day and you and Mommy can do all sorts of fun things together, like making cupcakes and going to the Jolly Gym and getting our fingernails painted and maybe have lunch at your favorite place. But today you need to rest, and Mommy needs to work."

Lara's expression transformed from pouty to perky in an instant when Elizabeth described the fun they would have.

Elizabeth tried to plan regular one-on-one time with each of her kids. She rewarded each with their own "Special Day" when they earned enough points by picking up their toys, trying new foods, going to bed without arguments, and playing well together. She realized it had been awhile since she and Lara had enjoyed a girls' day. She loved her children and knew that she needed to make them her priority, even though that was a big order when her business kept her so busy.

"I feel better, Mommy, so can we do Lara's Special Day today?" Lara asked, her blue eyes wide and pleading.

"I thought you were really, really sick, Lara. Is your tummy all better?"

"It feels good as new," Lara chirped.

Elizabeth knew that kids could be resilient, but Lara had set a new record for the shortest tummy ache recovery she had seen yet.

"Well, today is a school day for you and a work day for me," Elizabeth said. "We can have Lara's Special Day on Saturday, as long as you're not still sick. So why don't we talk more about our plans when I get home from work? Now, let's get you ready for school!"

She gave Lara a big hug, kissed her head, and whispered in her ear. "I love you, my princess."

Morgan arrived at IdeaWerx five minutes before her scheduled appointment with Elizabeth. She wanted to be punctual but dreaded having to spend even one more minute than necessary under Rosaria's evil glare. We hovered in the elevator lobby a bit longer, while Morgan looked at the time on her cell phone.

"Listen," I said impatiently, hitting the button to summon the elevator. "I sincerely doubt that Rosaria is looking forward to spending any time alone with you, either. Just go up there and sit in the waiting area for Elizabeth and don't say anything to get Miss Rosie's panties in a twist."

"She probably wears briefs. Big, white cotton briefs." She thought for a moment and then turned and whacked me on the arm. "And what do you mean telling *me* not to get her started? I suppose you think it's all my fault that she hates my guts?"

"No, I just think you two clash like stripes and plaids. All you can do is keep your distance." I felt badly for Morgan. She really had tried to chip through Rosaria's crusty exterior, but Rosaria had a titanium shell. Once or twice, I'd even considered a little spell, but that was highly frowned upon by my peers. Our job was to guide, not manipulate, I'd been told countless times. Well, *maybe just this once,* I thought now. Would it really be so bad to put a little lightness in Rosaria's heart?

The elevator door opened while I was pondering, and we walked down the hallway and entered IdeaWerx. Rosaria was at her usual post, guarding the entry to the inner workings of the company. Ordinarily, Rosaria would do her best to ignore Morgan. Today, she fixed her gaze on my girl but without the usual dagger eyes. She got up from her desk and came out of her office.

"Good morning," Rosaria said, in an almost pleasant tone. Boy, that had to hurt, I thought.

Morgan was getting the same vibe, which caught her by surprise. She had prepared herself to swap pointed barbs with the testy woman, but there didn't seem to be much fight in Rosaria today.

"Elizabeth just called and she's running a bit late, but she should be here in about fifteen minutes. Do you have time to wait?" Rosaria asked. She wasn't in the running for Miss Congeniality, but neither was she shooting poison-tipped arrows at Morgan. Maybe one of my colleagues had taken on this case after all!

"Sure, I have a little time. The gallery opens later on Tuesdays. " Morgan was trying to figure out what was behind this sudden shift. "Um, thanks for asking."

"No problem," said Rosaria, who turned on her sensible, thick one-inch black heels and started to walk back toward her office. She stopped. *Uh, oh,* I thought. *Here it comes.* She'd gotten Morgan to let down her guard and was now going to go for the jugular. I was ready to protect my girl but hoped I wouldn't have to use magic to do it.

"Morgan," Rosaria started, "I've been thinking about our conversation the other day. You were right. I have judged you by the way you look. I work really hard, and you seem to get what you want just by smiling at people, and I resent that. I resent women who get by without doing the work. But maybe I haven't been fair."

"Is that what you think?" said Morgan, her voicing rising a full octave. "You think that I don't work hard? Let me tell you, if you knew the boss I have to deal with, well, she's a royal bitch and most people can't stand her. My job is basically to keep people from having to deal with her directly, which means I have to spend my days listening to her complain about how the entire planet has disappointed her, and then try to convince everyone else to do the things that I need to get done, and do whatever I can so they don't bail—well, the good ones, anyway—because Celeste has insulted them for the gazillionth time. Trust me, you've got it a lot easier. At least Elizabeth shows you respect. You resent me? Well, I am envious of *you!*"

Rosaria appeared stunned. Her eyes were wide and her jaw dropped. It was as though Morgan had just chucked a glass of ice water in her face. She had seen Celestial Sky Gallery the night of Siobhan's reception, and she thought Morgan had the easiest job in the world: Just show up, smile at people, and throw parties on someone else's credit card. It didn't seem all that hard, more like play than work. She hadn't met Celeste, although she'd caught sight of her walking away with her underwear exposed. All Rosaria could think then was, *Why would a woman want to walk around with her underwear stuck up her butt?* Rosaria just didn't get the point of thongs.

"Just because Elizabeth is a nice person doesn't mean my job is easy. Those programmers back there are impossible. They're like little kids. I have to remind them of everything. 'Don't forget we need those reports.' 'Don't forget we need that update for tomorrow.' 'Don't forget the client is coming in.' 'Don't forget to wipe your butt!' And I know they call me 'Tightass' behind my back and make jokes about me all the time. Elizabeth doesn't see any of this, because my job is to keep things going smoothly. She doesn't have to worry about the stupid things. That's my job."

Morgan and I watched Rosaria and listened to her rant. When she seemed to come to an end, I elbowed Morgan to respond. She faltered a moment, trying to find the words. "Wow!" was all she could muster.

The two women stood and stared at each other, each waiting for the other to speak.

"Oh, for God's sake, say something, Morgan," I gasped.

"Rosaria, I'm sorry, I had no idea." Morgan's voice held genuine empathy. "I'm sorry you have to take such abuse. You should talk to Elizabeth. She wouldn't want you to feel this way."

"No!" Rosaria's chin was pointed upwards in a defiant pose. "I am a big girl and I can take care of myself. And don't you go telling her, either. That's all I need, for you to show me up once again."

"What do you mean, show you up?" Morgan was completely amazed by the anger, candor, and hurt that Rosaria had finally exposed. She was seeing Rosaria in a different light, realizing there was more to her than a tightly-wound mass of bitch genes.

"Oh, please, like you don't know," Rosaria said. "You come in here with your, 'Oh, I want to make something of myself' and Elizabeth gets all excited about helping someone in her career. I show up here every single day. I never call in sick. I never ask for favors, for a raise, for anything; I just do my job. And that's all I thought I needed to do. But you get all this attention from Elizabeth, like you're her long-lost daughter or long-lost employee or something. And I'm just stupid old Rosaria who has no goals, no wishes, who doesn't ask for special attention or for Elizabeth to be my mentor. So, yes, you show me up, and I don't know what to do about it. But you know what? I'm tired of trying. If you want my job, take it. I'm tired of all the crap, and I don't want to compete with you anymore!" As Rosaria became more and more worked up, her Hispanic accent grew more pronounced. This was one fiery Latina, not the bland grump we had been seeing.

Morgan was stunned. She had never intended to compete with Rosaria, nor had she ever contemplated taking Rosaria's job. How had she been so completely misunderstood? And how had she misjudged *Rosaria* so completely?

In her stilettos, Morgan towered over Rosaria, and she found herself looking down at the woman—literally, but not figuratively. She took one of the seats in the lobby to gather her thoughts for a moment. Rosaria stood with her arms folded, waiting for Morgan to confirm every suspicion she had just voiced.

I took the chair next to Morgan, crossed my legs, and surveyed the situation. I could honestly see why Rosaria would feel threatened: Morgan was everything she wasn't—at least, on the surface. Morgan was stylish and appeared confident (although I knew that was far from reality). She was likable and outgoing, and she wasn't afraid to ask for help.

Rosaria had none of those qualities, but she had never wished for them, either. That was, until now. She had spent most of her life believing that working hard and not making waves was what made a good employee. She never expected anything in return. Elizabeth was quick to praise her and paid her fairly. That was all she needed. Was it her ideal job? No. But it was better than some of the jobs she had had in the past—waiting tables in a diner for really bad tips, for example, or entering orders into a computer day after day within a sea of tiny cubicles where the most interesting part of her day was the subway ride to and from work. During that commute, she'd looked at other women, professionals who were dressed beautifully, who probably had jobs with nice offices and made important decisions. She'd looked at their briefcases and wondered what they carried. What deals were these women working on? How many people reported to them? What changes did they make in their worlds?

Rosaria had secretly wanted to be one of those high-powered women in an expensive suit with a fancy leather briefcase, someone whom people listened to and respected. When she'd taken the job at IdeaWerx, she'd seen Elizabeth as one of those women— powerful, confident, and a born leader. She'd hoped to learn from Elizabeth, to gain some of her wisdom and find a way to be like her.

But instead, Rosaria had just watched and followed. She didn't have the confidence to lead, challenge, or make a difference. When Elizabeth entered the room, the programmers took notice. They listened to her every word, heeded her suggestions, and showed her respect. All that Rosaria got from these co-workers was ridicule. When she tried to exert authority, they scoffed at her. It had never occurred to her to ask Elizabeth to give her guidance on leadership. She thought she should just watch and learn. Yeah, and that was working just fine, huh?

And then Morgan had waltzed into the office with the nerve to ask *Rosaria's* boss to mentor her! So Elizabeth would help a complete stranger while Rosaria worked diligently and without notice. It was no wonder she resented this intruder.

Morgan sat with her hands folded on her lap, looking at her entwined fingers as she searched for something to say. A few times, she opened her mouth to speak but stopped. Morgan at a loss for words? I was speechless!

Rosaria waited. She had said far more than she'd ever intended and wished she could take it all back. She'd unleashed her fury on Morgan and realized that perhaps she had been unfair. She looked at Morgan, who seemed genuinely pained by Rosaria's revelations. But Rosaria believed she had said more than enough. It was Morgan's turn.

"I don't even know what to say, or where to start," Morgan said, her voice cracking. "I came here because I had heard Elizabeth speak at a conference, and I thought she could give me some answers. I didn't come here looking for a job—not yours or any other—but for some direction. A friend told me about mentoring and got me all excited that I could find the help I needed in someone who had it all together, because I sure didn't. So I came here, and Elizabeth agreed to help me." Morgan looked up from her lap and made eye contact with Rosaria. The two women held each other's gazes as Morgan continued, "I am sorry that I made you so unhappy, Rosaria. I'm not a mean person. At least, I don't intend to be. Okay, maybe to mean people. Anyway, I really, really am not trying to take your job, and to be honest, I don't think Elizabeth would be happy with anyone but you, because you are really good at what you do."

At long last, the Latina released her firm grip on the scowl that seemed permanently fixed on her face. She walked over and sat down next to where I had parked myself. I rose from my chair so I could get a better perspective on the situation.

"Thank you," Rosaria said. Those two words, spoken to the woman who had posed such a threat until just moments ago, did not come easily from Rosaria's mouth. "I guess I owe you an apology, too. I've been a real bitch to you, and I know it."

"You can say *that* again!" I snickered.

"Shut *up!*" Morgan replied.

Rosaria looked at her, confused.

Once again, Morgan scrambled to cover up her misstep. (I have to admit I enjoyed watching her fix these little faux pas.) "I mean, shut up, you are *not* a bitch, Rosaria."

There was an awkward moment as each woman tried to determine the next move. It was like watching two fifth graders sizing each other up at their first dance.

"So, listen, Rosaria, let's start over, okay? Let's erase all the crap that has gone on between us and see if we can be nicer," Morgan said.

I thought I heard the facial muscles crackling as Rosaria broke into a smile. Whoa! She had beautiful white teeth, and no fangs with blood dripping off them.

For her part, Rosaria suddenly saw Morgan in a different light, too, as a person who was nice, and just happened to be pretty. *Not her fault, I guess,* she thought. She extended her hand to shake, and Morgan reached out and took it.

"Where I come from, friends hug!" I said, and pushed Morgan smack dab into Rosaria, who reflexively reached out to grab Morgan, as much in an effort to steady herself as to prevent her newfound friend from a fall.

It was at this particular moment that Elizabeth came rushing in the front door. She was looking at a text message and not watching where she was walking, which led her straight into the tangled mess of Rosaria and Morgan.

"Oof, oh, excuse me," she said without registering the scenario she had just tumbled into. When she realized that Morgan and Rosaria seemed to be having a warm moment, she was completely taken aback. "Hey, look at you two! Are you hugging or wrestling?"

Morgan and Rosaria split from their awkward embrace.

"Sorry, Elizabeth. Um, Morgan and I were just talking," Rosaria stammered, unsure of what to say or do at this moment.

"Well, hallelujah, ladies. I was hoping you two would find a way to become friends," said Elizabeth, with a big smile that assured Rosaria that she approved of a little public display of friendship.

Morgan jumped into the conversation. "I know things have been, well, awkward, but we've ironed out our differences. At least, I think we have," she said, eyeing Rosaria questioningly.

"Yes, I think so," Rosaria said.

"Good. Well, maybe you can use this new unity to make some major progress on our party. Listen, I know I'm late for our meeting, Morgan, but I have to catch up on a few quick calls. Can you maybe wait a little longer? I'm really sorry, but my daughter needed some Mommy time this morning, and I just couldn't say no."

"No problem. Rosaria and I can discuss a few details for the party," Morgan said with a smile.

"Great! I'll just be about ten minutes. Thanks!"

As Elizabeth hurried down the hall to her office, she was thankful that Lara seemed to be the only girl who needed Mommy to step in and take charge today. Elizabeth had been preparing for the day—very soon, she'd thought—when she would have to intervene with Morgan and Rosaria and make the girls play nice with each other.

But it didn't seem necessary now.

Morgan and Rosaria looked at each other with fresh eyes. Cleansed of all the pent-up emotions, they prepared to start a friendship.

footnotes

Anger, frustration, and resentment are like toxins. When you allow them to fester, they eat away at your life. Joy becomes an exception to your rule. When you want something to be better for you, make it happen. Grumbling, moaning, and sulking will not change your situation; it will just make it more unpleasant and longer lasting. You are the only one who can affect change.

Think about what makes you angry, resentful or frustrated. No one has to have that type of power over you – and if they do – snatch your power back! When negativity rises up inside you – think about some strategies to harness that emotion. Besides, nobody wants to hang around a Betty Buzzkill.

Write in your journal about your emotions and how you can better handle them. Is it confronting a person who has hurt you? Conquering a fear? Learning to forgive? Controlling your reactions? Learning to listen so you hear what the other person is trying to tell you?

Ask for what you want. Make a plan to achieve it and then put into action those tasks that will help you reach your goals. Waiting, wishing, and hoping is useless unless you have a Fairy Godmother. And I can tell you, there are just not enough to go around!

CHAPTER thirty-four

"I dreamt I was in that home makeover show and when the crowd yelled 'Move that bus!' and I went inside, it was like a huge walk-in closet. There were lights everywhere, and my shoes were all organized, and my favorite ones were on these pedestals that were all lit up, like they belonged in a museum or something, and all the clothes still had tags on them. It was all bright and new," bubbled Morgan.

"So that's your dream house, huh?" asked Sam, poking at the cherry tomato on his salad, which avoided his spear and rolled onto the table. He picked it up with his fingers and popped it into his mouth.

Although Sam had grown up with three sisters, he'd never understood the fascination with clothes and shoes and closets that they all shared. His entire wardrobe fit in a closet and one dresser, with room to spare. His most valued garments were his Boston Red Sox and New England Patriots hats and jerseys, which had their own section in his closet. So, he thought, he could maybe understand a little why some clothes could feel important to a person.

"That's the funny thing. That's not my dream house. Yeah, I want big closets—I mean, who doesn't?—but this dream didn't feel like it was about my stuff or shopping or designer bags—although, don't get me wrong, the bags were amazing—but I think it was maybe more about my life," Morgan said earnestly.

"What do you mean? Your life is in a closet?"

She rolled her eyes and gave Sam the "don't mess with me" face. He bowed his head like a dog that had just been slapped on the nose.

"No. I think it's because my life is a makeover. Everything in my life right now feels shiny and new, like clothes with the tags still on because I haven't worn any of them yet. But in the dream, I wanted to. I wanted to go through everything and try it on and see how it looked. You know, it wasn't even as though the closet was *crammed* with stuff, so this dream wasn't about compulsive shopping or even about being a clothes whore— um, sorry." She paused for a second and Sam smiled. "The clothes were few but fantastic! I think that says that your life should be about quality, not quantity."

"I think that's a good way to read it," Sam said, nodding. "So, it sounds like the changes you're making are doing a lot for you. You seem much happier and more confident than back when you were lying on the floor in my doorway."

"Puhhlease! That was maybe the worst night of my life. I was upset and confused and cranky."

"*Oh*, yeah," he agreed, a bit too vehemently.

"Let me give you a little tip here, Sam. When a woman says something bad about herself, you *never* agree. You either say nothing or you say, 'Oh no, you weren't cranky at all' or 'Those pants look amazing on you' or 'No, really, I love what you did with your hair!' Got it?"

"You'd think that after growing up in Estrogen Land, I would have learned something," Sam said, smiling, as he sipped his beer. "Okay, Morgan, you weren't cranky. And you looked amazing, in a rain-soaked sort of way." He thought again about what she'd said and decided to push back a bit. "But wait just a minute. You said it was the *worst* night of your life. Wasn't there maybe one little thing that didn't totally suck?"

Morgan looked at him, recognized he was fishing for a compliment, and took his hand in hers. She looked at him with longing and replied, "Oh, how could I have forgotten?" She stroked his hand with her thumb and added, "That pizza was amazing!"

Sam playfully slapped the back of her hand and went back to attacking his salad.

"Anyway, I do feel much better, thanks to you and a few others. Elizabeth is giving me some good advice, and I seem to have found a way to connect with Rosaria, and then there's Divinity, who is, oh . . ." Morgan stopped herself mid-sentence. At long last, I had become a real part of her life, one she counted among the people of value. I was touched. I patted her on the shoulder as she tried to regroup.

"Thank you, Morgan. I think you're special, too," I said gently. I decided not to push the moment but would grab my hug later, when no one else was around.

"Who is Divinity?" Sam asked.

"She's a friend. I actually met her earlier on the night I ended up at your apartment. We've gotten to know each other and, well, she's different, but she's been helpful in my getting better perspective on things."

"Hmm, maybe I can meet her sometime."

"Hmm, maybe you can," Morgan said with a smile. "So what's going on with you?"

"Not much," he replied. "I've been trying to get some new clients for the firm."

"Is business slow?"

"No, we're doing fine, but I just want a new challenge. I feel like I'm always doing the same thing for the clients I'm working with and it's not very exciting," he answered. Sam enjoyed tackling challenges—which probably made Morgan that much more intriguing to him—and he had lately been managing clients whose major issues had been solved. His appetite for building solutions wasn't being adequately fed.

"You ought to talk to Elizabeth. She's in an innovating mood right now and might be ready to spark some marketing for IdeaWerx."

"That's a good idea. I met her at Siobhan's reception. I liked her energy." Sam hadn't discussed business with Elizabeth that night. As much as he enjoyed a good networking opportunity, his mind hadn't been in business mode that evening.

"I wonder if I could get through her guard dog, though. Since you and Rosie the pit bull are now buddies, maybe you could put in a good word for me," Sam suggested.

"Ohmigod, if she heard you call her that, she'd probably smack you!" Morgan tried to picture Rosaria as a Rosie. Maybe without the sensible shoes and the frumpy clothes. Maybe if she laughed once in a while. "You know, I wonder . . ."

Morgan looked up from her Cobb salad, dressing on the side, and imagined a new and improved Rosaria. What was under that hard shell? What would Morgan unearth in Rosaria if she went digging?

"Uh, oh, you have a scheming look there, Ms. Demarest. What are you plotting, and please tell me I *don't* have to be involved." Sam wasn't a game player and definitely didn't do well with lying.

"I was just thinking that maybe I could help Rosaria be a little bit more 'Rosie'; that is, if she's willing to loosen up a little. She hinted that she isn't happy with herself. Maybe if we changed the packaging a little bit, she'd have a fresh outlook on life."

"And how do you propose nudging her into being your science experiment?" Sam had seen Rosaria only briefly at the gallery reception. She could certainly use a little help in the style department, but if she was as surly as Morgan said—and he had little doubt she was exaggerating—then she might not want to change her "packaging". You couldn't turn a grizzly bear into a teddy bear, he thought, and was afraid that Morgan might be getting ahead of herself and overstepping the boundaries of her revised relationship with Ms. Rosaria Vega.

"I don't know. I'll hint around. Makeovers can be a blast, or even just a spa day. When you pamper yourself, you come away feeling like a new person." Morgan drifted off to a spa in her mind. She imagined the full treatment, with the facial, massage, pedicure, and manicure—and an eyebrow waxing!—followed by getting her hair done and a trip to see Karina at Neiman's for a make-up refresher. "Seriously, Sam, you don't know what you're missing."

"I think there are some things that I just don't need to know or experience. Getting a pedicure is one of them," he pronounced, although he was a bit curious about what having your feet massaged felt like.

"Don't look now, Sam Baxter, but I think your Neanderthal is showing," Morgan whispered across the table. "This is the twenty-first century. Men get manicures and facials and, yes, even pedicures."

He made a gesture like he was tucking his shirt back into his pants. "Pardon me for exposing myself."

"Do *not* apologize for that!" I burst in. I had been wandering the restaurant, checking out the dishes and the dishing—some serious gossip was happening in the corner—and returned just in time to hear Sam's words. "My goodness, girl, is this a bad boy after all? What do we have here? Mr. Sam-Bam-Thank-You-Ma'am?"

Morgan was sipping her drink and snorted a healthy amount of Pepsi through her nose, then spit even more across the table and onto Sam's shirt.

"What *is* it with you and my shirts?" Sam teased, wiping the soda spray from his pale green oxford. "If we're going to keep seeing each other, I might have to start wearing bibs."

"If?" Morgan asked. "Is that a question, an invitation, or a challenge?"

Sam pondered a moment. This woman intrigued him. She was funny, smart, beautiful, and lighthearted. And given the fact that everything that was on her mind came through her lips, she seemed honest, too.

Sam pushed back his chair and stood up as if he were about to leave. He stepped over to Morgan, bent over, and brought his face so close to hers that he could see the flecks of gold in her hazel eyes. He put one hand on the back of her neck and stroked her hair as he brought his lips to her ear. "Given the way you and I connect, I would say the answer is 'yes' to all three."

With one hand on her neck, he cupped her face with the other and drew her mouth to his. His kiss sent heat through her entire body, curling her toes. Heck, just watching it curled *my* dang toes!

footnotes

Networking is a great way to make connections. Remember the *"Six Degrees of Kevin Bacon"* game? Well, it's based on the concept that says we are all just six connections away from any other person in the world. Whether you believe that theory or not, you can't argue that finding friends of friends of friends is a surefire way to broaden your opportunities. Take advantage of networking events. Use your Facebook page to ask for help with challenges. Reach out to the connections in your friends' networks. You never know when and where the next great thing is going to occur. As the saying goes, reach for the moon, because even if you don't make it, you'll land among the stars!

CHAPTER thirty-five

Rosaria was feeling strange this morning. Lighter. And her jaw was unclenched.

Ordinarily, she arrived at work a minimum of fifteen minutes early, prepared to do battle with the world. Her days began with a brief production meeting that included the entire team of programmers, each of whom needed to be reminded, day after day, that his or her presence was required. Inevitably, at least one of them was late, and the delays cut into her daily schedule, which started her off in an angry mood. If Rosaria could be on time every day, she reasoned, certainly the others could follow her lead.

Rosaria knew—although she would never admit it to anyone else—that she was in a chronically bad mood. She was tired of battling everyone and everything just to get her tasks accomplished. Their failures to comply became her failures to achieve. Yes, everyone was getting in her way. But where was this "way" even leading her? What were they preventing her from doing? More tasks? Rosaria knew that there was something more for her to do—and to be—but had not yet given herself the luxury of dreaming. Dreaming was frivolous, and there was no time to imagine what could be—not when what *must* be was staring her square in the face every day.

At her desk, she looked at today's schedule (which wasn't necessary, because she habitually memorized every task and appointment, and prepared a priorities list for the following day before she left her desk each afternoon—or evening, as was usually the case). Morgan was coming in to talk about the plans for the launch party. They had made some progress, having chosen the theme and caterer. Morgan was brainstorming ideas for activities and entertainment. Rosaria had already developed the guest list and segmented it by the value of each individual and his or her potential for building IdeaWerx's business. Her top tier VIPs would receive personal notes in their invitations, all of which would be hand-addressed, and Elizabeth would do the personal follow-up after the invitations were sent.

Rosaria looked at the notation for Morgan's appointment on her calendar: "MD". She'd used only Morgan's initials, which, in her mind, had meant giving Morgan the least possible acknowledgement. But now she was seeing the woman in a different light. Not as an adversary, nor a flitty little flake. Maybe that was why she was feeling a bit lighter this morning. She had one less burden to carry on her shoulders.

The morning production meeting took place at eight-thirty, as always. And, as usual, one of the staff—Benjamin—waltzed in late. Elizabeth, to her credit, started the meeting on time, but then had to backtrack to catch up with the inconsiderate fool who couldn't seem to have his butt in the chair on time. Rosaria looked at Benjamin and pictured him with a shock collar around his neck, herself holding the controls. Zap! She smiled at the image of him twitching and contorting in his chair.

Morgan arrived at nine-fifteen, as scheduled, and Rosaria was thankful that at least someone respected the clock. They sat in Rosaria's office, going through their notes, checking on progress from their last discussion, and batting around ideas to make the party memorable to the guests so that when they considered their choice of software developer, IdeaWerx would be at the top of their minds. Morgan discovered that she actually enjoyed swapping thoughts with Rosaria; there was a creative individual cloistered underneath Rosaria's rigid exterior. Granted, Rosaria didn't release the inner "Rosie" willingly, but she showed brief glimpses when she offered things like, "Maybe we could have paper on the walls and markers so that people could write graffiti, maybe ask questions or answer others. Elizabeth loves having her white boards for what she calls 'ideating.'"

"I love that!" exclaimed Morgan, who noted the thought on her smartphone. Her enthusiasm seemed to startle Rosaria, but also pleased and encouraged her. Morgan was more excited by Rosaria's own "ideating" than by the idea itself, although it definitely sounded like a unique addition to the festivities.

After they spent the scheduled half-hour discussing the party, Morgan decided to poke around a bit to test her theory about the makeover. "Rosaria," she said, "this is a totally different subject, but I was thinking of going for a spa treatment and wondered if you might want to come along. We could use the time to talk more about the plans and also give ourselves some much-needed pampering."

Rosaria looked at Morgan as though she'd just suggested they strap on bungee cords and dive naked from a bridge at rush hour. She pondered a moment before responding, and she realized that Morgan was extending a friendly invitation, something that was truly strange to her. It did not compute, and her mind struggled with the foreign concept. While she processed the thought, Morgan looked at her hopefully.

"I don't know," Rosaria started, very slowly. Then she recalled the gift certificate in her drawer. She reached in and pulled it out, examining the envelope in her hand. "Actually, Elizabeth gave me this gift certificate to her spa. I suppose I should use it. I've never been to a spa. It's not really the kind of thing I would do with my time."

"Ohmigod! This is perfect, Rosaria! Obviously Elizabeth wanted you to experience the spa, and you have a perfectly good gift certificate just sitting there. I'm not even going to ask how long it has been percolating there in your drawer. Okay, so listen, let's plan to do this as soon as possible. Weekends are out because we'll be stuck in with crowds. And it's somehow more decadent to go on a weekday. How about Thursday? Can you get some time? I don't work Thursdays, and I'm sure that you never ever take a day off, so Elizabeth shouldn't mind if you took some time, right? Just tell her we're going to be working on the event planning and need to do some field work, which is true, too."

Rosaria wasn't convinced. She was also inexperienced at asking for favors from her boss, or from anyone, for that matter. "I don't know . . ."

The ringing of her phone interrupted her pondering. She picked up the receiver and heard Benjamin's voice: "Hey, Rosaria, can you send me the meeting notes from today? I think Elizabeth mentioned a contact I need to have, the guy I need to call about the networking issue."

"It's Terry Mozzetta. And the 'guy' is a woman," Rosaria corrected him, with controlled anger.

"Whatever. Can you just shoot me that info? Thanks."

He hung up before waiting for her response. Rosaria replaced the receiver and stared at the phone. She could feel the fury bubbling up inside. If the heat of her anger could come through her eyes, the phone would have melted like butter on a hot frying pan. Once again, she was being called upon to make up for the team's weaknesses. And, in return for helping, she would get nothing but another snide remark passed from one person to the other, behind her back. What was the point?

Morgan saw the change in Rosaria's face, from calm to contorted. In the past, she would never have pried into Rosaria's business but decided to test the boundaries of their new and improved relationship.

"Something wrong?"

And that was all it took. Rosaria was clearly ready to let out her pent-up frustration, because she let loose with a verbal tirade about the inconsiderate, irresponsible idiots she had to contend with every day. She told Morgan about the incessant tardiness at the daily meeting and how it sparked her anger every morning.

"Why don't you just lock the conference room door when the meeting starts and put a sign on the door, like 'Meeting in Progress. Do Not Disturb', and tell everyone that if they're not there on time, they'll be locked out?"

Rosaria's first reaction to the suggestion was to knock it down, but before she could put words to that thought, she considered it again. "Not a bad idea. But I'd have to get Elizabeth to agree."

"I think she would appreciate you handling it. She seems to believe in delegating responsibilities. Why don't you pass it by her and see what she says?"

"I will. Thanks."

Rosaria's mind once again returned to processing the spa invitation. Her brain put the idea of pampering on a mental scale and weighed it against the worth of being the caretaker for the thankless men in her office. Fun versus frustration. It was an equation she had never considered.

She looked at Morgan with a smile that slowly spread across her face as she again envisioned Benjamin writhing from the maximum jolt on his shock collar. "I think Thursday will be fine," she said in her friendliest tone. And she made a mental note to delay sending Terry Mozzetta's contact information to Benjamin. She was suddenly feeling like taking a little time for herself, rather than wasting it on wiping the noses of the office boys.

footnotes

The problem with being as diligent a caretaker as Rosaria is that you forget to take care of the one person who really matters: yourself. When life starts throwing you an onslaught of mudballs, take it as a sign that you need to step back and give yourself a break. You're probably tired—emotionally and physically—and that fatigue is taking its toll on your ability to make good decisions and productive use of your time. When you make your daily To Do list, be sure to schedule in at least fifteen minutes of uninterrupted "Me Time" . . . and make that an appointment you can't cancel!

CHAPTER thirty-six

"Mmm mmm mmm," I said as I looked around the lobby of the Three Birches Day Spa. I felt as if I had walked into a dream. Three white birch trees—thus, the name—grew from the center of the atrium's bamboo floor and rose up to the sun beaming through the skylights. The furniture was a blend of ergonomic seats and plush sofas, with a color palette of soft greens, rich browns, and pale gold to mirror a woodland setting. "Am I in the Garden of Eden?" I asked. "Where is Adam? And bring me an apple!"

Morgan ignored me. She had been there before so the splendor of the surroundings was nothing new to her. Still, how could you not marvel at this ambience tucked in a corner of downtown Chicago?

"I feel like a wood nymph. Where are my wings when I want them?" I skipped over to one of the trees and pretended to hide behind it, peeking at Morgan, who was doing her usual "Oh-Divinity" eye roll. Of course, this tree was not a redwood and could not, therefore, hide my wonderfully full figure. I ran over to the currently unoccupied sofa and threw myself on it. As a Fairy Godmother, I am weightless, of course, but I can still enjoy a soft cushion under my backside.

Morgan touched her Bluetooth headset so it would appear she was on the phone. "Dee, you need to pull yourself together if you're going to stick around. I can't have you distracting me while I'm with Rosaria. She already thinks I've got a screw loose. I don't need to confirm it."

"Well, aren't *you* the party pooper," I said, sticking my tongue out at her. "Who's Betty Buzzkill *now*?"

"No. I am just trying to avoid any weirdness. As if having a Fairy Godmother isn't weird enough to begin with," Morgan replied, looking straight at me. "And how come you can't make yourself visible to other people?"

"I never said I *couldn't*, just that I'm *not*. There's a difference," I explained, shifting on the soft couch to get maximum comfort.

"Oh, I see. So making me look stupid talking to an invisible person is just your way of helping me? Real nice," Morgan replied, shaking her head at me.

"Listen to me, young lady. I've been in this job since long before you and your mama and your grandmama and your grandmama's grandmama were around, so I think I know what's best. The fewer people who see me, the more I can focus on you and less on talking with them. It's my job to make you the center of my world, girl, and I don't need those other connections. Everything I need is right up here," I said, tapping the side of my head.

"Well, I guess that makes sense . . . in a twisted sort of way. But tell me why you chose me as a client. Not that I don't appreciate your support here, Dee, but was I such a mess before?"

"Honey girl, it's not that you were a mess, but I could see that you had so far to go and could use a little help."

"Can you see into my future?" she asked hopefully, her brows shooting up like someone had just pinched her.

"I can see into your past but not your future," I explained. I saw the disappointment on her face, so I added, "I know that you possess a gift that will one day help other people. This is your journey, Morgan, my dear. I am only here to help steer you through some of the obstacles. And I assure you that my boss never makes mistakes when choosing our clients. Whatever you were meant to achieve, it will help the lives of others, not just your own. Directly or indirectly, that is not for me to know."

As Morgan considered my explanation, I pointed toward the door of the spa, where Rosaria was entering. She walked in purposefully but stopped as soon as she caught sight of the magnificent atrium. Her mouth dropped open. We watched the reaction from a distance, and I nudged Morgan to go over and welcome her. It appeared that Rosaria's feet were stuck in one spot, as if she had been painted into a corner.

"Hi, Rosaria. What do you think?" Morgan asked.

"This is amazing!" Rosaria beamed. "Who would think to do something like this in the city? I feel like I just stepped onto another planet."

"I know. It's beautiful. They make you feel great from the moment you walk in the door. But come on, it only gets better from here. Let's check in and get started!"

Morgan headed toward the reception desk, but Rosaria was still standing in the same place.

"Rosaria, you have to come with me. They don't do manicures and facials here in the lobby," Morgan teased. She slipped her arm through Rosaria's and led her toward the reception desk. I expected Rosaria to flinch at human contact, but she allowed herself to be led like a child. She was in foreign territory, and I imagined her defenses had been left at the door. This was going to be an interesting day!

Since Rosaria was a bit uncomfortable about having the spa treatments, I called for reinforcements, in the form of mimosas, which she clearly wasn't accustomed to, either. But halfway through her second drink, the champagne did the trick and I saw her shoulders relax and a smile creep up on her face.

Morgan and Rosaria were led to the spa's nail salon. Morgan opted for a French manicure, but Rosaria, to our mutual surprise, chose a vibrant red polish called Fiery Flame. The two women sat side by side while the manicurists filed and painted. Having never paid much attention to her nails, Rosaria's manicure was a bit more extensive than Morgan's.

"So, what do you think so far?" Morgan asked. "Are you enjoying this?"

"It's different," Rosaria replied as her manicurist massaged her hands and forearms. "But, yes, I think I like this."

"Did you feel that?" I broke in, wobbling back and forth like the floor was moving. "I think the walls are a-trembling. The earth is moving. And this woman is having—watch it now—*fun!*"

"You know, it's okay to do nice things for yourself once in a while, Rosaria," Morgan said. "You should never feel guilty about putting yourself first. If you don't do it, no one else will."

"It's just not something I can do. That was not how I was raised. You don't waste your time and the money you work hard for on something that is so . . . so frivolous," Rosaria replied. She was clearly conflicted that she was indulging herself instead of sitting at her desk. And I was sure she was calculating the cost of such guilty pleasures and thinking about what bills she could pay with the money.

"I understand, Rosaria, but life is full of hard times. I know you don't realize it, but

I've had them, too. And I've learned that if I don't remind myself that there are fun things that make me happy, I would just be miserable. Stuff like this is a reward for all those times when you've had to deal with rotten people or situations or just bad luck."

Rosaria considered Morgan's words. She weighed them against her practical side. There was a catfight going on in her head.

"Hey, Rosaria, it's okay," Morgan said in a hushed tone as she leaned toward her budding friend. "Go ahead and release your girl side."

Rosaria jerked her head in Morgan's direction. At first, I thought she was going to fire back with some crusty retort. Instead, Rosaria broke into a smile. She beamed at Morgan and then looked back at her newly polished fingernails.

During the pedicure, the women again sat side by side, their feet soaking in the warm, churning waters of the footbath. Rosaria was becoming chattier. She told Morgan more about her life, which totally revolved around her job. Rosaria had a few friends in her neighborhood, but they now had husbands and families. Most of her time with them involved either babysitting or being the third wheel at dinner. And none of them, she admitted, would ever go to a spa.

"Rosaria, think about it. You're young and single—free to do as you please. This is the time to give yourself little treats like this. Think about the emotional value of this investment," Morgan pushed. Emotional value? Investment? Who *was* this talking? "Give yourself permission to be nice to yourself. Shove off the guilt. That's just negative energy."

Rosaria pondered Morgan's words. She wanted to accept them as gospel, but it was all in such direct contrast to her belief system. She had not lived a joy-filled life. All she knew was hard work at all costs. But she had to admit that this was fun. And it was a damn sight better than the thankless job of playing Mommy to the lame guys in her office. She admired her nails and watched the pedicurist apply polish to her toenails. Yeah, things needed to change, she thought.

From the nail salon, they went to another area for facials. Rosaria, who did not like having her face touched, was wary, but the champagne was still working its magic. She didn't resist and actually enjoyed the experience. I even heard what sounded like a pleased little purr coming from her.

"While we're here, why don't we get your brows done?" Morgan suggested after they finished their facial. Now *that* was a bold move, I thought. Bravo for Morgan!

"What do you mean?" Rosaria asked suspiciously.

"They can clean up and reshape your brows, which will show off your eyes better. You really have great eyes, Rosaria." Morgan avoided the word "waxing", knowing it would put an end to the chance that we could all say goodbye to Rosaria's glaring unibrow.

Rosaria looked in a nearby mirror and rubbed her forefinger over her brows—well, *brow*, since it was one long, continuous caterpillar crawling from one temple to the next. She looked around at the brows on the women around her, and then back at Morgan. She smiled and simply said, "Sure."

The attendant guided Rosaria to a small room with a large chair that looked as if it had been rescued from a dentist's office and re-upholstered to look more chic. Rosaria sat down and stretched out.

Morgan distracted her while the attendant prepared the wax and applied it to the bridge of her nose, where the brows should naturally be separated. The warmth of the melted wax seemed to relax Rosaria, who lay there with her eyes closed and her hands folded together over her stomach. She had no idea what was coming.

This was like watching conjoined twins become detached, I thought as the tiny woman applied a gauzy strip to the warm wax. Then she settled her feet and prepared her grip. And in one fast movement, she ripped the strip from Rosaria's face, along with a patch of dark hair.

"Ouch!" Rosaria screeched. She sat bolt upright and shouted at the petite attendant holding a strip filled with Rosaria's brows. "What the hell are you doing?" She ran off a string of words in Spanish that I could only assume were not compliments.

Morgan tried to hold back a grin. She put her hands on Rosaria's shoulders to steady her as she tried to jump from the chair. "That's the worst of it," Morgan told her, looking at the red splotch that appeared where the eyebrows used to connect. "Seriously, some day you will thank me for this."

"You are an evil bitch!" Rosaria said, but with far less venom than the words might suggest. "I will get you for this!"

The attendant brushed a milky lotion on the spot to ease the pain. Slowly, she approached Rosaria with tweezers, intending to finish the job.

Rosaria held up a hand in protest. "Oh no, you don't! We are done here!"

The woman froze, looking at Morgan.

"Rosaria, you can't walk away from a task halfway through. That's what you're asking this woman to do, to leave her job undone." Morgan tried to appeal to Rosaria's powerful work ethic.

"I'm sure she can get a job with the CIA getting prisoners to talk." Rosaria practically spat out the words through her gritted teeth.

"Look on the bright side," Morgan added. "At least you're not getting a Brazilian wax."

I crossed my legs at the mere mention of those words. Rosaria gave Morgan her evil stare and then turned it on the attendant. "I don't even want to *know* what type of torture that involves."

Rosaria wiggled and twitched as her brows were plucked. At one point, she grabbed the wrist of her torturer and said in a low voice, "Be careful. I *know* people."

When the most painful part of the beautification process was done, Rosaria leaned forward in her chair to get a look in the mirror. She squinted and then rubbed her index finger along her newly shaped brows. The caterpillars that used to live above her deep-set brown eyes had been tamed. No, they were gone. What remained were two shapely brows that gave room to show off her beautiful eyes.

"What a difference!" Morgan gushed, squeezing Rosaria's shoulders excitedly.

"Okay," Rosaria said, raising one of her lovely brows. "You were right about the eyebrows. But I will get you back for the pain. Somehow. Some way. When you're not expecting it."

"You say that now, but you will thank me later, once the trauma has worn off." Morgan took a closer look at the reduced, reshaped, refined brows on Rosaria's face and smiled. "Oh yeah, you'll thank me, girl."

The women settled their bill. Rosaria's gift certificate covered just about everything. She had expected to have enough left over for another pedicure, which she had particularly enjoyed, but was shocked to discover how much the services cost.

"Okay, we have another stop," Morgan said, again slipping her arm through Rosaria's. Morgan effortlessly hailed a cab and gave the driver the address.

"Where are we going?" Rosaria asked with concern. Rosaria had asked Elizabeth to give her the morning off so she could run some errands with Morgan. Elizabeth had seemed genuinely pleased that the two women were finally working as a team, and when Rosaria had promised to return to work in the afternoon, Elizabeth had told her to take her time. So, Rosaria thought, perhaps a bit longer would be okay.

The cab stopped, Morgan paid the driver, and the women exited. Rosaria looked around to see where they were, and Morgan grabbed her arm and said, "This way." They entered a hair salon, where Morgan was warmly greeted. She introduced Rosaria to her stylist, Daniel, who gave Rosaria a close study.

"I see real potential here, sweetie," he said, as he lifted a few strands of Rosaria's hair. "You have nice texture. Color needs a boost. I'm thinking highlights."

"Nothing too bold, Daniel," Morgan cautioned. She saw Rosaria gaping at the images of over-styled models on the walls.

"Please," he dismissed her. "This is my craft, dear. Have you ever been unhappy when you left here?"

"No. You're a genius, Daniel. I bow to your greatness," Morgan teased. Daniel was clearly receptive to fawning. He smiled, turned, and slinked away, motioning Rosaria to follow, which she did, looking over her shoulder to make sure Morgan was close behind.

"How do you think I'd look with orange highlights?" I asked, browsing some photos as we walked.

"Like a very scary jack-o-lantern," Morgan replied in a hushed tone.

Daniel fussed over Rosaria, complimenting her skin and bone structure. Rosaria was soaking up the attention like water on a dry sponge. Because her hair was always pulled back, I had never realized how long it was. When Daniel released the clip that held it in a tight twist, it was like watching those scenes where the dowdy secretary tossed away her glasses and let down her hair to reveal a seductress. Rosaria wasn't exactly a seductress, but she certainly had the physical attributes if she could just learn how to use them!

"Are you sure about this?" she asked Morgan, as Daniel applied foils to her hair.

"Absolutely! You are going to be gorgeous! Daniel is an artist and knows exactly how to make a woman look fantastic."

Daniel smiled approvingly at Morgan and kept applying the pasty mix to Rosaria's hair, covering each one with foil until Rosaria looked like a science experiment. Once the highlights were done, Morgan advised Daniel to keep Rosaria turned away from the mirror. "This has to be a total surprise," she told them both.

"Let's hope it's a good surprise," I added, unsure if Daniel would go over the top. So far everything looked good, but now he had scissors in his hand and a gleeful look in his eye, like a starving man about to dive into a two-pound steak. He snipped, fluffed, dried, feathered, scrunched, poofed, and spritzed. The three of us stood back and gave Rosaria's new look a studied glance. Morgan was absolutely giddy, and I had to admit that this style was a five-hundred percent improvement. Daniel spun Rosaria around to look in the mirror.

Rosaria did a double take, staring. She reached from under the cape that covered her up and touched her newly coiffed hair to see if the image in the mirror was her own. Her brown hair had been altered to a rich auburn, with several hues of golden highlights artfully placed around her face. Her hair fell in soft layers around her face, which was transforming from disbelief to pleasure.

"What do you think?" Daniel and Morgan said in unison.

"Wow!" was all she could muster.

"I agree. She looks gorgeous." I walked over and whispered in Rosaria's ear. "You look gorgeous!"

She smiled, genuinely moved. "I—I didn't know I could look like this." Her voice was choked with emotion, and Morgan looked ready to cry herself.

"We're not quite done, Rosaria," she added.

"But I have to get back to work," Rosaria resisted lightly. "Elizabeth will wonder where I am."

"Let her know you've been delayed. This is important!"

Rosaria dialed Elizabeth but got her voicemail. She left an apologetic message that said her tasks were taking longer than she'd expected. She hung up, feeling better now that she had reported in to her boss, but a bit concerned that she hadn't actually spoken with her. Meanwhile, Morgan settled the bill with Daniel, using a gift certificate she had been saving. She gave him her usual generous tip and whispered something in his ear. When Rosaria got off the phone, she reached for her wallet and asked Daniel how much she owed.

"This one's on the house, sweetie," he said. "Just take good care of that gorgeous hair!"

Rosaria thanked him and offered a pleasant smile. Then she shot Morgan a questioning look when she saw Daniel's far-too-obvious wink to Morgan, who just shrugged it off.

"Morgan, I do have things to do today. I don't like to fall behind," said Rosaria.

"This is important, too, Rosaria. We are recharging your batteries so you can be even more productive when you get back to work," she said.

It sounded good, but Rosaria wasn't buying it.

"I am already so distracted that I can't even remember my To Do list. I hope this isn't going to take much longer," she replied. But Rosaria had already caved, a sign that she was truly enjoying herself. Still, she had at least issued a warning shot that she hadn't forgotten her responsibilities.

"Not to worry. One more stop and then we can get you back to work!" Morgan said cheerfully.

Outside the salon, they walked two blocks to Neiman Marcus. When they entered the store, Rosaria stopped dead in her tracks. "Oh, no! If you're going to try to get me to spend a fortune on a new outfit, I can't. That's just too far. I have bills to pay, and I am very careful about managing my budget."

"Take it easy. We are not clothes shopping. I brought you here to meet my friend, Karina."

They wove through the maze of make-up counters, where heavily painted women eyed them curiously. I was sure a few of them were dying to get their brushes on Rosaria, the woman with a beautiful hairstyle and no makeup. But Morgan led us purposefully to a counter where an attractive woman in her mid-forties was straightening up the display. Karina was about five feet eight inches tall, slender and stylish. She looked like an ex-model who had matured beautifully, without the help of Botox. Her makeup was artfully applied with a delicate hand, looking very natural.

"Karina, I'd like to introduce you to my friend." Morgan paused. "Rosie!"

Rosaria looked at Morgan. I was ready for her to correct the "mistake", but Rosaria just extended her hand to Karina instead.

"Hello, Rosie. So nice to meet you!" said Karina, who was simply dressed in a beige silk blouse and tailored black slacks—with beige stilettos that brought her height to about six feet.

"Rosie and I are having a chick day. We just came from Three Birches and Daniel. Now I'd like for you to show Rosie how easy it is to do some simple makeup," Morgan said.

Karina directed Rosaria to take a seat on the elevated stool. She looked at her face from a few angles and asked about her normal skin care regime.

"I wash my face twice a day," was Rosaria's response.

"You have beautiful skin, but you're going to want to take care so that it stays that way as you get older. Now, how much time do you want to spend doing your makeup?" Karina asked, still assessing Rosaria's face.

"None. I don't do make-up."

"But you *will*," Morgan added. "Let's keep it simple, Karina."

In the next few minutes, Karina gently applied a light concealer and a powdered mineral foundation to Rosaria's face. Morgan had never looked closely at her new friend, mainly because Rosaria was usually shooting eye daggers at her. But Morgan had to admit that Rosie had lovely features—almond-shaped dark eyes, pouty lips, and sculpted cheekbones. Karina worked soft brown lines on Rosaria's lids and dabbed on subtle golden highlights under her newly discovered brows. She added mascara and brushed blush to her cheeks and above the brows. Then she finished the look with lip gloss in a shiny shade of cranberry. Morgan and I watched the transformation in complete amazement. I wished we'd had the foresight to take a "Before" photo to show the stunning impact of this makeover.

Karina handed Rosaria a mirror. Rosaria looked at herself, then held the mirror farther from her face to get a broader view. She shifted her head to the left and then to the right, and dabbed lightly at her glossy lips.

"Rosie, I have to say that you look absolutely incredible!" gushed Morgan.

Rosaria continued to gaze into this magic mirror, afraid that if she put it down, she would turn back into the pre-Cinderella frump she had been this morning. "I don't know what to say," she stammered. "I had no idea this would make such a difference."

Rosaria's eyes brimmed with happy tears. Karina handed her a tissue.

"Be careful! Just dab! You don't want to smudge that gorgeous face!" Morgan told her. She took a tissue and dabbed at Rosaria's eyes for her. Rosaria grabbed Morgan's hand and held it tightly for a moment, her damp eyes sending a simple, heartfelt message that words could not adequately convey: thank you.

footnotes

Why do so many women see pampering as frivolous and impractical? You take your car to be tuned up. You take yourself, your kids, and your pets for annual checkups. But you don't look after your own emotional needs.

Recognize the importance of "Me Time" and give yourself permission to enjoy those moments, guilt-free, on a regular basis. Whether you just sit quietly and enjoy a cup of tea from a china cup, take up a hobby, go for a walk, take a bubble bath, or just linger in bed for an extra fifteen minutes, the times you take to recharge your emotional batteries are an investment in your well-being. And there is nothing frivolous about that!

CHAPTER thirty-seven

Rosaria had been looking at her watch every ten minutes since we'd left the spa. She had clearly not shed the guilt of taking time off work for personal reasons—although, God knows, she deserved it since she had never done so in the three years she had worked for IdeaWerx. But old habits die hard. And I suspected this one might never hit the pavement.

Rosaria looked fabulous—from the neck up, and, of course, her hands. Her perfectly pedicured feet were fully ensconced in her faux leather, low-heeled nun shoes, so no one could appreciate them. If Rosaria were to get arrested right then, her mug shot would be totally hot. But the clothing was a complete and utter fire extinguisher! I knew that Morgan felt the same way, but she was battling Rosaria's clock-watching and there simply wasn't time to shop for a new outfit.

If Rosaria were my charge, I would have helped her out with a little of my special talents, but she wasn't. Still, I thought, Morgan must be wishing that Rosaria's look could be complete. So, by whipping up a little fashion help, I would actually be supporting *my* girl. Sounded like reasonable rationale.

As we came around the next corner, I shot a quick elbow to Morgan's side, not so much that it would cause her to double over, but so I could grab her attention, which was currently focused on Rosaria's very sad shoes. I jerked my head in the direction of the store window to our right. It was another upscale resale store, and there in the window was a dress that would be ideal for our now-lovely Latina. The abstract jersey print of black, grey, and yellow had a somewhat plunging—depending on your cleavage—neckline, long sleeves, and a fitted waist that dropped to a gently flowing skirt that would reach just above the knee on a woman of average height. On Rosaria, it would head farther south, but it could work.

Morgan pulled up in her tracks and jerked Rosaria by the arm, pulling her backward and slightly off-balance.

"Hey! What are you doing?" Rosaria yelped.

"Come on. We have a quick pit stop," Morgan told her, pulling her toward the door of the store.

"No!" Rosaria declared, setting herself firmly. "I have to get back to work. This has been fun, but I don't have any more time."

"Five minutes, Rosie. Give me five minutes. You look amazing, but we need to finish what we started," Morgan explained.

"Oh, I suppose you're going to give me another lecture about how it's just not right to prevent someone from finishing their task, right? Well, that worked once today. No more. Morgan. I'm going to work *right now!*"

This was a critical moment, and Morgan was losing the battle. I had to do something. With a flick of my wrist, a puddle appeared by the curb where Rosaria was standing, her hands planted on her hips. That was when a passing cab splashed a spray of mud that hit her full on the back. It managed to miss her perfectly coiffed hair, but her dress, legs, and shoes were soaked.

She jumped away from the curb in horror, spewing a litany of expletives at the cab in both English and Spanish.

"Okay, now you *have* to change your clothes. And it just so happens we can take care of that right here, in this store, in just a few minutes," said Morgan calmly. She walked over and put her arm around Rosaria's shoulder, just above where the muddy mess had landed. She gently moved the other woman into the store, with Rosaria looking about as happy as a mugging victim.

Once inside, Morgan made a beeline to the dress in the window. She asked the saleswoman if her friend could try it on. Rosaria stood there, arms folded in defiance across her chest—not moving, not browsing, not caring. The woman removed the mannequin from the display and disrobed it. She handed the dress to Rosaria, who snatched it and headed for the dressing room.

"What size shoes do you wear, Rosie?" Morgan called as she headed to the footwear display.

"Six," came the growled response from behind the dressing room door.

Morgan picked through the shoes and ogled a pair of hot pink stilettos in perfect condition. "Ohmigod! These are amazing!"

She slipped them on and achieved a state of footwear euphoria. The price tag said eighty-five dollars, but she knew that, brand new, they would sell for about four hundred. She tucked them under her arm and kept searching for a pair for Rosaria.

"Excuse me," I said. "I don't believe we are here to expand your wardrobe, Morgan. Back away from the stilettos. We need to find something for Rosaria."

"Listen," she practically spat at me through gritted teeth, "I have been really good lately. I haven't bought a thing for myself. And if you know what's good for you, you will back off right now."

I expected her head to start spinning around and her eyes to glow red. I put up my hands in fearful surrender. I should have known better than to come between a fiery shoe ho and her hot pink stilettos.

It was hard to find a size six among the selection, so—without Morgan's knowledge—I once again helped things along. In just a few minutes, she found a pair of black Gucci pumps with a two-and-a-half-inch heel. Not exactly a stiletto, they functioned as a starter pair to transition Rosaria from low-heeled boring footwear to something that made a statement, like, "Stand back. Here she comes!"

Morgan slipped the shoes under the dressing room door. "Try these on. They'll look great with that dress."

"Isn't there something with a lower heel?" Rosaria asked. "I can't walk in these."

"You'll learn. Trust me."

"Hmph," came the mumbled reply.

A moment later, Rosaria emerged. She wobbled on the shoes as if they were stilts but otherwise looked stunning. The dress's v-neck accentuated her ample but not-too-full bust. The soft lines of the skirt exposed a small waist and curvy hips—fuller than Morgan's tight little tush but not quite J-Lo badonka-donk. And, since the woman was far too cheap to pay for a cab, all that walking earned her a pair of legs that deserved to be displayed and admired, not hidden under lengths of lifeless skirts. Morgan and

I were both stunned. Rosaria Vega was a real looker.

"Whoa! Why have you been hiding that figure, Rosie?" Morgan asked.

"This is ridiculous! I don't dress like this. Isn't there something in here that is more appropriate?"

"We could see if there's a convent nearby," I offered.

"The clothes you have been wearing are designed for Rosaria. We are here to dress Rosie, a woman of style, confidence, and beauty!" Morgan shot back.

The saleswoman had been listening to this exchange and finally added her two cents. "May I say something? I think that dress is perfect for you. Your friend is right. You have a beautiful figure, and you shouldn't hide it. Most women, including me, would kill to look as good as you do right now. If you don't buy that dress and those shoes, you are making a huge mistake."

"Thank you," Morgan said to her, making no attempt to mask her smugness.

All heads turned at the sound of the door opening. A tall, handsome man, about thirty years old, stepped in. He was dressed in a lavender shirt with a navy tie and slacks. His dark beard was closely cropped to his tanned skin. "Excuse me," he said in a deep voice. "I'm looking for the coffee shop that's supposed to be near here."

As he spoke, his blue eyes darted in our direction. I think we all wanted to shout, "Pick me! Pick me! I like coffee!" Even Rosaria was clearly affected by this man's hot looks. She blushed, fidgeted, and tugged at the hem of her dress.

The saleswoman smiled flirtatiously and gave him directions. He turned and headed toward the door. In passing, he shot an appreciative look at Rosaria and said, "Nice dress."

We all watched him leave. The view was almost as pleasant as watching him come in. When the door shut behind him, everyone turned to look at Rosaria.

"Okay," she said, "I'm buying the dress, the shoes, the whole thing. And what else have you got?"

"More importantly," I added, "who feels like going for coffee?"

footnotes

The Marines have a saying: "No man left behind." On the battlefield, you don't abandon a fellow soldier in need. Take a lesson from this. When you see a friend making a mistake, step in and help. Sure, a fashion emergency isn't life-threatening, but when you realize how potent the right combination of clothing can be to a person's mindset and outlook—particularly one as stifled as Rosaria's—step in and help your fellow would-be fashionista make the most of what she has going for her!

CHAPTER thirty-eight

Benjamin had not received the meeting notes he had requested from Rosaria, and he knew that Elizabeth would soon be expecting an update. He had sent Rosaria two emails and left a voicemail reminding her that he needed Terry's contact information, but Rosaria still had not responded. He finally had to resort to going to her office—a place that none of the programmers ever wanted to enter because, as they all knew, she was one POB (Pissed Off Bitch). Why did Elizabeth put up with her sour moods and constant griping? Rosaria acted as though she was the only one in the company with a brain—though, since most of the programmers had advanced degrees and, to the best of his knowledge, Rosaria hadn't yet earned her Bachelor's, he doubted very much that she was the genius here.

The tall, lanky man was sitting at Rosaria's computer—doing a search for the meeting notes, which were, of course, filed under "Meeting Notes" on her desktop—when we arrived back at IdeaWerx. He didn't see us come in, but Rosaria certainly caught sight of him invading her space. She started to charge forward, but Morgan held her back.

"Let's just give this new look a test drive, shall we?" she whispered to a red-faced Rosaria. She motioned for Rosaria to follow behind her.

"Hi," Morgan said cheerfully as she walked in on Benjamin. She had met him and his colleagues on a prior visit when Elizabeth had given her a tour of the offices. Morgan had wanted to see the product they would be celebrating at the upcoming party, and he had given her a demo of the software program.

Benjamin was just hitting the Send button to email the long-awaited document to himself. He looked up briefly. "Hey, Morgan, what's up?"

"Not much. What are you doing?"

He rose from Rosaria's chair and came around the desk. "I needed a file from Rosaria's computer and she hasn't been here all day. I couldn't wait, so I came and got it myself."

He gave a quick nod of acknowledgement to the attractive woman standing behind Morgan. *This place is starting to fill up with hotties,* he thought. *So glad that Elizabeth is bringing in some women who don't look and act like frustrated man-haters.*

"Luckily, she's very organized, so it wasn't hard to find. But if you see her . . ."

He stopped. His brain finally processed the image before him and registered Morgan's companion as Rosaria. "Hey, uh, Rosaria. How you doing? Wow. Um. You look really different. You got your hair done, huh? Really, really nice."

Combine shock with salivating lust and that would just about describe Benjamin at this moment.

He blinked repeatedly, made some strange faces, and continued, "So, well, wow. Um. I'm sorry I went into your computer, but I needed Terry's contact information, and, well, I hope you're not mad."

She stared him down, saying nothing. She was either enjoying his surprise at her makeover or just seething to a boiling point. Morgan and I waited and watched, neither one of us sure how she would respond.

"I understand, Benjamin. I'm sorry you had to go out of your way," she said, controlling her temper with far more restraint than I would have believed she could manage.

Benjamin was clearly relieved. While Rosaria thought he considered her an annoyance, he actually feared her wrath. I wasn't sure which caught him most by surprise: her new and enormously improved appearance or this lack of extended claws ready to shred him.

"No . . . no problem. Um, thanks. And really, Rosaria, you look great. Really, really great!" He backed out of her office, never taking his eyes off her. Once he passed the threshold to the hallway, he made a hasty retreat.

"He's running back there to tell the guys about your transformation," Morgan said. "Just wait. There will be a steady stream of them coming in here for lame reasons, just to check you out."

"Great. I really want to be the object of their nerdish curiosity," she said flatly.

"Better than the object of their ridicule, though," Morgan reminded her.

Rosaria's phone rang. She picked it up, muttered a short "right away", and hung up.

"Excuse me, that was Elizabeth. She doesn't sound very good." Rosaria paused nervously. She wondered what Elizabeth would think of this new look. Certainly, she would approve. She was the one who had given Rosaria the gift certificate to get spruced up a bit. *She'll be glad I used it,* Rosaria thought. She grabbed a notepad and headed down the hall, still wobbling on her stilettos-in-training.

Morgan started to follow after Rosaria, but I stopped her.

"Where do you think you're going?" I asked, blocking her passage. And believe me, I can put up a good blockade.

"I want to see Elizabeth's reaction," she said, looking at me as if I should know that obvious fact.

"This is not a sorority. It's a place of business. If you want to get all girly-girl, you do it after hours," I chided her.

"Seriously? Are you kidding me? I did all this work and I don't get to see the finale?" Morgan's voice pitched up about an octave and a half. If I pushed it, she might hit a note that only dogs could hear.

"Seriously. You don't belong in there. Just wait right here. And I'm guessing there will be enough noise that you can get the gist of it anyway."

"Yeah. You're probably right," she conceded.

"Ooh, I bet that hurt coming out of your mouth, huh? Do you need a breath mint now?"

She returned my fire with, "No, but you might want to take a chill pill."

Meanwhile, Rosaria had walked into Elizabeth's office and sat down opposite her. Elizabeth was typing something into her computer as she started to speak.

"Well, I'm glad you're back. This has *not* been a good day . . ." Her voice came to a halt as she looked up and saw the new and improved Rosaria. "What . . . ohmigod, look at you! Holy . . . You look completely different! I wouldn't recognize you if I ran into you on the street."

She sat and stared at Rosaria, assessing every change as only another woman can. She took in the absence of the unibrow, the highlights in Rosaria's hair, and the glossy lips. She could only see the dress from the waist up because Rosaria was seated, but it was clearly a complete shift from the frumpy cardigans, oversized blouses, and boring skirts she usually wore. And the neckline! Who knew that Rosaria had such shape?

"Morgan took me to the spa, and I used the gift certificate you gave me. Then we went to her hairdresser, and, well, it just kept going from there," Rosaria said, feeling relieved that Elizabeth seemed to approve of the new look.

"Wait—that's how you spent your 'morning' off?" Elizabeth asked. "I thought you were going to be back after lunch. I've been waiting for you for over three hours. If you had wanted to take a full day to go off and play dress-up, then you should have told me so I wouldn't be counting on you."

"I'm—I'm sorry, Elizabeth. I tried. I just didn't think—"

"No, you didn't think, did you? Well, this is a workday—for me, anyway. I've been sitting here all day, doing my job *and* yours. I can expect this type of silliness from Morgan, but you, Rosaria, are better than that!"

When Morgan became excited or agitated, her voice got chirpier. Elizabeth's became deeper and louder. So her harsh words carried down the hall, all the way to Morgan's waiting ears.

Morgan was stunned by the cutting remark. "Silliness?" she repeated to me. "I can't believe she said that! I thought she had some respect for me. I had no idea she thinks of me like all those other people who have underestimated me."

Morgan started to head toward Elizabeth's office to confront her. And I didn't stand in her way. It was good for her to stand up for herself, and I knew that she found Elizabeth rather intimidating, so this burst of fiery confidence felt like a positive step—even though the consequences might get ugly.

But Morgan stopped. Instead of charging into Elizabeth's office, she turned around and headed for the lobby, where she started to pace.

"I'm too angry to talk to her right now, but I think Rosaria is going to need a friend. I can't believe Elizabeth could be so selfish and cruel! Rosaria has been so loyal, so hardworking, and she finally takes a little time for herself and this is what happens! I would think that another woman would understand how important this is to Rosaria. I mean, she put herself out there and let me change her all around, and she was feeling good about it, really good." Morgan looked at me for reassurance that she hadn't imagined the whole thing. I nodded and let her continue. "And then Elizabeth just slaps her in the face. Total smackdown. I just can't believe it!"

Rosaria hurried down the hall, her head down. She sat at her desk and started typing on her computer, quickly wiping a tear from her cheek. She completely ignored Morgan, who had come in and sat before Rosaria. Morgan looked at her friend, wanting to say something but unable to find the words.

"Rosaria, I'm sorry. I heard what Elizabeth said, and she is totally wrong," she started.

Rosaria's head snapped up. The daggers had returned to her eyes. "No!" she spat out. "She's not wrong. I was. I shouldn't have listened to you. I do one thing, *one thing*, that goes against my every instinct, against everything I believe in, who I am, and you see what happens? God is punishing me for being foolish and trying to be someone I am not." She was choking back tears of anger, hurt, and frustration.

"God is not punishing you. Elizabeth is. And I guarantee you that Elizabeth is *not* God. You just let her push you around, and it's not fair. You had every right, every damn right, to take time off and do something for yourself," Morgan said.

"I didn't do it for myself. If it was for myself, I would have stayed here and done my job, like I am supposed to do," Rosaria replied, hitting the keys with such power that I was surprised a few of them didn't pop off. "I did it because I wanted to try to be friends. And you can see where *that* got me. Just leave me alone, Morgan. Leave me alone!"

Slowly, Morgan got up and walked out of Rosaria's office. She lingered in the hall, trying to decide her next step. *We made so much progress today,* she thought. *I can't believe it all ended this way.*

And with that, she made her choice. Morgan headed down the hall and marched into Elizabeth's office. She stood in front of the desk, choosing not to sit. Elizabeth looked up at her, questioningly at first and then with anger.

"Yes?" she said.

"Silliness, huh? So you think I'm just some stupid girl who has nothing better to do than play 'dress-up'. That's what you think of me, Elizabeth? Am I really that much of a useless idiot in your eyes?"

"I see that eavesdropping is a skill I didn't give you credit for. Well, don't expect me to stand up and applaud you, Morgan. While you two were off playing, I was here dealing with a major catastrophe. It must be nice to always have someone else picking up after you. I wouldn't know. I work for a living. I work damn hard," she seethed.

"I thought we were friends, Elizabeth. I thought you had some respect for me. Clearly, I was mistaken. What kind of mentor *are* you?" Morgan asked, as though she were seeing Elizabeth's beautiful exterior peel away to reveal some venom-spitting demon.

"Let me remind you, Morgan, that you came to *me*. I did not seek you out."

"No, you're right. I thought you were someone special," Morgan said.

"I didn't ask to make your dreams come true, Morgan. I'm *not* your fairy godmother!"

"No. You certainly aren't."

Morgan turned on her four-inch stilettos and stomped down the hall. At some point, when she was calmer, I would tell her how proud she had just made me. And that I was certain that her dreams *would* come true.

footnotes

Putting people on a pedestal is a grave mistake. Eventually, they will fall. And when they do, your belief system can come crashing down with them. Everyone makes mistakes—even mentors. Be prepared that everyone—including a mentor whom you might have elevated to a pedestal—can be wrong. While it's important to set expectations, reality will sometimes dash them. Learning how to deal with those disappointments is what will keep you moving forward. Take out your journal and make a list of the mentors in your life. You may have just one person, or different mentors for different aspects of your life: spiritual mentor, financial mentor, fitness mentor, business mentor, health mentor, etc. Write them down. Then, next to each one, list the help they provide as well as what you still hope to learn from them. Keep building on this list and remind yourself of your needs and expectations. And cut them a little slack when they occasionally have a misstep.

CHAPTER thirty-nine

Elizabeth was sitting alone in her office, feeling lousy about the way she had treated Morgan and Rosaria. She had let a bad day get the best of her, which brought out the worst in her.

The morning had started with yet another race to get the kids ready for school, another fashion battle with Lara, and another delay while they searched for Erich's missing homework. Meanwhile, Tom sipped his coffee in the kitchen, perusing a report and oblivious to the chaos that had become the hub of her life. Once she got the kids out the door to the carpool driver du jour, she poked her head back into the kitchen and grabbed her car keys and briefcase that were on the counter by the door.

"Hey, sperm donor!" she snapped. "Your offspring have left, and I'm going to work. Have a nice day. I can see how stressed you already are."

She slammed the door, stomped down the paved walkway to her car, and got her shoe stuck in a crack. She managed to pull it out with an overly strenuous yank that was driven by every frustrated muscle in her body. But the damage was done. The leather on her heel was scraped away.

She let go with a roar and marched ferociously to her car for the drive to work. At the Starbucks drive-thru, she had to wait behind an indecisive coffee customer. "Oh, just pick one, for crying out loud!" she grumbled, inching her car ever closer to the wishy-washy woman's minivan.

Finally, Elizabeth got her coffee and drove away. She took a sip, expecting her heavenly hazelnut nectar but discovered it was a plain old black coffee. No cream. No hazelnut.

"Idiots!" she growled. "You put a cup in front of the dispenser and press a button. Is that so hard to do correctly?" She slammed the cup in the holder next to her with such force that the lid popped off, splattering her with coffee.

"Damn it!" she yelled. "What else? What else?"

At the next light, she grabbed some napkins from the glove compartment and dabbed at the splatters. Luckily, she was wearing a navy blue jacket and slacks, so the stains would not be too noticeable. But still, the combination of heat and dampness against her skin did not make for a comfortable ride. She considered turning around and going home to change but decided she didn't feel like confronting her husband. And if he was still sitting there, oh so comfy, sipping the coffee that was just right, and enjoying a peaceful moment thanks to her ability to herd the kids from bed to breakfast to car, she might just shift into banshee mode. *Never let 'em see you sweat,* she thought. *I'm not going to let him see how ticked off I am. I will just decide here and now that the rest of the day will be fine. It will be great, in fact. This has all been a series of annoyances, and these, too, shall pass.*

But they didn't. She had a conference call to do at ten and had trouble with the conference line. Rosaria wasn't there, so Elizabeth had to improvise. She texted and emailed the two customers who were supposed to be on the call, then dialed the customer service line for the conference call company so that a representative could calmly advise her that they were having "unforeseen technical issues".

"Unforeseen? So this has never, ever happened before?" she said with forced control. "I am the first one who has been unable to dial in and access the line that I pay for? Well, isn't that great for you guys to be so reliable but terribly, terribly unfortunate for me as I am missing an extremely important phone call!" The timber of her voice escalated with each word. By the end, she was shouting.

"I am very sorry for your inconvenience, and I assure you we are doing everything we can to repair the problem as quickly as possible," came the reply, obviously scripted yet a bit frazzled.

"Well, that does me no good whatsoever. Do you have an alternate line I can use in the interim?"

After a moment of scrambling that included some horrific on-call music, Elizabeth was given a different call-in number and password, which she hastily scribbled down. She hung up while the agent was once again apologizing. Elizabeth then emailed and texted her clients the new dial-in information, and they were shortly able to begin their conference. But she was the tiniest bit irritated that Rosaria hadn't been here to handle the mishap. Of all days, Rosaria had to pick this one to take time off.

Shortly after lunch, Elizabeth received a call from Evan Euler, the CIO at Palladex. Right on schedule, she thought, noting that he had promised to call her on this date with his decision. Her heart started pumping as she waited for the good news. She pictured the celebration that would follow in her office once Rosaria returned. Elizabeth would order the champagne herself, rather than wait for her trusty assistant, just to surprise her and handle the task on her own. She appreciated everything that Rosaria did for her and made a mental note to be a bit more forthcoming with praise.

"*Hello*, Evan. So nice to hear from you! I hope you've been well," she cooed.

"Very well. Thanks, Elizabeth." He paused. She noticed an edge in his voice. He was probably just dragging out the drama a bit longer, making the poor girl wait. She smiled, thinking she'd probably do the same thing. *We're two of a kind,* she thought. "So I told you that I would call you today with our decision about software development. And, as I'm sure you guessed from our last meeting, we were very impressed with your presentation and your company."

Her smile grew. Here it comes, she thought.

"But we've had a change of heart. Our CEO is on a major cost-cutting initiative, so we've decided to outsource the development to another company," he said.

Elizabeth paused. She couldn't have heard correctly. Where were the words she expected—"Congratulations!" and "Let's get started"? Her brain felt like a pinball game with ball bearings banging around, trying to find a place to land.

"I'm sorry?" she said, hoping this was a joke.

"We've chosen an offshore company that can do the work for considerably less. I'm sorry, Elizabeth. I really did fight for you. I would much prefer to keep the work here, but I didn't have much choice." Evan was faltering a bit now.

The little weasel, Elizabeth thought. *Yeah, he fought for me, all right. I bet he bent over like the spineless yes-boy he really is.*

"Well, I have to say I'm disappointed, Evan. Like you, I believe in investing in our own country so that our citizens can benefit, particularly in this tough economy," she said, as politely as she could manage.

"And I agree, but it's the same tough economy that is causing us to scale back on our expenses," Evan countered, a bit more defensively now.

"I understand, and I hope that you might reconsider the choice in the future, if this economy lets us all get back to business as usual."

Elizabeth tried to relax her tone. She might be able to salvage the relationship. She was already calculating the next step for follow-up in two months to see how things were going. She had a feeling that Palladex might not be as thrilled with the outcome and be ready to pony up the budget dollars later, just to cut their losses. At least, she hoped so.

"I certainly will, Elizabeth. As I said, I was impressed by you and your company. This decision is by no means a reflection on your capability," he replied in earnest.

"Well, thank you. I appreciate that. And I wish you well and thank you for giving me the opportunity to present you with an option. Best of luck, Evan."

"To you, too."

Click. That ended the conversation and Elizabeth's hopes of making a great, big win for her business. So much for showing her ex-colleagues how far she had come. So much for having the money to hire more management staff to give her a break from her long work weeks. Well, her invisible husband was just going to have to be more involved at home, because she needed more help if she was going to keep working away at realizing her dream.

Speaking of invisible, she looked at her watch and realized it was almost two o'clock. Rosaria had said she was only taking off the morning and would return after lunch. Where the heck was she? Rosaria never used personal time, so Elizabeth assumed this must be something important. Maybe her mother was ill and Rosaria had to take her to a doctor. Or maybe it was Rosaria who was sick. Elizabeth thought about the relentless worker who had been such a valuable employee the past three years. If Elizabeth could only clone Rosaria, she thought, she'd have an office that was a model of efficiency and productivity. But then she pictured an army of Rosarias scurrying through the halls, heads bent down to push away all obstacles. Humorless frumps who lived to serve.

Elizabeth shrugged off the image. It was scary to think of work being so un-fun. She loved Rosaria and knew enough about her past to understand why she was so serious. The young woman seemed to fear that, if she enjoyed herself, something bad would happen. Ridiculous! Rosaria needed to learn how to lighten up. And Elizabeth had hoped she would be able to show her a brighter world. But she was always too busy with her own life to be the role model she had hoped would influence Rosaria to come out of her titanium cocoon. Maybe she should suggest they go to the spa together and use that gift certificate. Right now, Elizabeth relished the idea of a full-body massage.

A few minutes before three, Elizabeth heard someone come into the lobby. There was some murmuring, and she recognized Rosaria's voice. She thought, *I'll give her a few minutes to settle in and then see if everything is okay.* She felt her heart race as she imagined all sorts of things, like breast cancer or some rare disease that could require her to take time off, because Rosaria usually juggled her regular appointments around a lunch hour.

After a few minutes, she rang Rosaria's office and asked her to come in. She didn't know who the other voice down the hall belonged to, but she wanted privacy with Rosaria. When Elizabeth saw the masterful makeover, she was stunned. Rosaria looked like a new woman—a new, attractive woman with a great little figure. And then it registered in her brain that Rosaria was not sick. She hadn't been at a doctor's appointment. She didn't have a life-threatening disease.

She had been getting a makeover.

And Elizabeth became angry that Rosaria had made her worry for no reason whatsoever. And when she also realized that the other voice she had been hearing belonged to Morgan, she became enraged. So, Morgan with all her fancy clothes and youthful energy had been able to light the spark in Rosaria when Elizabeth herself couldn't. She realized those two were closer in age—actually, the same age—than Elizabeth's forty-two years, but Rosaria's seriousness had always made her seem much older.

All the frustrations and anger of the day welled up inside Elizabeth and erupted like a volcano. And the molten hot words that spewed from her mouth turned the newly sculpted Rosaria into a pile of simpering remorse. For Morgan, who had more confidence than Rosaria, Elizabeth managed to sever the bonds that had been strengthening between them. She hadn't realized how much she'd been enjoyed their relationship until she watched Morgan stomp away without looking back.

footnotes

When you've had a hard day, it doesn't take much to send you screaming over the edge. Unfortunately, we often take out our frustration on the easiest target. That could be your spouse, partner, best friend, child, parent, or co-worker. Losing your temper is inevitable, but how you manage the damage control is what defines you as a person, leader, and professional. Deal with your own mistakes as you would with those made by others. Acknowledge the mistake, explain the problem that caused you to erupt, and be big enough to offer a sincere apology.

CHAPTER forty

After the confrontation with Elizabeth, Morgan left the building and started walking down the block. I knew she was upset when she didn't hail a cab, as was her custom when her journey covered more than two blocks. I hurried to keep time with her brisk pace; for a woman in four-inch heels, she was in some kind of serious sprint. The farther she got from Elizabeth's office, however, the more she slowed. I doubted Morgan knew where she was going. She was just following her feet. The physical activity was keeping her from screaming, crying, or both. I knew her brain was reeling, so I made no attempt at conversation.

Her stilettos led her to her dad's ex-apartment. Her ex-city home. But now it belonged to Sam. Given the way her relationships with Rosaria and Elizabeth had soured so quickly, she was hesitant to risk a fall-out with Sam as well. What if her bad mojo infected their budding romance? Did she dare risk it?

She looked up at Sam's building and then started walking down the sidewalk, away from the entrance.

"Where are you going now?" I asked, confused and frankly a bit tired of walking.

"I—I don't know," she said, stopping again. She turned back toward the building, took a few steps, and paused. "What if I screw this up, too?"

"Now, *why* would you even think that, Morgan?" I asked, truly surprised at this waffling of her confidence.

"Because that's what I do, Dee! Look at everything I've done. I got Rosaria in trouble with Elizabeth and lost Elizabeth as a mentor, which isn't such a big loss, given how she thinks of me. I'm sure I won't be doing her party now, so I've got to build my experience elsewhere. But I guess I can't rely on one person to make things right," she said, thinking out loud.

"Actually, you can," I said.

"Well, sure, I guess as my Fairy Godmother, that would be *your* job," she replied.

"That's not what I meant. The one person I was referring to is *you!* You, Morgan, are the only one who can change your life. You are the only one who can make things happen for yourself. You are in charge, Morgan—no one else. It's not bad mojo, bad luck, or lousy timing. You are the one who holds the key," I said, with a blend of preachiness and affection rolled into one.

Morgan looked at me, processing the words and calculating her choice. "Okay."

"Okay, what?" I asked.

"Okay, I'm making a decision, and I'm going upstairs to talk to Sam."

I followed her into the lobby. She waved off the doorman, who recognized the purposeful stride of a determined woman and let her keep walking. There was no answer when she knocked on Sam's door. She looked at her watch. Not even five o'clock yet. Of course, he was probably still at work, like most people were at that hour.

She sat on the floor in front of his door, contemplating what to do next. Should she call him? What if he was not heading straight home after work? She pulled up her knees and tucked her head down, taking a few moments to rethink the day's events and gather her thoughts.

"Can I just say something here?" I asked, knowing full well I was going to speak, regardless of her response. "You didn't do anything wrong today, girl. You helped a friend who was in serious need of a pick-me-up. The fact that Elizabeth got all hot and bothered about Rosaria taking a few hours to herself is her own problem and not yours. You're blaming yourself for something that you shouldn't."

"I should have just stayed out of it. I should have left Rosaria alone. And I should never have assumed that Elizabeth could see me any differently than the flake that I am," she mumbled into her knees.

"She was wrong for what she said, and you shouldn't let her words completely erase all the good lessons you've learned."

"All my life, people have been treating me like a dumb blonde. No one ever raised the bar or expected me to be anything other than pretty or silly or frivolous, so that's all I've ever been. I didn't have to be an 'A' student or a star athlete, or even the most popular girl in school. I got used to being nothing more than average. But Elizabeth is this special person, and she had faith in me. I thought she saw through all the stuff on the outside. But how can I believe anything she said when it was all built on a big, fat lie?"

Morgan's angry voice was tinged with pain. She must have been on fragile footing to let Elizabeth's words cut her so deeply. I knew that Morgan could be a formidable force, but how do you communicate that to someone whose confidence was so wobbly?

"You've come a long way from the confused little girl who relied on everyone else to take care of her, Morgan. You have started down a path, you've built goals, and you have a vision for yourself. If that vision is for real, you don't need anyone else to approve. You've just got to believe in yourself," I said. "You are kind of a funny Cinderella story. You weren't living in an attic and getting beat on by a nasty stepmother and two ugly stepsisters. Your biggest enemy was yourself."

"Are you calling me an ugly stepsister?" Morgan asked, looking up at me with moist eyes.

"Puhhlease! Honey, those girls were just ugly to the bone, in looks and spirit. No, I mean the only one who has been holding you back from being your Cinderella is you. When you believed in yourself, you made things happen. Good things. And you will keep making your life better as long as you keep trying. Don't let other people cause you to doubt yourself. Their issues are *their* problems, not yours, and you have to accept that. Morgan Demarest, your Cinderella story is the transformation you are making from the girl who believed she was only second-best to a successful, confident career woman."

"I don't know," she said.

"You don't know? You don't *know*? Do you even remember who you were the last time you were sitting out here in this hallway, feeling so sorry for yourself because your boyfriend threw you out? Your biggest worry was your Prada wrap and a handbag."

"And those killer shoes," she added.

"Yeah. The shoes. But back then you defined yourself by the clothes. Now you define yourself by the person. I'd say that's a Cinderella transformation," I said.

"Well, there's just one thing," she said slowly.

"And what is that?" I asked, exhausted from all the cheerleading.

"I've always wanted a pair of glass slippers." She smiled at me, and her eyes sparkled. And there was the Morgan Demarest I had grown to love.

"Why, my dear, you're wearing them," I pronounced in my very best Fairy Godmother sweet voice.

She looked down and saw that her four-inch black leather Louboutins had been replaced with crystal clear stilettos. She stretched out her legs to marvel at the crystal footwear.

"Well, this has become a familiar sight," came a voice from down the hall. Morgan saw Sam strolling toward her from the elevator, smiling that smile that spread to his sparkling eyes. She jumped to her feet and met him with a powerful hug that almost knocked him off his feet.

"Wow, what's that about?" he asked in a voice muffled by her head against his face.

"Just glad to see your smiling face. It's been a rough day, but it's over." With her arms wrapped around his waist, she looked up into his eyes and whispered, "Now what does a girl have to do to get a drink around here?"

He opened his apartment door and made a grand wave to usher her in. His eyes followed her with genuine appreciation, all the way down to her feet.

"Hey, nice shoes!" he exclaimed. "Where do you find this stuff?"

"Oh," she said with a coy smile, "I've got people."

footnotes

You are the mistress of your destiny. You can blame others for wronging you or place expectations on them to lift you up, but in the end, the responsibility for your life, your success—or your failure—is your own. Confidence and self-worth comes from inside. It can be *boosted* by others, but doesn't start in the *minds* of others. When you believe in yourself, others will, too. To give yourself a needed boost now and then, create a playlist of at least five songs that lift your spirits. When life gets you down, take a break, close your eyes, and listen to those songs. Music can be very healing!

CHAPTER forty-one

On her way home from work after the horrific day she'd had, Elizabeth stopped off at Fred's, the pub at Barney's, for a dirty martini—make that extra dirty after the way she'd handled herself. She needed to cool off, and her favorite bartender, Clarence—known throughout the city for his divine martinis—would certainly offer her some sympathy before she plowed into her next target at full force.

Elizabeth had had enough—her work life was suffering because of the dysfunction at home. *Balance*, she thought. It wasn't a myth. And damn if she was not going to bring it back! It was time for her hubby to suck it up, put on his big boy panties, and help out around the home front. She handled far too many of the responsibilities and planned to demand that he either jump in or get out.

After cooling down for half an hour, she headed home. Prepared for Tom to put up a fight, Elizabeth was surprised at his reaction when she confronted him in the kitchen, less than a minute after she walked in the door. Tom was completely clueless about his lack of participation. Since Elizabeth didn't ask for his help, he'd assumed it was like everything else she did:

"I just thought you wanted me to stay out of your way and let you handle things," he said. "You have systems for everything and I feel like I shouldn't rock your boat."

"Systems? Tom, I am shooting from the hip most of the time. In case you didn't notice, these kids didn't come with instructions. I just keep trying to find a way to get through each day," she answered, fighting back the mixed emotions of anger and sadness.

Tom apologized and promised to do more, starting with getting the kids to bed that night.

The next morning, Elizabeth finally enjoyed a stress-free start to her day as Tom got the kids out of bed and ready for school. Of course, Lara picked this particular day to be an angel: "Yes, Daddy" was the response to his suggestion for what she should wear; Elizabeth always had to argue the choice. And magically, Erich seemed to be organized. So Tom looked at her as if this job was simple and she had manufactured the chaos herself. *Whatever*, she thought. The novelty would soon wear off and her little Stepford kids would resume their normal, childlike behaviors. In the meantime, she'd get the help she needed and wanted.

Now it was time to make things right with Rosaria.

On her way to work, Elizabeth stopped and picked up an extra coffee—black, no sugar, the way Rosaria took it. It was a brisk morning, and Elizabeth's perfectly blended hazelnut coffee was already coursing through her veins like an intravenous dose of caffeinated joy.

When she arrived at the office—twenty minutes earlier than usual, thanks to Tom's help—the door was unlocked, and Rosaria was already at her desk. She had regressed to the Rosaria of two days ago, before her makeover. Her hair was in a severe bun, and she had pinned back the layers that had framed her face, which was now scrubbed clean of any makeup. She was dressed in a beige pullover with a brown plaid skirt. And Elizabeth was sure that, tucked under the desk, Rosaria's feet would be ensconced in the ever-present sensible shoes with the rubber sole and short heels.

Elizabeth's heart sank. She knew she was responsible for botching the transformation. She thought about the lovely young woman who had walked into her office yesterday, smiling and even proud—both rare feats for Rosaria. And in one fell swoop, Elizabeth had extended her claws and shred Rosaria's happiness like tissue paper.

She walked slowly into Rosaria's office, placed the coffee cup in front of her, and sat down. Rosaria instantly snapped to attention.

"You're here early, Rosaria . . ." Elizabeth started.

Rosaria jumped in defensively. "I'm trying to catch up on yesterday's work. I plan to stay late tonight and make sure that everything is done."

She was trying so hard to please, Elizabeth saw—which only made her feel worse. She held up a hand to halt her. "Rosaria, you don't need to make up the time. I was wrong to lash out at you yesterday. It was clearly a special day for you, and I ruined it because of my lousy mood. I'm very sorry I hurt your feelings. I hope you will accept my apology."

Rosaria listened to her, afraid or unable to speak. She had expected Elizabeth to remind her of her duties and had been prepared to "yes" her as much as possible. She needed her job and didn't want one day of bad judgment to ruin it. But this reaction came as a complete surprise. Elizabeth was apologizing to *her*? But *she* was the one who had blown off most of the day just to have fun. And yet her *boss* was sorry? It didn't compute in Rosaria's all-work-and-no-play brain.

"But, Elizabeth, you were right," Rosaria finally responded. "It was a silly waste of time, and I should have been here working. It will never happen again."

"I was afraid you'd say that."

"Excuse me?"

"Rosaria, you *should* be doing things like that. You need to get out and have fun. You live to work, and you should work to live."

"I don't understand," Rosaria said, trying to sort out the logic.

"You are young and single, and yet I don't think you enjoy that wonderful situation. And you're beautiful, Rosaria—with or without the hair and makeup. You have inner beauty, and for some reason, you feel a need to hide it away. If you put more fun in your life, the joy would show on your face and in your whole being. I know that you have a hard work ethic, and as your boss, I totally respect that. But as your friend—and I hope you still consider me a friend—I have to say that enough is enough! Give yourself permission to have fun. Go out and get a manicure at least once a month. Go shopping, for goodness sake. Go out for drinks or a movie or dinner or whatever, with your friends."

Elizabeth paused, waiting for Rosaria to respond. Instead, they just looked at each other, neither one blinking.

"Okay, so let's rewind," Elizabeth said. "Next week, I want you to take a day off. Go back to the spa, if you want. Go shopping. Go to a museum. Just do something that you've been wanting to do but keep finding an excuse not to. I'm telling you that I insist that you take a day off, but only—and I really mean this—if you promise to do something fun! No doing chores, no sitting around your apartment. Get out and do something!"

Rosaria's confused mind slowly put together the picture that Elizabeth was trying to paint. Have fun. She didn't even know where to start, although she had to admit that getting her hair and makeup done had been enjoyable. And she *had* liked the surprised look on Benjamin's face. And then there was that man in the upscale resale shop. Maybe there *was* something to being more girlish. She did a quick inventory of her friends and wondered whom she would invite for a day of leisure. She whipped through them like a dealer fanning a deck of cards, dismissing each one for various reasons: she works, she's got the kids, she wouldn't enjoy it. And then she came up with the perfect person: Morgan. Morgan had an infectious spirit and knew how to find fun in just about anything.

But Rosaria had pushed Morgan away after the fiasco yesterday afternoon. Pushed? No, it was more like she'd hurled her out of the ring like a crazed wrestler. Morgan was probably as upset with her as she had been with Elizabeth. And yet, Elizabeth's apology made everything nice again. Maybe she could do the same with Morgan. After all, Morgan had had good intentions. If it weren't for Elizabeth's rebuke, all would still be well between them.

"Rosaria," Elizabeth broke into Rosaria's thoughts, "in spite of what I said yesterday, I am happy and really proud that you took a risk with your appearance. You stepped outside your comfort zone, and that was a huge step for you! I had no right, *no right* to lash out at you the way I did. On any other day, I would have gotten all girly and giddy, but yesterday was terrible for me. We didn't get the Palladex contract, which topped off a list of rotten things."

Rosaria's face turned to shock when Elizabeth mentioned the Palladex deal falling through. Like her boss, she'd thought it was pretty much a sure thing.

"I know, I know," Elizabeth said, responding to Rosaria's surprise. "They opted to cheap out and go offshore. But I thought about it last night, and I believe you get what you pay for. They'll get the job done cheap, but I expect it won't be all that easy. Anyway, it's not worth getting upset over one loss. There are plenty more clients out there to go after. I'm considering that whole experience just good practice."

Elizabeth smiled at Rosaria and stood up, but she didn't turn to leave just yet. She thought for a moment and then added one more thought. "I have to confess something else, Rosaria. I was envious that you and Morgan went off and had so much fun. You might not know it, but I love a good makeover myself!"

Rosaria's face relaxed, and she smiled, just a bit.

"But yesterday wasn't just any other day, and I let it turn me into a nasty shrew. I took it out on you. Looking back, I should have let your fun make me feel better, but I didn't."

Rosaria was fighting back tears, which caused Elizabeth to feel the same emotion bubbling up inside.

"No, Elizabeth, you were right," Rosaria said. "I let myself get caught up in a stupid fantasy. What was I thinking? I'm not her. I will never, ever be *her!*"

"Rosaria, you are beautiful, inside and out. You don't need to change who you are, because you're great."

Rosaria looked down at her desk and shook her head.

"Rosaria, look at me," Elizabeth commanded gently. "For three years, I've been trying to encourage you to allow yourself to blossom into the person you can be. And I'm not talking about the clothes or the hair or the makeup." She paused and added with a smile, "But those were *killer* shoes!"

Rosaria looked up at her boss and broke into a grin.

"I'm jealous that I've tried for three years to draw you out of that shell, and Morgan did it one afternoon. I'm trying to be her mentor, when she probably should be mine."

Surprising herself, Rosaria stepped from behind her desk and gave Elizabeth a hug, hesitantly at first but then strengthening when Elizabeth hugged her tightly in response.

"I'm human," Elizabeth said. "I make mistakes. I just try to hide them from you. But yesterday, I made a huge one."

"That's really okay, Elizabeth. I'm sorry I wasn't here when you needed me. I will try not to let that happen again," Rosaria said.

"Oh, I'm a big girl and can take care of myself," Elizabeth said, waving her off. "But you know what I *do* need?"

Rosaria shook her head, waiting for a request to organize something, research something, or call someone.

"I'm getting really tired of staring at the same old painting on the wall in my office. I need something new. Let's take a ride over to Celestial Sky and see if they have any more of Siobhan's colorful works so I can brighten this place up!"

Finally, Rosaria burst into a smile that lit up the dreary little office.

"And," Elizabeth added, "I have to stop on the way back and pick up some mascara and moisturizer. Care to join me at the makeup counter?"

footnotes

Life is so much more than a job—or it should be. When the things you do from day to day become a drain on your brain, it's time to inject something new. Or at least take a break from whatever it is that's sucking up your energy like a vacuum. Give in to those new, exciting moments when you feel tired, shabby, unappreciated, or just plain bored. Schedule fun time into your week. Give yourself a pick-me-up. Try something new—even if it's just a different route to work or a different recipe for dinner. Better yet, forget about cooking, and go to that restaurant that you've been meaning to try. Or, of course, you can buy yourself a new pair of shoes, just for the sheer pleasure of it! Whatever it is, take a break from the blah.

CHAPTER forty-two:

A YEAR LATER

Morgan was sitting at a traffic light when her phone rang. She tapped the hands-free button on her steering wheel and heard her father's voice.

"Hey, Pony Girl! Just calling to see how things are going. Are we still on for brunch this Sunday?"

Edward was particularly cheery this morning. His mood had steadily improved over the past year, along with his business—thanks to a little help from Sam. Sam's friend, Dante Simeone, had been looking for office space for his new public relations business, so Sam had put him in touch with Edward, who had a plethora of vacancies in his buildings. Edward bartered the rent in exchange for PR help, and the move paid off: Dante managed to grab some good media coverage on the hook of small businesses trying to grow in a sluggish economy, and angled Edward in as a creative developer who supported small businesses. Once Edward took his focus off snagging the huge companies and developed projects that supported entrepreneurs, he started seeing his revenues grow. Although the bottom line was not as lucrative as his pre-recession numbers, Edward was thankful that he had brought his business back from the edge of disaster. Networking with Dante and his connections had brought him closer to a growing community of spirited, innovative entrepreneurs, including a few who were looking to invest in the growing trend of family-based retail centers, the alternative to traditional indoor malls.

Edward had learned valuable lessons from his near-bankruptcy experience. He discovered he could work leaner, reducing his overhead without compromising results. Yes, he had to take on more responsibility himself—for the time being—but he was used to shouldering extra work. Edward winced as he recalled how his workaholicism had cost him his marriage. But he would never let his career hurt his relationships again. In fact, the whole experience had brought him closer to Morgan than ever before. Somehow, they had both used their life and career challenges to grow together and grow stronger.

He had moved back to the city from Hinsdale once Claire returned from her epicurean adventure, which had taken her from Tuscany to Provence. She had started a small catering business with a friend six months ago, and it was starting to catch on. Luckily, her daughter was building an event planning business that frequently needed a talented, creative caterer. A little nepotism never hurt!

"Yes, Dad," Morgan said to him now, "I've got reservations for eleven. Does that work for you?"

"Sounds great. Is Sam going to join us?"

"I believe so. I told him to bring Anthony. I'd love for you to meet him. He's such a great kid!"

"That'd be great. Sam has told me so much about Anthony, and I'd like to meet him. So, how's business going, sweetheart? Anything new?"

After planning the sweet-sixteen party for Celeste's daughter, several other mothers had contacted Morgan to do their parties—a twenty-fifth anniversary, a baby shower, and a Gatsby garden party. She continued to do the artists' receptions for Celestial Sky, as she still maintained a part-time job with Celeste, while she cultivated her business venture. Even Pavlo had sent some business her way. He ran in posh circles and had recommended her services to a high-profile actor who had become a patron of Pavlo's work. Now Morgan was planning a high-ticket birthday party for the actor's five-year-old twins. With any luck, she'd connect with other celebrity parents at the party and take her venture to a higher level.

Morgan chatted a bit longer with her father, until another call buzzed. She apologized to her father but said she had to take this one. He clicked off and she picked up the other call.

"Hey, what's up?" she asked, with a concerned tone.

"Everything is fine. I just wanted you to know your mother is here setting up. The flowers arrived and look great. You're going to love the tulips!"

"How did you manage to get tulips in Chicago at this time of year?" Morgan asked. Tulips were plentiful in the spring and even into the summer, but by mid-fall they were hard to come by, which probably meant she was spending more than budgeted.

"Don't worry. I got a good deal!"

"You're reading my mind again, Rosie. You know how that scares me!" Morgan said, laughing.

"Oh, and I got the hotel to chip in some gift certificates for the spa and the restaurant so we can use them for the extra-special VIP guests," Rosaria added.

"I knew there was a reason I partnered with you," said Morgan.

When her business had begun to grow, Morgan had recognized that she needed the kind of organizational talents that Rosaria possessed. Rosaria saw a task and went after it with full vigor and a mind for results. While Morgan excelled at schmoozing clients and coming up with creative approaches for events, Rosaria was the get-it-done person. They were a formidable pair!

Elizabeth regretted losing her capable assistant but recognized that Rosaria had an exciting opportunity to blossom into the young professional that Elizabeth had always known was lurking somewhere inside that all-business, no-frills exterior. She had hoped that Rosaria would grow within IdeaWerx but couldn't fault her for her choice.

Elizabeth had apologized to Morgan that day after the argument in her office. She explained that she had let the fallen deal with Palladex make her so angry she had to lash out at someone. She'd wanted that contract and shared with both Morgan and Rosaria that she'd felt she needed the project to underscore her success. That was the first time that Rosaria had ever seen her boss's confidence shaken. It proved to her (again) that things—and people—weren't always as they appeared on the outside.

Morgan reinforced that belief. The two women had become close friends. Morgan sparked the lightheartedness in Rosaria, who discovered the power of laughter—and shoes. Rosaria had managed to graduate from her stilettos-in-training to the real thing. The two of them had made it their quest to scour every upscale resale shop in metro Chicago to find the most exquisite shoes at the best prices. They tried to outdo each other and often called to describe their latest score.

"Blahniks. Red. Peep toes. Seventy dollars!"

"No! You didn't! Hey, can I borrow them next Saturday?"

For her part, Rosaria was a master of precision. She infused time and project management skills into Morgan. She taught her how to keep track of appointments, tasks, and goals; maintain a log for following up with prospects; and stay on top of schedules, budgets, and promises.

And then there was me. I had hung around for a little while, just in case Morgan needed me. And on occasion, she did. Usually it was just for a reality check when life spiraled out of control or to give her a kick in the butt when she experienced moments of fear just because things were going so well. Morgan often assumed that a string of good luck meant disaster was on the horizon.

But it soon became obvious that my work with Morgan was done. There were other women out there who needed my wisdom, insight, and incredible fashion sense. There was always a call for *Stiletto 911*, and who am I to say no to a woman in need of a makeover?

footnotes

You can make your own dreams come true when you take stock of what you want, make a plan, and pull together the people and resources you need to make it happen. The power is within you. For more help with improving your communication style, setting goals, managing conflict…go to .

Set your focus on achieving those goals that have real meaning to you. And remember, if the stiletto fits, strut in it!

Epilogue

The traffic lights were favoring Morgan this morning, so she would arrive early at the conference center. To ensure she was always on time, she had learned to add a buffer into every trip, whether she was taking a cab, driving, or walking. Yes, Morgan had discovered that she enjoyed walking. She was able to feel closer to her surroundings and noticed more details, like the gardens blooming in the spring and the brisk wind in her face that signaled the onset of autumn in Chicago.

And she also enjoyed the ability to do more window-shopping. With her event planning business, she found that browsing helped to jumpstart her creative juices. Morgan often saw things in windows—whether it was items for sale or just for display—that gave her ideas. She loved finding new ways to use common things, like clothespins, paint cans, and vintage picture frames. Her innovative invitations had been drawing raves from clients. They were passing her name along to anyone who remarked at their uniqueness. Morgan thought about offering the invitations as a side service, for people who didn't need—or couldn't afford—her as a planner. She liked coming up with the ideas but needed to find someone to do the actual crafting. *Hmm*, she thought. That sounded like a good task for Rosie. No doubt she could find the perfect person.

Morgan was thrilled with her partnership with Rosie. The young woman had truly blossomed. Aside from the exterior changes—which had launched an active dating life—she had developed confidence. Rosie worked just as hard as ever but was clearly jazzed by being a partner in a business that she found stimulating and rewarding. Who would have thought that those two opposites would become such a winning pair?

Morgan pulled the Mercedes up to the curb at the main entrance of the conference center, where attendees were milling around, waiting for the exhibit hall to open. Digimart was one of the biggest technology expos in Chicago and drew about thirty-thousand people who came to see the hottest gadgets, software, and electronics. Elizabeth was launching a new productivity software program—the first that IdeaWerx had done under its own name. Elizabeth had recognized that her team had great ideas that should be put to good use. So, in addition to creating programs for her clients, Elizabeth's company had jumped into developing its own products.

Rosaria's replacement ended up being two people: one to run the office systems and another to tackle marketing. Morgan was quick to point out to Rosie that it took two people to fill her now-high-heeled shoes.

The launch party that Elizabeth had originally asked Morgan and Rosaria to organize had been put on hold when she'd lost the Palladex deal, but her new marketing director had reignited the idea to court prospective clients. Morgan and Rosaria had delivered a stellar event that met every objective—people had a memorable experience, which put IdeaWerx on the top of their lists. And today they were putting on another event at the expo. Elizabeth was taking steps to be a player, rather than just hope to become one. And Morgan and Rosaria would benefit from the contacts they could make in the business world as a result of this reception.

Morgan remained in the car for a moment, enjoying the fine leather on the steering wheel of the luxurious Mercedes. She reached for the door handle, but Sam got there first. The door opened, and Sam gave Morgan his hand to help her from the car. She slipped the keys into his palm and gave it an extra squeeze.

"Thank you for letting me use the car. It was amazing! I felt like a millionaire driving it!" she said.

"Well, one day maybe we'll be able to actually own one of these. I was just thrilled to be able to rent it. Anthony is going to be psyched to go out in style on his birthday today. We're heading out of the city and doing some exploring."

"Well, have fun, and tell Anthony I've got a gift for him, but he has to come and get it in person! Are you bringing him to brunch on Sunday?"

"Yup. We're all set."

Sam slid behind the wheel, turned the key, and listened to the subtle whir of the engine. He pulled away as Morgan threaded her way through the crowd. She heard the whispers from people in the crowd as she walked past.

"Who is she?"

"She must be married to one of the execs."

"Are you kidding? She probably *is* one of the execs."

"Check out those stilettos!"

"I saw those at Neiman's. They cost about a week's salary."

"Maybe *your* salary. Mine goes to pay the bills."

"Wouldn't it be nice to have that kind of money to throw around?"

"Yeah, but she was probably born into wealth."

If only they knew, Morgan thought. It had taken a lot of work and focus—and a little help from her friends—to go from the rain-soaked Prada ho to a successful businesswoman.

The wisdom of her mentor and friend echoed in her head: *Life is under no obligation to give us what we expect.*

So true, she said to herself with a slight nod. *You make your own destiny. And if you don't like it, make a new one.* Which was exactly what she, Morgan Demarest, had done over the past year.

She looked around, wondering if Divinity would pop up. Instead, she saw a young woman watching her, standing away from the whispering crowd. Morgan noticed something in the woman. She had an interesting way of pulling together a distinctive look. It was colorful without being gaudy. Her accessories were not expensive, but well put together. And she was carrying an unusual handbag that Morgan couldn't place. It looked like hand-painted artistry, but she couldn't be sure at this distance.

Still, it wasn't just her appearance that caught Morgan's notice. This woman, who was probably the same age as Morgan, looked curious and yet restrained. When Morgan caught her glance, the woman's eyes held hers for a brief instant and then looked away.

A movement behind the woman distracted Morgan. Was that Divinity in the crowd? Before she could get a good look, the person vanished. Morgan's Fairy Godmother hadn't been around for months, and Morgan was surprised at how much she missed her jabs and jibes. She assumed that Dee had taken on another woman to "save". Was it the woman she'd just spied in the crowd?

Morgan smiled at the thought of someone else coming to grips with Divinity's unusual ways. But she had to admit that Divinity had, indeed, saved her. Not by magic, but by guiding her to walk in the shoes of a successful woman—which would always be stilettos!

The End

A new beginning.

ABOUT THE AUTHORS

Vivian Valtas Schmidt

Vivian Valtas Schmidt is an entrepreneur, philanthropist and author who has a deep passion for helping others. She has a love for family, stilettos, adventure—and not always in that order. Add this to her ability to conquer obstacles and you have a woman who proves all naysayers in the world wrong.

After graduating from Youngstown State University, with a degree in Mathematics Education, Vivian earned her MBA from the Fisher College of Business at Ohio State University. She holds a teaching certificate, is a Certified Peer Mediator and holds the CLF (Chartered Leadership Fellowship) designation from The American College. Vivian is on the Board of Managers for the Valentine Boys and Girls Chicago and is a member of National Association of Women Business Owners. She has also volunteered for a variety of non-profit organizations that benefit children.

Whether she is hard at work, volunteering, biking across Chicago, skydiving, or spending quality time at home with her husband and son in Chicago, Vivian Valtas Schmidt stands tall in her stilettos and radiates confidence everywhere she goes.

Sue Publicover

Sue has authored many books, ebooks, articles, and blogs, but you won't see her byline. She's a ghostwriter who has written about everything from potty training and foot ailments to Generation Y and social media. She now makes herself visible to the world in this first novel with Vivian Valtas Schmidt. Founder of Wordsmiths, Etc., Sue has been writing for more than 25 years. Sue is also a marketing therapist with a passion for finding creative solutions and helping people unleash their own potential as marketers. When she's not writing, she can be found strutting her stilettos on the ballroom dance floor, swimming with dolphins or manatees, lounging beachside with a view of the cabana action, or in search of her next adventure.

STILETTO 911

www.ingramcontent.com/pod-product-compliance
Lightning Source LLC
Chambersburg PA
CBHW070331260626
47160CB00003B/1006